The Palm Reader

ANTOINETTE ZAM

Copyright © 2023 Antoinette Zam
All rights reserved
First Edition

PAGE PUBLISHING
Conneaut Lake, PA

First originally published by Page Publishing 2023

ISBN 978-1-64544-872-3 (pbk)
ISBN 978-1-64544-871-6 (digital)

Printed in the United States of America

To my husband.
With all my love, babe.

In the acknowledgments in my first novel, *Scarred by Death*, I stated that the inspiration for my writing was my beloved mother, Sylvia. Again, I give the thanks and undying love to the woman who raised me and inspired me to follow my dream. Mom, although you are no longer with me, you remain alive in my heart and in my writing.

CHAPTER 1

Dashing down the back stairs, Kathy entered the kitchen. Surprised to see her husband, Derek, naked from the waist-up.

"Good morning, sweetheart. You're up early."

"The baby was up early. Before he left for the park with Fanny, he upchucked on my shirt."

Kathy smiled. "What time did you get in last night?"

"Around one. I wanted to check on Mr. Goldman. He now has the heart of a forty-year-old, literally."

"Was the person who passed, an organ donor, or did you have the miserable task of confronting the family?"

"Organ donor. Are you packed?"

"Almost," Kathy replied. "Do you think I should cancel if the baby isn't well?"

"Absolutely not. Lauren would have my head. Fanny and I will be fine. I don't know how you manage. I'm exhausted just feeding the five their breakfast."

"I owe it all to Fanny."

Kathy cared for the children, the house, the gardens, and her husband's needs, without help. Two years ago, Kathy contracted a virus, which landed her in bed for three weeks. When she was back on her feet, Derek insisted Kathy find a nanny to help with the children. She knew Fanny was the right one twenty minutes after meeting with her. One year later, Fanny moved into the guest house. Fanny's only child, her son, lived with his family in California. With her extended family and friends living in Connecticut, for now, Fanny would remain on the East Coast.

"I hope Gabe isn't giving Fanny a hard time. Are you sure he was feeling well enough to go to the park?"

"He was asleep five seconds after Fanny placed him in his carriage."

Kathy smiled. "The house is so empty without the children running through the halls."

"Enjoy it while it lasts. In a few minutes, they will be crashing through the front door."

"You did tell Fanny to have them home before ten, right? Lauren gave me strict orders. She's leaving with or without me."

"You will be ready to go," Derek assured her. "I'll make sure of it. I don't want to spend a minute more than I have to with our dear friend Lauren. By the way, Jenny told me you hired her to work next week. You have no faith in me, do you?"

"You're a doctor for heaven's sake. Of course, I have faith you can handle five screaming kids all by yourself. Anyway, Jenny needs the job to cover her college expenses."

"With what you're paying her to help around here, she'll have enough for college and a townhouse."

"You don't fool me, Dr. Derek Charles Wilson. Your bark is worse than your bite."

"Speaking of Jenny, she told me her mother lost her job. Said her mom is having a rough time finding another."

"I spoke with Mr. Baker at the bank," Kathy said. "He told me he was looking for an office manager. Jenny's mom starts on Monday."

Derek wasn't surprised by the news. "You have a big heart, and there isn't a jealous bone in your body."

"What?"

"Well, you're giving your husband carte blanche to spend an entire week with a good-looking twenty-year-old."

"Running after five little ones, you won't have enough time to tie your shoes," Kathy said with a grin.

"True. Five children, at the zoo with all those animals, I must have been out of my mind."

Kathy couldn't take her eyes off Derek's naked chest. To keep from tearing off the remainder of his clothes, she asked, "Did Nina give you the schedule for the book tour?"

"She did. It's in my briefcase."

Kathy sighed. "I don't think you and I have been apart for more than a week since we were married."

"Nina arranged for me to be home every weekend. I'll only be away two consecutive weeks during the six months."

"I wouldn't be going away, if Casey—"

"You're going," said Derek, interrupting her. "If anyone needs a break, it's you."

"Thanks, but if anyone needs a break, it's you. Surgeon, seminar speaker, and soon-to-be a best-selling author. I know your book is going to be a great success. I hope Nina received a nice sign-on bonus for signing you."

"I'm sure she did. As far as the book being a great success, I don't know how many laymen would be interested in the technical skills involved in replacing a heart. It isn't *Wuthering Heights* or a juicy sex novel."

"With the Net promoting your book, you might be surprised at how many laymen will read it," Kathy countered.

"Nina thinks the money will be rolling in by this time next year."

"You did arrange to have half of the book's sale proceeds donated to medical research, right?"

"I did," he replied.

Kathy walked toward Derek and kissed him. "I love you."

"I love and adore you. Go finish getting ready. We wouldn't want to upset the witch."

Derek watched Kathy take two steps at a time to reach the top landing. When she was out of sight, he reached for the list of instructions Kathy had left to care for the kids. After reading five lines, he placed the list down and looked out the kitchen window. He smiled. The garden was so lovely this time of year. Not a plant or a single bush was placed in the garden without Kathy's final approval. Emanuel, the gardener, did the hard labor. But, in the spring and fall, Kathy put on her garden gloves and helped Emanuel prep the garden for planting.

As Derek stared at the bounty of color in the garden, his thoughts turned to Nina.

*****

Nina, from her hotel balcony, glanced toward Connecticut and wondered if Derek was asleep, with Kathy cradled safely in his arms. With a soft sigh, she couldn't help herself from thinking about the first time they'd met.

After meeting with a client at the Hilton, she'd decided to take a stroll around the hotel. The door to the conference room was open, and her eyes were drawn toward the speaker, who was an attractive man. She glanced at the easel announcing, "Cardiac Seminar, Speaker: Dr. Derek Wilson." Before entering the room, she lingered at the door for several minutes. Ten minutes after sitting, she was well versed on the mechanics of the human heart. When the seminar concluded, she walked toward the speaker.

"Dr. Wilson, my name is Nina Halt. I work for the publishing firm Flynn and Bachman. Have you heard of the company?"

"Can't say that I have."

"I'll come right to the point. Did you ever consider putting your surgical techniques to paper?"

Derek smiled. "Writing?"

"Yes, as a learning tool for upcoming surgeons."

"Sorry, Ms. Hilt, with my busy schedule, I don't have time to write a book."

"The name is *Halt*. You wouldn't have to literally do the writing. My company would hire a ghostwriter to help in the process of getting your techniques to print."

"Thank you, Ms. Halt—"

"Do you have a business card, Dr. Wilson?" Nina presented Derek with her business card.

Derek retrieved a business card from his pocket and handed it to her.

"I want to run this idea by my boss. If there is an interest, would you consider meeting with us?"

Derek smiled. When Dr. Wilson smiled, Nina thought, *He is extremely handsome.* A warm feeling rose within her, and she felt flushed.

Embarrassed by the moment, Nina spoke quickly. "If there is an interest, I'll be in touch. Goodbye, Dr. Wilson."

Nina immediately spoke with her boss, Joe. He knew of Dr. Derek Charles Wilson. He was one of the top ten heart surgeons in the United States.

Joe's instructions to Nina was "Get the doc to sign on the dotted line."

After fifteen calls to the number Derek had provided, he returned her call. Derek agreed to meet with Nina and her boss, Joe, at the hospital. Dr. Wilson was operating at six in the morning that day. He would be available to meet with them at eleven. During the meeting, Derek said he had already discussed the book with his wife, Kathy, and she thought it a great idea. Joe wasted no time in presenting Derek with a contract. Derek said he would have his attorney review it. His lawyer requested several changes be made to the contract. The changes were made, and Derek signed on with the publisher.

Nina earned a nice commission for signing Dr. Wilson, but her greatest challenge was finding a ghostwriter. He or she had to be the right fit for the good doctor. She arranged for Derek to meet the twelve she had selected. Derek rejected every one of them. Frustrated, Nina reached out to a friend. The friend recommended Keith Paulson.

Convincing Derek that Keith Paulson was the best in his field was another challenge. After several heated discussions, Derek agreed to meet Mr. Paulson. Nina crossed her fingers and prayed that Keith was the one.

While Derek was meeting with Keith, Nina waited in the doctor's lounge. Working on her laptop, she checked her watch several times. An hour later, her cell phone buzzed with a text from Derek asking her to join them. When Nina entered the office, Derek was speaking.

"Mr. Paulson, transferring a foreign heart into a patient whose heart has just been removed—I think you would agree—takes skill and precision. But what you don't know, and what I have figured out, is how to speed up the process in connecting the new heart, without complications such as bleeders or dissection of a main artery. Any surgeon facing complications in the operating room can quickly find himself, or herself, exhausted by the task of trying to save one's life. These tricks of the trade—that I've learned the hard way—will allow the surgeon to spend more time watching, waiting, and hoping the new heart is satisfied with its new surroundings rather than correcting surgical errors. Without a medical background, I don't know if you're the right man for the job."

Frozen in place, Nina tried to find the words to change Derek's mind. Coming up short, she heard Keith say, "Dr. Wilson, my specialty is writing, yours is surgery. Is it possible for me to join you in the operating room? We can meet afterward, and you can put into words what I have witnessed, and I will put your words to paper. If you are not satisfied with my work, we can part as friends."

Derek pondered the suggestion. "Do you faint easily, Mr. Paulson?"

"I do not, sir."

"Then we have a deal."

Derek invited Nina to join Keith in the gallery of the operating room. Nina was not taken back by the incisions made into a human body, the cracking of the chest bone, or the amount of blood. She rested her head on her hands and watched Derek give life to a lifeless body.

Several days after the surgery, Keith and Derek met. Two weeks later, Keith presented Derek with fifty transcribed pages. Derek placed the pages in his briefcase. Three days later, Derek returned the pages to Keith. The pair would not be parting ways any time soon.

Nina entered her hotel room and caught sight of the bed and the ruffled sheets. Derek had arrived late the prior evening; he was needed at the hospital. His late arrival gave her time to work and complete the book tour schedule.

When he arrived, she presented the schedule to him.

"Nina, why can't we go to California after Hawaii? Why Texas, then Hawaii?"

"Derek, we've gone over this a hundred times. The hotels can't accommodate the dates. Do you enjoy making my life a living hell? You will be home with your family every weekend, except two. You will be home the week prior to Christmas and the week after. The book is flying off the shelves! You will have to consider a European and Asian tour."

"If the book is selling, it can sell itself in Europe and Asia."

"Why! Why, did I step into that conference room?"

Derek walked toward Nina. Placing his arms around her waist, he drew her to him. "Isn't it your job to reel in the client?"

Nina chuckled. Reaching up, she ran her fingers through his hair.

Derek asked, "Can you forgive me for being difficult?"

"Of course, I forgive you. How could I resist those puppy-dog eyes?"

Derek placed a strong kiss on Nina's lips. Lifting her in his arms, he gently laid her down on the bed.

The lovemaking was erotic and new to Nina. She allowed Derek to do things to her, and she to him, that she wouldn't have dreamed of doing with another man.

Lying in his arms, Nina sensed something was wrong. She left the comfort of Derek's arms saying she needed a shower. She invited him to come along, but he declined.

Showered, she entered the bedroom naked.

"Nina, we have to talk." Derek patted the bed.

Her legs grew weak as she slowly walked toward the bed. She sat at the end of the bed keeping a distance between herself and Derek's naked body.

"Nina, we both know this has to end. I must ask that you don't join me on the book tour. Seeing each other day after day wouldn't be right."

A chill ran down Nina's spine. Forcing a smile, she said, "I wasn't looking for a fairy-tale ending, Derek. I went into this relationship with my eyes wide open. I know Kathy and the children mean the world to you."

"No hard feelings?"

"No hard feelings," Nina lied. "You're not the first married man I've been involved with, and I know I'm not your first affair. Anyway, the ring, a home, a family, not my thing. I'm married to my career. I'll tell Joe that I'd be wasting my time following you around the country when I could be signing another client. I'll work on finding you a replacement, obviously a male. A female could not resist your good looks."

Derek reached for Nina's hand. "Thanks for the compliment, but—"

"But what! You don't think you're handsome? Come on, have you looked in the mirror lately?" Nina smiled. Rising, she gathered her clothes. From the corner of her eye, she could see Derek enter the bathroom. He emerged fully clothed.

"I should be getting home." As Derek walked toward her, she stopped him and asked, "Do you know when I became attracted to you?"

"No."

"The day you invited Keith and me to watch you at work. The young girl, what was her name?"

"Angela."

"Yes, Angela. She was twelve years old. Didn't have a chance in hell of surviving. You held a beating heart in your hands. Two hours later, the color returned to Angela's cheeks. I think of her often. I want to remember her growing old with her many children and grandchildren surrounding her bed when that heart stops beating. God gave her life, and you gave her a second chance."

"I'm not a god, Nina. I'm just a man."

Nina frowned. "I'm not very religious, but I do remember the Ten Commandments, and I've broken the first. 'I am the Lord your God: you shall not have strange gods before me.'"

Derek placed a kiss on Nina's head. "I'm so sorry, Nina. I hope we can remain friends."

She sighed. Their last kiss was not on her lips but the top of her head. The tears fell gently onto her cheeks, as she scolded herself for breaking the golden rule.

Nina had been hit on by married men in the past. She'd avoided crossing the forbidden line until she met and fell in love with Dr. Derek Wilson.

Nina reflected on the time that Kathy wanted to meet with her and Keith. Derek arranged a lunch. The three arrived early, and seconds later, Derek's cell buzzed. Kathy was running late. While Keith and Derek were discussing the book, Nina took notice of several men at the bar. Someone had caught the gentlemen's eye. Curious, Nina glanced in the same direction as the men. A beautiful blond woman was walking toward them. Derek rose.

"Sweetheart, you look beautiful. Nina, Keith, this is Kathy." Derek rushed to greet his wife. He placed a kiss on her lips. After the kiss, he asked, "Traffic?"

"No. Scotty didn't want Mommy to leave the house."

Kathy extended her hand. "Nina, we finally meet. Keith, the ghostwriter, truly not a ghost."

Keith slurred his words, mesmerized by the woman's beauty. "Mrs. Wilson, it's a pleasure to meet you."

That day would forever haunt Nina. Meeting the wife did not stop Nina from loving the husband. Kathy was not only beautiful but smart. Nina realized thirty minutes after meeting Kathy that the revisions to Derek's book were her doing.

The second time Derek and Nina lay together, after a few drinks, the conversation of infidelity came up. Nina wanted to know why Derek would cheat on a wife that he adored. Derek solemnly confessed that he had cheated on Kathy one other time in their marriage. After their first was born, with a nurse at the hospital. Nina's name would now be etched in Derek's mind alongside the nurse's name.

Nina sobbed. She'd fallen in love with Derek. Her dream of having him to herself for six months was just that, a dream. She hated Kathy. She wanted the life that Kathy possessed. She wanted to wake up every morning with Derek at her side. She had no one to blame but herself. She had crossed the forbidden line. Now she had to endure the pain of falling in love with a married man, who would never return that love.

*****

Derek poured himself another cup of coffee. Leaning on the kitchen sink, he cursed under his breath, *Fuck*. The affair with Nina had lasted a month. *A month*, he repeated. *What the hell was I thinking?*

He wanted to believe Nina when she said she wasn't looking for a fairy-tale ending, hoping she meant what she said, "No hard feelings." He never meant to hurt Nina. He was going to end the affair sooner but didn't. He had been walking on egg shells ever since the first night he and Nina were together. He feared that Nina would call Kathy, destroying his perfect life. Nina reassured him that she had no intentions of hurting his family.

Hurting Derek could backfire on Nina as well. Flynn and Bachman wouldn't look too kindly on Nina sleeping with a client, especially a client they believe could make it to the *New York Times* bestseller's list. Nina had as much to lose as he. Derek did the right thing breaking it off. He was sure that a few months from now, Nina would forget she'd ever met Dr. Derek Wilson. Who was he kidding? He knew the woman was falling for him. If she wasn't so damn eager to please, the affair would have ended after the first night.

He tried to stop himself from thinking of the six months of sexual fantasies he could have conjured up with Nina as the recipient. Derek didn't consider himself a perverted man, but he did enjoy pushing the envelope. Nina, shockingly, was a very willing partner. Nina was top in her field, a woman in power. But in his arms, she was powerless. He controlled her, made sexual demands of her that he would never dare ask of Kathy. Power and being in control heightened his sexual appetite.

There was only one woman that Derek ever had to fight for, and it was Kathy. He fought hard to have her. In college, freshman-year chemistry class, she was seated before he arrived. He couldn't take his eyes off her. After class, he tried to get her attention, but she didn't notice him. That was a first for Derek. He would flirt with the other girls in class, hoping Kathy would notice him. Nothing. He convinced himself it was a ploy. With his ego deflated, Derek gave up hope. Kathy earned an A+ in the class; he an A. Two years later, he would find the strength to approach her, and she agreed to a movie and a burger.

Derek never thought of himself as having a larger-than-life ego. He and Kathy were married for four years; their firstborn was two months old when his ego was inflated by another and caused him to do unforgivable deeds.

A mother in her twenties, with two children at home, had been on the heart transplant list for two years. Her condition was grave. The head surgeon informed the team that Dr. Wilson would be performing the surgery. Derek didn't fear the task he was given. He was fearless. Three hours later, he received a pat on the back from the head surgeon. Derek kept vigil over the woman for three days. On the fourth day, she was conscious and smiling.

At twelve midnight that day, Derek left the hospital for home. His first surgery was a success, and he was walking on air. He wanted to share the news with Kathy. He knew she'd be asleep, and he didn't have the heart to wake her.

"Heading home, Dr. Wilson?"

Derek turned. Sighting a pretty, blue-eyed redhead, he asked, "Julie, right?"

"Yes. It's hard to tell who is who in surgical garments. I'm impressed."

"I make a point to note the names of the surgical team, prior to surgery."

Julie smiled. "Great job on Mrs. Flint. The odds were against you."

"Excuse me?"

"You must have figured it out, the only reason Dr. Hecht gave you a shot with the knife was for training. The odds were against Mrs. Flint recovering."

"Mrs. Flint is a person, not a racehorse."

"I'm sorry to sound so cold, but you do know about the betting pools, right? The odds were against you. Everyone was sure only a miracle could have saved Mrs. Flint's life."

"A betting pool?"

"Yep. The odds were fifteen to one that you would fail. I was one of the few that bet you'd pull it off, and Mrs. Flint would make it to see another day. Harry bet she'd live a long life. He won $150. I split $100 with Will."

"These pools—betting on patient's lives is an acceptable practice?"

"No, Dr. Wilson. But you have to admit, being part of a life-and-death surgical team can be depressing. Betting on patients started long before I joined the team. And in our defense, we only bet on hopeless cases."

"And that makes it okay?"

Julie walked toward Derek. "It's obvious you're clueless about the betting pools. I like working here, Dr. Wilson. I hope you aren't going to rat the team out."

Derek stared into Julie's blue eyes. "I wouldn't want to piss off the surgical team, so your secret is safe with me."

Julie glanced at her watch. "I'm off in twenty. Can I buy you a drink with my winnings? There's a pub on Fifth whose doors are open till three in the morning."

Derek paused, thinking, *It's only a drink.* "One celebratory drink, at Charlie's, on Fifth. See you in twenty, Julie."

After five drinks, Julie and Derek checked into a hotel not far from the pub. Derek met Julie six times over a three-week period. Riddled with guilt, he knew the affair had to come to an end, and it did. As he was returning a medical chart to the surgical station, several nurses were hanging balloons and a farewell poster.

"Is someone leaving?" asked Derek.

"Julie. Her last day is Friday. Her husband was offered a position in Seattle. She's joining the surgical team at Seattle General."

The last time Derek saw Julie was at her farewell party. He raised a glass of champagne, along with the staff, and wished her well. Ten years had passed before he crossed the line once again, with Nina.

CHAPTER 2

Lauren placed a plate stacked high with pancakes on the kitchen counter. Pouring herself a second cup of coffee, she sat at the counter. Staring at the plate of pancakes, she decided they looked too good not to indulge. To avoid the extra calories, she did not spread butter on them and placed a small amount of syrup on the side of her plate. After one bite, she reached for the syrup bottle and generously dowsed the pancakes with the sugary liquid.

Savoring each bite, Lauren concluded pancakes came in a close second to an orgasm. With her mouth filled with food, she shouted to her children, "Breakfast!"

The door to the garage opened. Lauren jumped seeing her son. "Josh! I didn't see you go into the garage."

"I said, good morning, Mom. Sometimes I feel like the invisible man in this family."

"Stop being so dramatic, Josh. Where is your sister?"

"Last I saw her, she was trying to decide which jacket to pack. She is way over the fifty-pound limit."

Lauren sighed. "If she is over the weight limit, your father will be furious."

"Wow, look at this spread."

"I went a little overboard with breakfast. I wanted this breakfast to be special."

Josh flopped into the seat he had claimed as his own since the age of three. Stacking five pancakes on his plate, he dug in. Thinking her son handsome, Lauren wanted to reach over and rustle his thick head of hair. A gesture Josh put a stop to after his ninth birthday.

"Did you pack your hiking boots?"

"I don't think we will be doing much hiking, Mom. This trip is all about the arts."

"Visiting art museums is tops on Kelly's list, and Michelle has arranged to visit quite a few. Your father has set aside a few days for hiking."

Kelly entered the kitchen. "Art museums, music to my ears. Wow, Mom, blueberry pancakes. What's that on your plate?"

"Pancakes."

"You're always watching your weight. Do you know how many calories you just ate?"

"A lot."

"Yogurt and blueberries would have been a healthier choice."

Ignoring her daughter, Lauren asked, "Are you packed?"

Kelly grabbed a yogurt cup from the counter. "Packed."

"Under the fifty-pound limit?"

"I guess."

"Kelly, take the black backpack, just in case you have to transfer some clothes. You'll find it in my bedroom closet."

"Great idea, Mom. That reminds me. Mom, can I borrow your sexy black sandals?"

"Absolutely not. I've already packed them for my trip."

"Fine. I'll take the pair Aunt Kathy bought me?" Kelly left the kitchen in a huff.

Jake called from the foyer. "The doorbell isn't working."

"We're in the kitchen."

Josh sighed. "Why does Dad insist on ringing the bell to enter a house that he still owns?"

Lauren shrugged her shoulders.

Lauren and Jake had told the children that the house was going to be sold when they went off to college. One year was an eternity to Lauren. She longed to move to her family's place on Cape Cod. Lauren, an only child, inherited the house upon her parents' death.

Jake hugged his son from behind. "It's a great day to fly, not a cloud in the sky."

"There could be a storm kicking up in the Atlantic, Dad."

"I've already checked, son. No storms on the horizon. Where is your sister? She can't still be packing? Josh, tell your sister, if it isn't packed, it is not going. I told Michelle we would be back by twelve."

"Twelve? The flight leaves at six tonight."

"Two hours to the airport, no traffic. Check-in could take an hour or more. Best to be early."

Lauren smiled at her son. "It's going to be a long day."

Josh agreed. Rising, he called to his sister. "Better get a move on, sis. Dad is leaving in twenty minutes."

Jake sat down. "What, a feast?"

"Hungry?"

Jake declined.

"Hi, Dad." Placing a kiss on Jake's cheek, Kelly hugged her father.

"Hi, sweetie. Are you packed? Fifty pounds, correct?"

"Dad, you're such a worrier. Mom gave me a great idea. She said to take the black backpack, just in case I have to transfer some clothes."

"Great, more bags. We are heading out in twenty, missy."

"I'll bring down my luggage. I wouldn't want to upset your schedule, Dad."

Lauren chuckled. "When I was Kelly's age, I thought my parents were clueless."

"Amy, Lex, and I thought my father lived in a bubble. The man hated change."

Hearing Jake refer to his siblings made the hair on Lauren's arms rise. Jake's family only tolerated Lauren because she was Josh and Kelly's mom.

Lauren wrote her first book when Kelly was three, and her second book, two years later. By the fourth book in the series "Millennium Agent," Lauren began to lose that loving feeling for Jake.

During the early days of their marriage, the two occasionally argued. When the book tours began, so did the shouting matches. After the fourth book, Jake asked if Lauren could hold off on writing the fifth. His complaint—she was spending too much time away from the children, him, and their home. That was when the marriage began to collapse.

Lauren argued, "Jake, are you insane? You want me to give up writing? How selfish of you! I would never ask you to give up something you enjoy. If I'm not mistaken, my income for the last two years exceeds yours, so if either of us must give up their job, it's you."

Jake backed off, leaving Lauren to her writing and book tours. The couple drifted apart. Lauren began to refer to sex as "guilt sex." Lauren confronted Jake. "Jake, I know you're unhappy. You signed up for a wife, children, and the white picket fence, not an author. We started out on the same path, but somewhere along the road to happiness, we lost our way. It's time to consider letting go."

No one marries expecting the marriage to end. Jake and Lauren's marriage had a good run while it lasted. Several months later, they spoke with the children. Two months later, Jake moved out.

"How are Gus and Amy? Gus still hugging the bottle?"

"Gus joined an AA group. My parents refer to Amy's house as the dry house."

"There are liquor stores on every corner in Boston. If Gus wants to tie one on, he doesn't have to go far unless your sister finds a way to close every liquor store in a hundred-mile radius."

Jake laughed. "I'm sure she tried. Gus has been clean for fifteen months."

"I've always liked Gus. He still treats me like family. I can't say the same for the rest of your family. I do miss chatting with Amy. We were close until—"

"Why don't you give her a call?"

"No way! Give your sister a chance to gloat. 'Hi, Lauren, I guess you weren't as unforgettable as you thought. My brother sure did find a winner in Michelle.'"

"She might surprise you. Dealing with Gus's problem has mellowed out Amy. She's not as quick to judge others."

"Maybe now, but when you and I separated, she made it very clear that Christians do not divorce. Family secrets should remain in the closet, such as your uncle Hank. We all knew he had a second family two towns over, earning him the nickname 'Every Other Year.' Your cousin Greg and his best friend, how long have they been living together, eighteen years? Hypocrites, the lot of them, except for you."

Jake smiled.

Dropping a sensitive subject, Lauren asked, "How is Michelle feeling?"

Jake met Michelle on a first-class flight to Paris. Michelle occupied the seat next to him. Jake graciously asked if she preferred window or aisle. Michelle preferred the window seat. They switched. A conversation began, and Jake soon discovered that Michelle was an art appraiser. Once a month, she traveled to Paris for work. Jake, hearing of Michelle's profession, proudly announced that his daughter, Kelly, began painting when she was three. Now in her second year of high school, Kelly's dream was to be accepted to an art academy in Paris in her junior year. When the flight landed, the couple exchanged business cards. Jake took a chance and called Michelle two days later. During their stay in Paris, she and Jake met several times for dinner.

Arriving home, they continued to see each other. Six months into their relationship, Michelle told Jake it was love at first sight for her. Jake confessed the feeling was mutual. Realizing his happiness was with Michelle, Jake called his attorney to say that he was ready to sign the divorce agreement.

Three months after the divorce was finalized, Jake told Lauren he'd met someone. Anxious to introduce the children to Michelle, he asked Lauren's opinion. Jake was happy, and Lauren was happy for him. She gave her permission for Jake to introduce the children to Michelle. Jake made a reservation at their favorite restaurant and broke the news. Preparing himself for the fallout, to his surprise, the children asked, "Does Michelle make you happy?" His response, yes.

After the children were introduced to Michelle, she called Lauren. Other women would have thought Michelle's tenacity as pushy. Lauren thought Michele's call was sincere, welcomed, and considerate. During their conversation, Michelle assured Lauren, she wanted the children to accept her as a friend, nothing more.

Michelle was eight years younger than Jake. Lauren assumed that Michelle wanted a child of her own. When Jake and Lauren met to discuss the trip, Jake informed Lauren that he asked Michelle to marry him. With pride, he told Lauren that Michelle was pregnant.

The pregnancy, Lauren would attest, did not force a marriage proposal. It was obvious to Lauren, Jake loved Michelle. Jake had always wanted a third child, so Lauren knew the baby wasn't a surprise. Michelle insisted that Lauren be the first to know, saying, "Lauren should be aware of situations that will impact her children's lives."

"Michelle is doing well. When we return from Paris, we have our first sonogram the following Wednesday."

"I bet she's excited."

"She is. This isn't my first go-around, but I'm a little anxious to hear the heartbeat."

"Michelle is a keeper, Jake."

"She is a keeper. I never thought I could love someone as much—I'm sorry, Lauren."

"Don't apologize. I'm happy for you, Jake. You deserve to be happy. I wish I could be there when you tell Josh and Kelly the news."

"There's another reason for the trip. You know that Vince Di Marco requested that Michelle be the person to appraise his work. Well, during their conversation, Michelle told Di Marco of Kelly's interest in studying at the art academy in Paris. Di Marco wants to meet Kelly. Michelle thinks their meeting could land Kelly a spot at the academy."

For the first time since the divorce, Lauren was jealous. Kelly's dreams would not materialize with her mother's help but from her stepmother's connections. As Jake went on about Michelle's accomplishments in the art world, Lauren remembered when she happily called Jake to say her first novel was accepted for publication. All Jake could muster-up was *congratulations*. Suppressing her feelings, Lauren smiled and asked, "October is right around the corner. Do you have a date for the wedding?"

"October 25."

Lauren's phone buzzed. "It's Kathy. I'll be right back."

"Hi, Kathy, what's up?"

"Just called to say, as requested, I'm packed and ready to go."

"Great."

"That reminds me, I should go over the children's itinerary with Derek."

"Isn't that Fanny's job?"

"Do I have the right number? Is this Lauren Hicks? The Lauren Hicks, who nags the hell out of me, that my husband, Dr. Derek Charles Wilson, should be spending more time with his children?"

Taken back by Kathy using Lauren's maiden name, Lauren Hicks, Lauren wondered if Kathy had given up on Lauren and Jake reconciling. Kathy couldn't accept that she and Jake had divorced. She believed that one day they would come to their senses and realize they couldn't live without each other. Jake would kiss Michelle goodbye and return home to Lauren and the children. Lauren couldn't wait to see the expression on Kathy's face when she heard Jake's news.

"I can't believe Dr. Dick is spending an entire week with the brats."

"He's not going at it alone, Lauren. He has Fanny and Jenny to help. Anyway, the man is a doctor for heaven's sake. I'm sure he can handle five kids."

"He's a heart surgeon. He handles one heart at a time."

Kathy laughed. "You're angry, why?"

"Jake's in the kitchen. He came to pick up Josh and Kelly. I'm a little concerned about this trip."

"It's too late to change your mind. Jake would never agree to—"

"I'm not changing my mind. Anyway, in a year, Josh will be off to college, and Kelly, hopefully, will be studying art in Paris. It's time to cut the umbilical cord."

"True. Then don't second-guess your decision. Derek spoke with Jake last week. Derek said Jake is really excited about the trip."

Oh, Kathy, if you only knew the truth, thought Lauren. "I'm sure he is. I've got to go. I'll see you at ten tomorrow. Ten o'clock sharp."

"Oh, Derek was hoping we'd have lunch with him and the kids."

"Funny. Dr. Dick doesn't want to spend a minute more than he has to with me, or I with him."

"You will come in to say a proper goodbye to the children and Fanny. I don't want you to lean on the car horn to avoid seeing my family."

"I promise to come in, kiss each brat on the head, say a proper goodbye to Fanny, and give the middle finger to Dr. Dick."

"Dr. Dick loves you, Lauren."

"Bullshit. I've got to go. Jake wants to be at the airport by two."

"What time's the flight?"

"Six."

Kathy laughed. "You can't change the spots on a leopard nor Jake's fear of being late."

"That's one of Jake's annoying qualities. I have to go. Say hi to Dr. Dick."

"Will do. Wish the kids and Jake a safe trip from Aunt Kathy."

Lauren entered the kitchen. "Kathy says hi."

"I spoke with Derek last week."

"Kathy mentioned you did. Does Derek know about your plans?"

"Of course."

"Well, he hasn't shared the news with his wife."

"I'm guessing he has a lot on his mind. You know, he's not thrilled about the book tours. I don't think Kathy and Derek have been apart for more than a week since college."

"You might be right. Kathy said Derek insisted he'll be home every weekend. There are only two conflicting weekends that he won't be home."

"I'm sure he'll fly Kathy out to him."

"Kathy leaving her children? No way! Dr. Dick will have to do without his precious Kathy for two weeks."

"I'll never understand why you give Derek such a hard time."

"I don't have to remind you that I was never a fan of Dr. Dick. I tolerate the man because he is married to one of my best friends."

Jake smiled. "Kathy and Derek are a perfect match in looks, smarts, and you can't deny their love for each other."

Lauren sighed. "I guess."

The first time Lauren met Kathy Quinn was in college. Kathy is the smartest of all of Lauren's friends. She was valedictorian of Northwestern University.

Kathy was a natural beauty—blond hair, a China-doll face, the bluest of eyes, and a shape that turned men's heads. Five feet six in stature, her long and sleek legs, and her perfect round breasts drove men wild. She was hated by women and adored by men.

Kathy earned her degree in the sciences, specializing in chemistry. Her professors were sure they were in the presence of the woman who would discover a cure for cancer. But Kathy had plans of her own. She dreamed of the perfect husband and a house filled with children, created by their undying love for each other.

Every guy who crossed her path fell head over heels in love with her. In college, out of her many suitors Edward Garson tried to convince Kathy that there wasn't a man on earth who could love her more than he. Eddie, as he was known in college, came from money. Eddie's great-grandfather made his fortune in oil. Future generations of the Garson clan were taught well on how to invest their fortune. Children who would not be born for decades would enter the world setup with a sizable trust fund. If Eddie thought his fortune would entice Kathy to remain with him, he was greatly mistaken. Wealth was the furthest thing from Kathy's mind. Finding the love of her life, rich or poor, was all Kathy cared about.

Kathy didn't come from money. The money her family earned came from hard work, not hard labor. Kathy's parents earned scholarships and graduated from Princeton University, where they met and fell in love. Kathy's mother, a well-known divorce attorney, appeared on several talk shows. Kathy's father respected his wife's accomplishments but chose a simple life as a psychology professor, at the University of Michigan. Kathy had one sibling, a brother five years older, a tech nerd, who Kathy rarely saw. He lived and worked in London at a prestigious tech firm.

Derek came from a middle-class family. His mother and father were blue-collar workers. Derek excelled in school, especially in science, earning him a scholarship to Northwestern University. His dream, to be one of the ten best heart surgeons in the United States. He was a master with a surgical knife, and his fortune would be earned by his craft. What Derek possessed that Eddie could never achieve was, Derek was equal to Kathy in looks and smarts.

Derek's dream of dating Kathy came to fruition when Eddie's father, not happy with Northwestern, convinced his son to transfer to Yale. Eddie feared two things in life–losing Kathy and disappointing his father. Derek made his move as soon as Eddie's limo was no longer visible. Several months later, Kathy wrote Eddie a Dear John letter.

Lauren was a hard-ass; Kathy, a sweetheart. Lauren didn't think Kathy should date Derek. Before setting his sights on Kathy, Derek was well on his way to bedding every sexy girl on campus. His reputation as a womanizer preceded him. Lauren expressed her feelings to Kathy. "Kathy, the guy is good-looking and smart, but he's also possessive, self-centered, and extremely conceited. Mostly, I don't trust the guy. You're an intelligent girl, Kathy. Use your head. The guy is a player." Lauren was convinced that Kathy was setting herself up to have her heart broken. Derek proved Lauren wrong. Once Kathy and Derek were an item, Derek the playboy ceased to exist.

Kathy introduced Lauren to Jake Croft. Lauren wasn't looking for an exclusive relationship, but she agreed to one date with Jake. Lauren surprised herself, feeling a strong attraction to Jake. One date led to several dates, ending with them marrying two years after graduation. Kathy introduced Jake to Derek, and a close bond was formed.

Jake was a successful businessman. He was offered a position with Google right out of college, where he earned his master's and a PhD. With hard work and determination, Jake was now the CEO at Google's Boston location. But with all his accomplishments, he didn't think his success was equal to Derek's telling Lauren, "The man saves lives."

Lauren returned to the present. "I have to hand it to you, Jake, forty six years young, and you're expecting your third child. I'm sure Michelle will want another. Her biological clock is ticking. You realize next September, you'll drop off you're oldest at college while patting your youngest on the back, hoping for a burp."

Jake laughed. "I didn't mind changing a diaper or two. I'd bet I've changed more diapers than you."

"I bet you have. You know, I made it a point to feed the kids their dinner fifteen minutes before you came home from work. If they pooped, you'd say, 'You've had them all day, sweetie. I got this.'"

"You didn't fool me, Lauren." Jake chuckled. "Kelly took the worst poops."

Jake and Lauren began to laugh. When the laughter subsided, Lauren said, "I don't think you will have that problem with Michelle. She doesn't seem like the type to let her child sit in a dirty diaper."

"I feel extremely lucky. You're a great mom, and I have no doubt Michelle will be a great mom."

Changing the subject, Jake asked, "Are you looking forward to seeing the girls?"

"I am. I haven't seen Kathy or Elle in months. You know, Elle is working in Washington?"

"I do. Last time we talked, she said she dropped the guy she was dating."

"Jacques."

"Yes. Jacques."

"You know Elle—love them and leave them. Hey, why do you think your friend Derek didn't tell his precious wife your plans to marry and about the bun in the oven?"

"I don't know why he didn't tell her, but I'm guessing you wouldn't mind telling her yourself?"

"Well, if it's fine with you, I wouldn't mind sharing the joyous news."

Josh walked into the kitchen. "I heard you guys laughing. What's so funny?"

Lauren came up with a story to protect Jake's secret. "We were discussing, out of the two of our children, who took the worst poops. Kelly won."

Kelly entered the kitchen. "Josh, you're so gross. Why are you guys talking about poop?"

"I wasn't talking—forget it. Dad, our luggage is in the foyer. I need the car keys."

"Great. I'll take care of the luggage. You and your sister, say goodbye to your mom."

Kelly came in for a hug. "Mom, I'm going to miss you. I wish you were coming."

"It's only three weeks, sweetie. Don't forget to thank Michelle and your dad for planning this trip. And promise me, you won't wander far from your family, young lady. There are crazies everywhere."

"I promise I won't wander off. I love you, Mom."

Lauren gave her little girl a bear hug. When they parted, Kelly's eyes were glassy. "Have a great time, sweetie." To avoid Lauren seeing how upset she was, Kelly rushed off to help her father.

Josh smiled at Lauren. "Mom, we are going to miss you. It feels strange going on a trip without you. Anyway, Dad isn't fooling anyone. This trip, I'm guessing, will be a life changer."

"My lips are sealed. This trip is really important to your dad and Michelle. You like Michelle, don't you?"

"I do. She makes Dad happy, and that's all that matters, right?"

Lauren hugged her son. "Your parents are happy, Josh."

Josh and Lauren's eyes locked. "Have a great time with Aunt Kathy and Aunt Elle. Remember, don't drink and drive. I know how the wine flows when you gals are together. Assign a designated driver."

"Look at you. All that nagging paid off, designated driver. You do listen."

*****

Lauren placed the packed suitcase on the floor, exhausted from the day; she collapsed onto the bed. Reaching for the remote, she turned on the TV. It was time for her favorite TV show, *Jeopardy*. After answering twenty questions correctly, Lauren's cell phone buzzed. It was Elle.

"Hi, Elle?"

"Hi, Lauren, how are you holding up?"

"Holding up?"

"With the kids away, I thought you might need a friend to talk to."

"I haven't had too much time to miss them. It's only been a few hours. Before long, I will be an empty nester. I'm going to miss this house."

"So it's definite—you're selling the house? Good decision. Did the kids call before the flight took off?"

"They did. Josh said his dad was right, there was traffic getting to the airport. Two hours to check in. and the security line was long."

"I agree with Jake. Since 9/11, flying can be a nightmare."

"I guess."

"I spoke with Kathy. She said you read her the riot act. If she isn't ready to leave by ten tomorrow morning, you're leaving without her."

"Correct. With or without her."

Elle laughed. "Looking forward to seeing you guys. Be careful driving."

"Before you go, did you speak with Alice?"

"No. I'll give her a call tomorrow."

"I'm not looking forward to seeing Alice. I don't know what Casey was thinking when she got involved with that woman."

"We're doing this for Casey?"

"I guess."

*****

Naked, Lauren ran to answer her cell phone.

"Lauren, I've called twice. Were you out?"

"I was in the shower. Why are you calling, Kathy? Don't tell me one of the brats is sick, and you're not going. I swear, Kathy, I will have you killed if you cancel!"

"I'm not calling to cancel. I just wanted to check on you. With the kids gone, I thought you might be lonely."

Lauren spied the clock on her nightstand. "Elle called two hours ago to check on me. I'm doing fine since they've only been gone nine hours."

"You should feel blessed having Elle and me as friends. We worry about you, alone in that big house, the children on vacation with a woman we hardly know."

Lauren had to control herself from shouting, *a reconciliation is never going to happen, my dear friend.* "I do feel blessed to have you and Elle as my BFFs. I told Elle we will be there by six o'clock, just in time for dinner. You know what that means, right?"

"Yes, on the road by ten, not a minute later. Come early, Derek will have coffee waiting."

"I don't have time for coffee with Dr. Dick, and I'm sure he's hoping that I don't overstay my welcome."

"Not true. I've often said, you two are so much alike it's scary."

"Dr. Dick and I are like night and day. If he says black, I say white. It's been that way since Christ was a cadet."

"You're cut from the same mold."

"I'm nothing like Derek, and I hate you for comparing me to him."

"You can't hate me. We're blood sisters forever. Remember?"

Lauren smiled, thinking back on that night in college. After a few too many drinks, Casey pricked her index finger, demanding the girls do the same. Kathy and Elle immediately followed Casey's lead. Lauren, of course, protested. Casey teased Lauren. Frustrated, Lauren pricked her middle finger and pointed it at Casey.

Lauren whispered into the phone, "Blood sisters, forever."

*****

At four in the morning, Lauren found herself staring into her coffee cup. When she broke the stare, she retrieved a thermos and filled it with coffee.

She wanted to call Elle, but it was too early. She'd call from the car.

Lauren glanced at her reflection in the mirror. Satisfied, she reached for the suitcase that she had placed by her bedroom door the night before. Passing by her children's rooms, she sighed. Both rooms were spotless. Why, she was thinking, couldn't it always look this neat? Shortly, her babies will be off on their own. The clothes spilling over the hamper, the untidy bed, hair in the bathroom drain, toothpaste stuck in the bathroom sink, books, and video games spread on the floor will forever be memories. The punishments she dished out for not helping around the house will be long forgotten. Where does the time go? Descending the stairs, Lauren placed the suitcase by the front door. Staring at the door, she was reminded of the day she and

Jake took ownership of their dream home—Jake carrying her over the threshold and their little ones following behind, laughing, as Jake mimicked Lauren was too heavy to carry. Lauren could feel her eyes begin to well. To stop the tears from falling, she set the house alarm, picked up the suitcase, and opened the front door. Locking it, she closed the door behind her.

It was five thirty when Lauren entered her car. She dialed Elle's cell. Lauren's call went to voicemail. She left Elle a message. Placing her cell phone on the passenger's seat, she started the car.

Alone on a dark highway, Lauren mentally scripted her next book. Her thoughts were placed on hold when her cell phone rang. She hit the speaker button. "Hi, Elle."

"I was heading out for a run. I grabbed my phone and saw your message."

"I was feeling a little down, and you're the only person that I know who is up this early."

"Lauren Hicks Croft, a little down? This must be bad."

"I guess being without the kids—Elle, do you think I was wrong putting my career before my children?"

"Lauren, is this about the kids, or the trip that's got you down?"

"I'm not going to lie. I'd rather be boarding a plane to Bermuda."

"I have to agree, Bermuda might be a better choice."

"I might make a left turn and head to the airport. Wouldn't surprise a soul if I didn't show. You know I don't give a rat's ass what people think of me. I'm a heartless hard-ass and proud of it."

Elle smiled. "I know you better than anyone, Lauren. Deep down, you're a soft cuddly teddy bear."

"You're the one with a heart, Elle, not me. I handed Jake his walking papers six months after I knew my marriage wasn't working for me. You leave love notes saying it wasn't the guy's fault but yours."

Elle thought of Jacques. "Maybe I should have given one of those many suitors a chance. I might have a kid or two of my own."

"You don't need a man to have a child. You're still young. For sure, you'd be a great mom. It's not too late. Not to bring up a sore subject, but I thought the last one, Jacques, was the one. He proposed, didn't he?"

"Three times to be exact. After the third time, I left him a love note."

"I hate to pry, but I'm guessing Jacques didn't want to move to the good old USA, land of the free, home of the brave."

"Never asked."

"Wow."

"Career first. I was offered my dream job, anchor woman, six-o'clock spot, Washington, DC. Didn't have time to worry about hurt feelings."

"And they call me the hard-ass. Kidding aside, adoption, not a wild idea. There are so many children in need of a good home."

"I should adopt a child from one of the third-world countries, like Angelina and Brad."

"I love the idea. I'll start the paperwork."

"First, work on getting Kathy out of the house by ten."

"I'm not kidding, Elle, with or without her. I'm leaving by ten."

"I can understand why Kathy doesn't want to leave home. If I were married to Derek—"

"I know we rarely disagree, Elle, but Derek doesn't do it for me."

"Why do you give the guy such a hard time? I think it's because you guys are so much alike."

"Kathy, Jake, and you are convinced that Derek and I butt heads because we are alike. Listen, I tolerate Dr. Dick because he's married to one of my best friends."

Elle chuckled. "If you say so. Be careful driving. Good luck getting Kathy out of the house."

Lauren disconnected and repeated to herself, "Dr. Dick and I are nothing alike."

CHAPTER 3

Dressing for her run, Elle's thoughts were consumed by Jacques and her BFFs. Elle smiled, questioning Lauren's dislike for Derek. It was plain to see that Derek and Lauren were cut from the same mold, but neither would agree. Elle chuckled, wondering, if Derek had written a book just to one up Lauren.

Reaching the street, she took off running. She ran along the Potomac but hardly noticed her surroundings. Washington has charm but lacks the charm of Paris. Paris caused Elle to think of Jacques. She wiped all thoughts of Jacques from her mind and concentrated on her friends and their personalities. Lauren and Derek—self-centered achievers, strong-willed, and impulsive. She too was an achiever, but she did not consider herself self-centered. Impulsive, yes; she walked away from the only man she ever truly loved.

Clearing her mind of Jacques for a second time, she began to think of Kathy and Jake. Those two were definitely cut from the same mold—both caring, sweet as apple pie, and humble to boot. Casey was a combination of the four—strong-minded, definitely. Many times when the ladies had a tiff or two, Lauren would refer to Casey as a controlling bitch. Elle traveled to third-world countries taking on many fights to end hunger, thirst, and injustice. As a journalist, Elle reported the news, but when her job was done, she took her leave, wishing the people well. Casey would have stuck around to make sure the job got done.

In college, Elle tired easily when a girl would whine about a boy who didn't give her the time of day. Casey would patiently listen to the girl's woes and gave the best advice a friend could offer. That's what attracted Elle to Jacques, his disposition was similar to Casey's.

It happened again, thought Elle. Jacques had entered her thoughts for a third time. Elle's Fitbit buzzed. She'd run farther than she'd intended. Finding a bench, she sat. Looking out over the Potomac, she spied a boat making its way down the river. A short time ago, it was another boat and another river, the Seine River, in Paris. She missed Jacques so much it hurt.

She thought about her first job out of college. She was a go-getter girl for a small network in Detroit. Her big break came when Mr. Pratik gave her a shot as a traffic reporter. She didn't like the job much, but she did enjoy flying over the city in the company helicopter. When Mr. Pratik retired, Ms. Weston replaced him. Ms. Weston, an activist for women's rights, gave Elle her first major break. She was sent to Washington, DC, as a news reporter. Two years later, Ms. Weston asked if she would be interested in reporting the news from Iraq. She jumped at the chance. After three years, she tired of the muddy streets and the cold shelters and asked for a transfer. Ms. Weston offered her the anchor position in the Paris office.

One month after moving to Paris, she met Jacques Pascal. Several months later, Jacques convinced Elle they should move in together since neither spent much time in their own apartments. After two years, Jacques proposed. At the same time, the Washington, DC, six o'clock news anchor's position became available. Elle phoned Ms. Weston to inform her that she was the ideal person for the job. Ms. Weston agreed.

Elle jogged home. She showered, dressed, and poured coffee into a thermal cup. There was a major accident on I-95. Looking up at a cloudless sky, Elle decided to board the ferry to Cape May. She made her way to the top of the boat. Leaning over the railing, she watched the waves slap against the side of the huge vessel, and thought of Jacques. *Cruel* was the only word to describe leaving as she did. How many times had Jacques asked, "Elle, *pourquoi?*"

Her response was "This is my dream job, Jacques. Anyway, Paris is your home. It's not mine. The job is in Washington, DC, which happens to be in the USA, where I was born and raised. Listen, it's been a great two years. You're a great guy. Stop beating yourself up. You didn't know that this opportunity would come knocking, and I never thought that I would want something as much as I want this job."

The writing was on the wall. Elle wanted the job more than she wanted a life with Jacques. His efforts, over a two-week period, to get Elle to change her mind caused her to move to a hotel. Two days later, she would board a plane for home.

Elle spied the Cape May coastline. Seeing the lighthouse in the distance excited her. The Jersey Shore was where Elle spent most of her summers during college. College, her friends, a summer job at the Jersey Shore kept her far from her family in North Dakota. That was her plan, the day she left home for college.

This was Casey's hometown. Casey's mom and dad wanted to sell their home and retire to Arizona. Casey offered to buy her parents' home. Casey's sister and brother lived on the West Coast, and living there didn't appeal to Casey. After graduation, Casey continued her art education in Manhattan. She was talented, and a local art gallery on Fifth Avenue agreed to display her paintings. With the money she earned over an eight-year period, she paid off the note held by her parents and moved back to her childhood home. She began to paint sunsets, landscapes being her favorite, the ocean, beaches, dunes, and cottages—popular with the natives and tourists. Shortly after moving back home, she met and fell in love with Alice.

Casey, the controller, had landed Lauren, Kathy, and Elle summer jobs at the Jersey Shore. Elle smiled, reminded of her BFFs, college, and those god-awful summer jobs. The first job being the worst. Casey had convinced Lauren, Kathy, and Elle that working in New Jersey would give them a chance to meet their idol, Bruce Springsteen. Bruce was known to drop in at his favorite pub in Asbury Park and belt out a few tunes. Their intentions were to frequent the bar as often as they could. Of course, since they worked around the clock, with only Sundays off, and too exhausted to travel to Asbury Park, the closest they ever got to their idol was when Bruce performed at the Conference Center in Wildwood. From their nosebleed seats, they sang along with Bruce and screamed their dying love for him. And how can she forget their first apartment that Casey had rented sight unseen, an apartment they shared with three girls from Poland—three bedrooms, seven residents. Controlling Casey convinced the Polish girls to take the larger bedroom, which could easily accommodate three girls.

The BFFs waitressed at a motel restaurant, serving breakfast, lunch, and dinner. Their shift started at six thirty in the morning. They would set the alarm clock to go off at five because after four lukewarm showers, the water ran cold. The Polish girls elected to sleep late and never complained about the shower water being cold. Lauren crudely explained, "Heck, they live in Poland. It is fucking freezing there."

On rainy days, the roof leaked. There were pots scatted around the apartment to catch the water. They listened to the weather report daily. When there was rain in the forecast, they raised their mattress to avoid coming home to a wet bed. There were no blinds or shades on the windows, so they purchased dark-colored sheets and nailed them across the windows to block out the morning sun.

Lauren complained the most and swore she'd never return. She'd find a job in Cape Cod and live at her parents' home where there was hot water, blinds on the windows, and no leaking roofs. As their second year of college was drawing to an end, Casey's mom told her of a friend who needed to fill several waitress positions at his restaurant in Cape May. The hourly rate was decent; they would keep 80 percent of their tips, one day off during the week and Sundays. It was a sweet deal, and Elle and Kathy were in. Lauren held out until she heard that Mrs. Collins, a friend of Casey's mom, would rent them the upstairs rooms in her home.

Mrs. Collins had two rules, no boys in the house, but they could invite a few friends to spend time in the backyard, which overlooked the ocean. Eleven p.m. was the cut-off time for friends who visited. Casey swore to Lauren, there would be hot water to shower, no leaking roofs, and blinds on the windows. Lauren caved in two weeks before the spring semester ended. Elle was convinced that Casey, if given the chance, could convince the Lenape Indians that eighteen dollars, not twenty-four dollars, was a fair price for Manhattan.

There were many suitors that frequented Mrs. Collins's home. Kathy, being the most popular, introduced the girls to really good-looking guys. Lauren had a fling with a soccer player from Germany. Elle fell hard for a guy who played in the band at the local pub. Kathy became good friends with a local boy who knew he was way out of her league. They enjoyed being together knowing they would part as friends when the summer came to an end. Casey flirted with a few of the boys but nothing serious. The following summer was a repeat of the prior summer, and the last summer they would work at the Jersey Shore.

Kathy had taken herself out of the dating scene once she and Derek's relationship began. With graduation on the horizon, the BFFs had bigger fish to fry, a master's degree and a career path.

As the ferry drew closer to the shore, Elle removed her sweater and wrapped it around her waist. Excitement and stress were what she was feeling—excited to see her BFFs and stressed about her split with Jacques. She knew that her friends would reassure her that she had made the right decision.

The ferry whistle blew, announcing their arrival. Elle descended the stairs, got into her car, and waited for the attendant to lower the gate and usher her forward. Back on the road, she lowered the car windows and breathed in the salty air.

CHAPTER 4

Kathy entered the kitchen to find Derek staring at the gardens. "Admiring my work, or should I say Emmanuel's work."

Leaning on the counter, she tried to slip on her sandals without untying them. Hearing her voice, Derek turned. "It would be easier if you untied them first."

"I can wiggle into them. Done."

Derek smiled. "You look beautiful."

Kathy walked toward Derek. "So you think I'm beautiful, do you?"

"I do. Those sandals are sexy. They're turning me on."

"Are they, Dr. Wilson?"

"I can take you right here on the counter."

Kathy moved in closer and started to tease Derek. "What's stopping you?"

Derek glanced at the clock on the wall. "The witch won't be here for another thirty minutes, plenty of time for a little roll in the hay."

"So what's holding you back?"

Derek hoisted Kathy over his shoulder and headed for the stairs.

Kathy was laughing. "Thirty minutes, not a minute more."

As Derek climbed the stairs, he said, "To save time, I won't remove the sandals."

The manic breathing of intercourse was slowly returning to normal. Derek rested his head on Kathy's forehead. Moving his fingers up and down the curves of her hip, he whispered, "I love you." Kathy's head was resting on his shoulder, her hand on his chest, and her leg stretched across his torso. He was becoming aroused. "I can never get enough of you, Mrs. Wilson."

Kathy chuckled. "Aren't you tied of making love to the same woman?"

The question had made him flaccid. He positioned himself to be face-to-face with her. He replied, "Never. I love you, Kathy. I'm not perfect. There are times I do things—"

"What are you talking about? I know you love me, and in my eyes, you are perfect. You're a great father, an adoring husband, and we love each other."

Kathy smiled, and Derek's heart leaped out of his chest. "I want you to remember how good we are together when you're barhopping with the girls."

"You're jealous. Well, you don't have a thing to worry about. Every part of me is yours, especially from the waist down."

"If something should happen that would make you second-guess my love—"

The doorbell sounded.

"You'll have to save that thought, Dr. Wilson. Answer the door. I'm going to rinse off."

Derek released Kathy. "It's probably the witch." Derek stepped into his jeans, slipped on his flip-flops, and reached for a shirt. Devilish Derek then decided not to wear a shirt.

Since the Wilsons did not answer the door on the first ring, Lauren leaned on the doorbell.

Derek swung open the door. "You're annoying."

"Do you always answer the door half naked?"

"Nothing you haven't seen before."

"Where's your wife?"

"She'll be right down." Walking past Lauren, Derek asked, "Coffee?"

"I don't have time for coffee."

"You're talking to a doctor. I can down a cup of coffee in thirty seconds. Come on."

Lauren took a seat at the kitchen counter.

"The house is quiet. Where are the kids?"

"At the park with Fanny."

"Park. I'm leaving in fifteen. You better text Fanny. You and I know your wife is not leaving until she's kissed those brats ten times each."

Derek smiled. "She really loves those kids."

"Every mother loves her children. Kathy's obsessed."

"I heard that." Kathy hugged Lauren. "I've missed you. Haven't we missed Lauren, Derek?"

Derek whispered, "Like the plague."

"Ditto," Lauren retorted.

"Stop it, you two."

"Are you ready to go?"

"It's only 9:45 a.m., Lauren." Derek texted Fanny—at that moment, Derek's phone buzzed. "They're on their way."

"Great. My bag is in the foyer. I need to get my cosmetic bag. I'll leave you two to catch-up."

With Kathy out of sight, Lauren questioned Derek. "Speaking of catching-up. Jake told me he spoke with you last week, and you know about the wedding and the baby. Can I ask why you didn't tell your wife?"

"I didn't have the heart. She was hoping for a reconciliation."

"Chicken."

"Hey, I didn't tell you to leave Jake and break Kathy's heart."

"I didn't mean to break anyone's heart. I just wanted to sit at my computer and write. Are you excited about the book tour?"

"No. I don't like being away from the family."

"And I did? Don't answer that question. I might have to hurt you."

"I'm a surgeon, not a writer."

"I hate to throw salt on an open wound, but when the book tours started, my marriage collapsed."

"My marriage is solid as a rock."

The front door crashed open.

"Your children are back."

Descending the stairs to the foyer, Kathy placed her cosmetic bag next to her suitcase and greeted her children. "Did you have fun at the park?"

In unison, the children answered yes. "Mommy, where are you going?"

"Scotty, we talked about this. Mommy is going away for a while."

Scotty began to cry. "Don't go, Mommy." Kathy reached down, taking the child into her arms. She kissed his cheek. Scotty wrapped his arms around Kathy's neck.

Derek and Lauren watched the scene unfold before their eyes. Gabe, the baby, began to sob in Fanny's arms. With her free arm, Kathy took Gabe from Fanny. Mary, the third child, wrapped her arms around Kathy's leg. Eric's and Peggy's eyes began to well with tears.

Lauren greeted Fanny with a kiss on the cheek. "Hi, Fanny. Bye, Fanny." Turning her attention to the children, Lauren kissed Eric and Peggy on the tops of their heads, patted Mary's head, and ignored the sobbing Scotty and baby Gabe.

"Get in the car, Kathy. Doc, can you get the children off your wife so we can hit the road?"

Derek took control. "Scotty, let go of Mommy's neck." Scotty removed his grip. Kathy lowered a sobbing Scotty to the floor. "Mary, let go of Mommy's leg." The child released her grip. "Kathy, give the baby to me." Kathy kissed Gabe several times before handing him off to his father. "Go! Be careful. Have fun."

Lauren took hold of Kathy's arm. She pushed Kathy out the door and into the car. Lauren waved goodbye to Kathy's family as she rounded the car to access the driver's side.

Lauren cursed when the car wouldn't start. "Fuck!"

"You have to put your foot on the brake before you press the start button, Lauren."

"Your family upsets me so much that I can't even remember how to start my own car."

Lauren peeled out of the driveway.

"I think that went well."

"What went well?"

"How the children handled my leaving."

"You think that went well?"

"Yes. Last week, I had a hair appointment. All five children hung on to me. It took me thirty minutes to convince them I'd be back before lunch."

"Then I agree that went well."

CHAPTER 5

Elle stood at the hotel counter second in line to check-in.
"Good afternoon. How can I help you?"
"My name is Ms. Kessler. I'm checking in."
The attendant keyed in Elle's last name. "Here you are, Ms. Kessler. The reservation was for three rooms on the same floor."
"Correct. My friends will be checking in later today." Elle glanced at the gentleman's shirt and discovered his name was Dave.
"You and your guests have booked the entire week. How fortunate the weather for this week calls for sun, some clouds, but no rain. Now we both know that could change on a dime, but we're going to cross our fingers that the weather report is correct."
"Yes, we are, Dave."
Elle unlocked the door to her room. Tossing her suitcase on the bed, she opened the sliding glass doors and stepped out onto the balcony. After a long and lingering stare at the ocean, she spied the children playing in the park and their mothers in casual conversation.
One mother was begging her two-year-old to eat half his sandwich. Elle thought about her own bad eating habits created by her choice in careers. She ate on the run. A banana here, an apple there, maybe a salad, if she had the time. When she moved in with Jacques, he wouldn't let her leave the apartment without eating breakfast knowing it would be her only meal till dinner. Jacques was a great cook. If he didn't have time to cook her dinner, he'd take her to his favorite restaurant. He would order two bottles of his and Elle's favorite wine. They'd talk about their day, laugh, eat, drink, and watch the people strolling past.

"Jacques," she whispered to herself. Stepping back into the room, she retrieved her cell phone. Ten messages from Jacques. She wanted to retrieve his last message, but she didn't want to hear the sadness in his voice. She would return his call later in the day. Her stomach growled. She retrieved her swimsuit, flip-flops, and a cover-up from the suitcase. A few minutes later, she exited the elevator and walked toward the outdoor restaurant.

Lounging by the pool, cell phone in hand, she called Lauren.
Kathy answered. "Hi, beautiful. It's Elle, Lauren."
"Put her on speaker."
Kathy pressed the speaker button. "Hey, Elle, are you at the hotel?"
"I'm sitting by the pool."
"Sounds nice. We're on the Garden State not far from the Wildwood exit. We would have been there sooner if this one didn't have to take ten pee breaks. I guess her bladder is shot to shit after pushing out five kids."
"You only stopped twice, Lauren, stop being so dramatic."
Elle smiled.
"Elle, did you call Alice?"
"Not yet, Lauren, but I will."
Kathy asked, "Did you make a reservation for dinner?"
"I did. We have a seven o'clock reservation at Beach Creek."
"Must be a new restaurant."
"It's fairly new. Listen, to avoid the traffic coming into Wildwood, I'd take the Garden State to the last exit. Your GPS will get you to the hotel."
"Aye, aye, Captain."
After speaking with her friends, Elle decided to take a walk on the beach. On her walk, she made two calls—one to Sam Preston, the driver she had hired for the week; and Alice. Alice answered on the first ring.

*****

"Did Elle tell you she ended it with Jacques?"
"I guess you were hoping for a fairy-tale ending."

"This is a first for us. We've been on the road for five hours and haven't discussed Elle's breakup with Jacques."

"What is there to discuss? It's Elle's MO. When the boy gets too close, she walks."

"I don't understand her. I really thought Jacques was the one. I was hoping she would give up that demanding job and settle down."

"You do realize this is the twenty-first century. Not every woman wants to marry and have a flock of kids. Some women enjoy their independence and their jobs. I know that's hard for you to believe, but it's true."

"Some women choose to do both. You did."

"Are you forgetting my marriage ended in divorce?"

"It's just a matter of time. You and Jake—well, you guys love each other."

"Just a matter of time! What do you think is going to happen? You're still not hoping for a reconciliation, are you?"

"When two people love each other—"

"Let me stop you there. I was going to wait till we caught up with Elle before I dropped this bomb. Jake and Michelle are getting married in October, and Michelle is pregnant. And Dr. Dick knew, and he didn't bother to tell you."

Lauren glanced at Kathy. Her mouth hung open. "What did you say?"

"Jake is marrying Michelle, and Michelle is having Jake's baby."

"Can't be. He still loves you, Lauren. He doesn't love Michelle. I mean, Michelle is a nice enough person, but she and Jake—"

"Kathy, Jake and Michelle have been dating for two years. I know Jake better than anyone. He's happy, and Michelle is the one that makes him happy. He's over the moon about the baby. Derek and I see how happy Jake is. Why can't you? I did Jake a favor when I divorced him."

"That's not true, Lauren. He was miserable when you guys broke up."

"I'll admit, he didn't want to separate, but it didn't take him long to figure out that being married to me—he wasn't happy, Kathy. Listen, Jake and I share two beautiful children. We will always love and respect each other, and I think you should try to accept that he's made his choice."

"I would never be unkind to Michelle. Jake is Derek's best friend, and Michelle, well, the few times I've been in her company, she's a nice person, but she's not you. How did Josh and Kelly take the news?"

"Don't know. Jake and Michelle, as far as I know, might be telling the kids at this very moment. The kids are fond of Michelle."

"And that doesn't bother you, not even a little."

"If you're asking if I feel threatened, then no. Was I a tiny bit bothered by how fast my children accepted Michelle? Yes. I'm not afraid of losing my children's love. As the saying goes, blood is thicker than water."

Kathy agreed.

Lauren didn't tell Kathy the whole truth. Did she want to be the one who visited art museums with her daughter? Of course. She had arranged for her travel agent to plan a surprise trip to Paris and to Italy with the children. She had to put the trip on hold however when her last novel wasn't selling to the satisfaction of her publisher. While she was promoting her book, Michelle connected with Di Marco. With Josh going off to college in a year, and hopefully, Kelly's wish to study in Paris coming to fruition, Lauren knew that her plans to travel with her children may never happen.

"I don't know how you can be so strong. If Derek and I divorced and he was remarrying, I'd be so worried that my children might like their stepmother more than me. You know, when Jake and Michelle marry, you're going to have to share the children."

"Kathy, my children aren't babies. In one year, they will be off on their own. I really don't think Michelle is out to steal my children. If anything, she should be happy they won't be a bother."

"I guess, but we really don't know her that well. What if after they marry, she turns into the Wicked Witch of the East?"

"Then problem solved. My kids can complain to their loving mother how awful their stepmom treats them."

"If Michelle turns out to be the wicked stepmom, it can work in your favor."

The girls cracked up laughing.

*****

When they entered the hotel lobby, Kathy embraced Elle. "Elle, you look fabulous."

"I look fabulous. You haven't aged a day since college, Kathy."

"Move over, beautiful. I need to hug my girl. Notice anything different about me, Elle?"

"Not a thing, Lauren."

"And they call me the bitch."

"Wait. Did you lose weight?"

"Ten pounds, girlfriend."

"Oh, Lauren, you're always watching your weight. I don't know why. What are you, a size 8?"

"Six, Kathy, size 8, if it's a European cut. Nice tan, Elle. That deep-dark color doesn't happen from one day in the sun."

"Jacques and I spent a weekend in the south of France, before I"—Elle glanced at her watch—"where does the time go? We only have two hours before dinner. I need a shower. What about you guys?"

Arm in arm, the girls strolled toward the elevators.

*****

At Beach Creek, men's heads turned as the three gals in their sexy beach attire walked past. At the bar, a young man nearly fell off his barstool to offer Kathy his seat. When his friends noticed the women, they offered to buy them drinks. The girls graciously declined the offer. Creating a bar bill, the ladies ordered the drink of the day, three blue lagoon martinis. Twenty minutes later, they were seated at a table overlooking the bay.

Ordering another round of martinis, Elle wanted to be brought up-to-date on Derek's book, Jake and Michelle's relationship, and the children.

"Derek is still a hunk. The book tours start the week after I return. Oh, I met Nina, you know, the woman who was instrumental in signing Derek and Keith, the ghostwriter. Did I mention to you guys that Nina is very attractive? If not, she is. The children are fine and growing like weeds. Fanny is great. The kids miss their aunt Elle. They were excited to hear you will be spending Thanksgiving with us this year. That's it for me, but Lauren has news. Tell Elle the news, Lauren."

"What! Oh yes, but before I tell you the news, Elle. I need some advice. My last novel, well, sales are down. The publisher thinks I need to promote the book. My agent, Craig, thinks we should find a new publisher. I think we should stay put. Cutting down on the book tours might be the cause. Do you think my agent is right? Should I let him scout out another publishing firm?"

"Didn't you sign a contract?"

"I did, Elle, but only for five novels. Craig understands my feelings. The company believed in me when no one else did. Now if they said, 'Adios, Lauren,' then I'd move on without regret."

"I'm sorry, Lauren. I wish you would have told me. I—"

"Don't feel sorry for her, Elle. When Lauren says her books aren't selling, it means she is shy of selling a million copies. Lauren, you're a loyal person, and the firm has been good to you, so ride it out. If they drop you, it's their loss. Now tell Elle the news."

"Jake and Michelle are getting married on October 25. Mark the date. And they are expecting a little bundle of joy in February."

"What, a baby! I'm not shocked at the marriage proposal. They have been dating for two years but a baby? Is Jake happy? How did Josh and Kelly take the news?"

"Jake and Michelle are over the moon. Josh and Kelly don't know yet but will soon find out. The kids like Michelle. I don't think they will have a problem with the two marrying but the baby. At their age, they might be embarrassed by the arrival of a tiny sibling."

In unison, the ladies nodded. Elle and Kathy agreed.

"Being here, I'm reminded of our college days"—said Lauren—"barhopping with my BFFs, Kathy getting all the attention, as she did tonight."

Kathy sighed. "The gentlemen have moved on to women closer to their age. I must be losing my charm."

Lauren laughed. "Oh, I'm sorry, sweetie. But, gravity has a way of sneaking up on us. I hope I'm alive to see your breast and wrinkly ass sag."

"You forget, Lauren, I'm married to a surgeon. I'm sure he can set me up with the best plastic surgeon in town."

"Kathy, the cat lady. I can't wait."

"I don't think you will ever see that day, Lauren. Kathy will be the prettiest elderly woman in the nursing home."

"Thanks, Elle."

Elle was mesmerized by the yachts in the bay. "What happened to all the fishing boats? Look at the size of these yachts."

"I'm guessing the fishermen got out of the stock market before it crashed in 2008. And now are the proud owners of these monstrosities."

"You're probably right, Lauren."

While they ate dinner, Kathy ordered a fourth round of drinks.

"Elle, did you speak with Alice?"

"Yes, I did, Lauren. The service is at ten, followed by a luncheon."

Kathy sighed. "Alice hates us. I know for sure she hates Lauren and me. She tolerates Elle."

"In my opinion, she's insecure. She's jealous of the special bond the four of us share."

"I don't know if she is insecure, jealous, or both, Lauren. Honestly, I really don't care what Alice thinks of me. I'm here for Casey."

"Elle's right. We are here for Casey. If it weren't for Casey, I'd be sunning in Bermuda, not Wildwood."

"Enough talk about Alice. We're here to have a good time." When the waitress returned to remove the dinner plates, Kathy ordered yet another round of drinks.

*****

It was eight in the morning when the ladies exited the elevator.

Lauren whispered, "I need a cup of coffee, fast." She retrieved an aspirin bottle from her purse. "Juice and a couple of these should help." She offered aspirin to her friends.

Elle moaned. "How many drinks did we have?"

"Last count, we had eight. Those drinks were sweet but deadly."

Kathy whined, "I have pain behind my eyes. Is that normal?"

"You'll be fine. There's Sam. Elle, I'm not going anywhere until I get food into my stomach."

"Good morning, ladies."

"Sam, did you have breakfast?" asked Lauren.

"Yes. The wife cooked me up two fried eggs, rye toast, Canadian bacon, and coffee. I like my coffee dark."

"I think I'm going to throw up."

"You are not going to throw up, Kathy. Sam's right. We need a strong cup of java."

Sam checked the time on his watch. "We should be on the road in forty minutes."

*****

"Sam, it's nine fifteen. Will we make it to the church by ten?"

"If there is no traffic, Ms. Kessler, but that's unlikely this time of year. Don't worry your pretty little heads. Church services never start on time."

*****

Arriving five minutes after ten, the ladies exited the car and climbed the church steps.

At the entrance, Kathy was startled by the number of people already seated.

"The church is packed. We'll never find three seats together."

"There's Alice. Kathy, hurry before she notices us. Down this aisle, next to the lady in the white hat. I think we can squeeze in."

"Too late, Lauren. Alice."

"Elle, Lauren, Kathy, so nice of you to come."

The ladies ignored the sarcasm. "Nice to see you too, Alice. Excuse us, there are three seats—"

"I've taken care of the seating." Getting the attention of an usher, Alice asked, "John, can you show the ladies to their seats? Kessler, Wilson, and Croft."

"There must be a mistake," said Lauren.

John looked over to the seating chart. "Kessler, Wilson, and Croft first row."

The ladies glanced over John's shoulder. "The very first fucking row—is she kidding me?"

"Lauren, we're in a church for God's sake. Using the F word in church is a sin."

John raised an eyebrow. Kathy apologized for Lauren's cursing.

Kathy was first to enter the pew, followed by Lauren, placing Elle next to Alice.

When Alice entered the pew, Elle remarked, "I didn't know you and Casey had so many friends."

"Then you truly didn't know the woman, Elle."

Lauren moved forward in her seat, positioning herself to comment on Alice's condescending barb. Kathy placed her hand on Lauren's knee. "Let it go."

A priest and his young attendant stepped onto the altar. The young man placed a picture of Casey upon an easel. And the urn with Casey's ashes upon the altar. After lighting several candles, he took his place next to the priest.

Elle stared at the photo of Casey. Kathy whispered, "She looks so young." Elle remembered precisely when the photo was taken—the day they graduated from Northwestern.

Father Charlie began to speak. "Good morning. This mass is said in commemoration of the first anniversary of Casey Brice's passing."

Casey and Father Charlie were good friends. He bestowed upon her four of the seven sacraments she received during her time on this earth. After hearing of her condition and during the most challenging days of her life, he visited often. He was a great comfort to Alice, at a time when comfort was all one could offer. The sadness in Father Charlie's voice didn't go unnoticed by the congregation.

The Palm Reader

As Father Charlie spoke, the ladies revisited the day they first heard their friend was going to face the greatest battle of her life. Alice stood, interrupting their thoughts. Standing at the podium, she cleared her throat several times, before speaking.

"Good morning. I want to thank you for coming. I know Casey is looking down from heaven and smiling. It's been a tough year for me and Casey's family. Such a young life taken too soon. Casey's mother and father could not be with us today. Casey's father, like his daughter, is facing a battle of his own. I want to thank Casey's brother and sister for taking time away from their parents, to be with us today."

Alice glanced in the direction of where the ladies were seated. The ladies immediately realized that Casey's siblings were sitting behind them. *Embarrassing*, was the word to best describe their feelings of being placed in the first row, where Casey's flesh and blood should be sitting.

Alice continued. "I read an article recently where a woman described her relationship with her best friend. She wrote, she had one sister whom she loved, but as sisters do, they often fought and were critical of one another. She had a best friend named Sally. Sally was there for her in the good times and in her darkest hours. There are three women here with us today that Casey called her BFFs, forever." Alice glanced in the direction of the first row. For the first time, the ladies felt blessed to have been placed in the first row. With their backs to the people, they avoided the curious stares and acknowledgments.

"Casey shared her life with me, but her secrets with her BFFs. The four women shared a special bond as BFFs do." Alice's eyes began to well with tears. "Over the year, I questioned what my girl was thinking when she requested that we celebrate the one-year-anniversary of her passing. As this day drew closer, it was difficult for me, and I'm sure for you as well to say goodbye a second time." Trying to control her grief, Alice faked a cough. "As my sweet girl requested, today we will celebrate her life, not the sadness. I will do my best, my love, to remember only the good. I ask, dear friends, that you do the same."

When Alice was seated, Elle handed her a tissue.

*****

Scattered throughout the yard were tables draped with white linen tablecloths. In the center of each table sat a glass vase of yellow roses, Casey's favorite flower. A glass of champagne was given to each guest. The guests were asked to join Alice at the shoreline.

Alice made a toast to honor Casey. Lifting the lid off the urn, she passed the urn to Casey's siblings. Lauren, Elle, and Kathy looked on. When the urn was returned to Alice, she passed it to Elle; Elle, to Lauren; Lauren, to Kathy. Alice released the remaining ashes. She then asked her guests to join her for lunch.

After conversing with Casey's siblings regarding their father's health and offering empathy for their mom, Lauren spotted an empty table.

"No one is sitting at that table, let's—"

"Lauren, over here."

Brian, Casey's male BFF, was waving them over to his table.

"Sit. I've been dying to talk with you. Jeff, this is Lauren Croft, the writer. This beauty is Kathy, married to the hot heart surgeon. Elle just landed herself the anchor spot on the six o'clock news in DC. Ladies, this is Jeff."

Sitting, the ladies smiled at Jeff.

"Elle, I have to know. Did the Parisian follow you to DC?"

Elle, shocked by the question, asked, "Casey told you about Jacques?"

"Girlfriend, of course, she told me. She was over the moon about your relationship with Jacques. She thought he was the one."

"She wasn't the only one," said Lauren.

Kathy scolded Lauren. "Stop it."

Elle glanced at her friends. "In answer to your question, Brian, no. The Parisian still lives in Paris."

"Honey, you're not one of those fools who thinks long-distance relationships can work? Take it from me, sweetie, when the urges come calling, you'll forget the Parisian ever existed."

Lauren could see that Elle wasn't comfortable discussing her love life with Brian, so she interjected, "Brian, New Jersey acknowledges same-sex marriages. Are you and Jeff ready to take the plunge?"

"Lauren, we haven't even celebrated our first anniversary."

Jeff cut Brian a quizzical stare.

"What!" said Brian. "We haven't even had our first fight, so marriage is definitely out of the question. Lauren, how's the book going?"

"It's going."

Alice approached the table and sat. "Lauren, I was surprised to see you. I was sure you wouldn't show."

The expression on Lauren's face revealed her true feelings. She'd rather be sitting on the sand in Bermuda.

"By the look on your face, I'm guessing, here is the last place you wanted to be. So why did you come?"

"I couldn't let Kathy drive here all by her lonesome, Alice. But truth be told, this is the last place I wanted to be. I said my goodbyes a year ago."

"I'm sure it took great strains to shut down your computer and think of someone other than yourself."

Alice was sparring for a fight. Lauren was ready for the challenge. Elle quickly put a stop to a trashing match, saying, "Alice, it was a lovely service. Casey would have been proud—"

"I'm sure she would be since she planned the entire day several weeks before her passing. She even chose the flowers. I guess she didn't trust that I would remember her favorite flower was a yellow rose."

"That's how she earned her nickname, the controller."

"If I'm not mistaken, Lauren, you came up with the nickname."

"Yes, I take full credit. I'm sure we can all agree, it suited her."

While Alice was contemplating a comeback, Elle reached for her purse. "Alice, the service was lovely. The food was delicious, and it was wonderful to see you. It's been a long day. I think we should be going."

"Before you ladies rush off, there is one more piece to the puzzle. Your BFF left a letter. After the guests leave, I'd be happy to share the contents of the letter with you or not."

"A letter?"

"Yes, Kathy, a letter."

"Have you read this letter, Alice?"

"No, Kathy, I haven't. The instructions were for us to read it together. Now if you are interested in what your friend had to say, you can wait till everyone leaves, or you can come back tomorrow. If you go, stay, or never come back, makes no difference to me."

Lauren hissed. "This is ridiculous. I loved the woman, but she definitely wasn't thinking clearly. She plans an anniversary celebration of her passing, followed by the spreading of her ashes. Now a letter to her lover and BFFs. This is crazy. I'm out of here."

"I'm curious, Lauren. I'd like to hear what Casey wrote. What about you, Elle?"

Elle glanced at Lauren. "I agree with Kathy."

"Well, you two can stick around. I'm leaving. Whatever is in the letter can't be that important if we had to wait a year to read it. Unless Casey had a child she kept hidden from us, which I doubt."

"Elle and I will stay, Alice."

"Of course, you will, Kathy."

"Lauren, it's only a few more hours. Please stay."

It was against Lauren's better judgment to stay, but the letter had sparked her curiosity. "If I leave, Sam will have to come back for the two of you, which is a waste of his time and our money. I'll stay."

*****

When all the guests were gone, including Brian and Jeff, the girls sat at the backyard table watching the men from the rental company collapse the last table. Alice and one of the workers went into the house. Ten minutes later, she returned alone with four wine glasses and a bottle of red wine.

"I thought we might need a little something to relax us." Alice filled the wine glasses to the brim and offered a glass to each of the ladies. They accepted. Alice raised her wine glass in the air and made a toast. "To God, thanks for the slight breeze today. It was the perfect day to spread your one true love's ashes." Collapsing in the chair next to Lauren, she said, "Wouldn't you agree, ladies?"

Taking pity on Alice, Elle questioned, "I know it's been a hard four years, Alice, but knowing she is no longer suffering, must be a relief?"

"Nope. It's the pits losing the love of your life. Let me ask you, ladies, does it get any easier knowing that you deserted your friend when she needed you most?"

Lauren shouted, "We didn't desert our friend!"

"You didn't! Then where were you when she took her last breath?"

"Alice, the last time Lauren and I spoke with Casey, she said the doctor gave a thumbs-up. Do you remember, Lauren? We were so happy to hear she was feeling better."

"You really thought she was getting better? Are you insane, Kathy? She had stage 4 cancer. Her last MRI showed it was rapidly spreading. Do you remember me calling the three of you? I called to tell you she was slipping away."

"You don't have to bite her head off. Do you feel better having told us what you think of us? If so, then why don't you just read the letter, so we can be on our way?"

"You bet your ass, Lauren. It feels great to finally say that I think you three are lower than dog shit in my book."

"I knew this was a mistake. I'm leaving." Lauren reached for her purse.

"Just like you, Lauren, always running away from a bad situation."

"I didn't run, Alice. As Kathy said, last time we spoke with Casey, she said she was feeling better. We thought there would be more time—to say goodbye."

Alice laughed.

"If you're trying to make me feel guilty, Alice, it's not working."

"I wasn't expecting a hard-ass like you, Lauren, to feel guilty about deserting your BFF."

Elle reached for Lauren's arm, motioning her to sit. "Alice, why don't you read the letter?"

Alice was red in the face. There was so much more she wanted to say, but instead, she reached into her pants pocket to retrieve the letter. Seeing Casey's handwriting on the envelope caused Alice to choke up. She tore open the envelope. Opening the letter slowly, she glanced at it briefly and read.

Hi, love and my BFFs,

By now, my ashes are working their way into the ocean, which if I were alive would freak me out because you know how it infuriates me when people desecrate my beloved beach and ocean. Before I start, I must apologize to my love and soulmate, but I am sure all will turn out well.
Dear BFFs, remember, blood sisters forever. This is why I ask that you agree to my last dying request because there isn't anything we wouldn't do for one another.
Girls, I'm assuming Alice has made her feelings toward you known. Honey, did it really feel that great to tell the girls what you think of them? I'm guessing not in the least. You were there, and your face was the only face I wanted to see when I took my last breath.
Lauren, Elle, and Kathy, forgive me for lying, but I didn't want you there to see me at my worst. I wanted you to remember me as we were during our college days.
Alice, sweetheart, did we really want Kathy sobbing like a baby; or Elle, asking way too many times if I were comfortable; and Lauren, wondering if she should be taking notes and writing about my death in her next novel? Only kidding, Lauren, but I know how your mind works.

Everyone chuckled except Lauren.
Lauren grunted, "It's amazing how you all think I'm made of stone. But she does have a point. Sad stories sell."

Alice continued to read.

> Today ends the mourning period. From this day forward, I want you to think of the happy times. And that brings me to my last request. Lauren, Elle, and Kathy, I'm sure you booked the entire week for vacation, as I requested. And there was a reason for my request. I want you to spend the entire week with Alice.
> Honey, I don't want you to book a room at the same hotel as the girls. No, I just want you guys to spend the days and, hopefully, some of the nights together getting to know each other. Why? Because after today, you will all go your separate ways and never really get to know what a wonderful woman Alice truly is.
> Girls, I know you always wondered why I chose Alice. If you spend this week with her, I know you will come to love her, as I did.
> I don't have to be there to envision the looks on your faces, but you all share one thing in common—you love me, and I know you will not deny a dead woman her one last request.
> I'm depending on you. Don't let me down.
>
> Love you all, Casey.

Alice dropped the letter onto her lap and swore.

Elle whispered, "I wasn't expecting—"

Alice shouted, causing the girls to flinch. "No way. Casey knew how I felt about the three of you."

"Casey wasn't thinking straight when she wrote that letter."

"For once, Lauren, I have to agree with you."

"Alice, you must have done something really bad to get stuck with us for a week. What did you do? Set the cat on fire?"

"Shut up, Lauren."

"It hasn't been five minutes, and the two of you are at each other's throats. Look, the three of us are here for the week. Of course, we'd have to agree to put the bitterness aside, but I think we can do this," said Kathy.

"You want me to put the bitterness aside and spend time with three gals who hate my guts?"

"Alice, we don't hate you."

"You didn't think I was good enough for Casey, and you made your feelings known, Kathy."

"You were so different from all the other women Casey dated. It just surprised us that Casey—"

"Didn't choose the prettiest gal in the room?"

"Don't put words in my mouth, Alice. What I am trying to say is, we were wrong to judge you."

"It's too late, Kathy."

"It's never too late, Alice."

"Kathy, the woman hates our guts. I don't think it's a good idea for us to spend a week together hashing over the same shit."

"Lauren, it was Casey's last request. I think we can manage to spend one week together. Alice, I'm sorry you had to go through Casey's passing alone. But if it were Derek, I'd want his last moments to be with me and only me." Softly, Kathy added, "It's only a week."

*****

Alice reluctantly agreed to spend an entire week with the women she hated most in the world. Attached to the letter Casey had written was a list of suggestions for a fun week.

Alice chuckled. "She wants us to spend a day at the amusement park."

Kathy gasped. "I don't think my stomach can handle spinning rides."

"It was Casey's last request, Kathy. The amusement park sounds like fun."

"If I vomit, I hope it's on you, Lauren."

The women choose the fifth suggestion on the list to start the week. They agreed to meet on the beach in front of the hotel at ten, the following morning.

*****

It was a hot day. The ladies stood in the heat for as long as they could, waiting for Alice. They placed their beach chairs close to the entrance to the beach so Alice wouldn't miss them. Kathy glanced at her cell phone. "It's eleven o'clock. Where the hell is Alice?"

"I'm guessing she's had a change of heart. Are you forgetting the woman hates us?"

Elle stared at a figure approaching. "Not so fast, Lauren, I think that might be Alice."

Kathy and Lauren turned. Seeing Alice, Lauren began to laugh. "What the hell is she wearing? She's covered from head to toe. Did she listen to the weather forecast this morning?"

"Shut up, Lauren, before she hears you."

"Beautiful day." Alice started to set up her beach chair and umbrella. After organizing her space, she collapsed into her beach chair. "Lauren, stop staring at my outfit. I burn easily."

Lauren decided to take the high road. "I can sympathize, Alice. Jake would lather up with sunscreen, and after several hours in the sun, he was as red as a cooked lobster. Every summer, I'd poke fun at his long-sleeved shirt, and he'd call me a witch."

"You're getting quite the reputation, Lauren. Jake and Derek think you're a witch, and Alice thinks you're a bitch. You might need a personality adjustment."

"I'll get right on that, Kathy."

"Alice, since Casey wanted us to get to know each other better, did you know that Lauren's nickname for Derek is Dr. Dick?"

"Casey did mention Lauren and Derek's dislike for each other. Said it began in college." Lauren and Alice shared an uncomfortable glance.

"I don't think they dislike each other. I think they—" Kathy was interrupted when Elle's phone rang.

"It's work. I have to take the call."

Lauren scolded, "Hang up the phone, Elle. No calls on vacation. Your rules not mine."

"Hush, Lauren."

Lauren shouted, "Work is not on Casey's list!"

*****

On Monday, Alice arrived at the beach in a short sleeveless dress. The temperature was five degrees higher than the day before. After several hours, Alice removed her dress to reveal an impressive body.

"Wow, Alice, your body is rock-solid. That explains why Casey was attracted to you."

"It wasn't my body she was attracted to. It was my charming personality that caught her eye, Lauren."

"We can agree to disagree regarding your charming personality."

While munching on snacks and drinking wine out of plastic cups, Kathy asked, "How did you and Casey meet, Alice?"

"I'm sure you think I was the pursuer, but it was Casey who made the first move. You're familiar with the art gallery on Main Street? Well, Casey approached me to ask my opinion on a painting I was admiring. It was a painting of a mother and daughter, sitting on a very colorful beach towel, at the beach, with their backs to the artist. Each with a hand affixed to their bonnets. I said the painting was beautiful. The colors in the piece were magnificent. But what I admired most about the piece was the definition of the back muscles of the mother and child. I said, 'It must have been a windy day because they are struggling to keep their bonnets intact.' She responded by confirming it was an extremely windy day. It was then I realized, she was the artist. She invited me to lunch, which lasted three hours. When we left the restaurant, she gave me her business card, saying, 'If you're interested in purchasing the piece, give me a call.' She began to walk away. I told myself to let her go. This woman was clearly out of my league and straight. But my heart overruled my head, and I called out to her. As she walked toward me, I said, 'Let me give you my number. I'm really interested in the piece, but

I'm not sure I can afford it.' She took my number, said goodbye, and walked off. Several days later, she called to ask if I were free on Saturday. We met for an early dinner. Around seven, she asked the waitress for the tab. I offered to split it, but she wouldn't hear of it. I assumed the night hadn't gone as she planned, and she couldn't wait to see me off. Outside the restaurant, before I could say good night, she asked if I'd be interested in going to the cinema. *Steel Magnolias* was playing, and she hadn't seen it. Of course, there wasn't a woman on the planet who hadn't seen the movie. So I lied and said I hadn't gotten around to seeing it myself. When Sally Fields breaks down at the cemetery, Casey reached for my hand. I glanced at her, and her eyes said it all. That's when I knew she liked girls."

Kathy sighed. "I love a fairy-tale ending."

Ignoring Kathy, Elle said, "She fooled me. I didn't know Casey liked girls until I tried to hook her up with a boy from my chemistry class. She laughed and said, 'Elle, you're more my type.' I was floored."

"I knew."

Lauren asked, "When did you find out, Kathy?"

"Two days after we met. I'm guessing, Lauren, you didn't have time to read the college pamphlet. There was an article on page 21. It said, "Don't assume all girls like boys, and all boys like girls. Asking could avoid an uncomfortable situation with a roommate.' So I asked."

"Why didn't you ask that to Lauren and me, Kathy?"

"Because I knew you weren't, Elle. The music Casey loved, the posters she hung, the way she set up her side of the room. So I took the advice offered in the pamphlet and asked. She told me she didn't have a sexual preference and was hoping by graduation, she'd figure it out. I dropped the subject."

"When did you find out, Lauren?"

Lauren raised her eyes to the sun to avoid eye contact with Alice. "I don't remember. She might have told me. I'm not sure." Wanting to drop the subject of Casey's sex life, Lauren asked Alice, "Did Casey ever share with you when Elle and Jacques met?"

"No, I don't believe she did."

Elle smiled. "I was able to find my way out of the desert, but I couldn't find my way around Paris. My first day on the job, I was scheduled to arrive at six. First mistake, I decided to walk. Second, I went to the wrong building. It was six in the morning, not a soul on the street. Frantic, I searched for someone to help. After five minutes of pure agony, Jacques turned the corner in his running gear. I called to him. 'Monsieur parlez vous anglasis?' (Sir, do you speak English?) He stopped, smiled, and then started rattling off one sentence after another in French. I put up my hand to stop him. 'Je ne parle pas Francais.' (I do not speak French.) He laughed and continued to laugh. It didn't take long for me to realize, he was mocking me. I became angry and said, 'Are you forgetting who saved your sorry asses in World War II?' Stunned, he started to apologize, in English, and said, 'I'm sorry. This is—how you say, a bad habit. I try to rattle the Americans who I know can't speak a word of French. But yours is such a lovely face, so please, will you forgive me?' I told him I had no time for his antics, as I was going to be late for work. He looked at the address and said, 'Come, follow me.' As we walked, he explained that the building was at the other end of the street. When we reached the building, I thanked him and said *au revoir*. A few days later, he was waiting at the building when I arrived for work. The rest is history."

"I love that story. In fact, I think I'll use it in my next novel. The main character will not be as kind as Elle and rush off to the States. She will stab her lover to death and then vanish. Why? Because the lover was getting close to finding out she was a secret agent."

"Leave it to you, Lauren, to take a beautiful love story and turn it to shit."

"Don't knock it, Kathy. My depraved writing has made me a wealthy lady."

"Did you ever think of writing a love story, with a fairy-tale ending?"

"Listen, Kathy, if you want a bullshit love story, write one yourself. God knows you have the smarts."

"I might just do that, Lauren. Because sometimes a woman just wants to put all the crime and hate aside and wrap her arms around a beautiful romantic novel, with a fairy-tale ending."

"I agree with Kathy," said Alice. "But I do have one request. Can the main characters be lesbians?"

The ladies cracked up laughing.

CHAPTER 6

The night before the last day of their vacation, while dining at a restaurant in Cape May, they reflected on their time together. The ladies talked about how amazing it was that they were able to set aside their differences and enjoy the week.

Kathy sighed. "Well, ladies, we did it. We managed to spend the week together and not kill one another. I have to hand it to Casey. If the angel of death were knocking at my door, my first thought wouldn't be of my friends liking each other. Casey was one smart cookie. She knew if the letter was read after her funeral, knowing how her lover felt about her BFFs, this week would not have happened. The one-year-anniversary memorial was for our benefit."

"I thought the one-year-anniversary memorial was ridiculous. But I will admit, the week has been fun, although I could have done without the church service."

"I agree, Lauren. Seeing Casey's photo on the altar, the rosy color in her cheeks, the warmth in her eyes, and her smile that could light up Times Square can't ease how the cancer changed her appearance—the sunken cheekbones, the clay-colored skin, teeth that were too large for her face. Alice, I am truly sorry for not being—"

"No, enough with the apologies, Kathy." Alice reached for Kathy's hand. "Earlier this week, you said if it were Derek, you'd want the last moments of his life to be spent with you and you alone. You were right. I was given the privilege to hold that sweet girl's hand at the end. Casey only lasted as long as she did because she knew I wasn't ready to let her go. Once I accepted that the suffering had to end, she took her last breath. And I began to breathe again."

Releasing Kathy's hand, Alice glanced at Lauren. "We agree our girl was controlling, so why should the end be any different? She devised a plan, and it worked. The BFFs and the lover are breaking bread together, and it feels right."

With the elephant in the room gone, the ladies planned their last day together. The amusement park was the only thing that wasn't checked off Casey's suggested list.

*****

"Are you girls insane? Do you see the size of that roller coaster?"

"Come on, Kathy, it will be over before you know it."

"All right, Lauren, but if I vomit on you, you'll only have yourself to blame."

*****

"You were a trooper, Kathy."

"My eyes were closed the entire time. That was the last ride, correct?"

"We hit every ride in the park, except for the baby rides."

"Look! Kohr's ice cream."

"Ice cream. I wouldn't be able to hold down an ice cream, Elle."

"Kathy, it is Kohr's. Are you forgetting how many ice creams we devoured during our summers at the shore? You can't visit Wildwood and not have a Kohr's ice cream, Kathy."

"Not ice cream, but I will have one of those pink cotton candies."

Elle placed an order for three vanilla orange twist ice cream cones and one pink cotton candy. The ladies found an empty table. While enjoying their treats and casual conversation, Elle spied a sign that read "Palm Reader."

"Let's have our palms read."

"What did you say, Elle?"

"Let's have our palms read." Elle pointed her finger toward the building. On the glass window the words *Palm Readings and Tarot Cards*, were scrawled in white paint.

"No way. I don't believe in that bullshit," said Lauren.

"Casey frequented that establishment often."

"What! Casey did? Why, Alice?"

"I don't know, Lauren. Maybe she was hoping for a better outcome."

"Doesn't sound like Casey."

Elle smiled. "Well, if Casey had faith in the palm reader, who am I to disagree? Kathy, you in?"

"Do you really want to have your palm read, Elle? I'd rather head back to Alice's place, start up the grill, and down a few bottles of wine. It's our last night together."

"How long can it take to have our palms read, ten minutes each? Come on, this can be fun."

"What the heck, I'll give it a go."

"Thanks, Alice." Elle began to plead with Lauren and Kathy.

"Elle, you're too old to whine. Come on, Kathy. If Elle doesn't have her palm read, she'll whine the entire night."

*****

Black and purple linens, combined with strings of black beads, loosely hung before an open door. Finding their way inside, they were confronted by the darkness of the room. Elle's eyes quickly adjusted, and she spied a light shining in the back of the store. It was coming from an open door to the left of the room. A young girl ran from the open door. Spotting the ladies, the young girl asked, "Do you want your palms read?"

Kathy's maternal instincts emerged. "Don't be frightened."

The girl stared at Kathy. Boldly the girl said, "Frightened of you? I'm not frightened of anything or anyone."

Elle stepped forward. "Hi, my name is Elle. What is your name?"

"My name is Isabella, but my friends call me Bella."

"What a lovely name." As Elle walked toward the child, she was taken back by the child's beauty. An enormous amount of curly latte hair was falling slightly beyond her shoulders. Her eyes were a beautiful shade of green. Her complexion, olive.

"This is my friend Kathy—"

"Bella, did you hear me call you? Go. I need you to help with the baby."

The child ran off. The ladies were startled by the older woman. Her hair was wild, black with silver streaks, waist length. Her eyes were hazel flexed with yellow. Her wrinkles were few. Elle guessed the woman was in her early sixties.

"How can I help you?"

"Are you the palm reader?"

"Yes. Tarot cards and palm readings. Ten dollars for palm reading. Twenty for tarot cards."

"We want to have our palms read, if you have the time?"

The woman's eyes glanced over her establishment. "Did you make an appointment? No, well—this is your lucky day. As you can see, I'm not busy. Sit."

There was a round table in the middle of the room. The table was covered with a purple table cloth, and a medium-sized crystal ball sat in the middle of the table.

Lauren leaned over Elle's shoulder and whispered, "How old do you think she is? She looks ninety, but I'm guessing sixty-five?" Elle told Lauren to hush.

The ladies stared at the crystal ball. The woman took notice. "It's a prop, nothing more. The people who visit my establishment, if they don't see a crystal ball, they don't think we are legit." The woman placed a small purse on the table. "Palm readings cost ten dollars."

Kathy retrieved forty dollars from her purse and handed it to the woman, who then locked eyes with her as she accepted the money.

"So your people are gypsies?"

"Yes. You're the pretty one."

Kathy was confused by the woman's statement. Breaking eye contact with Kathy, the woman spoke to Alice. "I know you."

"We've never met."

"You're right. We have not met. Your friend, the sweet girl, she showed me a picture of you. And a picture of the three of you. Since I have not seen her in over a year, I'd say the cancer took her life."

"And you would be right."

The Palm Reader

"Sad. Give me your hands."

Alice presented her hands to the woman. The gypsy woman took her time reading Alice's palms. "Hasn't been an easy year, has it? You loved the sweet girl, but like the year, your relationship wasn't an easy one. Loving her brought much pain to your life." The woman dragged her index finger along Alice's hand. "This is your life line. As you can see, you will live a long life. You will have to find a way to trust again."

"Trust again?"

"Your love for the sweet girl placed a web around your heart. You will love again, but the ghost of your first love will place a strain on future relationships. You have trust issues. If you want to share your life with another, you need to find a way to overcome your issues. I'm told therapy helps." The woman released Alice's hands.

Lauren's eyes were fixed on Alice. The woman motioned to read Lauren's palm. Lauren was reluctant to offer her hands.

"I don't want to disrespect your profession, but I'm a nonbeliever."

"You're the writer. The sweet girl spoke of you often."

"Casey. Her name was Casey, and yes, I was her friend. The writer."

"Yes. You write about strong women—women who prefer to live by their own rules, not the rules set upon them in a world created by men. The female characters in your novels aren't your typical stereotypes, mothers, wives, and daughters. No, they're free-spirited."

"You've read one of my novels?"

"Your friend left several books. But no, I read the outline. Don't care much for books about strong women. I like romance novels. The ones that make you cry, but in the end, everyone is happy."

Kathy burst out laughing. "See, Lauren? Everyone likes a good romance novel now and then."

The woman ignored Kathy's outbreak and continued. She dragged her index finger along a line on Lauren's hand. The woman didn't move her finger. Lauren stared at the woman and wondered if she had fallen asleep or, worse, died. The woman opened her eyes and said, "This line represents a wall of your novels and the wall you hide behind."

Lauren drew back her hand. "Listen, lady, no disrespect, this line is just a line, not a wall of novels, and believe me, I have nothing to hide."

The woman locked eyes with Lauren, causing Lauren to shift in her seat. She broke the stare by offering Kathy's hands to the woman.

Kathy drew her hands back.

"I don't bite."

Kathy laid her hands on the table, palms up.

"You have children. More than three." The gypsy woman studied Kathy's palm. "A successful husband. You are happy."

"Yes, I am very happy. My husband wrote a book. Do you think it will be a success?"

"He is already a successful man."

"Yes. He is. But this book, if it is a success, the money will help many people."

The old woman sighed. She didn't break eye contact with Kathy, saying, "Happiness can cloud the truth."

"What do you mean?"

The woman studied Kathy's right hand. "This line represents a cloud. The cloud is thick, making it harder to see beyond it. I sense the truth lies behind the cloud."

Now the woman made eye contact with Elle, who extended her hands.

"Wait—I need to know—"

While holding Elle's hands, the gypsy woman began to answer Kathy's question. "Happiness is good, but there are times we allow happiness to overshadow what is right in front of us. You have to look beyond the happiness, to find the truth."

Kathy locked eyes with the woman. Feeling uncomfortable, she didn't ask another question. The woman looked away and stared into Elle's eyes. "You allow your demons to control your life."

Startled by the woman's words, Elle chuckled. "You think I'm possessed by the devil?"

"No, not the devil, but evil, yes. For many years, you have buried this evil. If you don't face the demon, you will never be able to move on. You are stuck in the past."

The Palm Reader

The woman didn't wait for Elle to respond. "I have read your palms. Now go."

"I knew this was a bad idea. She thinks Elle is possessed by demons. Let's get out of here."

Kathy and Alice followed Lauren's lead, and together, they moved toward the entrance. Elle lingered, locking eyes with the gypsy woman.

"Elle!" shouted Lauren. "Let's go."

Elle turned away from the woman and walked toward the entrance. Pushing the curtain aside, Elle glanced over her shoulder hoping to make eye contact with the woman. The gypsy stood and turned her back to Elle.

*****

The woman entered the kitchen. Seated at the kitchen table, newspaper in hand, was her husband. A handsome man, a few years older than the woman. He lowered the newspaper and said, "Last night, the moon was full. Your sightings are stronger when the moon is full. All four got their money's worth. How many times have I told you, woman, when the moon is full, raise your prices? We could use the extra cash. Now tell me what you saw?"

"Old man, you know better than to ask."

"The one you told to face her demons will be back."

*****

Sam kept a close watch on the ladies from the rearview mirror. "You ladies are awfully quiet."

"It's been a long day," said Elle.

"Speak for yourself. The day was going just fine until Elle got it into her head that we should have our palms read."

"Lauren, you agreed to go."

"Alice agreed to go. Kathy and I were shamed into going."

Sam laughed. "You ladies had your palms read by the woman next to the Kohr's ice cream stand?"

"That's the one. She's a fake, right, Sam?" said Lauren.

"I don't believe in all that voodoo, but if you ask my friend Bob, he'll tell you the woman is the real deal. Bob's first wife was a sweetheart, a good woman. At the age of thirty, she passed away, brain aneurism. Bob's greatest wish was to find a woman equal to his first wife and start a family. He had his palm read by the gypsy. She told him love was in his future. Bob met Grace. After six months of dating Grace, Bob visited the old woman for a second time. She told Bob that Grace was not the one. Bob didn't listen. He thought Grace was a treasure, so he asked her to marry him. Six months into the marriage, Grace's sweet demeanor disappeared. She was a miserable woman who presented Bob with two spoiled and miserable daughters."

After hearing Sam's story about Bob's miserable life, the car ride to Alice's house was solemn.

*****

Brian greeted the ladies. "How was the amusement park? Did anyone vomit?"

Alice was going to respond, but Brian cut her off. "Sorry, love, I'd love to stay and hear all about your insane day, but Jeff and I have dinner plans. The steaks are prepped for grilling. Corn and a salad are in the refrigerator. The potatoes are par boiled. The white wine is chilling, red on the counter. I've got to run. You ladies have a great night."

Brian was out the door before Alice could thank him for his help.

Elle, on Alice's request, retrieved the white wine from the refrigerator. Kathy removed four wine glasses from the wine rack. Lauren grabbed the two bottles of red wine from the table. Alice brought two bags of chips, and the four ladies headed down to the shore to watch the sun set. They sat in silence. When dusk had fallen, Alice rose and said, "I'll get dinner started."

Elle followed Alice. Kathy and Lauren sat stoic finding the waves crashing on the shoreline comforting. After what seemed like an eternity, Kathy said, "We should go up."

The Palm Reader

The ladies ate in silence, which was slowly driving Alice wild. After dinner, Alice asked if anyone wanted coffee. The ladies declined coffee and opted to refill their wine glasses. Alice had to put an end to the madness. "You ladies haven't been your chatty selves. I bet I can figure out what's wrong. The gypsy woman got under your skin."

"I thought it was going to be fun to have our palms read. The typical words you assume you will hear from one in her profession is 'You're going to live a long life, find love, and live happily ever after.' Instead, she thinks Elle is possessed. Lauren hides behind a wall created by her novels. And I can't see the truth because there is a thick cloud of happiness blocking the view. What the fuck?"

"On that note, I have to agree with the gypsy. It is humanly impossible to be happy twenty-four-seven, Kathy."

"Of course you would agree with her, Lauren. Alice, why did you allow Casey to visit that woman?"

"I was her partner, Kathy, not her mother. Seeing that woman brought back a memory I was trying hard to forget."

"And what was that, Alice?" asked Elle.

"Casey made me promise that when the end was near, I'd bring her home to die. She wanted to take her last breath looking out over the ocean. Of course, I swore to her that she'd die at home. The last time Casey visited with the old woman, she told Casey I wouldn't keep that promise. I didn't."

Kathy did her best to console Alice. "Alice, don't beat yourself up. Anyone in your shoes would have done the same. The hospital was better equipped to make her comfortable at the end."

"Kathy's right, Alice." Elle glanced at Lauren, hoping she could muster up a few kind words.

Lauren shrugged her shoulders at Elle. Elle wanted to wring her neck. Lauren didn't find the words Elle was hoping for, but Lauren gave it her best shot. "You shouldn't beat yourself up about not keeping your promise, Alice. We're human. We make decisions based on what we can live with."

Alice stared into her wine glass. She reached for the wine bottle and poured, filling her glass to the brim. "What you and Casey shared, Lauren, was special. I would think you of all people—whatever, I didn't want you there anyway."

Kathy and Elle locked eyes. "Alice, I thought we were over pointing fingers. You seem to be placing all the blame on Lauren when Elle and I are equally at fault."

Alice and Lauren shared another uncomfortable stare. Kathy took notice.

"That's the third time I've caught you staring at one another," said Kathy. "Alice, I think your hatred of Lauren goes deeper than her not showing up at the hospital. You keep saying that Lauren and Casey shared a special bond. What special bond did Casey and Lauren share that excluded Elle and I?"

"Kathy's right, Alice. I've also noticed you and Lauren locking eyes. What's going on?"

Alice didn't respond.

Since visiting with the gypsy woman, Lauren subconsciously had been questioning the meaning behind the gypsy's words. Kathy and Elle wanted answers to why Alice disliked her. If the answer was to be told, she wanted Elle and Kathy to hear the truth from her.

"Casey and I were lovers in college."

Stunned, Kathy said, "What the hell are you talking about, Lauren?"

"We were lovers in college."

"You and Casey were lovers in college? On what planet, not this one, because you couldn't keep a secret like that hidden from Elle and me."

"It lasted six months."

"Six months in college you and Casey were lovers? And Elle and I didn't have a clue unless—Elle, did you know?"

"I didn't, I swear. Lauren, why didn't you tell us? Never mind. Whatever happened between you and Casey was private. But why tell us now, after all these years?"

"I would have taken the secret to my grave, Elle. But you both were wondering why Alice detests me. That's why."

Kathy chuckled. "Because you and Casey had a fling in college, ridiculous."

"It started in college, and then there was the summer after Jake and I divorced."

Kathy sat up in her chair. "What! Again, after you and Jake divorced?"

"The kids were at camp. Jake and Michelle—I thought being at my summer home would help the loneliness. Kathy, you were very pregnant with Scottie. Elle, you were an ocean away. So I reached out to Casey and asked if she could come spend a week or two."

"And?"

"And we rekindled the relationship."

"You slept with Casey when she was with Alice? Lauren, how could you?"

"I don't know, Kathy. It just happened."

"It just happened. So are you trying to tell us that your marriage fell apart because you were in love with Casey?"

"I wasn't married to Jake when I slept with Casey, Kathy. We were single in college, and I was divorced when we reconnected."

"You were lonely, so after messing up your own marriage, you decided to destroy Alice's relationship with Casey? Who the fuck are you, Lauren?"

"I'm the same person, Kathy, your BFF."

"No. You're a selfish bitch."

"Kathy, let Lauren explain."

"Explain what, Elle? She had a fling in college with Casey, fine. She isn't the only woman who tested the waters in college. But after she divorces Jake, she finds herself alone and lonely, so she calls Casey to warm her bed. It's a wonder that Alice hasn't punched her lights out."

"Kathy, it takes two to tango. If Casey truly loved me, she wouldn't have crossed the line. I believe Lauren was Casey's one true love."

"Alice, that isn't true. What happened between Casey and I was a mistake. She loved you."

"What did happen, Lauren? If you were Casey's one true love, as Alice believes, was she your one true love?"

"No. Alice assumed I was Casey's one true love when Casey didn't return home after two weeks. She decided, not because I asked, to remain at the Cape until Labor Day. What Casey and I shared wasn't love. I made my feelings known, and Casey was fine with it."

"So you broke her heart. You sent her away like you did Jake."

"Listen, Ms. High and Mighty, you know why Jake and I drifted apart?"

"You told us you two drifted apart because you wanted to write, and he wanted a wife. But is that the truth, or is the truth you'd rather be with a woman? The gypsy woman was right. We've read your books. The heroine you write about in your novels is bisexual. Why Casey, Lauren? Why did you break our girl's heart? You couldn't find someone else to ease your loneliness? Unless Casey was a safer option. Career first, right? If anyone found out that Lauren Hicks Croft was a dike, that would affect sales."

Alice took offense when Kathy referred to Lauren as a dike. But this wasn't her fight, so she kept silent.

"So you sent Casey away with a broken heart. Alice, who truly loved our girl, forgave Casey for screwing around with you."

"Kathy!" shouted Elle. "This is between Alice and Lauren."

"Oh, Elle, stop defending her. You always take her side. She broke our girl's heart. Alice has every right to hate her. You should have been with Casey at the end, Lauren, asking for her forgiveness."

"I don't need Elle to defend me, Kathy. I never thought—"

"What! That Casey was in love with you, Lauren. She told Alice. Doesn't that prove you were her one true love?"

"I don't believe I was Casey's one true love. We all know Casey was a flirt. She came on to me. We had too much to drink. I should have stopped her, but I didn't. I had no idea Casey had called Alice to confess. If I would have known, I would have stopped her. I swear, Alice, I never meant to hurt you."

Kathy had a flashback. "I remember that day—the Tuesday after Labor Day. Casey called to say she was heading back home, and would I mind if she stopped by for a visit. I convinced her to stay for a few days. During her visit, Derek and I thought she wasn't her happy self. It seemed like she had the weight of the world on her shoulders. This was before her cancer diagnosis, so it wasn't that. I did question if something was bothering her. She said she was tired. Strange, since she'd just spent six weeks at the Cape with you. Her heart was broken, and you were the cause, Lauren. She was in love with you, and you broke her heart and hurt Alice. You're a selfish bitch."

"Fuck you, Kathy."

"You crossed the line, Lauren. You came between two people that were committed to each other."

"Doesn't sound like Casey was committed to Alice, does it, Kathy? Because if she were, I wouldn't be telling this story."

Lauren glanced at Alice. "I'm sorry, Alice. When you left Casey, she admitted to me cheating on you was wrong, I swear."

"You screwed the woman she loved, and now you want to make it right, by saying it was a mistake? Poor Lauren, she was lonely, and Casey filled that need without you having to come out to the world. Casey would never expose your little secret. She loved you, and you used her. That's what truly happened."

"Kathy, enough."

"Elle, are you not appalled by Lauren's actions? She's gay since college. Didn't bother to tell her husband, and she screwed her best friend when it suited her. Then she tossed them out like last week's garbage."

Lauren couldn't believe her ears. Kathy, her dearest friend, was condemning her for being human. The person that she thought would have her back always was driving the knife deeper into her heart. Lauren told herself, *Stay calm*. She'd wait for the right moment when Kathy was calmer to explain she wasn't the person Kathy was accusing her of being—a selfish bitch. "Kathy, I never meant to hurt anyone. You have to believe—"

"You hurt Casey when you sent her packing. Alice lost the love of her life, why, because you were lonely. You hurt Jake because you put your career before your marriage. You probably didn't want to share a bed with him. Jake doesn't know how lucky he is to have found Michelle. Derek was right about you, Lauren. He said Jake was happier without you."

"Kathy."

"What, Elle, are you going to say you never thought, not once, that Lauren is a selfish bitch?"

Before Elle could answer, Lauren shouted, "No, she doesn't think I'm a selfish bitch because not everyone is as perfect as you, Kathy. Fairy-tale endings aren't all they're cracked up to be. Life and shit happen. The gypsy woman said you need to find the truth. Well…if I'm a selfish bitch, then you're a fool."

"Go ahead, Lauren, condemn me, as you so often do. Remind me how useless I am because I don't have a successful career. Tell me how foolish I am for wanting to be a stay-at-home mom. How doting on my husband and children is a crime. Someday, Lauren, I will have my memories. All your children will have is the memory of Mommy's back as she closes the door behind her, off on another book tour. What kind of mother are you?"

"Wow, feel better getting your true feelings off your chest, dear friend?"

"You can dish it out, but you can't take it when someone tells you what they think of you."

"Oh, I can take it. I'm willing to admit when I make a mistake. I don't allow my happiness to cloud the truth in my life. I slept with Casey before and after I was with Jake. But I bet your precious husband can't say you are his one and only."

"Derek is a saint compared to you, Lauren. My husband would never cheat on me."

"Your saint is perverted."

"What the fuck does that mean?"

Lauren inhaled deeply. She didn't, did she, speak the unforbidden word *perverted*? Lauren had to put a stop to this argument immediately. "Nothing, Kathy. I'm done with this conversation. Hate me, judge me, call me a fake, a liar, and a cheat. I guess I deserve it. I'm tired, and I've had way too much to drink. Elle, can you call Sam? It's time for me to say good night."

"You're not going anywhere, bitch. Who the hell do you think you are calling my husband perverted when you're the perverted one? You fuck anything with legs."

"Kathy, what's gotten into you?"

"The gypsy woman has gotten into her head, Elle. She's trying to figure out the meaning of the old woman's words. What's wrong,

Kathy? Are you wondering if your fairy-tale marriage is a farce? You crucify me for having an affair when I was single both times. I'd say, that isn't cheating."

"You're calling my husband a cheat? Prove it. You say he's perverted? Prove it."

Lauren controlled her anger. "I don't have any proof, just a gut feeling."

"You bitch. You'd do anything to hurt me. You've always been jealous of the love Derek and I share. Why, because you were in a loveless marriage? I always thought Jake was too good for you. I pity your children. A good mother puts her children's needs before her own."

Elle stepped between Lauren and Kathy. Lauren was at her boiling point. Kathy had gone too far, and Lauren wasn't going to let her off that easily.

"Your husband is perverted. You want proof? I've got it. He forced Casey and me into a threesome in college."

Kathy screamed, "You're lying!"

"Lauren, don't. Kathy, Lauren—"

"It's true, Elle. Mr. Perfect has a dark side. I'm not sure Kathy is woman enough to satisfy a man with a dark side."

Kathy moved to strike Lauren. "Shut your dirty, cheating mouth."

"She's telling the truth, Kathy."

The three looked to Alice for an explanation. "Casey told me the story. Derek caught Lauren and Casey in the act in college. He gave them an ultimatum, agree to a threesome with him, or he'd spread the word that Lauren was gay. Word around school was Casey swung both ways, so Derek knew Lauren was the path to his achieving his threesome."

Kathy fell back in her chair. "You're lying. I need to call Derek."

Lauren feared, with Alice backing up her story, if Kathy asked Derek for the truth, he might deny everything. If he denied it, it would destroy Kathy or, worse, their marriage.

"Kathy, I'm begging you. Please don't call Derek," cried Lauren.

"I don't believe you, my husband—I have to call Derek."

"Kathy, please. I didn't mean what I said that you're not woman enough—"

"Why did you do it, Lauren? Why did you and Casey agree to a threesome?"

"Lauren refused. She was willing to leave school if Derek followed through on his threat. Casey convinced Lauren that after once or twice, Derek would lose interest," said Alice.

"Derek would never do that to his friends. What really happened, Lauren? When Derek walked in on you and Casey, did you talk him into a threesome for his silence?"

"No, Kathy, it wasn't my idea. Alice is telling the truth. Derek caught us together. He came up with the threesome. I didn't want to go along—"

"But Casey convinced you."

"Yes and no. I knew it was wrong, but I didn't want to leave school. I worked so hard to maintain my grades."

"You were worried about your grades, so you slept with my husband?" Kathy shouted. "How many times did you sleep with my husband, Lauren?"

"Kathy, I didn't sleep with your husband."

Kathy shrieked, "How many times, Lauren? If you won't tell me, I'll ask Derek."

"Why would you do that, Kathy? We all did crazy things in college."

"How many times, Lauren? I'm going to find out from you or Derek."

"Six times, maybe seven."

"Seven times. You slept with my husband seven times."

"Kathy, Derek wasn't your husband. You weren't even dating at the time. Actually, it stopped when you agreed to date him."

"If you thought Derek was perverted and had a dark side, as my friend, you should have told me. Instead, you chose to keep your disgusting secret."

"I wanted to tell you, I swear, but he begged us not to. Once Casey and I knew how much you two cared for each other, we put it behind us."

The Palm Reader

"You didn't put it behind you, Lauren. You hate Derek. It's obvious. What I thought was bantering was your dislike of him. You think he's a cheater, has a dark side, because you agreed to a threesome. That doesn't sound like you, Lauren. Allowing a man to convince you to do something you weren't comfortable with. Doesn't sound like the Lauren I know unless you're the perverted one, Lauren."

Lauren felt Kathy's friendship slowly slipping from her. Lauren was telling the truth when she said that she had placed those awful encounters behind her. Twenty years ago, Lauren wanted to tell Kathy the truth, but Casey insisted telling her would destroy their friendship. Twenty years later, her confession cost her a treasured friendship. She'd take Kathy's insults graciously and hope she'd get a second chance to explain.

"I was ashamed for allowing myself to be placed in an awful situation. The last thing I wanted was for others to find out. Derek is, and will always be, head over heels in love with you. Can't you just forgive and forget?"

"You slept with Derek, Lauren. I don't think I can forget or forgive. I now know you, for who you truly are." Kathy turned her back to Lauren. "I hate you, Lauren."

Lauren tried to stop her, but Kathy pushed her aside.

"Let her go, Lauren. Her world was just turned upside down." Elle followed Kathy to the front door. She retrieved her cell phone and called Sam. When Sam arrived, Elle said to him, "I'm going back with Kathy. Don't leave without me."

After Kathy's quick departure, Alice tried to console Lauren. Wanting to be alone, Lauren walked toward the ocean and collapsed on the sand.

Elle found Alice where she'd left her. "Where is Lauren?"

Alice pointed toward the shoreline. Elle wanted to go to Lauren to console her, but it was Kathy, she feared, who needed consoling.

"Alice, I'm going back to the hotel with Kathy. Can Lauren spend the night?"

"Yes, of course. I'm sorry, Elle. In the past, I would have welcomed hurting Lauren, but I couldn't let her take the fall for Derek's bad behavior, and Casey convincing Lauren not to tell Kathy the truth was wrong."

*****

Staring out the car window, Kathy showed no emotion on the drive back to the hotel. Elle wanted to reach for her hand; she didn't because she didn't want to cause a scene in front of Sam.

Elle didn't go straight to her room; instead, she followed Kathy to hers. When Kathy entered the room, she retrieved her cell phone.

"Kathy, can we talk before you make that call?"

"You think I'm calling Derek? I'm not. I'm calling the Atlantic City Airport and booking a flight for home. If that bitch thinks I'm driving back with her—"

"Let me make the call." Kathy handed Elle the phone and headed for the bathroom.

Elle made a reservation for one, on a flight to Greenwich, Connecticut, leaving at 9:00 a.m. She also arranged to have a car meet Kathy when she arrived. When Kathy emerged from the bathroom, Elle said, "Sam will pick you up at seven. The airport is forty minutes from here. It's a small airport, several flights in and out. Security shouldn't be an issue. I've arranged for a car to meet you when you arrive."

"Thanks, Elle." Kathy placed her suitcase on the bed and began to throw her clothes into it. She set aside an outfit for the following day. When she finished, she collapsed into the only chair in the room. Elle sat on the bed across from Kathy. Elle reached for Kathy's hands. She accepted the gesture and began to cry.

"Kathy, I know you're upset, and I don't want you to think what I'm about to say will give you the impression I don't feel empathy for you. But we all did things in college we are not proud of. Before you confront Derek with an embarrassing situation he would rather not relive, take a little time before you make your next move, okay?"

"What would you do, Elle, if you were me?"

"As I said, we all did things in college we regret. I dated that jerk Hugh Carlton. Everyone told me he was no good, but I knew better.

The Palm Reader

When we were in his dorm room, he forced himself on me. I said no, but he was going to have his way. I was so frightened I began to sob. I think he was afraid someone would hear, so he called me a dick tease and told me to leave. I ran, Kathy, thanking God that I wasn't raped that night."

"They were my friends, Elle. I trusted them with my life. Lauren slept with Derek, my husband."

Elle lowered herself to the floor kneeling before Kathy. She said, "Casey was gay and proud of it. I believe Alice when she said that Lauren wanted to say no. Derek, well, he was just being a guy. Lauren comes off as being invincible, but I don't think she could have handled the humiliation of being tagged as gay."

Kathy listened, but Elle surmised Kathy wasn't ready to forgive. The words she spoke were going in one ear and out the other.

"I'm happy Casey is dead. It would have hurt me to break my friendship with her, but Lauren's friendship, I can live without."

"Kathy, it's hard for me to wrap my head around what happened tonight. I can only imagine how hurt you are, but Lauren, you, and me, we are more than friends. Please try to—"

"Lauren has always been jealous of me and the life Derek and I share. I realize what he did was wrong. You said it yourself. We all did things in college we are ashamed of. I'm sure Derek regrets what he did. Doesn't every guy fantasize about sleeping with two women? Lauren accused me of not being woman enough to satisfy Derek. What friend says those words to another friend? One who is vicious, jealous, and a selfish bitch."

"Things got heated, Kathy. I'm not defending Lauren, but it was obvious to me that you had a problem with Casey and Lauren's relationship. You placed the blame entirely on Lauren. When Lauren knew the conversation was becoming heated, she tried to stop, but you insisted she tell you the truth. I truly believe Lauren wanted to save you and Derek the embarrassment of bringing up a subject I'm sure he regrets. Lauren said that once you and Derek were together, he begged them not to tell you. I don't know if I would have told you the truth."

Kathy stood and walked toward the balcony. Sliding the door open, she stepped out. Elle followed and stood beside her. "Kathy, Derek loves you. No. He loves and adores you. Don't let what happened over twenty years ago destroy what you have. Lauren has a way of coming on strong, especially with you. But you know she loves you and your family. Blame the night on too much wine and a confession that was better left unsaid. And me insisting we have our palms read."

"It's easy for you to defend Lauren, Elle. She didn't sleep with your husband. We both know, Elle. Lauren has always put her needs first. You wear blinders when it comes to Lauren. I refuse to allow that bitch to come between Derek and me. All these years, I thought Lauren was just clowning with Derek, but she was harboring ill feelings toward him because she wasn't strong enough—" Kathy paused.

"From what you just said, I'm assuming you aren't going to tell Derek you know."

"Of course, not. I am not going to allow that bitch to destroy us."

Tonight wasn't the right time for Elle to ask Kathy to forgive and forget. Elle had to respect that Kathy's feelings were normal. The woman just found out that her best friends and future husband slept together. That image would be etched in Kathy's subconscious forever.

Kathy ended the conversation by informing Elle that she was tired.

"Of course, I should go." As they entered the room, Elle said, "You have to promise that you won't leave without saying goodbye."

"I promise."

Kathy walked Elle to the door. Elle hugged Kathy and said, "I love you."

"I love you too, Elle."

"I'll meet you in the lobby at 6:00 a.m. sharp."

"Elle, you understand that what happened today, well, I'm never going to forgive Lauren. I hope it isn't going to affect our friendship?"

Elle smiled. "BFFs forever."

*****

Lauren tossed and turned the entire night. At four in the morning, she went to the kitchen and prepared a strong pot of coffee. Alice entered the kitchen at five.

While pouring herself a cup of coffee, Alice asked, "Did you get any sleep?"

"No. What happened last night?" Lauren didn't wait for an answer. "She's never going to forgive me. I hurt Casey, Jake, you, and now Kathy."

Alice sighed. "Things did get heated. But when you go after the cub, the lioness will attack."

"The cub being Derek, and Kathy the lioness."

"Something like that. In your defense, Derek and Casey were wrong. Derek for being a dick. The nickname fits him well. Casey should never have convinced you to give in to the guy, thinking eventually he would lose interest. It was Kathy agreeing to date Derek that stopped the threats. Who knows how long his threats would have lasted. I think you did the right thing not telling Kathy. If she stopped dating Derek, out of spite, he might have pinned you as gay," said Alice.

"Kathy was right when she said the 'Lauren she knew' would never allow a man to take advantage of her. But twenty-year-old Lauren didn't want to give up on her dream of graduating from a prestigious school."

"It explains why you hate the guy."

"I don't hate Derek. How can you hate a genius? But what happened between us in college is why, after all these years, I question the man's fidelity. I have to believe, he would never do anything to hurt Kathy. The man worships the ground she walks on. She is never going to forgive me. She accused me of sleeping with her husband. I feared losing her friendship twenty years ago, and twenty years later, I did."

"It's not an easy situation to get over."

Lauren glanced at Alice. "I'm so sorry, Alice. Every bad decision I've made is coming back to haunt me. You know, the only reason I told Elle and Kathy about my encounter with Casey was, I feared how the truth would sound coming from you."

"I guessed that was the reason. Lauren, the week we spent together, well…I've gotten to know you, and you're not so bad. You were right when you said Casey was a flirt, and I believe you when you said, she came on to you." Alice paused. "I never thought what happened to you in college was right. Maybe it's the female activist in me, but I just couldn't let Kathy condemn you without knowing the truth. I hope my backing up your story didn't cause more harm."

"I hope and pray she didn't call Derek. I fear the man will deny, deny, deny everything. If Derek thought the truth would cost him Kathy, I think he would lie."

"Last night you called him a cheat."

"I don't know for sure. Maybe Kathy was right. Maybe I have been harboring ill feelings toward Derek. All these years, occasionally, I might have thought about that time in college, but not to the point where I wanted to destroy Derek."

"Do you think she'll ride back with you?"

"Oh, Alice, she has to. We have to talk. I have to make her understand that Derek was just being a guy, and I know it won't be easy to explain why I agreed to—but I have to try, Alice."

*****

Entering Alice's home, Elle called out. "Good morning."

"I'm in the kitchen."

"Hi, Alice. Where's Lauren?"

"She's in the shower. How's Kathy?"

"She's on her way to the airport."

"Makes sense."

Elle collapsed in a chair. "Terrible end to a perfect week. How did things get so fucked up? Earlier in the day, we were laughing having a great time, then they were at each other's throats."

"I wish Casey had never told me about the college threesome. I don't want to crucify the guy, but Derek was wrong, and Casey was wrong to convince Lauren it was okay."

"You're right, Alice. Derek was wrong, and I know things got heated between Kathy and Lauren, but why confess now, after all these years? Kathy will never forgive Lauren."

Lauren entered the kitchen. "I promise, Elle, on the ride back, I'll explain why I didn't tell her the truth twenty years ago."

"Lauren, Kathy booked a flight for home. Her flight departs at nine."

"What! How could you let her go, Elle? She called Derek, didn't she, and he told her not to get in the car with me. That bastard."

"She didn't call him."

"She didn't call Derek?"

"No. She's not going to tell him, she knows. She's convinced that you've harbored ill feelings toward Derek since college, and this was your way of making him pay."

"That's not true. Elle, you shouldn't have let Kathy get on that plane. Now I'll never get the chance to explain."

"I didn't stop her, Lauren, because I don't think you can explain why you didn't tell her what happened twenty years ago."

"You've already chosen a side. I didn't tell her because she was happy, and I was afraid to lose her friendship. Or maybe I was ashamed that I went through with it."

"I haven't chosen a side, Lauren. I'm sick over this. You have to understand, twenty years ago, Derek wasn't Kathy's husband. He was just a guy. She had a right to make her own decision even if it costs you her friendship."

"Yes. At forty-two years old, that makes a whole lot of sense. At twenty, it was fucking scary."

"I don't want to argue with you, Lauren. I'm going to do everything in my power to help fix this. Kathy doesn't want to speak with you. I think you need to give her time to figure things out."

"Allowing Kathy to leave before I got a chance to talk with her might have been the biggest mistake of your life, Elle. When she gets home, are you sure she isn't going to confront Derek? No. If she confronts him and he doesn't tell the truth, you think their marriage will survive?"

"I couldn't stop her, Lauren. I never saw Kathy so upset. She has an image of you and Casey sleeping with Derek. That image will be with her forever."

"I know that, Elle. That is why she and I should have talked this over. Maybe I would have gotten through to her."

"You weren't getting through to her, Lauren."

Lauren ran her hands through her hair. Elle was right; an image of Derek and Lauren lying naked was forever burned in Kathy's mind.

*****

Kathy's plane was delayed thirty minutes. When she finally boarded, she was assigned a window seat. The attendant offered her a drink. The white wine fit her mood, bitter. She asked herself, *Should I have driven back with Lauren?* She wanted Lauren to hear it from her that their friendship was over, done, finished. No. She did make the right decision. If she would have driven back with Lauren, she would have turned the entire incident around by ignoring how much she was hurting. Lauren would have said, "If it makes you feel better, I'm sorry. Okay, I should have told you, but you weren't even dating the guy. Do you know how insane you sound accusing me of sleeping with your husband?"

Kathy didn't think herself insane. Her two best friends were forced into an awful situation by a guy she agreed to date. *Oh god, this can't be happening. Derek is a good man, a devoted husband, and father. He couldn't have done what Lauren accused him of doing, could he? But Alice had confirmed that Lauren was telling the truth. Lauren said she was going to say no, but Casey convinced her it would be fine. Bullshit. Lauren was just trying to make herself the victim. Last night, she confessed she was lonely after her divorce from Jake. She had no one to blame but herself,* thought Kathy. Jake had moved on with Michelle. Alice had forgiven Casey, and she and Derek were happy. These recent occurrences could have made Lauren bitter and jealous. And her jealousy was setting her on a path to destroy Kathy's marriage.

Kathy's head was spinning. None of it made sense. Lauren might be selfish and self-centered, but she wouldn't deliberately destroy a marriage. No. She might be crude, condescending, but never hurtful. Lauren's confession had burned the image of Lauren, Casey, and Derek together, in her mind forever.

Why was Kathy questioning Derek's devotion to her and his family? He did nothing that would cause her to think he was a cheat. Lauren was convinced he cheats, is perverted, and has a dark side. But why did Lauren attack her, saying she wasn't woman enough to satisfy her man? She had to stop questioning her husband's devotion. She couldn't allow Lauren's confession to ruin her marriage or her children's lives.

Her thoughts were interrupted when the flight attendant asked for her glass and requested that she fasten her seatbelt.

When she was able to use her phone, she called Derek. He answered on the first ring.

"Hi, I've missed you. Instead of me coming home, what if you and I spend two nights at the Hilton? You make the reservation. I'll meet you at the hotel in an hour."

*****

Elle parked the car. Walking along the boardwalk, she stopped and sat at the same table she'd sat with Alice, Kathy, and Lauren the day before. Keeping a close watch on the entrance of the gypsy woman's establishment, several young ladies entered the building. While she waited for them to exit, she thought of Kathy.

Kathy texted as she'd promised. She arrived safe and sound and was on her way to meet Derek. Confused, Elle wondered why Kathy was meeting Derek when she paid to have Kathy driven to her home. Lauren's words echoed in Elle's ears. *"Are you sure, Elle, that Kathy won't tell Derek?"* No, Elle wasn't sure. Kathy could have changed her mind on the plane. Kathy might have wanted answers and convinced herself it was best to confront Derek. If Kathy decided to stick with her original plan and not tell Derek she knew about the threesome, she still had to concoct a believable story of why she and Lauren hadn't driven back together. If Lauren and Kathy's friendship was over, the fabricated story would have to include that Lauren would never be invited to the Wilsons' home ever again.

Derek and Jake would definitely call Elle for an explanation. This mess was escalating by the minute. Elle envisioned Derek and Kathy's marriage falling apart, and Lauren's confession being their demise.

Elle noticed the young ladies exiting the building. She moved quickly. When she entered the dark room, her eyes immediately adjusted.

"Hello." When no one appeared, she raised her voice. "Hello!"

The woman entered the room. "Yes."

"Do you remember me? I was here yesterday."

"I remember you."

It was a hot day outside and five degrees hotter in the room. Elle began to sweat. She retrieved a tissue from her purse and began to dry her forehead.

"Come." The woman walked to the back of the room. Elle followed. There was a sofa, a lounge chair, and a coffee table at the end of the room.

"Sit. You need a drink."

Elle glanced into the room where the woman had gone. A kitchen, and off the kitchen were several rooms. Elle guessed they were bedrooms. In the kitchen, close to the entrance, was a large fan blowing cool air toward her. The woman reappeared with two tall glasses with ice and a pitcher of iced tea.

After filling her glass with iced tea, the woman handed it to Elle, who drank the sweet liquid quickly. The woman refilled her glass.

"This is really good."

"My mother's recipe. She didn't use tea bags. The tea leaves are from India. You can purchase them on Amazon. Just key in tea leaves from India, and a list magically appears. This is peach and ginger. I love Amazon. Order today, have it tomorrow."

Elle smiled.

"Why are you here?" asked the woman.

"The words you spoke after reading my palm kept me awake the entire night. Do you remember saying I had to face my demons?"

"You want me to explain?"

"No. Maybe. Yesterday, after my friends and I met with you, well, a perfect day turned into a horrible night."

"Why?"

"My friends. The pretty one, Kathy, and Lauren, the writer, they aren't speaking. I don't think they will ever speak again."

"And this is my fault?"

"No, of course, not. But your words kind of set the wheels in motion. Kathy questioned why she had to look beyond her happiness for the truth, and Lauren, well, she made a confession that severed her friendship with Kathy."

"I'm sorry to hear that, but they are not here, you are."

"Yes. As I said, the words you spoke kept me up the entire night."

"If you are here to say that the words I spoke were harmful, then you should have gone to the palm reader on Atlantic. She tells people what they want to hear."

"I don't doubt you. I don't know what you see or sense. All I know is, I was heading home, but I couldn't leave without seeing you."

"Your name is Elle, right?"

"Yes."

"Elle, I like you, so I'm going to be honest with you. I don't see dead people or speak with the dead. I am an honest gypsy. Some days, I don't sense anything. If I have an off day, I don't charge the people. I tell them to come back another day. You and your friends came on a good day. My husband thinks it was because the moon was full the night before. When I look in your eyes, Elle, what I see is pain—the pain of a lost love, a lost childhood, a person, an occurrence, something, or someone caused that pain. What it is, only you know. What the outcome will be after you have faced the demon, I do not know. Facing the problem may or may not bring you peace or lessen the pain. But my advice is to face the demon and break the control it has over you. Now go."

Stunned by the early dismissal, Elle stood. "Thank you for the iced tea."

The woman smiled.

*****

Kathy lay in bed, listening to Derek singing in the shower.

Yesterday, arriving at the hotel, she spotted Derek at the lobby desk, checking them into their room. She wanted to run to him.

Instead, she remained still and watched him from behind. When he turned, seeing her, he smiled. She remained where she stood. He rushed across the lobby, taking her into his arms.

He whispered, "I've missed you."

Kathy held on to him, breathing in his scent, she wanted to ask if what she'd discovered was true, but instead she asked, "How are the kids?"

Derek smiled. "They are good. In fact, they were very good. I had a great time with them. But now I intend to have a great time with their mommy." Derek glanced over Kathy's shoulder. "Don't tell me Lauren is self-parking?" Before Kathy could answer his question, he said, "I made a reservation for lunch. Or did I luck out, and the witch decided to head back home?"

"Lauren and I didn't drive back together."

Confused, Derek asked, "You didn't drive back with Lauren? How did you get here?"

"I took a flight from AC."

"Why?"

"I'm starving. Let's talk over lunch." Taking Derek's arm, she led him toward the restaurant.

While they ate, Kathy concocted her own version of the fight she and Lauren had. After finishing her version, which excluded Lauren's two confessions, Casey, and the threesome, she went on to say, "I just couldn't take her insults any longer. She criticizes the way I choose to live my life. This time, she went too far."

"Sweetie, I know Lauren thought you'd be the person to find a cure for cancer, but what Lauren thought didn't make a hell of a difference to you in the past. Why now? What did she say that caused you to jump on a plane and leave her to drive home alone?"

"She said things that were cruel and hurtful. I wanted to strike her. She dwelled on the same shit. Why would I choose wiping milk off children's faces when I could be saving the world? How could I watch my husband become a success while I raise his five brats and clean his mansion?"

"That doesn't sound like Lauren. Was she drunk?"

"Are you defending her?"

"No. We've always known how Lauren felt about you choosing your family over a career, and she might have made a few jokes now and then, but you never seem to let it bother you."

"Our friendship with Lauren is over. You should be happy. You didn't much like her anyway."

"Baby, Lauren is a part of our family. I might not always agree with her, but—"

"But what, Derek, you don't want to see her go?"

Derek's brows furrowed.

"Maybe you agree with Lauren. I should be out there saving the world."

"You know that's not true. I know you love being with the kids, and I appreciate all you do to make our home a happy one."

"But—"

"There is no but. Baby, you know if you wanted more than just raising our children and running our home, I'd support you 100 percent."

"Well, Lauren is out of our lives, and I need you to respect my decision. I don't want you to call her or Elle to find out what happened. You have to trust me. This is best for our family. If someday I wish to rekindle a relationship with Lauren, it will be my decision."

Derek reached for Kathy's hand. "Kathy, I've never seen you this upset. If you say your friendship with Lauren is over, then Lauren is no longer a part of our lives."

Derek's singing turned into him shouting his favorite song, "My Girl." Kathy knew it was for her benefit because he sang it to her often.

Kathy thought about the first time she'd noticed Derek Charles Wilson in chemistry class. He was leaning on the doorframe talking with an attractive girl. There was no denying the guy was handsome, but he had a reputation for breaking girls' hearts, and she avoided having her heart broken by ignoring him. Two years later, Kathy agreed to a burger and a movie. Her plan was to go out with the conceited jerk and then dump him. But the night turned out differently. Derek was sweet, charming, considerate, and handsome. Those puppy-dog eyes drew her in. He talked about his dream of saving lives, how he studied hard to earn a scholarship to Northwestern, how he wanted to make his mother and father proud. His parents were blue-collar workers; it pained them that all they could afford was a monthly allowance.

He shared, "Someday, I want to buy my parents a nice house. I want my mother to retire. My father says he'll never retire, but I don't want him to worry about the house or bills. I have a brother that is five years younger and a sister seven years younger. If I can, I want to make sure they have the same advantages that I have."

Kathy was smitten after their first date. Derek was always a gentleman. He didn't force himself on her, and Kathy had to know for sure, if he was committed to her. They fooled around, but intercourse didn't happen until both had graduated from Northwestern. They decided to move to New York after graduation. Kathy attended Columbia where she earned her master's, and Derek, Cornell. Kathy wasn't a virgin, but the first night she lay with Derek was the first time she felt truly satisfied as a woman.

The sounds of water splashing and the singing stopped. Shortly, Derek would be lying beside her. She glanced around the room focusing on the entrance. Fifteen hours ago, they'd entered the room. On a small round table sat a tray of chocolate strawberries, a bowl of whipped cream, and a bottle of champagne.

Derek pulled back the curtains covering the long windows. He called to her, "Kathy, come here."

When she was beside him, he stepped behind her wrapping his arms around her waist. He said, "Look at the size of that pool."

There were three bars surrounding the pool. The music was loud enough that they could hear the muffled sounds of the DJ playing "Who Let the Dogs Out?" The women were wearing strings as bathing suits. "You up for a swim?"

"I'll look like an old lady next to those women. My bathing suit covers my tits and ass."

"Come, I have a surprise for you." Derek presented Kathy with a gift bag. She sat on the bed. "What's this?"

"Open it."

She took out the first item. It was a navy-blue string bathing suit bottom. Reaching into the bag, she retrieved the top. "You expect me to wear this?"

"There's more."

Kathy looked in the bag and found a matching cover-up.

"I don't think you need it, but I wasn't sure you'd be comfortable—"

Derek was kneeling before Kathy; she looked into his eyes. "It's perfect."

"You like it? Great. There's one more gift, Mrs. Wilson."

Kathy looked into the bag and saw a long black velvet box. Opening the box, she gasped. "A diamond necklace! It's beautiful."

"Not as beautiful as you."

Wrapping her arms around his neck, she cried, "I love it. Thank you." At that moment, she hated Lauren even more than she did the day before. Lauren tried to ruin what she treasured—her life with Derek.

Kathy put on the bathing suit and admired herself in the mirror. Derek insisted she wear the necklace to the pool, and she agreed.

They drank, lounged, and sang to the music. The day was perfect.

When they went back to the room, they made love. Derek turned her on all fours, and she stopped him. Lying flat on her back, he entered her. He was in the moment, but Kathy couldn't stop herself from seeing Derek making love to Lauren.

*****

Lauren reached Exit 59 on the highway—the exit she would take to Kathy's home. She wanted desperately to exit the highway, but Elle's words echoed, "Let her go, Lauren. She needs time."

Lauren remained on the highway. Tears welled up in her eyes. *Kathy was hurting,* thought Lauren, *and it was her cruel confession that broke that sweet girl's heart. How much time did Kathy need before Lauren could call, asking if they could talk? How much time did Kathy need before Lauren could beg to be forgiven? How much time did Kathy need before Lauren couldn't bear to be without her friend a minute longer?*

An eternity, thought Lauren.

CHAPTER 7

Thanksgiving was one week away. Since September, Elle spoke with Lauren often and Kathy several times. Lauren asked if Kathy was well, hoping Elle would say Kathy was ready to talk. Kathy never mentioned Lauren to Elle, and Elle didn't push. During her last conversation with Kathy, she told her, she was going home to North Dakota for Thanksgiving. Kathy never questioned why.

Elle had spoken with Jacques. They were finally at a point where they were able to talk as friends.

The gypsy woman was in Elle's thoughts daily. There were nights where she tossed and turned, the gypsy's words invading her dreams, *face the demon*.

On the flight home, Elle thought about the conversation she had with her mother when she called to say she was coming home for Thanksgiving. *Elle, I don't think I will recognize you. How long has it been—seven or eight years? I've lost track. How long will you be staying? As you know, there isn't much to do in North Dakota, not for a girl who has traveled the world.*

The answer to her mother's question was seven years and six months, when she'd returned home for her father's funeral.

When Elle exited the plane, she saw lifted high enough for her to see was a cardboard sign with her name on it.

"Elle."

"Uncle Charlie, you look great."

Uncle Charlie lifted Elle in the air and swung her around. "You don't look so bad yourself, kid. It's been a while. Do you have any other luggage?"

The Palm Reader

"Nope."

"Good, then let's get the hell out of here."

In the car, Uncle Charlie began a conversation. "Level with me, kid, why the visit?"

"It's a long story, Uncle Charlie."

"So there's a story. Does this story have to do with a life-changing decision?"

"Such as?"

"Your mother thought you wouldn't be traveling alone."

"I see. Did she honestly think I'd get married or have a child and not tell her?"

"It's been, what, eight years? A lot can happen in eight years."

"Nothing much, Uncle Charlie. I mean, Uncle Charles. I don't want to upset Mom. You know how she hates when I call you Uncle Charlie. She'd say, 'It's Uncle Charles to you, young lady.'"

"Your mother has that stick so far up her ass—"

"Uncle Charles!"

"What! You know it's true."

Elle smiled. Uncle Charlie didn't question again why Elle decided to visit after all these years. As they drove, Elle spied the downtown area. Nothing much had changed. Mr. Lee's lumberyard was gone, replaced by a massive Home Depot. Taco Bell was new. The old strip malls were replaced with elegant buildings that housed boutiques, restaurants, art galleries, fountains, and rich green gardens filled with colorful flowers. A larger mall with various stores was located on the outskirts of Fargo.

Elle reflected on her grade-school days when Mrs. Cruz proudly described their home state.

> *North Dakota* is a Sioux word, meaning, "friend or ally." North Dakota is the least-visited state. November through March is snow season. It wouldn't be uncommon to see a flurry or two every month except July and August. Rain most common the rest of the year. Well-known people were born in North Dakota—Lawrence Welk,

Roger Maris, and Peggy Lee, to name a few. There are no towns or villages in North Dakota, only cities. The city of Rutland was the home of the 3,591-pound hamburger. Grand Forks holds a grand pasta party each year. The hamlet of Ruso has a total population of two in winter and four in summer. In Fargo, it's illegal to wear a hat while dancing.

So why did Elle's grandfather purchase 1,000 acres of land in Fargo? His fascination with bees, especially the honeybee. After earning his degree in entomology and biology, he headed to Fargo. Five years after arriving, her grandfather's bee farm was one of the largest producers of honey. Seven years later, he divided a portion of the land to grow wheat and sunflowers. At the age of twenty-eight, he married a local gal. Three years after they married, Uncle Charlie was born. Elle's mom was born two and half years later.

Elle wasn't as enthusiastic as Mrs. Cruz about the state of North Dakota, but she did love the city this time of year. The holidays brought out the horse-drawn sleighs. The sleighs would roam the city from the beginning of November to the end of February.

"Beautiful weather for this time of year."

"We're having a heat wave. How's the job going? Are there any perks for anchoring the six o'clock news in DC?"

"To get me to and from the studio on time, I get to live in a penthouse apartment owned by the network."

"Cool, free rent."

"So what's new with you, Uncle Charlie, still dating Elaine?"

"I am."

"The woman is half your age."

"I wish."

"Does it still drive Mom nuts that you refuse to settle down?"

"I think your mother has given up hope of me settling down. Elaine is happy with the way things are. Anyway, your mother wasn't the only one who thought someone might be joining you on this trip. Last time we talked, you were living with a guy in Paris. I'm guessing with the move to DC, that relationship might have ended, or not."

"I still speak with Jacques, but his career is in Paris, and mine, in DC."

"There has to be one guy in DC that would want to get to know the famous Elle Kessler."

Elle smiled. Driving through the gates inscribed with the family name, Beckham Farms, Elle glanced at the farmland to her left and right, now barren. Three miles down the road, she spotted the house. It was elegant and massive even from a distance. A bronze brick structure with large floor-to-ceiling windows surrounded the first floor. There were ten bedrooms in the house. At least six of the bedrooms had balconies—the master and her room having the largest. The back of the home had a surrounding porch, which overlooked the gardens; within the gardens was a pool and lounge area. Beyond the pool, two tennis courts and a horse stable; beyond the stable, the bee farm. When her grandfather resided in the home, the porch overlooked the stable and bee farm. As a wedding present to his daughter and her husband, the pool and tennis courts were added. Elle's father was athletic and enjoyed a daily swim, when the weather permitted. Trudy was a decent tennis player. Golf was played at the local country club. The couple was suited for each other.

Uncle Charlie turned onto the path toward the house. Coming to a stop at the main entrance of the house, the massive doors opened. Trudy stepped out first. Elle gasped. Her mom had always been an attractive woman, but it seemed as if she hadn't aged a day since last she saw her. Her mother wasn't a fan of plastic surgery. Trudy believed every woman should accept the inevitable. Elle was sure a tuck here or there was out of the question. From behind Elle's mom, Rose and Hutch rushed to greet her. Until the age of twelve, Elle's mother was her primary caretaker. When Elle turned twelve, her mother lost interest in her comings and goings. Rose rushed to greet Elle. Embracing her, Rose said, "Ms. Elle, it's been so long since we last saw you."

Elle released Rose and hugged Hutch. "You both look wonderful. How's the foot, Hutch?" Elle spied her mother's eyes glued to the car doors; when no one else emerged, Trudy exhaled.

"It's good, Ms. Elle. Doc thought I might lose it after the black mare stomped on it, but the Man Above had other plans."

Elle's grandmother was a religious woman, and her grandfather followed his wife's beliefs after they married. No surprise that Trudy would fall in love with the righteous Reverend Kessler.

"Enough, Rose. Elle must be tired after her long trip. Let's go inside. There's a chill in the air."

Elle followed her mother into the house. When they were face-to-face, Elle reached in to hug her mother. Trudy, uncomfortable by the embrace, released Elle. "You look great, Mom. Must be in the Beckham DNA. You and Uncle Charlie look great."

"Uncle Charles, Elle."

Uncle Charles rolled his eyes at Elle. "Sorry, Mom."

"Rose hadn't slept a wink when she heard you were coming home for Thanksgiving. She's spent two days cleaning your old room. Your room was painted three years ago, the curtains and bedding are new. I did have the rock-star posters removed."

"You didn't toss the posters, did you?"

"No. You can find them in your bedroom closet. Dinner is at six. I've invited a few friends. Charles, you did tell Elaine that dinner is at six, correct?"

"I did. We will be here sharply at six."

Trudy frowned.

"You've invited guest. I thought this weekend would just be family?"

"Elle, you called a week ago to say you would be home for Thanksgiving. The invitations went out the end of October. I couldn't cancel on the people who have spent every Thanksgiving with me for the past seven years."

"You're right, Mom, but I thought you and I would spend some of this time catching up."

"There will be plenty of time to catch up. I'm sure you could use a nap before dinner. Hutch, can you take Elle's bag to her room?"

"I can manage, Hutch."

*****

Elle settled into her room. She opened the balcony doors and took in the view. She could see the pool and tennis courts from her room. At the end of October, a tarp was placed over the pool. The tennis courts were professionally cared for. Seeing the pool brought back memories of Elle's childhood, sitting at the edge of the pool watching her father swim one hundred laps, her mother lounging in the sun reading a novel or a fashion magazine.

Trudy would caution, "Be careful, Elle, you don't want to fall in and be trampled by your father."

When her father finished his final lap, he'd call to her, "It's your turn, sweets."

She'd dive in and swim to him. On days when the temperature was unbearable, her mother would join them. She didn't much care for tennis but didn't protest when her mom and dad offered lessons because she knew they loved the sport. Looking beyond the bee farm, she remembered once lived her best friend, Liam. When the babies could sit on their own, without tumbling over, she and Liam were placed in the same playpen, while the young mothers of the parish enjoyed one another's company. She and Liam rode the school bus together, where they met three other children who lived close enough for the five to become best buddies. The Horton children consisted of two sisters, three years apart, and a brother the same age as she and Liam. The five frolicked in the pool June, July, and August.

Taking her mother's advice, Elle closed the balcony doors and rested. As soon as her head hit the pillow, she drifted off to sleep. Unfamiliar voices awakened her. After a quick shower and a change of clothes, she descended the stairs. Entering the living room, she chuckled. Her mother said she had invited a few guests. Elle estimated there were forty people. Getting her mother's attention by waving, Trudy walked toward her. In a loud voice, her mom introduced her, "Everyone, for those of you who have not had the pleasure of meeting my daughter, this is Elle."

Elle worked the room. She introduced herself to those she had never met and reminisced with those she did know. Uncle Charlie and Elaine arrived two minutes before everyone was escorted to the dining room for dinner.

Trudy and Elle sat at the heads of the table. Trudy placed several politicians closest to Elle. After two glasses of wine, Elle began to relax, finding herself enthralled and easily engaged in conversation with the guests closest to where she was seated. She agreed and disagreed with the different opinions on domestic and international politics. After dinner, the guests were invited to the drawing room. Elle sat close to the fireplace but found herself drifting off, so she excused herself saying it had been a long day. It didn't surprise her to learn, while offering a good night, that fifteen of the guests would be joining them for Thanksgiving dinner.

Thanksgiving Day, Elle woke, dressed warmly, and went for a walk around the grounds. She had considered packing her running gear but didn't. Arriving home an hour later, she joined her mother and their guests for a late breakfast. Thanksgiving dinner would be at five. The remainder of the day, Elle sat in her room and read. The guests said their goodbyes after breakfast on Friday morning. Elle thought it would be a great time to talk with her mother. But Trudy had plans, a business meeting in the downtown area. When Elle asked if she could tag along, Trudy told her she would be bored, then reminded Elle that dinner was at six, and Uncle Charlie and Elaine were joining them.

"Mom, you know I'm taking the red-eye back on Saturday. You do remember me telling you that I have to be back for the *Sunday Morning Show.*

"I remember, Elle. We can talk tonight during dinner."

When Trudy departed, Elle called her uncle. She needed to speak with Trudy privately, or this trip was a waste of her time.

"Hey, kid, what can I do for you?"

"Uncle Charlie, I need you to bow out of tonight's dinner."

"For me agreeing to be a no-show at dinner, you will have to take the blame for me canceling. I don't need your mother down my back lecturing me that I'm a selfish ingrate."

"I will. And in appreciation for bailing on you tonight and for the lift back to the airport, I want to take you and Elaine to dinner. Come by the house around seven tomorrow night, and I'll make a reservation at a restaurant close to the airport."

"When a beautiful woman offers to pay for dinner, a gentleman must graciously accept."

"Thanks, Uncle Charlie."

*****

Trudy arrived home at five thirty to find Elle sitting on the staircase. Startled, Trudy placed her hand over her heart. "Elle, I didn't expect to see you there."

"I was waiting for you."

Trudy started to climb the stairs. As she passed Elle, she said, "We only have twenty-five minutes to get ready for dinner."

"Uncle Charlie and Elaine aren't coming to dinner."

"Just like your uncle to cancel. Three days of family time is too much for your uncle to handle. I thought for you, his niece, he might have toughed it out. He has no respect for family, never did."

"I called Uncle Charlie and canceled the family dinner."

"Why would you do that, Elle? I instructed Rose to prepare a dinner for five."

"Well, I'll just have to eat for two."

Trudy gasped.

"Sorry, wrong choice of words. I'm sure Rose can freeze the leftovers. Tonight, it's just you and me. We need to talk."

Trudy stared at her daughter. "I haven't seen you in eight years, Elle. I know you've traveled the world, landed yourself a fabulous job, which I have offered my congratulations to you several times. You've confirmed you're not pregnant. Last time we talked, you said you had broken up with the guy you were dating. Did you already meet someone else? If so, I think you should give the relationship time before you jump into marriage."

Elle showed her ring finger. "Do you see a ring on this finger, no? You're right. The fifteen times we've talked in eight years, we've discussed my travels, the new job, and the ex-boyfriend, and we never dared to talk about my father."

"Your father. This visit is to discuss your father. The man is dead. What is there to discuss? If it's money, I think I've been more than generous. If Uncle Charles outlives me, you will divide the estate. If I outlive him, it's all yours to do with it as you please."

"Thank you. You have been very generous with Father's estate, but this isn't about money or lack of it. Your little act isn't fooling me, Mother. It's time to get your head out of the sand and talk about the past."

"I have no idea what you're talking about, Elle."

Trudy began to climb the stairs. Elle followed. When they reached the master bedroom, Trudy headed for the dressing room. Elle remained stoic taking in the size of the room. Stepping further into the room, she saw the chaise lounge where she and her mother would sit, while Trudy read out loud to her.

Trudy was always replacing Elle's name with the female heroine's name. "*Elle* let down her long beautiful hair, which the prince climbed to rescue his beloved." Elle was begging her mother to read the story again. Every night before dinner, she'd watched her mother apply a soft amount of powder to her face. Then she'd run the fluffy powder puff along Elle's nose, causing Elle to laugh. A touch of lipstick for the mother and a gentle touch of color for the child. Trudy would imitate the Wicked Witch of the East. "There, my pretty, we are ready to join your father for dinner." They would descend the stairs to find her father waiting. Repeating the same words every night. "There they are, my sun and my moon." Father would offer each of his girls an arm and escort them to dinner.

Mother entered the room and went to her closet. "Mother, we have to talk."

Frustrated, Trudy turned toward Elle. "This can't wait till dinner?"

"No."

"If you don't mind eating a cold dinner, then talk."

"That's why they invented microwaves, Mother."

Elle went to sit on the edge of the chaise lounge, motioning with her eyes for Trudy to follow. Annoyed, Trudy walked across the room and sat on the bed, folding her arms across her chest.

"All right, you have my attention, talk."

"You remember Casey, my college friend, stage 4 cancer. Before she died, she planned a one-year memorial service followed by the spreading of her ashes. I won't bore you with why Casey arranged for myself, Lauren, and Kathy to spend a week at the Jersey Shore. What I will tell you is during that time, for fun, we had our palms read. Do you know what the gypsy woman told me, Mother?" Elle didn't wait for an answer. "She said I had to face the demon."

Trudy frowned. "She told you to face the demon, and you came to visit because you think, I'm the demon?"

"No. Father is the demon, and you, his protector."

Trudy thought before questioning. "Why did your father need protection?"

"Liam."

Trudy pondered. "Liam! The Larson child. The boy that took his own life?"

"Yes."

"What does Liam's death have to do with your father or me, Elle?" Trudy began to rise.

Elle shouted, "Sit, Mother, I said we are going to talk, and I will have my way."

"You're acting like a child."

"Sit, damn you."

Trudy lingered for a moment before sitting.

"You protected him, my father, your precious husband, because you were afraid of losing everything."

"I'm assuming by everything, you mean, this house, money, and my position in the community."

"I caught him, Mother. Here in this house. My father had Liam cornered in the library. Liam's pants and underpants were down around his ankles. He was pleasuring himself while fondling a twelve-year-old boy. I screamed. Father zipped his pants up and then tried to convince me that Liam had soiled his pants. Liam pulled himself together. I could see the horror in his eyes as he ran from the house."

Trudy shouted, "No!" Her eyes began to well with tears.

"Yes, Mother. Your husband was a pedophile. The preacher of your precious community was a monster. And you, his protector. He told you, Mother, didn't he? He told you what I saw. He convinced you that Liam had soiled his pants, and you believed him. I know you did because that was the day you stopped loving me."

"Elle, please—"

"Do you know what it is like to live with blood on your hands? I do. At first, I didn't want to believe that my father, the man I adored, could ever abuse a child. So I blamed Liam. I told him that if his parents ever found out what he was, they would disown him. I told him never to come near me or my family again. I deserted him, and he hung himself."

"No, Elle, you're not to blame for Liam killing himself. You have to believe me. Your father never told me that you caught him with Liam. Elle, please give me a chance to explain. You're right when you say I was protecting someone, but that someone was you."

Trudy lowered her head. "I met your father at college. He was studying to be a preacher. There was an immediate attraction. Your father was charming, as you know. We dated for two years. He asked me to marry him before he left for the service where he served as a chaplain. Your grandmother, as you know, was a religious woman. Hearing of our engagement, she convinced my father that he should build a church in our community, with your father as its pastor. Your father returned from the service, and we were married in that church."

Trudy paused. "We were in love. Your father earned the respect of our community. I was teaching at the local school, helping out at the church when I could. Life was good. Then one day, there was a knock at the door. An old Army buddy, William was his name. Your father called him Bill. Bill was down on his luck and needed a place to stay for a week or two. My father had gotten Bill a few jobs around the city, but Bill never seemed to show up for work. I convinced your father that Bill was taking advantage of him and that he should ask Bill to leave. The following day, Bill was gone. But that wouldn't be the end of Bill. I remember the day I heard that Liam hung himself. I was sad, but my heart had been broken three weeks prior to his death. I was cleaning out your father's closet when I found a metal box, hidden and locked. I can't tell you why, but I broke the lock open. The box was filled with rent receipts for an apartment in the downtown area. On one of the receipts was an address. I never told your father what I found, but I was curious. So I went to that apartment. I knocked on the door, Bill answered."

Trudy began to sob.

"When I entered the apartment, I was taken aback by the smell. Bill was thinner than I remember, and there were needle marks up and down his arm. I spied two young teenagers playing video games. The boy, I guessed, thirteen, and the girl, eleven. At first, I thought they were Bill's children. He laughed and said, 'They're not my kids. They belong to the preacher.' Appalled, I asked, 'What did you say?' He said, 'By the look on your face, I'm guessing you didn't have a clue.'

"Bill was right. I didn't have a clue. I asked him if the children were your father's.

"He mocked me, 'You're kidding me, right? These are your husband's little playthings. The boy's his favorite.'

"I was about to faint when Bill caught me and placed me in a chair. Sitting across from me, he said, 'Listen, lady, I'm sorry you had to find out this way. But if I were you, I'd keep the preacher's secret to myself. He's a mean guy, promised me the world when we met in the service, got me hooked on drugs. That's how they take control of you. Came home to find out he was married. I begged him to leave you, but he had a nice setup that he wasn't ready to give up for this. I've been here all these years, right under your nose, your husband's little secret. When I got too old for him, he found these two. Their mother was a drug addict. Used to pimp the kids out, that's how she earned her drug money. When she was found dead in the street, the preacher took them in. He could have tossed me to the street, but he needs someone to look after them. I need the money, and whenever the preacher isn't around—well, we keep ourselves busy. You get the picture, right?'

"I slapped Bill—no, I started to beat on him. He pinned me down. This got the attention of the children. I turned to see them staring at me. I yelled for him to let me go. He shouted, 'Trudy, think of your girl! What if this little secret got out? What would happen to your daughter and your family? Once this hits the newspaper, the pillar of your community, the preacher, scum of the earth, would ruin you.' His words hit me hard. When I calmed down, he let me go. I ran from the apartment. I drove till midnight thinking what my next move would be. I was going to drive home, pack our bags, go to my father, tell him the truth, and leave the state. But I didn't. I drove home and slept. When I did find the strength to confront your father, he didn't deny a thing. I told him never to touch me or my child. I removed his name from any of our bank accounts. I took control of the house and church finances. That was what we agreed to for my staying. I was also thinking of my mother and father, and what this would have done to them. So yes, I did know about your father's double life, but I never knew about Liam."

"When did you confront him?"

"A little over a week after my finding out."

"You cut him off, and he turned to Liam. He was a sick bastard."

"I took to my bed for a week or more. I thought of killing him. I wanted him gone. I hated him. I hated myself."

"You left your bed to attend Liam's funeral. That bastard stood over Liam's coffin and prayed for his soul. Liam's parents were distraught. Liam's mother kept asking why. My father and I were the cause of her son's death. Liam's family was torn apart. Liam's mother took his siblings back to Nebraska. Liam's father died of a broken heart. A family destroyed by the demon. I know you say your silence was to protect me and your family, but what about the children in that apartment?"

"I know you hate me, and you have every right. I turned from you because I was ashamed. But I did right by the children. I got them out of the apartment and far from North Dakota. There was a woman in our church who had seven miscarriages. I prayed with her every time she lost another child. She and her husband never did have a child of their own. They moved to Virginia. We still communicated after they left the city. I told her of the children. I said they needed a home, a good foster home. They agreed to take the children in. I paid for therapy, schools, and support. All the couple had to do was love them, and they did. The children grew to be good people with families of their own. I still keep in touch with the family. Bill didn't last too long after your father deserted him. I read in the paper, he died two years later. Buried in a pauper's cemetery."

"And we who once loved the demon live to suffer in silence."

"Elle, you have to stop blaming yourself. You were twelve. You had nothing to do with Liam's death. You reacted like any child would have in that situation. You wanted to think your father was telling the truth. You wanted to lash out at someone, and it was easier to blame Liam. You had no idea how fragile Liam was at that time. Elle, you can hate me for being a coward and for deserting you. But I swear I didn't know about Liam. I couldn't bring myself to love you because I had made a deal with the devil. I'm saddened finding out you already knew what your father was capable of. I wanted nothing more than to protect you. My days are spent in fear—fear that another one of your father's victims will come knocking at the door. I'm so sorry, Elle, to confess, that the day you left this house, I was glad to see you go. Far from him and me."

"The children you found in that apartment never chose to expose you for protecting a pedophile?"

"I never stopped the two children from telling their story. It disgusts me to think that they think of me as their savior. They chose to protect me by not having my name dragged through the mud."

Trudy began to cry. "I don't expect you to understand or to forgive me, Elle. I allowed the shame to control my actions, and I have to live with my sins."

Elle was reminded of Lauren. Shame caused Lauren not to tell Kathy the truth about her encounter with Derek. Shame caused Trudy to protect and desert her child. Shame caused Elle to refuse Jacques's proposal. Shame caused Elle not to want children of her own. Elle thought of the gypsy woman when she said she didn't know if facing the demon would ease Elle's pain. It didn't.

"Elle, I want you to know that I never stopped loving you. I'm so proud of you. I know you're going to go back home, and I won't hear from you. I understand. Why should I ask you to respect me when I don't respect myself? Elle, I thought having your palm read was insane, but if the woman who told you to face your demon was standing here, I'd thank her for getting us to talk about the past. The talk wasn't the pleasant way we used to talk about princesses and princes on white horses, but maybe, if you find it in your heart to accept my faults, we can talk about good things and happy things."

Trudy lowered her head, a gesture which is performed when one can't face having hurt another. Elle saw the pain, a pain that she had seen many times as a reporter. In Iraq, Elle watched mothers who walked with their heads down and quickly moved their children along, so not to endure the lashes given to them by men in power. When finding a child who lived in an abusive home, in many cases, there was an abused wife. Control by fear was the thought process. Elle wasn't in a position to judge these women for remaining in an abusive marriage. What right did she have to condemn a woman who feared for her life or the lives of her children? Often, she wanted to give these women hope—that in time, things would change. But change came slowly and often reversed itself back to the old ways.

Elle stared at Trudy. She couldn't believe that her own mother had suffered such a fate. Elle's anger toward her mother began to subside. She went to sit next to her mother. Wrapping her mother in her arms, she rested her head on Trudy's shoulder.

"Mom, I came home to chastise you for protecting a pedophile. I never expected to hear that you were facing your own demons." Elle paused. "Mom, you saved two children who think of you as their savior. You confronted Father, which might have ended his madness. Your fear is that someone will knock on the door and condemn you, but not one person has come forward. Liam taking his own life and your discovery might have put a stop to the bastard. We'll never know. We will always blame ourselves for allowing Father to live out his life without serving time for his crimes. We are left to endure the sins of the father. Mom, we need each other to ease the pain of the past. I don't want us to be estranged one minute longer. What about you?"

Elle and her mom microwaved that night's dinner, which they ate in the master bedroom with Trudy asking a hundred questions about Elle's travels, Jacques, and how she landed the DC job.

The following day, mother and daughter visited Liam's grave.

CHAPTER 8

Kathy sat at the dais half listening to the director of the hospital, Dr. Weisman. The good doctor spoke about her accomplishments on the groundbreaking of the family care center. He went on to say that Dr. Wilson and his wife made it a life choice to give back to humanity.

"If you're asking yourself why Dr. Wilson is not sharing the dais with his lovely wife, it's because he is on a tour promoting his book, which is receiving an overwhelming acceptance within the medical field." Dr. Weisman spoke of Derek's book in detail. He went on to say that the Wilson family is donating 75 percent of the profits from the book for medical research and the construction of the family care facility. The audience applauded.

Kathy was asked to stand during the applause, but she chose to remain seated. Dr. Weisman then proceeded to walk toward the replica of the new facility on display. Kathy continued to smile, but thoughts of her son Scottie overshadowed the kind words spoken by Dr. Weisman. Two days prior, Scottie had contracted the flu. Kathy immediately isolated him from her other children. Tonight, she left a crying Scottie in Fanny's arms, to attend the dinner. Earlier in the day, Scottie's temperature had spiked to 102. She called the pediatrician who informed her that as the day went on, it wasn't uncommon for a child's fever to spike. Scottie had eaten half of the homemade chicken soup Kathy prepared. She placed iced wash clothes on his forehead, ankles, and wrists. Before leaving the house, Scottie's fever had dropped to 100. Fanny convinced her to attend the dinner. Kathy had called twice since leaving her home. Last time she called, Fanny informed her Scottie was fast asleep, and his forehead was cool.

Kathy's thoughts were interrupted when Dr. Weisman asked if she would like to say a few words. She stood and approached the podium.

"Good evening. Thank you for coming out to support this project. My husband and I are extremely grateful for your generous donations. Having five children of our own, Dr. Wilson and I felt a need for this facility. Today, I thought of those parents faced with the thought of losing their child. I'm sure those of you who have children would welcome a facility such as this one. I tell you this because tonight, I had to leave my son Scottie who is home with the flu in the arms of another, so I could be with you tonight." Kathy pointed at the replica of the facility. "This facility will offer a home to the parents and siblings of a child fighting for their life. Dr. Wilson and I ask that you be as generous as you have been in the past. I don't think you will be disappointed with the collection of paintings and sculptures that are being presented tonight for sale. Thank you and good night." Everyone applauded as Kathy left the stage with her purse in hand.

Arriving home, she went straight to her son. As Fanny had assured her, Scottie was sound asleep. She lay with him for fifteen minutes before checking on her other children.

Entering her bedroom, she stripped down to her underpants and bra. She collapsed on the bed and began to cry. Kathy found crying had become a daily emotion. She cried tears of happiness the day she married Derek and when her children were born. She cried at weddings, sad movies, funerals, and situations that required a good cry. She was emotionally drained by the amount of crying she had experienced this past year. The crying fits started after Lauren confessed her infidelities. Kathy's change in demeanor began around the same time. Some of the tears she shed daily were due to the fact that she agreed to oversee the family facility project, which took time away from her children. Dr. Weisman approached her several times over the past three years, asking if she was up for the challenge. She recused herself saying her children were her first priority.

The Palm Reader

After her split with Lauren, she asked Derek if he thought she should say yes to Dr. Weisman.

Derek said, "It's your choice, babe. But if anyone can get the job done, my money is on you."

Today, her face appeared on magazines, newspapers, and Facebook. Lauren, unless she now was living under a rock, couldn't avoid reading of her success—a success she wanted to rub in Lauren's face.

Kathy wondered how her absence was affecting her children. They had come to accept that Mommy had to attend meetings, meet with the mayor, and the county's planning board, smile, and flirt with inspectors to achieve the required permits to gain the approvals to break ground. Her own mother was able to handle a career and still made school sports, music concerts, and the National Science Awards. On several occasions, her mother had to apologize for missing an event because she was on an important case. And those were the times that Kathy had missed her the most.

Kathy turned on her side and pulled a tissue from the tissue box on her nightstand. She wasn't critical of mothers who had to work. She felt blessed that she didn't have to work in order for her family to survive.

Prior to her knowing of Derek and Lauren's escapades in college, her life was perfect. At least, that was what she thought until that awful woman read her palm causing her to believe her life was a farce. The one person she could depend on to tell her the truth had lied to her for twenty years. The image of Lauren and Derek intimate was causing her to have questions about the man with whom she was living. She had tried to convince herself that Lauren was jealous of her, especially her looks.

When Kathy was younger, she hated being the prettiest girl in the room. When she shared here fear with Derek, he laughed and said, "Sweetie, you're beautiful. Own it. I discovered early in life that my looks and charm were my greatest assets. You can't tell me you didn't blink those beautiful eyes or pout those sexy lips, on occasion, to get your way."

Kathy didn't think of herself or Derek as shallow. She couldn't deny that sometimes she did blink her eyes and pouted her lips to her advantage. What she couldn't wrap her head around was that her husband plotted an encounter with two of her best friends. The man she knew spent hours watching over a patient until the patient under his watch was out of the woods; that man was the man she loved, not the man Lauren said had a dark side.

Kathy left the comfort of her bed and entered the bathroom. Looking at herself in the mirror, she could see the start of dark circles under her eyes. She needed to sleep. Kathy hadn't had a good night sleep since returning home from Cape May. When she woke in the middle of the night, she found herself staring at her husband. Everything in her life had changed, especially her sex life.

Whenever she made love to Derek, she stopped him if he became too rough or if he chose a position, which she didn't find comfortable. Things that were standard in their lovemaking, she now questioned. She could see the frustration in Derek's face, and Lauren's cruel words would resonate, "Are you woman enough to satisfy your man?" On the nights she allowed Derek to have his way, she had to force herself to focus on the pleasure and not the actions. Visions of Derek and Lauren in each other's arms making love sickened her. Climaxing in the past was easy to achieve, she now knew the number of times she didn't reach her peak.

Kathy hated herself for demanding the truth from Lauren. If she had let it go, she might have avoided the sexual issues she was now experiencing. *Fuck you, Lauren, fuck you.*

Her success with the family care facility was the only thing that boosted her depressed mood. She hoped Lauren was jealous of her success. The greatest revenge was to outshine the shiners. She was being childish. If anyone would praise her success, it would be Lauren. Lauren would be thrilled for her. She'd donate the kitchen sink to make sure Kathy was successful. Often, she thought of confronting Derek about the encounter with Lauren and Casey. He might be able to convince her that what transpired was innocent. College antics, that's all. Why couldn't she accept the encounter as easily as Lauren, Elle, and Derek obviously did? People had made mistakes every day of their lives. Actions they probably weren't proud of. Men and women who cheated on their partners had been forgiven, but did their partners truly forget?

Kathy knew why she hadn't confronted Derek; she'd heeded Lauren's warning. If Derek should deny the encounter never happened, it would end her marriage.

Kathy's cell phone buzzed.

"Hey, babe, how was the dinner? Did you raise a shitload of cash?"

"I don't know. I left early."

"Don't tell me you caught the flu from Scottie?"

"No. I'm fine. I wanted to be home with our son."

"Is he lying next to Mommy?"

"No, he's in his own bed, sound asleep."

"Good. I'll be home around twelve on Friday. When I get home, I'm going to take over, and you and Fanny are going to put your feet up and rest. Kathy, I was thinking, if the kids are well, I would love you to join me on the California tour. A week away would do you good. You can lounge by the pool while I work. I really miss you, sweetie. I would offer Hawaii, but I know you'll never agree to leave the kids for two weeks."

Kathy sighed. "You're right, fourteen days is too long. I don't know, Derek. I don't think it's fair to leave the kids with Fanny for an entire week."

"You can ask Jenny to help. You said she can use the money."

"Jenny has to agree to stay at the house the entire week. Fanny can use a vacation. She's been talking about heading out west to visit her son."

"I'll call Fanny and Jenny. I'll use my charm and my wallet to convince them it's a great idea."

Good looks and charm—Derek's greatest weapon, thought Kathy. "If they agree, I'll consider going. A short vacation sounds good, but only if the kids are well."

"Babe, you're the best. I love you, see you on Friday. Get some rest."

When Kathy ended the call with Derek, she considered his offer. Six days alone with her husband might be what they needed to survive Lauren's confession and the palm reader's accusations.

*****

Lying on the bed with his cell phone in his hand, Derek stared at the ceiling. Earlier this evening, he called to check on Scottie and was sure Kathy hadn't gone to the dinner. He was surprised to hear from Fanny that Kathy had gone. He didn't like the fact that he was states away from his family when they needed him the most.

He couldn't wait for these god-awful book tours to end. Sales were going through the roof, and the money was rolling in. Kathy was right; the internet was a great source in promoting the book. Thousands of orders were being placed by medical colleges across the country and internationally. Hospitals ordered the book for training residents. The average Joe purchasing the book exceeded his expectations. Derek should have been elated with the attention but no such luck. The only thing on his mind was Kathy. He was still scratching his head when Kathy approached him to say she had called Dr. Weisman, saying she was ready to pursue the family care facility.

If Derek were being honest with himself, Kathy had not been herself since ending her friendship with Lauren. Derek sympathized with Kathy's mood. She treasured her BFFs, and now two of them were gone from her life. He was hoping that once the girls had kissed and made up, Kathy would be back to her normal self. The girls were still estranged, and he and Jake didn't think this issue was going to resolve itself any time soon.

Jake tried to get Lauren to explain what went down. Lauren said, after too many glasses of wine she might have come on strong condemning Kathy's life choices. Jake tried to find out what Lauren could have possibly said that would make Kathy end their friendship.

Lauren said, "*Jake, I take total responsibility for hurting Kathy. And you* and Derek need to back off. If Kathy is going to forgive me, it has to be her decision."

The Palm Reader

Lauren was right; it had to be Kathy's decision. Derek thought of casually mentioning to Kathy that her mood was a little off, after cutting Lauren out of her life. If he were being truthful, he wanted to confront Kathy because this break from Lauren was causing havoc in the bedroom. Why Kathy would allow her own pleasures to be affected by Lauren's vicious words was ridiculous. Derek couldn't make sense of why Kathy was turned off by sexual moves that were acceptable prior to her Cape May vacation.

Derek glanced around the suite. The Ritz-Carlton decorators didn't miss a beat in creating a romantic getaway. Derek stood and walked toward the private balcony. Looking out, he stared at the outdoor Jacuzzi, which was surrounded by thick shrubs for private bathing. There was also a Jacuzzi in the room. At night, you could soak in the large tub and look out over the ocean. There were lampposts close enough to the shore, so the reflection from the lights at night made the ocean sparkle. Each day, when he returned to the suite, there was cheese, crackers, strawberries, whipped cream, and champagne. He dreamed of sipping the champagne and licking the whipped cream off Kathy's breasts. These days, he wasn't so sure that she would welcome the gesture.

His cell phone buzzed.

"Hello."

"Derek, its Nina. You called?"

"Oh, Nina. What's up?"

"I don't know. You tell me."

"Oh yes, I did call you. Nina, I can't work with Jeff."

"Derek, Jeff is the third person you've asked us to replace. What's the problem?"

"He books too many signings, lunches with wealthy women, and dinners where I am asked to speak for well over an hour. I've tried talking with him, but I guess he's trying to impress your company."

"It's not Jeff's fault or the company's, Derek. The book is a success. You know that. I have a thousand requests sitting on my desk asking for you to speak at country clubs, hospitals, and university seminars. The list goes on and on."

"I know, but I can't go on like this."

"What do you expect me to do?"

"I don't know. You and I get along really well. Maybe you should step in."

"Derek, we agreed that I wouldn't join you on the tour."

"Nina, I promise you, business only, nothing more."

"I will talk with Joe. I'll call you tomorrow."

Nina hung up without saying goodbye.

Derek smiled. He knew the company would agree to whatever he wanted. He was their number one client at the moment. He ran his hand through his hair, maybe he was wrong not having Nina accompany him on the book tour. He glanced at the Jacuzzi and thought of Nina naked.

CHAPTER 9

The weather is picture-perfect, blue skies, seventy-five degrees, and the tourists are gone, thought Lauren. Usually, the weekend after Labor Day, you could feel a chill in the air announcing winter was on its way. At her favorite breakfast shop housed in her favorite corner of the room, she was on the internet staring at a picture of Kathy. The article praised Mrs. Wilson, wife of Dr. Derek Charles Wilson, and her accomplishments regarding the building of a family care facility adjacent to the hospital. Lauren smiled, saying, "You go, girl!" There was a photo of Kathy, alone, and one of her and Derek. Lauren stared at the photo, focusing on Kathy's eyes. Her eyes lacked emotion. In the picture of Kathy and Derek, he was smiling; she wasn't. Lauren was concerned, but there was nothing she could do about it. Lauren always brought up Kathy when speaking with Elle.

Elle's response was, "Kathy's been busy. She's got a lot on her plate—kids, Derek being away so often, and the hospital project. I've only spoken to her a handful of times. Most of my calls go to voice mail."

Leaning back in her chair, Lauren placed her hands behind her head. Over a year since she last spoke with Kathy, Lauren was happy Kathy had taken on the hospital project; the publicity kept her in Kathy's life. Lauren clicked on the donation icon. Anonymously, she made a generous donation.

Life was good, except for Kathy's departure from her life. Her fifth book in the series Millennium Agent was a success. She spent a fabulous three weeks in August at the Cape with her children before Josh left for his first year at Penn University. Kelly, with Di Marco's help, was studying at the Art Academy in Paris. Michelle and Jake married; Lauren did not attend. She scheduled a book tour that week to avoid an uncomfortable situation. Derek, Kathy, and Elle did attend. Baby Jack was born on February 3. Jack was a cutie. Lauren was smitten with the child. Josh and Kelly spoiled their baby brother, and Lauren was sure Jack was missing the attention with his siblings being away. Jake was happy, and seeing him happy eased the pain Lauren felt for turning his world upside down.

Alice and Lauren spoke often. Alice visited Cape Cod in June and spent a few days with Lauren. Alice had won Lauren over. When Lauren thought of Alice, she thought of her as a dear friend. Lauren had cable and often watched the DC evening news hosted by Elle Kessler. Elle's popularity was blooming. Once the network was sure Elle was their girl, they dressed her in designer clothes and shoes.

Yes, life was good but lonely. Being an empty nester was horrible. Losing two of her BFFs didn't help. Lauren closed the article about Kathy and opened the file named, MA book 6. Her agent was waiting for the final draft of the book. The deadline was October 24. Her agent was concerned she wasn't going to make the deadline, and Lauren thought he might be right. She started to type, and the words began to flow nicely. An hour later, she noticed the lunch crowd had emerged. Lauren had occupied the table longer than she should have. She began to gather her things when someone said, "I really enjoyed number 5."

Lauren looked up. An attractive, well-dressed woman, who appeared to be in her late thirties, was pointing at the book she had placed beside her computer.

"Lauren Croft, correct?"

"Yes. I'm glad you enjoyed the book."

"How long before the sixth book is published?"

"Did my agent send you?"

The pretty lady smiled.

"A draft of six is due to the publisher in October, then the fun begins. Did you want the table? I was just leaving."

"I just stopped in for coffee. I have an appointment in town. It's not till twelve thirty. Do you mind if I sit?"

"Please sit."

The woman sat. "In six, will she marry the tall, dark, and handsome guy?"

Lauren smiled. "She's a millennial. She doesn't need to be married."

"True. How could she take down the bad guys with a baby strapped on her back and a husband at home?"

Lauren chuckled. "Women have been juggling life, family, and career since year 1."

The woman agreed. Lauren couldn't help but notice the woman had a pretty smile, lovely eyes, and a pretty decent figure. "You're meeting someone in town. Business or pleasure?"

"Business. I'm meeting with the owner of the Thomas Gallery."

"Carl Thomas. I went to school with Carl. Nice guy. What is your line of work?"

"Sculptor."

"Wow. So you mold clay, or do you twist metal into something a novice stands in front of wondering, What is it? I'm sorry, the only sculpture I've come in contact with is a Mallard wooden duck my father purchased and sits above the fireplace in my cottage. My daughter is an artist, as we speak. She is studying at the Art Academy in Paris. She didn't acquire her talent from her father or me. I couldn't describe one brush stroke from another. She, on the other hand, can dissect a painting for hours."

"You are a well-known author, on the *New York Times* bestsellers list seven years in a row, and you don't consider yourself an artist?"

"My mother placed a book in my hands, out of the womb. By the age of three, I could read *My Dog Red* from cover to cover. I guess you can say writing is an art. I'd say writing is a desire to tell a story, and the praise you receive when someone enjoys what you have written is an amazing feeling. I'm sure you can relate. Sorry, I didn't get your name?"

"Shelby Nash."

"Shelby Nash. The name sounds familiar. My daughter subscribes to *Aperture* magazine. In the February issue, there was a flattering article about you and your work. One of your pieces was purchased by Justice Ruth Bader Ginsburg, a gift for Justice Antonin Scalia. She purchased a smaller one for herself."

"One of my proudest moments. She's a lovely woman. Never met Justice Scalia, but Justice Ginsburg spoke highly of her friend."

Lauren smiled. "You live in Manhattan, correct?"

"Yes."

"How long will you be visiting Cape Cod?"

"Four days. I'm staying at the Inn."

"Traveling with a friend or alone?"

"Alone." Shelby checked her cell phone for the time. "I should be going. It was nice to meet you, Lauren." Shelby extended her hand. "Can't wait for number 6."

"Nice meeting you, Ms. Nash."

"Please call me Shelby."

"Shelby, do you have dinner plans?"

"No."

"Would you like to have dinner with me at my place? My daughter's paintings are scattered throughout the cottage. I'd respect your professional opinion. But if you think my daughter is wasting her time, please keep it to yourself."

Shelby chuckled. "I'd love to have dinner with you, and I promise to keep my opinions to myself."

"Does six o'clock work for you?"

"Six works."

Lauren jotted down her address. "Do you have a car? If not, I can send a car."

"I drove here."

"Then I'll see you at six. Before you go, fish or steak?"

"Either is fine with me."

"Do you like salmon?"

"I do."

"Then salmon it is."

*****

The salmon was prepped for grilling. Lauren fried kale in olive oil, tossed a salad, and placed the triple cheese baked potatoes in the oven. She lit a fire and set the table. She checked her hair and makeup in the microwave glass. The outfit she had chosen was a loose white blouse over black slacks, a silver buckle black leather belt surrounded the blouse. She wore the black sexy sandals Kathy had given her for her fortieth birthday.

Tapping her index finger on the kitchen counter, she wondered if Shelby had changed her mind. It was six fifteen, and Shelby was a no-show. She removed the potatoes from the oven. There was a knock on the door.

"Hi."

Handing Lauren a wine bag, Shelby stepped inside. "I'm sorry for being late. The roads are dark. The speed limit was forty. I was doing twenty."

"Better safe than sorry."

"The guy at the liquor store said these are your favorites."

"And Chuck would know since I visit the liquor store quite often. I don't need to sign up for AA, but when writer's block sets in, a few glasses of wine keeps the juices flowing."

"I truly understand. Nice place."

"I inherited the house from my parents. I grew up on the Cape. Please sit. I'll be right back." Lauren removed the appetizer she had prepared earlier from the oven, scallops wrapped in bacon with a brown sugar glaze.

Lauren offered Shelby a plate and poured two glasses of wine.

"Is that one of your daughter's paintings over the fireplace?"

"Yes. It's my favorite. Cape Cod at its best."

"You're not wasting your money. She has talent."

"Thank you. Kelly is a strange one. When I watch her paint, I don't see a child or teenager and wonder if she is missing out on the fun, but when she puts down the brush, she says, 'I'm going to Penny's house, or let's go shopping. I can use a new pair of jeans.' From the age of three, she took a liking to painting. I had a friend who was an artist. Casey Brice. Many of her earlier paintings were sold at a gallery at the corner of Fifth and Lexington. Once Casey knew Kelly was interested in painting, she taught her everything she knew."

"I don't know of her. Does your friend still paint?"

"No. She passed away, cancer. Coming on four years, seems like yesterday."

"I'm sorry."

"How did your meeting go with Carl?"

"Great. Several of my pieces will be on display from the end of March through October."

"That's wonderful news." Lauren stood. "Relax, enjoy the wine. Dinner will be ready in ten minutes."

Shelby arrived in the kitchen a few minutes later, asking if she could help. Lauren grilled, while Shelby placed the prepared food on the table.

"I grill salmon five minutes on each side. If it's too pink for you, I can—"

Shelby cut into the salmon. "It's perfect."

During dinner, their careers were the topic of conversation. Shelby had moved to Manhattan after earning her master's degree. She donated her time a few days a week at the elementary school in walking distance from her apartment. Her pieces traveled the world, but she had only been to London and Paris.

"I was surfing the net for famous authors. Your name popped up. You're married?"

"I was married. I never got around to updating my profile."

"Do you still keep in touch with your ex?"

"Jake, of course, he's my best bud. We met in college. Married after we got our master's and landed jobs. I worked for two-years. Jake wanted children. Josh is our first, and then along came the artist, Kelly."

"Relationships are complicated. If you don't mind me asking, what changed?"

"I changed. I wanted to be a writer. I might be the only author that loves promoting the book. I'm a people person. The time I spent away from the family, well…Jake asked me to cut back. I didn't. I could see Jake wasn't happy, so we separated."

"I see."

"Jake remarried. Married the woman of his dreams. They have a son, Jack, cute as a button. Jake's happy, and I'm happy for him. What about you? Is there a special someone in your life?"

The Palm Reader

"There was. We broke up, eight months ago."

"And you can't find a tall, dark, and handsome guy in New York City?"

"I prefer an intelligent, good-looking, and curvy woman."

Lauren's eyes widened, and her smile began to fade.

"You're shocked. If you have a problem with me, I understand."

"No, not at all. My best friend Casey, the one who taught Kelly to paint, was gay."

"Some people aren't comfortable with my life choice."

"They're idiots."

Shelby smiled.

"I've made a lovely dessert. Would you like coffee?"

"I prefer tea if it's not too much trouble."

"Tea it is. Would you like to have dessert in the living room? The fire adds a comfy touch."

"Yes."

The ladies continued their conversation in front of the fire. After dessert, they opened another bottle of wine. Shelby shared how supportive her parents were when she came out. Coming out cost her the loss of a few family members and friends. She was most comfortable with people that accepted her for who she is. She chose to live in Manhattan because it was a city of diversity. Shelby checked her phone for the time.

"I can't believe it is twelve fifteen. I should go."

"You should stay the night. The roads are dark. We finished two bottles of wine, and by the looks of you, I'm sure we can find a pair of Kelly's pj's that will fit."

"I shouldn't."

"Why not?"

"I have a meeting at eight tomorrow."

"You have an alarm on your phone. Set it. Please stay. If anything were to happen to you driving back, I wouldn't be able to forgive myself."

"All right."

Lauren placed fresh linens on Kelly's bed, while Shelby changed into a pair of Kelly's pj's.

"I'll take these with me and purchase another pair for your daughter."

"That won't be necessary. Good night."

*****

Lauren woke early the following morning. She prepared coffee, retrieved the newspaper, and was sitting at the island when Shelby entered the kitchen with bed linens and pj's in hand.

"I'll take that." Lauren asked, "Eggs, bacon, toast, and juice for breakfast? I defrosted several muffins."

"Coffee and a muffin is fine. I'm not fond of eggs. Thanks for letting me stay."

"My pleasure." Lauren placed a plate of muffins in front of Shelby and poured coffee into her cup.

They ate in silence. Shelby checked the time and stood. "I had a great time, Lauren. For your kindness, I'd like to treat you to dinner."

"It was my pleasure, but—"

"Carl recommended Rico's."

Lauren didn't have the heart to say no. "I'll make a reservation at Rico's. You won't be disappointed."

*****

Shelby enjoyed Rico's. She complimented the chef, saying the seafood fra diavolo was amazing. At nine on Saturdays, Rico's had live entertainment. The ladies sang along and danced to the music. At twelve that night, Lauren said good night to Shelby and asked if she was free for brunch and a Sunday drive. After a fun day, Lauren dropped Shelby at the Inn at nine and offered to cook her dinner the following night. Shelby accepted Lauren's invitation to dinner.

Steak was on the menu. Lauren was at a loss. She'd already cooked potatoes, and so she searched the net and came up with a mushroom risotto, asparagus, a fresh tomato salad, and her famous lemon cello cake for dessert.

Promptly at six, there was a knock on the door.

"Come in. You know the way. How was your day?"

"Good. The contracts are signed and dated. I picked up a book at the bookstore and read for a few hours."

"Which one? I've read most of the books at the bookstore."

"Ruth Bader Ginsburg's *My Own Words*. When you brought up the article in *Aperture*, it reminded me that I've been meaning to read her book."

"It's a great book."

At ten that night, Shelby said her goodbyes to Lauren. They exchanged cell numbers, and Shelby jotted down her address in the city.

The following weekend, there was a knock at the door. When Lauren answered the door, she was surprised to see Shelby.

"Hi, I should have called. I had nothing going on this weekend, so I jumped in my car this morning and wound up here."

Lauren didn't know how to respond to Shelby's hasty decision to drive to the Cape. "Come in. How was traffic?"

"A little hitch at the GW Bridge."

"I wasn't expecting anyone. I was getting ready to scramble two eggs. If I remember correctly, you don't like eggs. I have frozen waffles in the freezer. I usually shop on Thursday, but the time got away from me yesterday. I decided to shop tomorrow." Opening the refrigerator, Lauren said, "Do you like breakfast sausages, Jimmy Dean's? They're turkey, not pork."

"Waffles and turkey sausages are fine. I brought wine." Shelby held up two bottles of wine.

"Great."

Shelby went to the car to retrieve her overnight bag. This time, she was prepared to spend the night. Saturday, they window-shopped before heading to the supermarket. Shelby convinced Lauren to order Chinese food before heading back. They ate in front of the fire, sipped hot tea, ate the cupcakes they bought at the bakery, and finished off with a red wine Lauren was dying to try.

"What are you doing for Thanksgiving?" asked Shelby.

"Thanksgiving?"

"I'll be in Japan on Thanksgiving. Why don't you come along?"

"Japan. You want to me to go to Japan with you? Thanks for the offer, but Thanksgiving is a family holiday."

"But your children are away."

"Josh and Kelly will be home for Thanksgiving."

"Can't they spend Thanksgiving with their father?"

"Jake, Michelle, the children, and I are spending Thanksgiving together for the next five years until the kids are finished with school."

Shelby looked wounded.

"Shelby, you're disappointed, I'm sorry."

Shelby moved closer to Lauren. "I am disappointed. I wanted to take you to Japan, all expenses paid. I lied earlier. It wasn't a spur-of-the-moment move my coming to see you. Lauren, I couldn't stop thinking of you."

"Shelby, I think—I'm not gay. What I am is a divorced woman with two grown children."

"There are a number of gay women who are divorced with children, Lauren."

"Yes, but I'm not one of them. I'm sorry if I led you to believe differently."

"The time we have spent together, you often talked about your friend Casey, lovingly."

"Of course, I loved her dearly as a friend."

"But when you speak of Casey, your demeanor changes. It's obvious that you shared more than just a friendship with the woman."

Lauren wondered how her demeanor had changed to reveal that Casey and she were more than friends. "Casey and I were as close as sisters. I never had siblings. My best friends are the sisters I never had."

"I apologize for misjudging you, Lauren. I thought the connection I was feeling was mutual. My instincts haven't failed me in the past. I hope we can still be friends?"

"Of course. Shelby, if I did anything that led you to believe I wanted more than just your friendship, I'm sorry. I'm curious, Shelby, what did I do to make you think I wanted more than to be your friend?"

"You invited me to your home thirty minutes after we met. You offered me to stay at your home. The brunch, the drive around the countryside, and whenever we sat on this sofa, the first time, and tonight, you moved closer to me each time. If you had said yes to Japan, I would have kissed you."

Lauren needed a few moments to digest her actions. "It isn't uncommon for a local to offer dinner to a visitor in this neck of the woods. I enjoyed the trip through the countryside and the brunch and the dinners and sitting on this sofa talking, but nothing more."

"When you first looked up at me in the coffee shop, maybe you didn't realize, you stared at my face and then worked your way down my body. I assumed you liked what you saw."

"You're a beautiful woman, Shelby."

Shelby smiled. "But you don't want to be intimate with a beautiful woman."

Lauren became confused by the warm feelings she was experiencing by Shelby's sexy smile. "I'm sorry if I made you feel uncomfortable."

"It is fine, Lauren. Good night."

Lauren couldn't sleep knowing Shelby was in the next room. She checked the clock; it was three in the morning. She couldn't wait for morning to come and Shelby to leave her home. She managed to drift off at 4:00 a.m. She dreamed of her and Casey lying naked in their dorm room. Seconds later, it wasn't Casey but Shelby in her arms. She forced herself awake at nine. She threw on a robe and headed downstairs. Shelby was in the kitchen sipping coffee.

"I'm so sorry. I know you wanted to get an early start. Did you eat breakfast?"

"I had an English muffin. I didn't want to leave without saying goodbye."

"I'm glad you waited."

"You're not going to apologize, are you? I'm fine, Lauren. You aren't the first woman who wasn't interested in me. Just the first I got wrong."

"I didn't sleep last night. Talking about Casey brought up a lot of memories." Lauren rinsed a cup and poured herself a cup of coffee.

She sat at the island. "I don't know why I feel a need to explain, but you were right. Casey and I were lovers in college."

Shelby began to speak. Lauren stopped her. "It began and ended in college, and then we reconnected after my divorce. Last night, when you smiled, I got a warm feeling, but I'm not ready to act on those feelings. I don't know if I ever want to go down that road again."

"Thank you for explaining, Lauren. I meant what I said. I hope we can still be friends. If you ever need a break from the cottage, you have my cell number. I'll make a reservation at my favorite Italian restaurant, not as good as Rico's but decent."

Shelby waved as her car pulled away from Lauren's cottage.

*****

Lauren stared at the calendar on her desk, November 1. Next to the calendar was Shelby's address. She wasn't sure if she wanted to add Shelby's contract information on her phone. She placed her phone down and began to type. The sixth book was complete and in the publisher's hands. Reviewing her notes, she couldn't seem to find the words to start the second chapter in book number 7. Frustrated, she rose and went to the living room opened a bottle of white wine and poured herself a full glass.

Wine in hand, she returned to her computer. She tried to concentrate on the notes she had jotted down for chapter 2 but kept glancing at the sheet of paper with Shelby's address. She had spoken to Shelby three times since she last saw her. Shelby was busy packing for her trip to Japan and asked if Lauren could spare a few days to come for a visit. Lauren declined saying she had plans. But Lauren missed Shelby and couldn't stop thinking of her. She chuckled to herself thinking of Shelby's smile and how it had set off a warm feeling within her.

Lately, Lauren was doing a lot of soul-searching since meeting Shelby. She often compared her feelings for Casey, Jake, and Shelby. In her confession to her friends, she confessed that she wasn't in love with Casey, not the way she loved Jake. Sex with Casey was spontaneous, fun, relaxed, and easy. At the beginning of their relationship, sex with Jake was spontaneous and lustful. After two kids and at the age of thirty-five, before sex, she began the regiment of brushing her hair, shaving her legs, making sure her private area was waxed, darker eyeliner, richer lip color, exotic perfume, and sexy undergarments were a must. With Casey, none of that mattered.

One question that plagued her constantly was, why did she reject Casey's love? Lauren had asked herself that question often. When she was with Casey, feelings of love, such as the love she felt for Jake, didn't evolve. Lauren reflected on Casey's explanation on how their relationship could work. She was going to spend more time in Cape Cod. No one would suspect what they meant to each other because of their bond as friends. It was obvious that Casey was in love with Lauren, but the feelings weren't mutual. Lauren explained to Casey that she had Jake and her children to protect. If people began to talk about what was going on at the cottage, it would spread like wildfires, and her family would be affected. It was one of the reasons Lauren hadn't acted on her feelings of spending the night or nights with a woman on the Cape. Then Shelby entered the picture, and she wanted to cross the line with Shelby.

That night, she thought what if she presented her concerns to Shelby. Would Shelby be open to a closet relationship, away from the public eye?

There was only one way to find out. She'd call Shelby in the morning to say that she would be in Manhattan this weekend.

*****

Lauren accepted the valet parking offered by Shelby's apartment building. The doorman took the car keys and verified Shelby was expecting her.

"Twenty-fifth floor, apartment 2512."

Lauren held her head high as she entered the elevator. She had a plan. They would go to dinner. She'd tell Shelby there were rules regarding Jake and her children. If Shelby couldn't live by the rules, then she would walk away. No harm done.

Antoinette Zam

For some unknown reason to Lauren, a vision of the gypsy woman flashed before her eyes.

Lauren rang the doorbell. Shelby opened the door. Lauren saw Shelby rushed in and took Shelby in her arms. Neither one pulled away. With each kiss, their desire grew. Shelby guided Lauren toward her bedroom. It was a night neither would soon forget.

CHAPTER 10

It was the end of January and the first of many cold days that year. Elle walked out of her office building and entered the company car provided by the network. On the drive home, she settled back and relaxed, thinking, *Washington has lost that special glow that begins with Thanksgiving and ends with the New Year.*

She smiled. Christmas was amazing. She never could have imagined herself spending Christmas with her mom in Washington. Trudy arrived the week before Christmas and left the Saturday after New Year's. Trudy was only gone a week, but Elle missed her mom. She missed waking up to a home-cooked breakfast and arriving home to the smell of a home-cooked meal, prepared with her mother's loving touch.

"Max, can you stop at the deli? I'd like to pick up a few groceries before heading home."

When Elle stepped from the car, a snowflake rested upon her cheek. The weather forecast called for six to seven inches of snowfall that night.

Elle entered the deli greeting Amin with a warm smile.

"Ms. Elle, so good to see you. What can I get for you?"

"Am I too late for soup?"

"I have soup in the back. What's your preference?"

"If I'm too late for your wife's famous Hindu soup, I'll settle for chicken?"

"Hindu soup, coming right up."

Elle grabbed a basket and began filling it with goodies for a long winter's weekend. She had no special plans for the weekend—the

New York Times on Sunday. If the snow wasn't an issue, a long run on Saturday morning. Sunday, lunch at Ester's, a local gal who in Elle's opinion made the best crab cakes in town. Later that day, she would head back home and read the latest Daniel Steel novel she had been putting off for a month.

Amin appeared with two large containers of soup. Elle selected several blocks of gourmet cheese, two loaves of French bread, and dessert. She paid the bill and wished Amin a good night.

Max handed off Elle's groceries to the doorman while Elle retrieved her Louis Vuitton briefcase. The briefcase was a Christmas gift from her mother. With the snow mounting, she walked with her head down. Lifting her head, she gasped seeing him standing there.

"Jacques!"

Jacques kept his distance. She walked toward him. There was no embrace when she reached him, just a smile.

"Hello, Elle."

"What are you doing here?"

"Business."

"Why didn't you call to say you were coming to Washington?"

"I wanted to surprise you."

The doorman impatiently held the door. "It's freezing out here. How long have you been waiting? Never mind. Come in before you catch pneumonia."

When they entered Elle's apartment, Jacques whistled. "Wow, this place is amazing."

"It is amazing. And it's all mine until the ratings drop."

"My friends who live nearby say you're doing a fine job."

"I try."

Elle offered Jacques a drink; of course, he chose wine.

"It's thirty degrees outside. You must be freezing?" Elle flicked a switch to light the fireplace.

"*Oui.* You Americans would say, I'm chilled to the bone."

Elle smiled. Jacques walked toward the fire to warm his hands.

Elle couldn't take her eyes off him. "Let me get you that glass of wine. Are you hungry?"

"*Oui,* a little."

"I hope you like Hindu soup."

"Hindu soup? I've never had, but I'll give it a try."

"If you don't like the soup, I have enough cheese and bread to last a lifetime."

Jacques smiled. Elle opened the bottle of wine and poured him a glass wondering if he would notice it was his favorite. He immediately asked, "Is this—"

"Yes. I have a case imported every so often."

"Does this mean you're happy to see me?"

Elle avoided an answer. "I have to change. Make yourself comfortable."

In her bedroom, she leaned on the door elated that Jacques was in the next room. Her heart was pounding. She questioned how the night would end. Zipping through her closet, she chose silk lounging pj's. She went into the bathroom to brush her hair. She powdered her face and applied a soft shade of pink lipstick. When she entered the living room, Jacques complimented her. "You look beautiful, Elle."

Embarrassed, she replied, "Thank you. I'll heat the soup."

"Can I help?"

"You can set the table. The dishes, silverware, and glasses are in the left cabinet."

Jacques did as he was told. While Elle cut the bread and cheese, she glanced at Jacques several times to convince herself she wasn't dreaming. Once Jacques finished setting the table, he sat at the round dining room table adjacent to the kitchen area. Surrounding the dining room were large glass windows, which overlooked the Potomac.

"This view is amazing," said Jacques.

Elle looked out the large windows. "It is an amazing view."

"That's the Jefferson Memorial and the Washington Monument, *oui*?"

"Yes."

They ate in silence until Jacques commented that the soup was good. He asked for her to pass the bread and cheese plate, twice. Fifteen minutes passed before Elle addressed the elephant in the room.

"The last time we spoke, you should have told me you were coming to Washington. I could have made plans to see the sights."

Jacques paused. "I was afraid you wouldn't want to see me."

"Last time I checked, I thought we were friends. Why wouldn't I want to see you?"

"By phone, yes, you are friendly, but in person, you might feel differently."

"For the past several months, we've been able to converse without arguing."

"As long as I don't bring up that I love and miss you."

Uncomfortable, Elle passed Jacques the bread basket again. "I have bread, Elle. What I don't have is you."

Elle lowered the bread basket.

"Please, Jacques, don't turn this night into an argument."

"I do not wish to argue with you."

"You said you had business in Washington. How long have you been here?"

"I arrived this afternoon."

"And you headed straight to my door, why?"

"I wanted to tell you face-to-face that I've been offered a job by an affiliate here in Washington."

Elle gasped. "You're moving to Washington?"

"I want to know where you and I stand before I accept the job."

Elle placed her napkin on her lap. "My feelings haven't changed, Jacques. I don't want to marry you or anyone for that matter."

"*Pourquoi*, Elle?"

"I don't want to talk about marriage."

"*Pourquoi?*"

"*Pourquoi!* Why the same question you have asked over and over for a year? I can't explain except to say, you don't really know me. I come with baggage. And if you knew the real me, marriage might be out of the question."

"You are the same girl I met and fell in love with in Paris, no? We were happy. When you were offered this job, everything changed. When I tried to come up with a solution on how we could make it work, you boarded a plane for home. What did I do or say that made you run?"

"I was offered my dream job, and I couldn't imagine a solution that would have worked. For your information, long-distance relationships do not work. You need to find a woman who wants what you want. I'm not that woman."

"You said, you come with baggage. Did you not have the same baggage when you met me?"

"I did. That's why I never accepted your marriage proposal."

"If you ever loved me or trusted me, you should have given me a chance to decide if I could or couldn't live with your baggage."

Elle didn't respond.

Jacques rose from his seat. He headed for the living room to retrieve his coat. Elle rushed after him.

"Where are you going?"

"I'm leaving. It was a mistake for me to come." Jacques's hand was on the doorknob.

"You haven't finished your meal. Can't friends share a meal together without discussing the future?"

"I don't want to be your friend, Elle. I want to be your husband. I want to spend my life with you. I want to have a family with you."

"I don't want children I can't protect."

"What are you saying? Why wouldn't you be able to protect our children? You are talking crazy."

Elle walked around the sofa and sat. "It's a long story."

Jacques's hand fell from the doorknob. "Elle, I didn't wake up yesterday morning and say, 'Let me catch a flight to Washington and force Elle to accept my marriage proposal.' I've been working on relocating for months. I came to ask if we could try again. You said, 'If I knew the truth, I'd think twice about marrying you.' If you want to share your story, I will listen. If not, I'll say goodbye."

"I don't want marriage or children, and you do. How is this relationship going to work?"

Jacques moved closer to Elle. "Are you unable to have children, Elle? Is that the reason you will not marry me? If you were unable to conceive, we could adopt. And if adopting is out of the question, then I would be happy just loving and sharing my life with you."

Tears began to well and gently rolled down Elle's cheeks. "I'm sure I can conceive, but I don't want children. Children need to be protected, and I'm not sure protection runs in my DNA."

Jacques looked confused.

"I'm sorry. It's unfair of me not to tell you the truth."

"Tell me, Elle, what has you troubled? Please *ma vie*."

Jacques threw his coat over the sofa and sat next to her. Elle didn't want to share her family's disgrace with Jacques, but if she told him the truth, he would be free to go on without her. He would forget Elle ever existed. He'd find a lovely girl to love and have a flock of beautiful children.

"Did you ever wonder why I never talked about my childhood?"

"You told me you were estranged from your parents. Speaking of them upset you, so I didn't push. I assumed, when you were ready to tell me why, you would."

"I'm ashamed to tell you why. I'm ashamed to tell anyone. I'm sorry for the pain I've caused you. It was wrong for me to love you when I knew there would be no future for us. I love you, Jacques. I loved our lives in Paris. It was wrong of me to hope that you'd be content with our arrangement and not ask more of me. It was wrong to lead you on. And yes, you do deserve to know the truth."

"If you are so sure I will walk away from you when I know the truth, then let it be my choice."

Elle lowered her head. "When I was twelve—" Elle told Jacques the truth. Finishing her story, she broke down sobbing.

Jacques took her into his arms, saying, "*Mon amour*, you have nothing to be ashamed of."

"All these years, I thought my mother had kept my father's secret. My mother wasn't a demon, Jacques. She was a victim, like me. She's done so much to right the wrong. She's a good woman."

"She is a good woman, your mama. And so are you, Elle. You mustn't let your father's sin stop you from being happy. I've listened to your story, *mon amour*, and my feelings for you have not changed. I love you, and I want to share my life with you if you will have me."

"I don't deserve you, Jacques. You'd be better off without me. I didn't protect Liam. I fear I'd have to pay for the sin and pain that I caused him. I can't take that chance."

"*Mon amour*, you shouldn't allow the fear to stop you from living your life. Liam wouldn't want you to chastise yourself for another's sin."

"I caused so much pain, Liam's and now yours. Can you ever forgive me?"

Jacques cuddled Elle in his arms. "I forgive you, and so does Liam."

"Do you really think we can make this work?"

"*Bien sur, mon amour.* I love you, Elle, and I know you love me. Now do I take the job or return to Paris?"

Elle smiled. Side by side, they watched the fire blaze until the morning light.

The following day after making love, they planned a future together in Washington, DC.

CHAPTER 11

Derek and Kathy arrived at the Ritz-Carlton at eight that evening. Nina greeted them as they entered the hotel lobby. Nina had arranged for their check-in in order to have time with Derek to review the itinerary for the following day. Derek politely asked Nina if they could talk in the morning, using exhaustion as an excuse.

In the elevator, Derek said, "That was the worst flight ever. A three-hour delay, turbulence, and I think the pilot was in training because the landing was rougher than the flight."

"If I wasn't wearing this pin-straight skirt, I would have kissed the ground when we exited the plane."

Placing his arm around Kathy's waist, Derek smiled. "You do look hot in that skirt." He lowered his hand and caressed Kathy's bottom. She felt herself warming to his touch. The elevator door opened to their floor, and the couple dashed off to find their room. When the door to their room opened, Kathy rushed in, removed the skirt, and bolted into the bathroom. When she emerged, Derek was sprawled naked on the bed. Kathy lowered herself on top of him. She was surprised that after an hour of lovemaking, not once did thoughts of a perverted Derek or Lauren naked entered her mind.

"I'm starving."

"You ate on the plane."

"I'm ordering a hamburger, fries, two cocktails, and dessert. Do you want anything?"

"Tea, yogurt, and fruit."

Derek placed the order while Kathy showered. Five minutes later, he joined her. After he washed the shampoo out of Kathy's hair, Derek cupped her breasts in his hands. They lowered themselves to the floor after making love for a third time. Resting their backs against the wall with the water streaming down their legs, Derek said, "I can never get enough of you."

Kathy chuckled. "Three times, and we've been in the room less than two hours."

"I promised you a good time, and I always keep my promises, Mrs. Wilson."

There was a knock at the door.

"Saved by the bell. I don't think I'm up for round four."

Derek tapped Kathy's leg, before grabbing a towel to wrap around his waist.

When Kathy left the bathroom and reentered their hotel room, she found Derek eating a juicy hamburger smothered with fried onion, cheese, and bacon. Kathy sat across from him; she extended her hand taking several French fries from his plate.

"I don't know how you do it. You eat whatever you want and never put on a pound. Aren't you the guy that preaches to his patients that fats are bad for the heart?"

"Sex is a great cardio workout. I probably burned three thousand calories pleasuring you."

Kathy smiled and said, "I'm going to call Fanny to see how the kids are doing."

They spoke with the children. Derek had read Peggy her favorite book so often that he was able to recite it over the phone from memory.

Kathy slept through the night without waking from the dream where Derek and Lauren are lying next to each other naked.

*****

The following morning, the couple ate breakfast in the lounge before Derek went off to go over last-minute instructions with Nina. Kathy had two hours to kill before she was expected in the conference room. She didn't have to attend the seminar, but she did want to see her husband at work.

Lounging by the pool, she was fifty pages from finishing Lauren's novel. She didn't want any part of being Lauren's friend, but she couldn't give up reading her books. She loved the way Lauren told a story. She kept Kathy on the edge of her seat until the very end.

The sun felt good on her face. Closing the book, she placed her face toward the sun and thought of Elle. Elle and Kathy spoke often, but Kathy avoided lengthy conversations in fear that Elle would question if she was ready to forgive and forget. So far, Elle had respected Kathy's wishes never to bring up Lauren when they spoke. Several times while they spoke, Kathy almost questioned Elle on how Lauren was doing. One year and eight months since she last saw or spoke with Lauren. With Elle living in a different time zone for five years and Casey's cancer diagnosis, Lauren and Kathy had bonded. When Kathy had good news to share, Lauren was her go-to person. She missed telling Lauren about her success with the family care facility. Lauren would be so proud of her. Kathy turned the book over and stared at Lauren's picture. Maybe Elle and Alice were right. Derek and Lauren were young and foolish. If only she could wrap her head around what had happened, things might be different.

Kathy spied the time on her phone. She gathered her belongings and went to the room to shower and dress.

When she entered the conference room, she saw Derek next to the podium reviewing his notes. She stood in the back and glanced around the room. The audience consisted of five gentlemen and fifty ladies. She smiled. She surmised the women wanted to meet the gorgeous Dr. Wilson, the handsome doctor they had seen on many talk shows promoting his book. When they read in their local newspapers that the good doctor was in town, they ran out to buy a ticket to the seminar. Kathy chuckled to herself. She then spotted Nina speaking with a gentleman. She thought the man looked familiar but couldn't place the face with a name. Derek stood in front of the podium. Seeing her husband, Kathy put all thoughts of the man speaking with Nina out of her mind.

Derek is amazing, thought Kathy. When the seminar ended, he was rushed by all the women in the room. Nina stopped them from approaching, saying they could purchase the book outside the conference room and then form a line. Dr. Wilson would sign their books and answer their questions.

Kathy chuckled. If her life ended today, Derek would have to buy an extra freezer for all the food dishes he would receive from the single and divorced women. Realizing she had to use the restroom, she left the conference room. A line of women blocked the ladies' room entrance, so she decided to use the bathroom in their hotel suite. She changed her mind about joining Derek and remained in the room to finish Lauren's novel, leaving Derek on his own to handle the flood of women demanding his attention.

Derek found her asleep. His kiss woke her.

"Hi, beautiful."

"It's my Prince Charming."

"Yes." He kissed her again and again, which led to him carrying her into the bedroom, for round four.

Lying in his arms, Kathy asked, "All those women wanting your attention must be exhausting. I can't believe all those women are in the medical profession."

"Are you a little jealous, Mrs. Wilson?"

"Should I be?"

"Not at all. And to answer your question, five were doctors and five surgical nurses. Do you know how many room keys I was offered? 'Dr. Wilson, I'm so impressed by the book I'd love to hear more about your profession. Do you have time for dinner or lunch? I'm free the entire day or tomorrow.'"

"Most men would love the attention."

"I'm tired of raising my hand to show them I'm married. Doesn't seem to bother them in the least. I have to shower. We have an early dinner reservation."

"Why so early?"

"We are having dinner with Dr. Harrison."

"The man Nina was speaking with was Dr. Harrison, right?"

"It's been a while. I wouldn't expect you to recognize him. I told Nina to make an early reservation, so we could spend the night catching up."

"His wife's name is Emma, and they have three children. Three girls, correct?"

"His wife's name was Emily. She passed three years ago. Three children—two girls and a boy."

"I'm so sorry to hear about Emily. They were a lovely couple."

"The big C put an end to the lovely couple."

*****

Kathy and Derek entered the dining room, arm in arm. Nina was first to notice the stunning couple. Her heart sank.

Kathy rushed to Dr. Harrison's side. "Dr. Harrison, I noticed you today talking with Nina in the conference room. Please forgive me for not stopping by to say hello."

"That is a sweet way of saying, you didn't recognize this old, wrinkled face."

"You are as handsome as ever." Sitting between Derek and Dr. Harrison, Kathy offered her condolences. "I am sorry to hear about Emily. I wish I had known."

"Emily wanted her passing to be private, just family."

"I understand. How are the children?"

"The children are doing well. My boy Tom is in technology. My daughter Nancy is a pediatrician. My daughter Debra is a lawyer. All are married to fine people and have blessed me with five grandchildren. Emily did a great job raising those children, with little help from me. I hope this man of yours takes the time to be with his children."

Placing her hand over Derek's, Kathy said, "He's a fabulous father. Just last night, our daughter Peggy wanted Derek to read her favorite book to her over the phone. Derek memorized the entire book. Dr. Harrison, why has it been so long since we've seen you?"

Derek answered, "That would be my fault. Joe called a number of times. I neglected to take his calls. Joe, I swear, if I knew it was you, I would have taken the calls."

"It's not your fault, Derek. When Emily was diagnosed with cancer, I cut myself off from the world to care for her. When I did call, I should have stated it's Dr. Harrison, Dr. Wilson's mentor."

Kathy reached for Dr. Harrison's hand. "I'm so happy you took the time to come and hear Derek speak."

"This young lady is the reason why I'm here."

Nina lowered her head.

"I called the publishing firm and asked to speak with his publisher. This lovely lady, finally, took my call when I said I was an old friend and Derek's mentor."

Nina had been quiet the entire time. Kathy had forgotten she was there. "I don't know what Derek would do, without Nina. Thank you, Nina."

"You're welcome."

"When Derek told me you guys had five children, I almost fell over. The last time we saw each other, you were pregnant with your second."

"The second—that was eons ago. This is the longest I've gone without being pregnant."

"Five children, and you don't look a day over twenty."

"She's a great mom," said Derek.

Nina lowered her head. "And what about you, young lady?"

When Nina realized Dr. Harrison was talking to her, she blushed. "I'm not married, so there are no children."

"A pretty thing like you, and no one has snatched you up?"

Derek stared at Nina, waiting for an answer.

"I'm married to my job."

"Nonsense," said Dr. Harrison. "Take my advice, young lady, find a man and have a few kids. You'll never regret it."

Kathy noticed Nina was uncomfortable with the conversation. Changing the subject, Kathy asked Nina how she chose her career. Kathy took notice that every question she asked Nina, Nina's answers were directed at Derek. Kathy thought it strange but concluded that Derek was the only person with whom Nina had a connection.

When Dr. Harrison said good night, Derek walked with him to the valet. Kathy and Nina were left on their own. "I can go for a nightcap. What about you?" Kathy got the attention of the waiter. "I'll have another pink martini. Nina?"

"I don't want anything. Thank you."

"All work and no play will get you to an early grave, Nina."

"I really should be going. We have an early day tomorrow."

"It's early. Please have a martini with me? We never get a chance to talk."

"I'll stay until Derek gets back."

Kathy ordered two pink martinis.

"These are delicious, aren't they? They take the edge off a hard day."

Nina didn't respond.

"I want to thank you for being so protective of Derek. This afternoon, when the women rushed Derek, you were like a lioness protecting her cub. Can you believe those women? I would only act that way if I saw Bruce Springsteen or Billy Joel or Channing Tatum."

Kathy thought her joke would prompt a smile, but Nina remained stoic. Kathy continued. "Knowing how much Derek hates touring, I'm sure you take the brunt of his bad moods. How do you stand him, Nina?"

"There are times he can be difficult, but if you want to be successful in my business, you have to have a strong backbone. I don't think he is comfortable with all the attention."

"Most men would be turned on by the attention."

"Derek isn't one of those men."

Kathy took offense by Nina's accusation that she, Nina, knew her husband better than his wife. "By one of those men, I assume those men would be men who stray? So I have your word that my husband is as faithful as a church mouse?"

Nina's face began to flush, and her eyes widened.

"I don't have anything to worry about, do I, Nina?"

Derek showed up just in time to release Nina from answering.

"I felt my ears ringing. Were you lovely ladies talking about me?"

"Yes. Nina assured me that you would never cheat on me."

Derek's mouth dropped open. "What?"

"I questioned how she handles your bad moods. Like today, when those women were hoping to get into your pants. Nina assured me, you're not one of those guys—the kind of guy who would cheat on his wife."

Derek's face went white. "Kathy."

"What? She didn't tell me something I didn't already know. Thank you, Nina. I didn't need reassuring, but it's nice to hear that my husband is faithful to me."

Derek glanced at Nina.

Kathy noticed Nina's sad eyes broke contact with hers and turned toward Derek's.

Nina rose. "It's been a long day, good night."

"Why are you rushing off? Did I say something to upset you?"

"No. I'm just tired, Kathy."

"Nina never stops working, Kathy. I'm sure she wants to go back to her room and make some phone calls before it gets too late."

"You're right, Nina. It has been a long day. Derek, we should go."

Kathy retrieved her purse and took hold of Derek's arm as the three made their way to the elevators.

*****

That night, the dream returned of Lauren lying in Derek's arms. While Derek slept, Kathy eased her way out of bed and walked toward the balcony. Slowly opening the door, she stepped outside. The moon was full, and Kathy was reminded of another night, the night Lauren ruined her perfect life.

Something had awakened the dream, and Kathy had a feeling it might have been her recent conversation with Nina. That Nina was a cold one. Kathy tried to welcome the woman into her life as a friend, but Nina kept her distance. She was an attractive woman and single. Nina was one of those women who chose career over marriage. Kathy wondered if marriage was becoming obsolete. From the way Nina hung on Derek's every word, Kathy was sure Nina needed to find Derek's clone. Or maybe she had found the man of her dreams, Kathy's husband. She had to stop herself from thinking every woman was out to win her husband's love. Nina was just doing her job keeping the client happy. Deep down, she might have thought Derek a conceited shit. Kathy decided to keep a close watch on Nina. The woman had to have a life outside work. If Kathy could find out what that life consisted of, the two might find they have a lot in common.

*****

For the remainder of their stay, Kathy had no intentions of attending another one of Derek's seminars, but if she wanted to get closer to Nina, she had to endure.

Standing in the back of the room as she had done the day before, Kathy watched Nina's every move. When Nina took her seat, Kathy noticed that Nina's eyes were locked on Derek. Throughout Derek's talk, Nina never took her eyes off him. She didn't glance at the audience to get their reaction or take notes. Derek had her full attention. Nina looked demonic, like a vampire in a trance. When Derek was finished, Nina rushed to his side. A few words were spoken between them. Derek must have said something to upset Nina because she rushed out of the room. Kathy followed. Nina entered the elevator, and the doors closed behind her. Kathy waited for the next elevator. When the doors opened to Nina's floor, Kathy had to concentrate on Nina's room number. Like a flash of light, Kathy remembered Derek saying Nina was in room 5116. She knocked on the door. No answer.

"Nina, are you in there?"

Still no answer. Kathy persisted.

"Who is it?"

Relieved, Kathy said, "It's me, Nina."

Several seconds later, the door opened. Nina's eyes were red.

"Kathy. Why are you here?"

"You rushed out of the room. Is something wrong?"

"I'm fine."

"You don't look fine. You've been crying. Is it something Derek said?"

"No. I'm just overworked. That's all."

Nina turned her back to Kathy and walked into the room.

"Do you mind if I come in?"

"Come in."

Nina walked toward the sofa and sat. Kathy pointed at the chair across from Nina. "May I sit?"

Nina nodded her head, and Kathy sat.

"I won't keep you, Nina. I just wanted to make sure you're all right." Kathy paused. "I'm a really good listener if you want to talk."

"I'm fine."

"You don't look fine. I noticed you rushed off after talking with Derek. Did you two have words?"

"Derek wants tomorrow off, so he can spend time with you. And that's impossible. The tickets have already been sold. I have no room to reschedule. The week is booked solid."

"I can fix this. Derek will keep his commitments. I promise."

Nina nodded her head.

"Nina, I've noticed how attentive you are to Derek. Is that part of the job or something more?"

Nina became defensive. "What do you mean?"

Kathy chuckled. "I love my husband, but there are times when he's talking about a difficult surgery, which I have no interest in, and I find I need to tune him out. You, on the other hand, have heard him speak so often I can't believe you're not on your computer checking emails or playing Candy Crush. You never take your eyes off Derek. If we were in high school, I'd say, you have a crush on the guy."

Nina's eyes began to well with tears.

"You do have feelings for Derek?"

"I'm sorry, Kathy."

"What do you have to be sorry for? Did you act on those feelings?"

"You mean did I sleep with Derek?"

"Did you sleep with my husband?"

"We've already had this conversation, just last night. I remember saying, you had nothing to worry about."

"So nothing happened, but you're in love with Derek."

"I have feelings for Derek, yes."

"Is it wise to be spending so much time with a man you have feelings for, especially if that man is married?"

"No, and I've tried, but Derek's gone through three people, and he's our number 1 client. My boss is convinced I'm the only person he can work with. I was told it is part of my job to keep the client happy."

"The company can't force you to remain here, but telling the truth why you want to leave can cost you your job. I'll talk with Derek—"

"No, please. There is only one tour left before we break for the holidays. After the last tour, I'm going to resign."

"You shouldn't have to give up your job because you're smitten with my husband. There must be another way?"

"Call it woman's intuition, but it didn't take you long to figure out I had feelings for Derek. I'd rather that he didn't know I fell in love with him."

Kathy was astonished by Nina's confession of loving Derek. Before her was a successful, self-confident, independent woman, demoralized for loving a married man. "I'll talk with Derek."

"I don't know how this happened. I've always separated business from my private life."

"I'm sure you have. I can't explain why women find Derek captivating. To me, he's Derek. I don't see him as some kind of sex god."

"You are like the human version of Barbie and Ken. You're perfect together."

"Well, I never thought of us as Barbie and Ken, but you might be right. Derek and I have a special love and bond."

Crying, ashamed, and humiliated, Nina lowered her head.

Kathy rose. "I'll convince Derek that I'd rather you weren't traveling with him. I'll do my best to come off as the jealous wife. I'll say I'm uncomfortable with you and him spending so much time together."

Nina lifted her head and stared at Kathy. Without speaking, they knew the only way Kathy could pull this off was if Derek knew Nina's true feelings.

"As far as the job goes, Nina, you're really good at what you do, and if your company doesn't see your worth, to hell with them."

The Palm Reader

Kathy closed the door behind her and lingered in the hall. Her heart ached for the woman on the other side.

*****

Derek found Kathy sitting on the balcony. "There you are. Why did you leave? I was going to invite my beautiful lady to a romantic lunch."

"Sit down, Derek. We have to talk."

"About what?"

"Nina."

Derek froze. "Nina."

"Yes, Nina. The woman is in love with you, Derek? Did you know?"

"Kat—Kathy."

When Derek spoke Kathy's name, there was a hint of guilt in his voice. Kathy sat up in her chair and faced him. "Do you have something you want to tell me, Derek?"

"It meant nothing, Kathy. I swear."

"You slept with her, didn't you?"

Derek looked confused. "She told you."

"You bastard! You're admitting you slept with Nina because you think I already knew. Nina confessed she was in love with you, nothing more. I can't believe I felt sorry for her. She looked me in the eyes and lied straight to my face. And you, you bastard, you cheated on me."

Derek fell from his chair onto his knees. "Kathy, I broke it off. Nina and I haven't been together in months. Kathy, please let me explain. I've never done anything like this before, I swear."

"This is the first time you've cheated on me since we've been married, and you expect me to believe you? Of course, why wouldn't I believe you? You've never lied to me before unless your threesome with Lauren and Casey counts as lying but not cheating because we weren't married at the time?"

The bile in Derek's stomach started to rise. "You know about the threesome. That's why you and Lauren—"

Kathy pushed Derek out of her way. Walking into the room, she retrieved her luggage from the closet and started to throw things into the suitcase.

"Where are you going?"

"Home, to our children."

"Kathy, you can't go. Please let me explain."

"Explain? I didn't ask you for an explanation, Derek. You're a fucking liar, a cheat, and the scum of the earth."

"No. Nina was a mistake."

"Is that what she is, a mistake? Lauren and Casey—were they also a mistake? How many mistakes have you made, Derek, after we were married? Forget it! I already know, hundreds, I'm sure."

"Nina was the first. I swear. Please let me explain."

Derek followed Kathy throughout the room as she gathered her belongings. "I don't know how or why I crossed the line with Nina. It just happened."

Kathy stopped in her tracks. "It just happened? You don't know why or how, but it happened? That's a sorry excuse for cheating on me. And Casey and Lauren, what's your excuse? You were young and foolish? Boys being boys? Fuck you! Get out of my way." Kathy pushed Derek aside. She retrieved her purse, checked for her passport, wallet, and keys—everything she would need when she arrived home.

"Kathy, you can't leave. We have to work this out. Think of the children."

"Did you think of the children when you screwed Nina? Did you think of how your perverted threesome would affect my friends for the rest of their lives? No. Your only thought was how to satisfy your demonic, perverted libido."

"Kathy, you know me. I'm not that person. I never meant to hurt anyone. What happened between Lauren, Casey, and me—yes, it was wrong, but I was a twenty-year-old jerk. Casey, Lauren, and I are friends. They never held what I did against me. What happened with Nina—I swear, it was the first time in our marriage that I—she even admitted it was wrong, and she agreed that it had to end. We ended it as friends."

"You shit! Lauren and Casey didn't spit in your face because they didn't want to hurt me. How could you threaten young girls into sleeping with you? That's sick. Did you ever think how your forcing Lauren into an awful situation affected her? She seemed pretty disgusted with herself when she confessed what you forced her to do. Did you think Lauren's bantering with you was friendly fun? The sight of you sickens her. And the woman in room 5116? She was a confident woman until you got your hands on her. Now she's just another idiot who fell for your charm and good looks."

"I didn't force Nina to have sex with me. I didn't make her fall in love with me. She told me she didn't want anything from me. She knew how much our family meant to me. I believed her when she said we could end this as friends."

Kathy stared at Derek. "After you discard these women, you truly believe they are your friends? I don't know you. I never knew you. You're perverted. You have a dark side that I wasn't aware of until now. Get out of my way." Kathy got her raincoat from the closet and grabbed her luggage. As she headed for the door, Derek stood in front of her.

"Stop. Kathy, please stop! Think about what you're doing? We have to talk. We have to work this out. You have to think of our children. Before you leave me and break up our family, give me a chance to explain, please."

"Get out of my way, Derek, before I scream and bring the entire hotel down on you and your best-selling book."

Derek began to sob. "Kathy, please don't leave me. Please let me explain. I love you, and only you, I swear!"

Seeing Derek on his knees, sobbing and begging, gave Kathy the satisfaction of knowing she had crushed the man who used and discarded women like last week's trash.

CHAPTER 12

After finishing the six o'clock news segment, Elle said good night to the staff. She went to retrieve her purse and the items she had purchased earlier in the day. During the day, Elle reported on news that was filled with death and destruction, which on a normal day would cause her to wonder if the end of the world was nearing.

Today, she didn't care about the world and its woes. Her heart was filled with thoughts of Jacques and how their lives were about to change. Jacques was due back later this evening. Since they had planned a life together, Jacques was traveling a few days a week to Paris. This was the last time he would have to make that trip. Monday, he would only report to the office in Washington. There would be a trip now and then to Paris, which would give Jacques time to visit with his family. His parents understood that their son's heart was in Washington but mourned his departure from his homeland and family.

Elle entered her apartment. She rushed into the bedroom. Placing her coat on the bed, she retrieved the package from her briefcase. She went into the bathroom, read the instructions twice, and then peed on the stick. As she waited, she prayed that the news would be good. Frightened, she lifted the stick and smiled. She jumped around the room. Her first thought was to call Jacques, but before sharing their news, she thought it would be best to make an appointment with her OB-GYN. What if the test was wrong? She didn't want to get Jacques's hopes up in case the test was faulty. She sat on the bed, and her joy turned to fear. She wanted to be pregnant. She'd missed two periods. Her breasts were tender, all signs that she was with child. The words *with child* brought back the joy she was feeling earlier. Her stomach began to growl. No more missed meals; she had to think of her child. She went to the kitchen, opened a can of soup, and placed it on the burner to heat. She made herself a salad and a sandwich of cooked ham and cheese. She ate two brownies for dessert. When she was finished eating, she crashed on the couch, stuffed from all the food she had consumed. Placing her hand on her stomach, she spoke.

"Mommy promises no more skipping meals, three meals a day, and dessert, because I love you." Tears began to well, and Elle couldn't believe that she had referred to herself as a mother. She was forty-one; she never thought she'd ever conceive. She quickly stopped herself, thinking she shouldn't get ahead of herself. She needed to make that appointment. She needed to be sure.

It was two in the morning when she heard his key in the door. Jacques was home. Fifteen minutes had gone by before he entered the bedroom. She knew he got a quick bite before coming to bed.

"Long flight?"

"*Mon amour*, I tried not to wake you."

"I can't sleep."

"What's wrong?"

Elle put on the light so she could see Jacques's face. He came and sat on the bed. She asked him to come closer. She lifted her body, fluffing the pillows behind her, then leaned back.

"What is it, Elle?"

She smiled. "I was too excited to sleep. I wasn't going to tell you. I don't want you to be disappointed if I'm wrong." Elle reached over and removed the stick from her night table.

"Is that what I think it is?"

"Yes. We're pregnant, or I think we're pregnant. I haven't been to a doctor. I also haven't gotten my period in two months."

Jacques took Elle into his arms and smothered her with kisses.

Elle chuckled. "I can't breathe, and I don't think that's good for the baby."

Jacques released her.

"I'm going to call my OB-GYN in the morning and make an appointment. I know this is exciting news, but I don't think we should start buying baby clothes until a doctor confirms I'm pregnant, right?"

Without a word, Jacques took Elle into his arms and kissed her lips. Elle wrapped her arms around his neck. When they parted, he said, "We are having a baby. I don't need a doctor to confirm we're pregnant. You're glowing, Mama."

The following morning, Elle called her OB-GYN. Her appointment was on Friday, at ten. Three days of wishing and hoping, which seemed to drag on. They woke early on Friday. Elle wasn't due at work until twelve. Jacques left for work that day at six thirty. The plan was that they would meet at the doctor's office at nine forty-five. Elle arrived at nine thirty.

When Jacques entered the office, he joined Elle in the waiting area. He smiled, saying, "It's going to be good news, I promise."

The doctor confirmed they were expecting, and a month later, together, the parents listened for a heartbeat. The sound of their child's heart echoed in the room. They kissed, hugged, and laughed. Jacques, being a Parisian, kissed and hugged Elle's doctor. They asked a million questions regarding Elle's age and eating habits; Jacques asked about sex. The doctor assured them sex, food, and age weren't a concern. At five months, the couple shared the news with their parents.

Trudy was elated. "November. Around Thanksgiving, that's wonderful. Is Jacques all right with me moving in before Thanksgiving, Elle?"

"We wouldn't have it any other way. I want you here, Mom, with me and my family."

Of course, the next question on Trudy's mind, was marriage. "Are you planning on marrying or choosing the Kurt-and-Goldie lifestyle? It works for them, and I'm sure it will be fine."

Jacques and Elle had already filed for a state marriage license. The next day, the two were speaking with the reverend at an Episcopal church. It would be a small wedding, followed by a fabulous dinner.

Elle had been thinking of Kathy and Lauren. Lauren, she spoke with frequently, but recently Kathy was harder to reach. Fanny assured her Kathy would return her phone calls, but she never did. Elle had left a number of voice mails asking Kathy to return her calls, but she didn't. It was the end of April. Elle was sure Kathy had returned from her trip to California.

Jacques asked, "A penny for your thoughts?"

"I was thinking of the girls. I haven't told them I'm pregnant. I haven't even told them about us or the wedding. With work and our life, I haven't had time to have a decent conversation. I know Lauren is seeing someone, but when I ask, she says she has to work a few things out before she can share her news."

"I don't want you to worry. It's not good for the baby. The next time you speak with Lauren, tell her your news."

Jacques was right. The next time Elle spoke with Lauren, she would share her news. If Kathy ever got around to returning her calls, she'd tell her as well.

CHAPTER 13

On her drive to the city, Lauren thought about her children. The school year had ended. Both children were living at the cottage. She was on her way to meet Jake for lunch. Kelly returned home, not as a child but a woman. Shortly after, she and Jake greeted their daughter at the airport. Kelly informed them she was continuing her studies in Paris and hoped they wouldn't object. Jake and she had discussed it and decided to agree. Lauren was concerned that Josh's grades would suffer because of his newfound freedom, but to her surprise, he did better than expected. He told Lauren he dated, but nothing serious. Upon his return home, Josh hooked up with an old girlfriend on the Cape. Little Jack was growing like a weed. Michelle had hinted that her biological clock was ticking. It wouldn't surprise Lauren if a baby announcement was lurking.

Lauren entered the restaurant and glanced around the room. She'd made a reservation for two several days earlier. Jake had texted he was running late; she requested to be seated.

While she waited for Jake to arrive, she became aware that her legs began to shake—a habit she developed as a child when placed in a bad situation. She kept a close watch on the door. Seeing Jake, she waved. Jake began to walk toward the table but was stopped by several business associates. He glanced at her mouthing, five minutes.

"I'm sorry. The meeting ran over schedule. Do you remember Harris? He was the comptroller at Goggle before he started his own firm."

"Name doesn't ring a bell."

The Palm Reader

Jake smiled. Lauren knew exactly what Jake was thinking, *I wouldn't expect you to remember Harris. You never took much interest in my career or coworkers.*

"Are the kids driving you crazy?"

"Nope. I love having them home. I know we've talked about Kelly continuing her studies in Paris, but do you think there might be another reason for her wanting to remain in Paris?"

"A boyfriend? It wouldn't surprise me."

"You know when we agreed to let her study in Paris, there was a good chance she'd meet someone and remain."

"In one month, she'll be eighteen. We really don't have a say on how she wishes to live her life."

"Josh has hinted he might want to live on the West Coast after college, working for Google. He's sure you can work something out for him."

"If he asks, I'll make a few calls."

"It's easier for you having the children living so far away. You have Michelle and Jack."

Jake felt empathy for Lauren. "I enjoyed living on the Cape in the summer, but I don't know how you handle the loneliness during the winter months."

"I don't think about it much. I pass my time writing. More people are retiring to the Cape. I've met a lot of interesting people. I joined a book club. There are lunches, dinners, and movie invites. I keep busy. You're a city boy. I bet your weekends are spent with Jack at the park, museums, theater, and shopping."

"You're right. I enjoy the hustle-bustle of the city."

"Do you regret marrying me?"

"Absolutely not. We had a good life. Two beautiful children. No regrets."

"You're one of a kind, Jake, not a hateful bone in your body."

The waitress asked, "Can I get you something to drink?"

"Dark beer and ice water. Lauren?"

"I'll have the same."

"Today's burgers are listed on the blackboard. Other options are listed on the menu. I'll be right back with your drinks."

Jake studied the blackboard. After a few minutes, he reached for the menu.

"The Bison burger, fried onion, and cheese sounds good."

"It does. Michelle's been cooking a lot of chicken and fish."

"Chicken and fish is the better health choice. I haven't had red meat in a while. I'm going for the Bison burger and fries. If you decide on the Bison, I promise to keep your secret."

Jake smiled. "Why not?"

The drinks arrived, and they placed an order for two Bison burgers, fries, and cheddar cheese on the side. They shared casual conversation during their meal.

When the plates were cleared, Jake said, "I enjoyed having lunch with you, Lauren. Now tell me what's on your mind? But before you do, I have news."

"Michelle is expecting."

"How did you guess?"

"A little birdie told me. Kidding aside, Michelle hinted her biological clock was ticking. How is Michelle feeling?"

"Great. We had a doctor's appointment the other day. It's a girl."

"It's a girl. That's great."

"Do the kids know? What about Derek, Elle, and Kathy?"

"The kids know."

Lauren wondered why their children hadn't told her.

"I've been trying to reach Derek, but he hasn't returned my calls. The last time I spoke with Elle, Michelle hadn't taken a pregnancy test."

"And Kathy?"

"Haven't spoken with her in ages. I guess you haven't heard from her."

"No."

"I don't want to pry, but you two were so close. What happened, Lauren?"

"I told you. I pissed her off. I don't want to talk about Kathy. That was wonderful news. I'm happy for you and Michelle. A girl, you must be tickled pink?"

"We are, but getting back to why you invited me to lunch, what's your news?"

"I've met someone, Jake."

"Lauren, that's wonderful. Do I know him? Does he live on the Cape?"

"It's not a he, Jake. It's a she."

Jake's facial expression of joy went cold. "What did you say?"

"I met a woman, and I'm in love. Her name is Shelby. I want to introduce her to the kids, but before I do, I wanted you to know. I was hoping for your support."

"You want to tell our children you're in love with a woman?"

"Yes. I know this is a difficult situation that is why I'm asking for your support. If the children see that you're okay with me loving a woman, they may accept Shelby as my partner."

"You're sleeping with a woman? How long have you known that you—"

"I know what you're thinking, Jake. I never slept with anyone while we were married, not a man or a woman. I met Shelby in August. Shelby doesn't hide her life choice. She wants us to be open with our family and friends."

"I don't give a shit what Shelly wants. You are not going to fuck up our children's lives. I won't allow it. I don't know how you got to this place, Lauren, but if you want to screw this Shelly woman, do it privately. Stay in the closet."

"Her name is *Shelby*, not Shelly. And we don't want to stay in the closet. Don't I have a right to be happy? I supported you when you wanted to introduce Michelle to our children, didn't I?"

"This is an entirely different situation, Lauren. If you told me you met Mr. Right, I'd be happy for you. Do you really think you're being fair to the children? Don't you see how your announcing your partner is a woman is going to affect them? Put yourself in their place. You know our children were hurt by the divorce, and now this. Mom was straight, but now she swings both ways. They are going to have questions—such as, did you prefer women and is that why you were so eager to get rid of their dad? Right now, I'm having a hard time believing that you met this woman in August. What if you kept this woman under wraps until you felt the time was right to come out as a couple? If these questions are running through my mind, it won't be long before the kids start asking the same questions. You messed with my head while we were married. As their father, I can't agree to support you and allow you to hurt and confuse the children."

"I never cheated on you. I broke up our marriage because we weren't happy. Look at you now—two babies and a wife who adores you. Everything you ever wanted I offered to you on a silver platter when I divorced you. Now it's my turn to be happy. With or without your support, I'm sharing my happiness with the children."

Jake sighed. "That will be the biggest mistake of your life. If the children were younger, I'd fight you in court, but they're adults. For once, Lauren, choose our children's happiness over your own. I tried to protect you, Lauren, but maybe it's time you knew the truth. Besides doing my job, I was both mother and father to our children. I dried their tears when they wanted their mother while you were off promoting your latest novel. School ended the third week in June, but you left for the Cape at the end of May. Why? To prepare our summer house. Who was there for them before they left for the Cape? Me. Why do you think I asked you to cut back on work for the kids' sake, not mine? When you realized I was unhappy, you asked for the separation. At first, I was hurt. I didn't want to leave the kids, but I no longer wanted to live with you. And, yes, I now have the life I've always dreamed of with a partner that is willing to compromise."

Jake paused. He'd hit the nail on the head. The word *compromise* didn't exist in Lauren's world. She couldn't deny that when she went off for two or three weeks, Jake was there to carry the load. He was high enough on the executive chain to drop the children off at school, work from home if necessary, and be there to tuck them in bed at night. Weekends were a great time for Lauren to work, so Jake had the privilege of driving them to school events. When Lauren returned home, she always gave the kids her undivided attention except for the times she'd zone out creatively and the sound of a child's voice interrupted her thoughts. "Mommy, it's your turn to roll the dice."

"I'm asking you to reconsider telling the children. If you love our children, just this once, think of someone other than yourself? If I haven't convinced you telling the children is wrong, then I hope your confession doesn't backfire. I would find no pleasure in saying, 'I hate to say I told you so.'"

Jake motioned for the waitress. He paid the bill in cash. Without another word, he got up and left the table. Seconds later, he walked out of the restaurant.

*****

Lauren was driving way over the speed limit. She wasn't concentrating on the road; she was furious with Jake. She'd known him twenty-years-plus, and this was the first time he had ever spoken his true feelings. Where was that man when they were married? For the first time in her life, he left her speechless. She couldn't understand why he was so upset. This was the twenty-first century, and it wasn't uncommon for a man to care for the children and the home. She had an astonishing career, which put food on the table and a hell of a lot of money in the bank. So she missed a few weeks here and there when the kids were younger. She had a good relationship with her children; they weren't scarred by her absence.

Jake had no right to tell her how to live her life. He had no control over what she shared with her children. They were adults; she thought they were smart enough to understand that Mommy is happy, just like Daddy. Hearing the siren, Lauren slowed down, but it was too late. The officer motioned for her to pull to the side.

"Good afternoon. Do you know why I stopped you?"

Lauren took several deep breaths before answering. She needed to calm down. "Yes, Officer, I was over the speed limit."

"Ten miles to be exact."

"Ten miles? I thought I was going faster."

"Ten miles over is fast enough. License, registration, and insurance card, please."

As the officer went to check her license, Lauren's cell phone buzzed. It was Shelby. She didn't answer. The officer returned.

"This is your lucky day. With no priors, I'm going to let you off with a warning. A kind gesture for keeping the law. Have a good day, and slow down."

"Thanks, Officer."

Lauren melted into the traffic, remained in the middle lane, and kept the sixty-five-mile-an-hour speed limit. She was an hour away from home.

She should return Shelby's call, but the way she was feeling, she didn't want to deal with Shelby's questions. How did Jake handle the news? When are you going to tell your kids? When can I meet your children?

Lauren began to sweat and decided to pull over. She sat in the car considering her next move. She loved Shelby, as she had once loved Jake. But Jake and she were bonded by the children. Each understood how their love created these two individuals, that they were bonded to protect and love. Shelby having no children of her own, how could she understand Jake's concerns? Lauren owed Jake the respect to heed his warning. Lauren knew that Jake wanted the best for her. Maybe Lauren did mess with his head, but she never meant to hurt him. She didn't want to mess with her children's heads or hurt them, but she loved this woman and was open to sharing their love with the world. Wasn't that what she promised Shelby, the first night they made love?

Lauren felt truly screwed. Her cell phone was in her hands; she needed to call her friends. She corrected herself; Elle was her only friend. Now that Jake knew the truth, she was gay or bi, why shouldn't she tell Elle?

Lauren jumped when her cell phone buzzed for a second time. Shelby. This time, she answered.

"Hi, I'm on my way home."

"How did it go? Did you tell Jake?"

"I told him."

"And does he want to be there when you tell the kids?"

"I really can't talk. As I said, I'm driving, and I've gotten pulled over once today."

"Oh, wow, did you get a ticket?"

"No. Did you know there's such a thing as being kind to a person with a clean driving record? Well, today was my lucky day."

Shelby chuckled. "Call me later. Love you."

"Love you too."

Lauren started the car, and when the traffic was clear, she entered the right lane.

Arriving home, she was happy to find the house empty. She called out several times to make sure the kids weren't there. Kelly was probably on the beach, painting. Josh was either sunning himself or flirting with the girls. She decided to return Shelby's call.

"Hi."

"Hi. How are you?"

"I've been better."

"Didn't go so well, did it?"

"Jake is really upset. I guess when you've been married, the first thing you don't want to hear from the woman you were married to is she's gay. Opens up a whole lot of questions and doubts."

"I'm sure it does. Were you able to convince him that you only started to like women, or did you tell him this was your second time? Obviously, before and after you two were married."

"If you are asking if I told him about my relationship with Casey, no."

"Aren't you afraid that Derek or Kathy might let the cat out of the bag once he tells them we're dating?"

"Shit. You're right. I'm sure if Jake tells Kathy, out of revenge, she might tell him about Casey."

"Did he agree with you that the children should know?"

"No. He doesn't think I should tell them."

"I see."

"Shelby, I haven't decided not to tell my kids. I promised you that we would have an open relationship, and I mean to keep my promise. I just need time to figure out how and when to tell them."

"It's never the right time, Lauren."

"I know, but Jake thinks the children might—"

"We've discussed this. There's a good chance your children might not accept our relationship. But you'll never know if you don't tell them."

"I'm stuck between a rock and a hard place. I don't want to lose my children, and I don't want to lose you."

"Whatever decision you make, Lauren, I can live with."

"If I decide Jake's concerns are valid and I don't tell the children, what happens to us?"

"I want to have an open relationship with you, but I understand that you have to consider your family."

"So if I'm not truthful about my relationship with you, I'll lose you."

"I don't want to put pressure on you, Lauren. If you aren't comfortable telling your children or friends, then we move on. There might be someone in your future who wants to remain hidden. Didn't you say Casey was one of those people?"

"I didn't love Casey. I love you, and I have to respect what you went through to be open about your sexuality. I can't deny I'm frightened of losing my children."

"Once you come out, you also have to deal with the public. You might lose a lot of readers once they know you're gay."

"I was concerned about my career when Casey wanted to move in, but when I committed to you, I put those worries behind me."

Josh entered the house.

"I have to go. Josh is home."

*****

Lauren tossed and turned the entire night. In the morning, she asked Kelly and Josh if they would make themselves available for dinner. She decided the children had to be told.

*****

"That was a great meal, Mom."

"I'm glad you liked it, Josh. Kelly, can you help me with dessert? Josh, why don't you start a fire? We'll have dessert in front of the fireplace."

Lauren placed a tray of brownies and three glasses of milk on the coffee table. Josh was spread out on the floor in front of the fire; Kelly, in the armchair with her legs tossed over the side.

"These are really good, Mom. Did you make them?"

"I did, my sweet girl. Salted caramel and peanut butter brownies. The recipe was in *People* magazine."

Josh reached for a brownie. "They are good."

"Isn't this nice, just the three of us, in front of a warm fire?"

Josh smiled. "Dinner, a special dessert, what's up, Mom?"

"Mom had lunch with Dad yesterday. Dad told her about the baby, and she thinks we need to discuss it, right, Mom?"

"Your dad did tell me about the baby, and I was thrilled for him and Michelle. Since you brought it up, sweetie, are you okay with the baby being a girl?"

"Are you asking if I feel threatened that I'm losing my position as Daddy's little girl?"

"Something like that."

"I was a tiny bit jealous when I first heard the news, but no different from how Josh felt when Jack was born."

"I wasn't jealous of Jack."

"You didn't feel threatened when Jack was getting all the attention?"

"No."

"I think we can agree that your dad loves his children equally."

"Mom's right. So, Mom, if none of us is upset that Dad is having another baby, what's on your mind?"

Lauren's children had her full attention. She stared into their eyes knowing she'd raised kind, mature, and compassionate adults. She was about to rock their world, but her relationship with Shelby wouldn't spawn more siblings to deal with. Lauren's thoughts drifted. Shelby was young and may want to have a child someday. Lauren thought this was a conversation they should have had before she announced to her children she was gay. Although she enjoyed sex with both men and women, so that made her life choice bi, not gay.

"Mom, you zoned out. Are you having one of your creative moments?"

"No, sweetheart. I want you and Josh to know that what I'm about to say doesn't change how much I love you guys."

"Mom, you're scaring me. Are you sick?"

"I'm sorry, Kelly. I didn't mean to scare you. I'm not sick." *Although*, thought Lauren, *sickness might trump gay.* "I'm seeing someone."

"You're seeing someone. Do we know him?" asked Josh.

"Mom, that's great. Does he live on the Cape?"

"No, in Manhattan, and you don't know her, well…Kelly, you know of her work. She's an artist."

Josh jumped up. "Mom, you're kidding, right?"

"I've met someone, Josh. Her name is Shelby, and I'm in love with her. I'd like to intro—"

"You're sleeping with a woman?"

"Josh."

"Answer me, Mom. Are you sleeping with this woman?"

"I know once you meet her, you'll see why I'm so happy."

"Is that why you invited Dad to lunch? You told him about this woman."

"Yes, Kelly. I thought your father should know."

"Who else knows?"

"Why is that important, Josh?"

"Because if Dad, Kelly, and I are the only ones that know, and let's not forget Michelle, we can put a stop to this before it ruins us."

"How can me finding love and happiness be a bad thing, Josh?"

"Are you fucking kidding me, Mom? You're a famous author, and Kelly and I are your children. When my friends at school find out you're gay, they will make my life a living hell."

Kelly remained stoic.

"Do you agree with your brother, Kelly?"

"You're gay, and you told Dad. He must be devastated."

"I assure you, sweetheart, I never cheated on your father. I swear. I met Shelby last August. Shelby wants to meet you guys. I think it's only fair that you meet the woman and see for yourselves how happy she makes me."

"You're insane. I don't want to meet your lover. I want you to break it off with this woman."

"I thought you wanted me to be happy, Josh."

"If your happiness means I have to accept that you sleep with women, I'd rather you be miserable."

"Poor Dad."

"Kelly, sweetheart, your dad is fine."

"Fine? How can he be fine? So you're saying you were straight when you were married to Dad, but now you're not. He doesn't believe you, and neither do I."

"I never cheated on your dad. I swear. What happened between Shelby and I, well…I began to have feelings for her, and I acted on them."

"Is Shelby gay, or did you two figure that out while you were dating?"

"Shelby is gay, Josh."

"And you allowed her to get into your pants?"

"Josh!"

"Shut up, Kelly. Are you listening? She let this gay woman have her way with her."

"All right, that's enough. I thought you were adult enough to handle the truth. Josh, I love this woman. I'm happy. Can't you just be happy for me?"

"No. You're not thinking of us. You're thinking of yourself. You have to break it off with this woman. I can't believe that you thought telling me would be okay. An image of my mother and this woman is forever burnt in my mind. The respect I had for you, Mom, is gone. You hurt my father. You hurt us. I don't think I'll ever forgive you."

Josh ran from the room taking two steps at a time until he reached his bedroom. He slammed the door so hard the house shook. Kelly began to cry.

Tears welled in Lauren's eyes and gently rolled down her cheeks. She glanced at her daughter, and moving closer to her, she said, "Sweetheart, I never meant to hurt you or your brother."

"Josh is right, Mom. You have to break it off with this woman."

"Kelly."

"Mom, you have to end it with this woman. Josh is right. I don't want your shit to invade my private life."

"I'm happy, Kelly. Isn't that what your brother and you wanted for me, to be happy?"

"We wanted you to be happy, but to destroy our lives for your own happiness is cruel. Being happy with a woman is not what we were hoping for. I agree with Josh. You have to break it off. If we can keep this affair between us, we can be saved from the disgrace. You have no other choice, Mom."

"Kelly, I want to be able to love this woman openly without shame."

"This is so overwhelming. I'm worried about Dad and how he must be feeling. Josh thought the world of you. All he's ever wanted is for you to be happy. How could you do this to him? An image of your mother sleeping with a woman isn't something he'll soon forget. Please end it, Mom. I can't talk about this any longer. I'm going to check on Josh."

Lauren wrapped her arms around her knees and cried. She wished she had listened to Jake. When she had cried all the tears she could muster, she went up to bed. Before entering her bedroom, she placed an ear on Josh's door. She could hear her children talking. In the morning, they might be able to come up with a solution that would work for the family.

It was five thirty when Lauren heard the car start. She jumped from her bed and ran to the front door. She watched as her children drove off together. She collapsed onto the floor and sobbed.

CHAPTER 14

Nina looked at her watch. The seminar was about to begin, and Derek was a no-show. She made her way to the podium, tapped the microphone three times, and then announced that Dr. Wilson was running late. She excused herself and headed for the elevators.

She lingered at the door wishing she was anywhere else in the world. She knocked and hoped Kathy wouldn't answer. Derek answered.

"You're not dressed. Did you lose track of the time?"

"I told you I needed a day off, Nina."

"And I told you that was impossible. I have a room filled with people expecting you to speak."

Derek walked into the room. Nina waited at the door.

"You can come in. She isn't here."

Nina stepped into the room.

Derek said, "You can close the door."

"I'd rather keep it open. Where is Kathy?"

"She isn't here. She left me. She knows about us."

To support herself from falling, Nina leaned on the door.

"Come in and close that damn door."

Nina entered the room, found a chair, and collapsed into it.

"She followed me to my room yesterday. I was upset, and she asked what was wrong. I told her you and I had words about you wanting a day off. She said she would speak with you."

"You also told her you were in love with me."

The color in Nina's face went from white to red. "I told her I had feelings for you, yes, but not the truth. How did she find out about us?"

With the saddest eyes Nina had ever saw, Derek said, "I told her."

"Why?"

"I wanted to spend time with her—a romantic lunch. But I was committed to signing those fucking books. I came to our room, hoping to find her. Since my plans for a romantic lunch didn't happen, I made a reservation at a fancy restaurant. I bought her a special gift. A bracelet to match the necklace I'd given her a while back. When I came into the room, I found her on the balcony. I was happy to see that she was taking time to relax. I sat on the foot of the lounge chair. Immediately, I knew something was wrong by the look on her face. I asked what was wrong. She said we had to talk. She asked if I knew you were in love with me? I panicked. I thought you told her. I admitted that I cheated on her."

Nina lowered her head. "She knows I lied to her. I told her nothing happened between us. I told her she had nothing to worry about. You would never cheat on her."

Derek cried, "I can't believe I risked it all. It was wrong to sleep with you. I can't believe I hurt Kathy, my precious Kathy." Derek sat on the bed, holding his head in his hands. "She'll never believe the affair meant nothing to me. She'll never trust me again. I lost her and my children for what, a cheap thrill."

Derek's words cut into Nina's heart—*an affair that meant nothing, a cheap thrill.* She allowed the lump in her throat to pass and asked, "Where is Kathy?"

"She went home."

"Have you spoken with her?"

"She won't take my calls. I was going to follow her, but I don't know what stopped me. She texted me, said to stop calling. I don't know what to do. I want to go home, but I fear I don't have a home to go to."

"You have to face her sooner or later."

"If she'll see me."

Nina felt the vomit rising in her stomach. She was the woman who had destroyed another woman's marriage. She hated herself, but she also had to find a way to get Derek to finish this tour and the Hawaii tour. At this moment, all she had was her career, and as Kathy said, "No man was worth destroying all she achieved."

"Derek, I know you're hurting, but there is a room filled with people excepting you to speak. If you don't, it's my ass on the line. You have to get dressed, finish this tour, and the next. You owe me that much."

"I'm sorry, Nina. I can't go down there and act like my life hasn't fallen apart. I can't. My marriage has to be my priority. You'll have to figure out a way to get me out of my commitment."

"Canceling now will ruin me. And the company won't let you off the hook that easily. You signed a contract. The time you'll waste in fighting a lawsuit you can't win will put more stress on your marriage, the children, and your career. And should I remind you what attorneys charge to go up against a large corporation?"

"Let them sue me. I don't care. Anyway, I'm not going down there to face those crazy bitches."

Nina looked at the man before her. Gone was the confident, charming, powerful man she was obsessed with. Kathy was right. Derek was just a man, nothing more, and Kathy, the only woman that could crush him. What an idiot she had become. No, she wasn't going to lose everything she achieved for this man. Hearing that she was just a cheap thrill and their time together meant nothing to Derek caused her to regain her confidence. She had to get this egotistical, narcissist human being dressed and in that conference room. She had too much to lose if she didn't.

"I can't go down there, Nina. And then you'll want me to do it again tomorrow and the next day and the following month. I want to go home to my wife and children. I have to go home."

"Do you think Kathy wants to see you right now? You have four days left on this tour, four days to give Kathy time to calm down. Kathy told me that you and she have a special love and bond. That love will get you through this. It won't be easy. It will take time, but if love conquers all, then maybe your marriage will survive."

Derek finished the four-day tour. He didn't know if he had a home to go back to, but he would soon find out once he returned home.

CHAPTER 15

Kathy paid the Uber driver, who graciously offered to carry her luggage to the front door. When she entered her home, she paused. Fanny came to greet her.

"The little ones are asleep. Eric and Peggy are at a playdate. They will be home at three. I'm so sorry you had to cut your trip short. How is your friend?"

"My friend?" asked Kathy. "Oh, yes, as well as can be expected. I'm going to arrange to see her at the end of this week."

"Of course."

Kathy hugged Fanny. As the tears began to well, she said, "I'm going to shower. It's been a long flight."

When Kathy entered the bedroom, she placed her suitcase on the bed. Then she collapsed to the floor and cried. She retrieved her phone from her purse. Ten phone calls and fifteen text messages all from Derek. She placed her hand on the bed and thought what would become of her, her marriage, and her children. Derek cheated on her. Nina lied to her. How many other women had Derek slept with? She had to be strong for her children. She had to pull herself together for her children's sake. She wanted to scream, throw things, and cut his clothes to shreds. But how would she explain her actions to Fanny and the children? She never lied to Fanny, but today, she had no choice. She told Fanny that she cut her trip short after hearing from a friend who received the big C diagnosis. Fanny knew most of her friends and would probably ask which one. Kathy would have to create a fake friend unknown to Fanny. The perfect life she once knew was destroyed by a cheating husband, a friend's confession, and a mistress who lied to protect her lover and herself.

Kathy wondered if the gypsy woman was working her magic so that Kathy would finally make sense of her palm reading. "Look beyond your own happiness, and you'll discover the truth." Had she been so happy that she overlooked Derek's late nights at the hospital or the late nights he spent with Nina working on the book? Was she so blinded by her perfect marriage that she missed all the signs that her husband was a perverted, cheating, and no-good bastard? *Why Derek?* she cried. She rose and lay on her side of the bed. She placed her hand on Derek's pillow. They were so happy, have a beautiful life, blessed with five beautiful children. What did Nina have that she didn't? She wanted to stop the pain in her heart, so she slapped her forehead several times. Was Derek telling the truth when he said Nina was his first affair since they married? A man who would force a threesome didn't sound like a man who would abstain from sex until he met Nina. Her phone buzzed; it was Elle. She sent the call to voice mail. There was a text saying this:

Call me, or text me.

She texted this:

I arrived home. Please do not call me or text.

The text was to Derek, not Elle. She missed talking with Elle, but the time wasn't right.

*****

Hearing of Lauren's plight, Shelby made her way to the Cape. Lauren spent her days on a beach chair staring at the ocean. She tried to contact Kelly and Josh, and neither had returned her calls. She thought of calling Jake, whom she was upset with since he didn't bother to call to say her children were with him.

Shelby walked to where she was sitting and sat next to her on the sand.

"I've lost my children. They hate me, Shelby."

"They don't hate you. They just can't accept the way you've chosen to live your life."

"Jake said telling them would be the biggest mistake of my life."

Shelby sighed. "Lauren, we've managed to keep intimate moments private, but you don't think your friends and acquaintances are questioning why I visit your cottage so often? It was only a matter of time when our friendship would be questioned by the public. Would it have been easier for the children to find out by another source, the media, a friend, or a vicious gossip?"

"No. That is why I wanted to be the one to tell my children, not some stranger. I thought they'd be happy for me, but I was wrong."

"It's only been a few days. When your children figure out hearing the news from their mother was your way of protecting them, they might come around."

"They said I should break it off now before someone figures out we might be more than just friends."

"I told you, Lauren, if you want to end it, we'll end it. I drove up to see that you were okay. Now that I've seen you, I'll be heading back to the city."

Shelby kissed Lauren on the cheek and headed back to her car.

The wind picked up, and Lauren wrapped her sweater tighter around her shoulders. In the past when she felt miserable, she wrote.

Lauren's cell phone buzzed. She retrieved her phone, and a ray of hope sprang within her.

"Michelle."

"Jake told me he hadn't called you to let you know the children are with us, so I decided to call. How are you?"

"Been better. How are they doing, Michelle?"

"Jake has spent a lot of time talking with them. Today, they took a drive to the lake. Lauren, I wanted you to know that Jake and I have also been spending a lot of time talking."

"I know it mustn't be easy for Jake hearing his ex-wife is dating a woman. Millions of questions must be running through his mind.

As I told Jake, I never cheated on him. I hope once he's had time to process everything, he'll remember, if there is one thing I'm not, it's a liar. Michelle, you're a mother. I wanted to be the one to tell my children. I didn't want them to find out through idle gossip. I still think hearing the truth from me was the right way. Jake said it would be the biggest mistake of my life. Turns out he might be right."

"I wish I had the answers, Lauren, but I don't. I agree that you deserve to be happy, and if this woman makes you happy, then we will have to find a way to get through to Josh and Kelly."

"They want me to break it off with Shelby, but that won't change how they feel about me. Kelly said the image of me and a woman being intimate was forever burnt in Josh's mind."

"I'm sure it is. They have a lot of questions. One, of course, was this the reason you divorced their father? I spoke with Jake. I told him that I believe you when you say you were faithful to him. I don't know how convincing I've been, but I know he'll come around. He knows how important it is to make the children understand that no matter how you choose to live your life, you are still their mother—a mother who has loved them unconditionally."

"Thanks, Michelle. If it's not asking too much, can you text or call and let me know how they are doing?"

"Of course."

The call disconnected, and Lauren felt relieved knowing that her children and Jake were spending time together. She knew once Jake wrapped his head around the situation, he would find a way to get the kids to come around.

When Lauren got back from the beach, she returned Elle's calls.

"Hi. It's about time you returned my phone calls. Were you out of the country?"

"I'm sorry, Elle. I've been busy."

"I've called Kathy numerous times. She hasn't returned my phone calls either. I know she's back from California because I spoke with Fanny. It's like you two have fallen from the face of the earth."

"Again, I'm sorry."

"Well, at least you returned my call. I have news. Is this a good time?"

"You have my full attention."

"Where do I begin? I'm pregnant."

"You're what?"

"I'm having a baby."

"Did you get artificially inseminated and didn't bother to tell me?"

"You don't answer my calls."

"You could have texted me."

"You wanted me to tell you I'm pregnant in a text?"

"No, of course, not. Elle, I'm blown away. I'm happy for you. No, I'm elated. You know my feelings. Any child would be lucky to have you for a mom. So you took my advice, you don't need a man to have a child? Well…actually you did need his sperm. I hope you chose an intelligent, good-looking, genius to father your child."

"I did. I chose Jacques."

"Paris Jacques?"

"Yes."

"You didn't want the guy, but you convinced him to supply you with his sperm?"

"No. Jacques is living in Washington. Let's just say, my prince wouldn't take no for an answer, so he arranged for a transfer to the Washington office. Jacques never gave up on us, and I'm glad he didn't. It's a long story, and one day, I promise to tell you everything, but now I just want you to know, I'm getting married. My mother and I are planning something simple."

"Your mom? I thought you and your mom didn't speak."

"That's part of the long story. The baby is due in November. The wedding is in two weeks. I want my two besties by my side. I'll be pissed if one of you refuses to attend my special day."

"Nothing can keep me away. I'm sure Kathy will feel the same."

"I knew I could count on you, and I'm hoping Kathy will do the same. She isn't going to allow you to upstage her."

Lauren smiled.

"How are the kids? I know college ended the beginning of May for Kelly and a week later for Josh. I know how much they enjoy summers at the Cape? Has Kelly been painting? How did Josh like his first year at college?"

Lauren thought this wasn't the right time to unload her woes onto Elle. "Josh is enjoying college and being home for the summer. Kelly is painting. Jake and I have agreed to allow her to continue her studies abroad. She leaves for Paris the second week of August. Same time Josh returns to school."

"I'm happy for Kelly, but it must hurt just a little not to have your girl home to stay."

"I'll keep myself busy practicing walking down the aisle. I'm so happy for you, Elle. You finally found the man of your dreams. You guys are pregnant, the best news ever. And your mom and you managed to work out your differences. I can't wait to hear your long story."

"I'd come spend a few days with you at the Cape, but with the wedding right around the corner, I don't have the time. I'd love to introduce you to the father of my baby. Do you think you can spare a few days for a visit to DC?"

"I'll text you dates that work for me. Elle, I'm so happy for you. You're going to make a beautiful bride."

CHAPTER 16

Lying in bed, Kathy stared at the ceiling. In the morning while the children were out with Fanny, she'd pack an overnight bag. She wasn't ready to deal with Derek. Earlier in the evening, she texted him to say that she wouldn't be there when he returned home. She said the time she spent with the children was great, but it didn't give her much time to think how to move forward with their present situation. He'd replied:

I understand.

She turned to face Derek's side of the bed. Tears began to well in her eyes. She hated him for hurting her, but at night alone in their bedroom, she missed him. There was no way that their marriage could survive Nina and the threesome. Knowledge of the threesome had softened the blow that Derek had cheated on her with Nina. Kathy had to face that her husband was a cheat, and Nina wasn't his first affair. He'd probably been cheating on her from the time she said, I do. The only answer to their situation was to separate and end their marriage with a gruesome divorce. Kathy would fight for the house, child support, alimony, half his money, and future earnings. Of course, she'd demand sole custody of their children. So Derek could go on with his perverted life without the interference of caring for his children. She began to softly sob into her pillow. "Derek!" she screamed. He always acted as if she was his world. She remembered how he pleaded for her to stay, talk, and work things out for the sake of their children. Why would she want to work things out with a husband that cheated on her, for her children's sake? Kathy didn't need Derek to make her feel like a woman. She could have any man she wanted, and he knew that. What did Nina have that Kathy didn't? She was smart, beautiful, and bore him five children. Sex wasn't an issue. Why? Was it Nina's success as a businesswoman that attracted Derek to her? Had Derek lost respect for her because she hadn't carved out her own career? She was honest with him when they'd met and married. She wanted a family to dote on. He said he was on board with her decision to be a stay-at-home mom. Then what changed? Had Kathy become complacent? Not interesting enough to hold on to her man? *I hate you, Derek. I hate you, and I miss you. I miss what we had. What didn't I give you that would cause you to look elsewhere?* The only answer was Kathy's husband had a dark side. He craved more than she was willing to give. If only Lauren and Casey had told her the truth, they could have saved her from marrying and having children with a perverted man like Derek.

When Fanny returned home with the children, she informed Fanny that while the children were napping, she was going to leave to spend a few days or a week with her sick friend. Derek would be home later that evening to help with the children.

*****

Derek arrived home to find Fanny sleeping on the sofa. Earlier, he called Fanny to say, his flight was delayed. Ascending the stairs, he went to check on his children. Finding them sound asleep, the tears began to well in his eyes. Entering the bedroom he shared with Kathy, he collapsed onto the bed. He hadn't heard from Kathy, and he worried if she had arrived safely. His tears began to fall as he wondered what would become of his life. He loved Kathy and his children, but he did not see this ending well for him.

Kathy was hurting; even though he hadn't heard her voice in days, her text said it all. She wasn't ready to see him or deal with his infidelity. When he was in California, he wanted nothing more than to come home and see her face. It surprised him that when he received her text, he was relieved that she wouldn't be there when he returned home. It gave him time to spend with his children under the same roof. Kathy would ask him to leave, and he would because he didn't want to cause her any more pain.

Finding out that she knew about his encounter with Lauren and Casey, which occurred when he was an egotistical young man, was embarrassing and humiliating for him. The affair with Nina only confirmed Kathy's fears that Derek might be a perverted predator. Mature Derek never forced a woman to have sex with him. Yes, the two women he crossed the line with were eager to please, but if he pushed the envelope and they weren't comfortable, he'd stop. He had stopped many times when Kathy didn't feel comfortable with a particular sex act. He respected her feelings.

How many times had he asked himself why. Other than the thrill and freedom to do as he pleased with Nina, the affair meant nothing to him. When the thrill was gone, he broke it off. Fate had ended his affair with the nurse, and he was grateful. That affair brought many sleepless nights. He forced himself awake, wet with sweat, his heart pounding because in every dream, the nurse confronted Kathy and told her the truth. Fear had reentered his world that Kathy might reach out to Nina to condemn her for sleeping with her husband and then lying to her face. In retaliation, Nina might confess his affair with the nurse. Before leaving California, that was a conversation he and Nina should have discussed. He thought of calling her, then changed his mind. Kathy knew his cell phone password, and changing it now would be a mistake. If Kathy saw he had called Nina, late at night, it would cause a slew of questions.

He went into the bathroom and showered. Sleep wouldn't come easily, so he thought of emptying his luggage. Changing his mind, he lay on Kathy's side of the bed. He breathed in her scent, which lingered on her pillow. He wished he could turn back time as far back to his college days. Wipe away ever forcing Casey and Lauren into a threesome. An action he never thought they would agree to. Lauren's response, he assumed, would be to tell him to fuck off. To his surprise, Casey came back to say he had to keep his word and never to tell what he saw. Even if they would have refused, he never intended to tell anyone. He made his threat, and if they would have said no, he would have gone on with his life. Casey and Lauren, even though he found them attractive, weren't on his list of women he desired to sleep with. Yes, it was fun and surprising when Casey wanted to continue. He thought if Casey was on board, so was Lauren.

When Lauren confessed the encounter to Kathy, Kathy made it sound like Lauren felt violated. Which could be true. Out of the three, Casey seemed very comfortable being part of a threesome.

What was confusing to him, if Kathy knew about the threesome, why didn't she confront him? Derek had noticed a change in Kathy's demeanor when she returned from her trip with the girls, but he thought it was due to Lauren's treatment of her. Lauren was condescending of Kathy choosing to be a stay-at-home mom. So when Kathy immediately took on the family care facility, Derek was certain that Kathy needed to prove to herself that she was more than a mom. There were so many questions he wanted answered, but the affair with Nina put an end to life as Derek knew it.

At six that morning, Fanny knocked on the bedroom door. "Dr. Wilson."

"Come in, Fanny."

Fanny entered the room. "You're dressed."

"Yes."

Fanny glanced at the suitcase standing in the corner. "I was going to start a wash, but you haven't unpacked."

"I'll unpack later this evening after the children are in bed. I will take care of the wash. I have an early surgery tomorrow, and then I'm free for the week. You are officially off duty when I return. Spend some time with your cousins."

"I could use some time off. Should I call Jenny to help?"

"No. We'll be fine."

He sighed wondering how Fanny would take the news when she returned, and he was gone.

*****

Kathy pulled into the driveway, exited the car, walked slowly to the front door, and knocked. A woman answered.

"Hello."

"Hi. Is Lauren home?"

"Yes, she is." The young woman called out, "Lauren!"

Kathy waited for Lauren to appear.

"I was out back. What's up?" With her head down, Lauren continued to dry her hands with a towel. Looking up, she was speechless to find Kathy standing at her door. "Kathy."

"Hi, Lauren."

The young woman rushed in and extended her hand. "Hello. So you are Kathy. I'm so pleased to meet you." Turning to Lauren, she said, "You weren't lying. She's even more beautiful in person. Come in."

Kathy followed Shelby's lead. She entered the house. Kathy stared at Lauren, her facial expression questioned, *Who is this woman*?

"Kathy, this is Shelby."

"It's nice to meet you, Shelby."

Shelby went to Lauren's side and placed her arm around Lauren's waist. Kathy took notice of the gesture.

"Are you hungry?" asked Shelby.

"I don't want to be a bother."

"Don't be silly. I was just going into town to pick up something to eat for lunch. I'm sure you two have a lot of catching up to do." Shelby grabbed her purse and the car keys from the hook. "I'll be back in an hour."

Lauren couldn't take her eyes off Kathy. "I can't believe you're standing in my living room."

"I should have called to let you know I was coming. It was wrong of me to just show up."

"Don't be ridiculous. You saved me the stress of wondering if you were coming to knock my lights out. I hope you're not here to knock my lights out, are you? Not that I would blame you. You know, for wanting to knock out my lights. But I am curious, were you heading to Canada and decided, oh, let me stop by and say hi to Lauren?"

"Something like that."

Whatever Kathy's reasons for being here, Lauren was thrilled to see her.

"All right then, whatever the reason for the visit, let's open a bottle of wine and catch up." Lauren hadn't felt this good in days. Kathy was in her living room. If Kathy wanted to blast Lauren out for the threesome, so be it. Lauren prepared a tray of cheese, meats, and crackers. She placed the tray on the coffee table. She retrieved two wine glasses and a bottle of red wine. Lauren unscrewed the cork and poured Kathy a glass of wine. Handing it to her, she smiled. "Cheers." Sitting on the armchair across from Kathy, Lauren knew something was wrong. "If you're waiting for Shelby to return with lunch, don't. She's not going to be back for hours." Lauren handed Kathy a plate. Kathy placed several cheeses, two meats, and crackers on her plate and began to devour her food, rinsing the food in her mouth down with wine.

"Last meal I ate was yesterday morning. I did have a bag of chips for dinner."

"I never knew how you got by with two small meals, but I didn't know you were down to one meal and a snack."

Kathy managed a smile.

"I'll address the elephant in the room. Did you wake up today and say, 'Let's go and visit Lauren on the Cape?'"

Lauren waited for Kathy to respond, but she just stared at Lauren and asked, "Is Shelby your new BFF?"

"She's more than a friend."

"When she placed her arm around your waist, I thought she was more than a friend. Are you happy?"

"I'm happy with Shelby, but my life is a little complicated at the moment."

Kathy frowned.

"Loving Shelby has caused me a greater loss."

Lauren went on to explain how another confession had destroyed others.

"Jake warned me, if I told the children, it would be the biggest mistake of my life, and it was."

Kathy didn't criticize Lauren's actions. "You can't allow your children to determine how you live your life, Lauren."

Lauren's eyes widened. "You don't agree with Jake that telling the children was a mistake?"

"They would have found out sooner or later. Does Shelby live on the Cape?"

"No. She has an apartment in Manhattan."

"How long do you think it would have been before your neighbors started talking?"

"Yes, exactly. Jake was horrified when I told him I was dating a woman. He had a million questions about our time together. Did I cheat on him, and the truth and answer is no. I never cheated on Jake, but he was right. Josh and Kelly were devastated by my coming out. Shelby wanted an open relationship, and I had to make a decision. You were right when you said I'm selfish. I leap before I think."

"Are you happy?"

"I am, Kathy. I love Shelby, and Shelby isn't willing to remain in the closet. The kids want me to break it off before we're found out. They are never going to accept us as a couple."

"You can't have it all."

"I wish I could, but I can't." Lauren needed to apologize for her behavior. "Kathy, I am truly sorry for hurting you. I don't know what happened that day. The gypsy woman got into my head. I worried that Alice was itching to tell you and Elle about my affair with Casey. Talking about Casey reminded me of the threesome with Derek. I should have told you the truth back then. And I was wrong saying those things about Derek. I should have respected that he was your husband. If there was one thing I love about the guy, it's how much he loves and cares for you and the children. Back then, Derek was being a guy, and you're right. I should have been strong enough to tell him to fuck off, but I didn't. There is no excuse for my behavior in college and my confession that day. The argument got heated. I wasn't expecting the reaction I got from you when you heard Casey and I were involved. Of course, it was wrong because Alice got hurt. One who is in a monogamous relationship would think cheating is wrong, so it now makes sense that you would have reacted as you did.

If you choose not to forgive me, I understand. But I am happy that you've given me a chance to say, I'm sorry."

"I'm not ready to talk about that night."

"Okay. When the children walked out on me, I so wanted to call you, but Elle said you and Derek were in California, and I knew you wouldn't take my call."

"I wouldn't have then, but today, things are different."

"You are different. For one, you're not lashing out, calling me selfish, which I am, scolding me for hurting my children, saying, 'How could you, Lauren? How could you put this woman before your children? What is wrong with you?'"

"It's been two years. I've changed."

"You might have changed, but I don't think you've tossed aside your morals. I'm sleeping with a woman, and I might never have a relationship with Josh and Kelly ever again. The Kathy I know would be appalled by my actions."

Kathy sighed. "It's your life. I have no right to judge you. I thought the kids might be here. I never expected to—I packed an overnight bag, but I shouldn't stay."

"Please don't leave. Shelby will be disappointed if she returns and finds you gone. Please, Kathy, please stay. I've missed you."

Kathy's eyes locked with Lauren's. "I wouldn't want to upset Shelby." Kathy rose and went to the car to retrieve her bag. Lauren and Kathy climbed the stairs together. Kathy placed her bag in Kelly's room.

"It's a beautiful day. Did you bring a swimsuit?"

Kathy turned to face Lauren. "No, can I borrow one of yours?"

"Follow me, but not the beige swimsuit. It cuts ten pounds off your stomach, and I've been drinking a lot lately."

Shelby arrived home to find the house empty. She prepared lunch and found Kathy and Lauren lounging at the beach. Kathy had fallen asleep, and Lauren had placed a blanket over her.

Shelby and Lauren walked toward the water to talk.

"Has she forgiven you?"

"I talked. She listened. Wasn't condescending about my coming out. Something's wrong."

Shelby looked over her shoulder. "I think you're right. She's out cold. I don't think she's had a good night's sleep in weeks. She's here, so that tells me whatever is going on, it's you she feels most comfortable telling. She'll open up when she's ready. It's really windy today. I'm heading back to the cottage."

Lauren moved her chair closer to Kathy to block the wind. She watched Kathy sleep.

What's wrong, girlfriend? she thought. Taking her pad and pen from her beach bag, she jotted down notes for her next novel. It was four o'clock when Kathy stirred.

"How long did I sleep?"

"Three hours."

"Three hours? Impossible. What time is it?"

"Four. I'm happy you're awake. The wind's pick up. We should be heading back."

The three enjoyed a lovely dinner prepared by Shelby. They drank wine while Shelby described when she knew she loved sculpting over painting. She shared with Kathy how supportive her parents were when she told them she was gay. Therapy helped her to overcome the fear of coming out to her extended family and friends. Shelby spoke with pride and elation that after years of therapy, she was able to face the world as a gay woman. Shelby's words only confirmed to Lauren that Shelby would never have agreed to an undercover relationship.

Kathy kept a close watch on Lauren. Lauren hung on every word Shelby spoke. Her smile said it all. She was in love. Kathy felt sorry for her friend. Loving someone as much as Lauren loved Shelby would bring her nothing but pain. The pain had already occurred. Loving Shelby had cost Lauren her children.

Kathy's mood lightened with every day that passed. On the fourth day, Lauren found Kathy in the same location, on a beach chair, staring at the ocean, wrapped in a blanket. Lauren placed her chair next to Kathy's. Wrapping a blanket around herself, she sat.

"It's just us and the seagulls."

"Is that your subtle way of saying, 'Kathy, let's talk'?"

The Palm Reader

"Why don't we ditch this beach and head to town and have lunch. Just you and me?"

"You and Shelby go. When it gets too cold, I'll head back."

"So that's a no to lunching in town? Then I'll move on. Thanks for not knocking my lights out and for being supportive of my relationship with Shelby. By the way, she thinks you're great. We've spoken of my children, but you haven't mentioned yours, not once since you arrived. Elle's been trying to reach you, and you haven't returned her calls."

"So you've spoken with Elle?"

"Two weeks ago."

"Derek fucked Nina. You knew he was a cheating bastard. So I came to the only person who has always told me the truth except when you should have told me the truth and stopped me from marrying a cheating, perverted pig."

Lauren was shocked. "I'm so sorry, Kathy. You don't think I spoke badly about Derek because I knew he was cheating?"

"Relax, Lauren, I'm not accusing you of knowing. You haven't even met the woman."

"I just assumed you might have thought I knew."

Lauren removed her hand from the blanket and placed it on Kathy's knee. "Is Derek in love with this woman?"

Kathy chuckled. "Derek doesn't love anyone but Derek. No, she was just another notch in his long list of lovers."

"Derek?"

Kathy turned to stare at Lauren. "You seem shocked?"

"Did you have him followed?"

"No."

"How did you find out about Nina?"

"The woman confessed she was in love with him. When I asked if she slept with my husband, she lied and said Derek was loyal. He was clueless about her feelings for him. Her company demanded that she remain with Derek throughout the tours, and seeing him every day was causing her great pain. I bought her story hook, line, and sinker."

"I'm confused."

"I asked Derek if he knew Nina was falling for him. The idiot confessed, thinking Nina ratted him out."

"Oh, Kathy."

Tears began to roll down Kathy's cheeks. "He cheated on me, Lauren. He broke my heart. You said he was perverted, and I believe he is. He has a dark side. I have to leave him. What other choice do I have?"

Lauren didn't respond. *Derek cheating on Kathy? Unbelievable,* thought Lauren. Even she, the woman who thought the man capable of cheating, couldn't believe her ears. Kathy asked, What choice do I have but to leave him? Which meant she might be asking Lauren to come up with another solution? Lauren had to hold off offering an opinion until she had time to think.

After Kathy had calmed down, Lauren said, "We're going to lunch, and I won't take no for an answer. We will talk again tomorrow, and together, we will come up with a solution. I promise."

Together, the friends walked hand in hand to the cottage.

That night, Lauren shared with Shelby Kathy's dilemma.

"He cheated on her? You always said you didn't trust him."

"What I said and what I believe are different. Derek adores Kathy. I don't know why the bastard cheated on her, but she believes he's done this more than once."

"Once a cheater, always a cheater."

"That sounds right, but there are times a man or a woman might stray. That doesn't mean they're screwing everything that walks on two legs."

"True."

"I don't know why I'm defending the bastard. If he were standing here, I'd choke him. He had it all—a beautiful wife, five beautiful children, and he screws this Nina gal."

*****

The following day, it rained. Shelby had a meeting that afternoon at the art gallery. Before leaving, Shelby prepared a brunch for Kathy and Lauren.

When it rained, the cottage was damp and cold. Lauren lit a fire.

Kathy wrapped herself in a blanket and lounged on the sofa. Lauren set before them the brunch Shelby had prepared.

"Shelby will be late, so we have the entire afternoon to talk."

"What is there to talk about? Derek cheated on me, and I am going to ask him to leave."

"You've decided to haul his ass to the curb before you have a chance to find out why? Like how long has he been with this woman, or was it a one-time-wish-I-didn't-but-I-did mistake?"

"He's been working with her for a little over a year. I don't think it was one time. I think he figured out Nina was in love with him, and he ended it."

"You think Derek was screwing this woman for over a year? I don't believe that."

"Let's not forget what Derek is capable of doing."

"Kathy, I fear that what happened between Derek and me in college is causing you to make a rash judgment on how to handle his infidelity."

Kathy chuckled. "Do you hear yourself, Lauren? Derek threatening you into a threesome is the same man that screwed Nina and who knows how many other women. So, yes, I believe he's been screwing this woman for a year."

"I know this is going to sound crazy, but it's hard for me to wrap my head around Derek having multiple affairs."

"He said Nina was his first affair and his only affair. A trapped dog will bend to your will when they have no way to break loose. He lied to save his own ass."

"There are ways to find out if he is telling the truth."

"He cheated on me, Lauren. It doesn't matter if it were one time or a hundred times."

"The other day, you said, you had no other choice but to leave him. Is that what you're planning on doing? Don't you want to know why he would risk it all for this woman?"

"I'm sure he found her attractive."

"Maybe, but I'm not buying it. There are times when two people are caught up in a moment, and shit happens. I'm not excusing his behavior, but the Derek I know loves you and his family. I know why you're here, because I always had my doubts because of what happened between Derek and me. And I should be convinced that he's cheated before, but I'm not. If it were me, I want to find out why before I tore my family apart."

"There is no other solution, Lauren."

"Kicking his ass to the curb isn't the only solution. A love like yours and Derek's just doesn't die. You owe it to yourself to find out if the man is a cheater or if this is the first time he's crossed the line."

"Are you asking me to live with a man who didn't respect or treasure what we shared? I had the perfect life, Lauren—a husband I believed loved me as I did him. When you accused him of cheating on me, I thought you were just being hurtful. Derek would never hurt me or break the trust we had. Well, I was wrong, and you were right. Do I want to know how many more women there were? No. One is enough."

"I'm definitely not the one to be dishing out marital advice. Defending Derek isn't what I do, and if he were standing before me, I'd choke the bastard. Therapy might help you to find out the answers you need to move forward, with or without Derek."

Kathy lowered her head. "I'm in so much pain, Lauren. I still love him. I miss him. I miss his touch. I miss his smell. I miss the way he makes me feel like I'm the only woman he would ever desire. Do you truly believe therapy or my finding out that Nina is his only affair will bring back the security I felt with him? I don't think so. And what if under every rock is another woman? Do I want to feel more foolish than I already do?"

"You're right. I don't want you to hurt more than you're hurting already. Forget everything I said. You deserve better."

"I can't forget everything you said because I've been toying with the same thoughts. I want back what Derek and I had. I want my children to be raised with both their parents. And I want Derek to hurt as he hurt me. The only way to hurt him is to take all that he loves away from him. I have that power, and everything inside me is telling me to move on those feelings. That is why I left. I haven't texted him to let him know where I am. I hope he's wondering if I met someone, and at this moment, I'm lying in a hotel room screwing the guy's brains out. I want him to suffer, and then again, it pains me to know he's suffering. I'm a mess."

"This love-and-hate experience is normal." Kathy closed her eyes. She looked tired, and Lauren decided to let her rest. They'd talk again tomorrow.

And they did. It was a pretty day, so Kathy and Lauren took a walk on the beach.

"I'm leaving on Saturday. I texted Derek last night to say I'd be home by three."

"I'll miss you."

"You have Shelby to keep you warm."

Lauren smiled. They walked without another word. When they returned to the cottage, Kathy sat on the porch swing and asked Lauren to join her.

"I'm not going to kick Derek's ass to the curb. I'm going to a therapist, not with him, but on my own. I'm going to suggest he do the same. I'm also going to find a way to look under every rock. I can't live without knowing if he's a perverted cheat. While I'm working on myself, if I discover there are no happy endings for me, I'm going to leave him. I'm hoping for a better outcome, but I'm not optimistic. Maybe you were right all along. I have been living in a fairy-tale world. It's time for me to grow up. As you said, no one can be happy 24/7. Everyone has shit in their lives. Well, the shit has finally hit home, and I can't run from the truth."

Lauren rested her head against Kathy's.

*****

Kathy, on the drive home and not too eager to see Derek, pulled to the side of the road and called Elle. She apologized for not returning Elle's calls.

"Elle, I wanted you to be the first to know that Lauren and I have reconciled."

"You did! I need details. Lauren called you, right?"

Kathy wanted to tell Elle that Derek was a cheat but asked about Elle instead. "Lauren suggested that I return your call. She said, if I love happy endings, yours would make my day."

"I can't believe Lauren didn't tell you herself. Are you sitting?"

Kathy looked down. "Actually, I am sitting."

"I'm getting married, and I'm pregnant."

"What? When? How? To whom?"

"Shocking, right? I'm marrying Jacques. I'm having his child. The wedding is in September. A small affair, and I want my besties by my side."

"Elle, do you love him?"

"Of course, I do. Can you spare two days to come to DC to meet Jacques before the wedding? Lauren's free."

"Yes. Anything for you, Elle."

For the first time in weeks, Kathy smiled. "You're pregnant! Elle, that's wonderful news."

"I'm over-the-moon happy, Kathy. And happier that my two BFFs were able to work things out. Life couldn't get any better. Wouldn't you agree?"

Kathy felt a lump form in her throat. "Yes, Elle, life is good."

CHAPTER 17

Derek was in the kitchen pouring himself a cup of coffee when he heard the key in the front door. Kathy was home, and his heart leaped in his chest. He heard her footsteps as she ascended the hall stairs. Then he heard the door closing behind her. His car was in the driveway, so she knew he was at home. She hadn't walked throughout the house in search of the children. He lowered his head and began to place the lunch dishes in the dishwasher. When he was finished, he went to fold the laundry.

*****

Kathy removed her sweater and placed it over the handle of her overnight bag. She removed her shoes and lay on the bed. She listened for her children's voices. Looking at the clock on the nightstand, she assumed her younger children were napping; the older children, at school. She stared at their wedding picture that was hung on the opposite wall. Before the day was over, she'd have to confront Derek. Every fiber in her body wanted to ask him to leave the house. Then she thought twice; if he left, she'd have to deal with the children's questions. She was exhausted and didn't have the strength to deal with her own children. She drifted off to sleep. She was awakened by the sound of children running through the house and Derek's voice announcing, "Finish eating your snacks. In two minutes, we are leaving to pick up your brother and sister from school." Kathy felt relieved that she was granted another thirty minutes of not having to deal with Derek or the children.

She stared at the ceiling the entire time. When her children reentered the house, they called, "Момму! Where are you?" They then charged up the stairs.

She waited several seconds before answering, "I'm in my bedroom."

Crashing through the door, the kids jumped onto the bed. "We missed you, Mommy."

She hugged her children and kissed them several times. "Mommy missed you guys. How was your day?" When she looked up, Derek was standing in the doorway holding the baby. He walked toward her and handed her the baby. She hugged Gabe and breathed in his scent. "Mommy missed her little man. Did you miss Mommy, Gabe?"

Gabe gave her a wet kiss and mumbled a word or two. She guessed he'd missed her as much as she missed him.

"Mommy had a long drive home. Why don't we let her rest?" said Derek. Reaching for the baby, he said, "I promised them pizza. Can I get you anything?"

"I'm fine."

He nodded. "All right. Why don't you guys go play, and Daddy will call and order the pizza."

"I want extra cheese," said Eric.

"I don't like extra cheese, Daddy!" yelled Peggy.

"I'll figure it out. Let Mommy rest."

Derek and the children left the room. After an hour, Kathy drifted off. She woke to Derek's voice and touch. "Kathy, I brought tea and cookies."

Kathy sat up. "Thanks, but I'm not hungry."

Derek nodded and turned to leave the room.

Kathy called to him. "Where have you been sleeping?"

He turned. "In our bed. I'll move to the guest room."

"I think that would be wise for now, but when Fanny returns, I want to avoid the questions. We can fool the children for a while, but they too will have questions."

"I'll do whatever you want me to do, Kathy."

Kathy stared at her husband; she wanted to scream at him. "Whatever I want, Derek, and what do you think that is?"

"I'd think you'd want me as far from you as possible, and if that's what you want, then I'll go."

"You're right. I don't need you, Derek. I've done a pretty good job on my own while you were off screwing your publicist."

"Kathy, please."

"Why don't you tell me what you are doing when you come home from the hospital at three in the morning or when you call to say you're going to be late?"

"Caring for my patients."

"Caring for your patients, but you found time to screw Nina."

Derek's eyes began to well. "Nina was a mistake."

Kathy saw the emotion in Derek's eyes. "A mistake, and you want me to believe that she was your only mistake?"

"Yes."

"A man with thoughts and actions such as yours just doesn't end his perverted behavior."

"If you're referring to what happened between Lauren, Casey, and me in college, I was twenty years old, Kathy. We weren't dating. I didn't even think I had a chance with you."

Kathy frowned.

"When you found out what happened with Lauren, why didn't you question me and let me explain?"

"I didn't want to believe that you would force any woman into performing for you."

"I made a threat. I never thought they would agree."

"You threatened Lauren. You were going to spread rumors about her. She would have been devastated, and she would have left college to avoid being targeted as a gay woman."

"I made the threat, yes, and if they told me, no, I had no intentions of telling anyone. It was a prank—that was all."

"You pulled a prank, and when they said yes, you went along."

"Kathy, I was young, stupid, and curious."

"And what is your excuse now that you're older, successful, and you have your devoted wife wrapped around your little finger?"

"There is no excuse. I fucked up."

"If you fucked up with Nina, I'm sure you fucked up more than once."

"No matter what I say, you're never going to believe me. I'm telling the truth. Nina was the first." Derek had no intentions of confessing his affair with the nurse. Hearing that he had crossed the line twice since they married wasn't going to ease Kathy's pain. The lie would go with him to his grave.

"You're right. I don't trust you. I don't think I ever will, not in this lifetime."

Peggy called, "Daddy, Eric pulled my hair."

Derek turned and left their bedroom. Neither Kathy nor Derek slept that night. They got through the following day with a lot of yes and no answers between them. Three days had passed of the same. On the fourth day, during dinner, Kathy announced that she was leaving tomorrow to spend two days with Aunt Lauren and Aunt Elle.

Peggy shouted, "Mommy, you're going away again?"

"Sweetheart, it's only for two days. I've been keeping a secret. The reason why Mommy will be away is to help Aunt Elle plan her wedding."

Derek raised his head from his plate and stared at his wife.

"Aunt Elle is getting married?"

*****

That night, Derek knocked on their bedroom door. Kathy swung open the door.

"What?"

"You reconciled with Lauren?"

"I did. She had you figured out all along. The night I found out about your threesome threat, she accused you of being a cheat. Said it wouldn't surprise her if you had a mistress holed up somewhere."

"Lauren said that about me?"

"Yes, she did. That's why I wanted nothing to do with her. One, she allowed me to get involved with you after she knew what you were capable of, and two, she had her doubts that you could be faithful to me. I thought she was jealous of the love we shared, and I hated her for calling you a cheat. When I found out that she was right about you, I thought it was only right to tell her I was sorry for what you had put her through."

Kathy turned her back to Derek and went back to packing her things.

"When will you be back?"

"What time do you have to leave on Sunday?"

"My flight is at four. I should leave by two."

Kathy smirked at him. "I'll be back before you leave. Fanny will be home before you return. You'll have to move back into the bedroom until we can figure out where we go from here. Are you planning on attending Elle's wedding? I thought you might feel a little uncomfortable seeing Lauren."

"I'll be at the wedding." Derek closed the door behind him.

*****

Kathy landed ten minutes before Lauren's plane arrived in DC. They hugged.

"This place is a madhouse. Let's get out of here. I can't wait to see Elle."

*****

"I can't believe you're here!" screamed Elle. "Jacques, come meet the girls."

Wearing a cooking apron, he greeted the girls with a sexy French accent. "I'm happy to finally meet Elle's BFFs."

He extended his hand to Kathy. She ignored his hand and went in for a hug.

Lauren followed, saying, "Congratulations, Jacques, you're marrying the finest lady on earth, and your child will be blessed with the best mom ever."

"Ditto," said Kathy.

Kathy put her arms through Jacques's and walked toward the kitchen. "Something smells delicious. Elle can't cook, so this has to be your doing."

"Jacques loves to cook. He's made a fabulous dinner of coq au vin."

"My favorite!" exclaimed Lauren.

Jacques opened a bottle of wine. Removing his apron, he said, "Ladies, enjoy the dinner. I will catch up with you later this evening." Taking Elle in his arms, he kissed her and wished her a lovely evening.

"Where are you going?" asked Kathy.

"I'm going to the bar to watch a soccer game with a coworker."

Before Kathy or Lauren could stop him, Jacques rushed from the apartment.

"I was hoping to get to spend more time with that hunk of a man," said Lauren.

"That's my fault. I wanted to catch up with you guys, so I asked him to plan a night out with a coworker. He'll be back by eleven. You can ask all your questions then."

"This is amazing. Does Jacques cook all the meals?"

"Breakfast and dinner. Tomorrow, we are ordering Chinese. I need a break from all the rich foods."

"One thing Jake and I had in common, neither one of us could cook. We got really good at ordering out. I'm an awesome griller—chicken, steak, or fish. I'm your gal."

"We know. Remember the night you tried to make chicken parmesan? Who can mess up chicken parmesan?"

"I didn't know you had to place the chicken in the egg and then a dusting of flour. I thought you tossed it all together."

The girls broke out in laughter.

"How are the wedding plans going?"

"Everything is done, thanks to my mom. Kathy, I hope Derek is able to make it to the wedding. If I'm not mistaken, he had one more tour. Correct? Derek will be in Hawaii. I'm so sad he'll miss the wedding."

"He'll be there, Elle."

Lauren glanced at Kathy wondering if things were better between her and Derek. Elle was still in the dark regarding Kathy's present situation.

"Elle, you said you would tell us how all this came about. Where should we start—with you reconciling with your mother or Jacques showing up on your doorstep?"

"I'd rather start with Jacques showing up on my doorstep, Lauren."

Elle began to tell her story, finishing with why she never thought marriage and children were conceivable. When she finished, the girls wiped away the tears that had formed hearing of Liam's suicide.

"All these years you blamed yourself for the boy's death? Elle, I am so sorry. No child should ever have to carry such a heavy burden. I often wondered why you never spoke about your parents. When I met them at our graduation, there seemed to be a distance between you. Now it makes sense. I'm happy you got to hear your mom's side and that you were able to heal."

"I owe it all to the gypsy woman, Lauren. If I hadn't visited with her that day and heard her say I had to face the demon, I wouldn't have reached out to my mother."

"And if I hadn't visited the gypsy woman, I wouldn't have fought with Lauren, and I wouldn't have known that my husband is a perverted cheat."

Elle glanced at Lauren; her eyes questioned, *What's going on*?

"You're not the only one who had to face a demon, Elle. I just found out that Derek cheated on me with his publicist, Nina."

"Derek cheated on you?"

"You're shocked, why? He's the same man that threatened Lauren and Casey into a threesome. The man has no boundaries."

"How did you find out?"

Kathy told her story, ending with, "I should have kicked his ass to the curb. Instead, when he returns from Hawaii, he's moving back to our bedroom until I decide what my next move will be. Fanny will be back from her vacation, and the children are asking why Daddy is sleeping in the sick bedroom."

"I'm so sorry, Kathy."

"Lauren suggested therapy. All those late nights at the hospital, I should have figured something wasn't right. He had me fooled."

Lauren and Elle made eye contact.

"Kathy thinks Nina isn't Derek's first affair," said Lauren.

"Lauren believes Derek is telling the truth. He's even got her fooled."

"She might be right, Kathy. Derek doesn't strike me as the type to have a string of women waiting for him to call."

"I hired a private investigator. I need to know how many women he's slept with."

"And if you find out there aren't any other women, what next?" asked Elle.

"I don't have a clue. The children adore Derek, and that is why I've decided to take Lauren's advice."

"I told Kathy for her children's sake she should give therapy a try, but I'm the last person that should be giving marital advice. What do you think, Elle?"

"Therapy is the only way that you're going to find out if your marriage can survive. I do suggest that before you work on your marriage, you figure out if you've come to terms with what happened between Lauren and Derek in college."

"I've forgiven Lauren."

"Is it because you now see Lauren as a victim and Derek the villain?"

"He is a villain."

"He was a twenty-year-old testosterone male," corrected Elle. "If you discover that Derek is leading a double life, which I would be shocked if he where, therapy is a must for you and the children."

"Since that god-awful night in Cape May, I've had a lot of time to think about the situation in college. Derek sat in the corner and watched until Casey invited him to join in. I don't want to talk ill of the dead, but I think Casey enjoyed the threesome more than Derek and I. I know I was wrong for not telling you twenty-something years ago, and I'm sorry. But the affair with Nina has to take top priority if your marriage is going to survive," said Lauren.

Kathy pondered Lauren's advice.

"Elle, I told you I also had a life-changing experience. I met someone, and that someone is a girl, not a guy. I'm in love." Lauren told Elle how she met and fell in love with Shelby and how her loving Shelby cost her, her children. "Josh and Kelly are living with Jake, but Michelle told me Josh has already returned to school, and Jake agreed to allow Kelly to spend time in Paris with a friend."

"Jake didn't try to stop them?"

"No. I think he felt the three of them needed time to work things out. Michelle said he spent a lot of time talking with them but couldn't convince them that how I choose to live my life doesn't change that I'm still their mother, which I think is a crock of shit. Jake was devastated when I told him I was in love with a woman. He's questioning if I was gay while we were married. If he ever found out about my affair with Casey, I'm screwed."

"There are only three people that know about your affair with Casey. He'll never hear about it from me or Elle. I don't think Alice has anything to gain by telling Jake or the children."

"I'm not worried about Alice, Kathy. She and I have become close friends. She spent three hours on the phone with me after my children walked out on me. Elle speaks with Alice at least twice a month."

"We've become close. I told her about the baby and my wedding. I sent her a save-the-date card."

"That's good news. Now that I'm back in the loop, I'll give Alice a call," Kathy said.

The remainder of the weekend, Kathy and Lauren put their woes on hold to dot on Elle.

Kathy returned home to her children, and Lauren, to an empty house. Shelby was on tour for four weeks. Lauren welcomed the time to think about how to regain a relationship with her children.

CHAPTER 18

Nina patiently waited for the cab that would take her to the airport. The Hawaii tour was over, and she was happy to be moving on. She resigned her position after the California tour had ended. A publishing firm in New York City made her a sweet offer, which she accepted. She loved the city of Boston but was happy to leave it behind.

"What time is your flight?"

Nina turned to see Derek standing behind her. The two weeks they had spent together in paradise was difficult for Nina. She felt betrayed by the man. Derek's words never left her; he lost the love of his life for a cheap thrill, and she was the cheap thrill he was referring to. To discover she meant nothing to him was humiliating.

"Six."

"Six thirty. We can share a cab."

"I'd rather we didn't," Nina said. "I wouldn't want Kathy to hear we shared a cab. It's been nice working with you, Derek. I'm sorry for the way things turned out. I don't think I'll ever forgive myself for hurting Kathy. I hope you'll be able to work things out with your wife."

Derek frowned. "I heard you're leaving the firm?"

"I was offered a sweet deal from Random House, thanks to you. Your success was my ticket to an executive position."

"Congratulations. I'm happy for you, Nina. Nina, I never meant to hurt you, and I wish things could have turned out differently."

"Like your wife never finding out?"

Derek sighed. "Kathy's hurting, and I don't have a clue as to how our marriage can survive the affair."

"You'll have to convince her that I was just a cheap thrill."

Nina's cab showed up in time for her to turn her back on Derek, leaving him to ponder how deeply his words hurt her.

*****

Derek arrived home the following morning, and the house was empty. He went to their bedroom and placed his luggage on the bed, then began to unpack. After he finished, he lingered in front of their bed and stared at the place where she'd lain the night before. He heard the front door open. One person had entered the house. He heard her footsteps as she climbed the stairs. Opening the door, she found him staring at their bed.

'You're home."

"The plane landed at six this morning. I've booked a shuttle to DC. What time is your flight?"

"I'm leaving at six this evening."

"Of course, how many shuttle flights are there to DC? Are the plans the same?"

"What plans?"

Derek turned to face her. In the past, they would have embraced, and if the house was empty as it was now, they would have made love. Derek couldn't stop staring at her; she was beautiful. She was wearing running gear. Purple and pink were the colors of her sweat suit. Her face was flushed, the way she looked after making love. He wanted to take her in his arms and beg to be forgiven. He couldn't live without this woman. The two weeks they'd spent apart were unbearable.

"Is this where I'll be sleeping when we return home from Elle's wedding?"

"The plans are the same. I thought we should talk before the children and Fanny got home."

Derek collapsed on the bed.

"I thought you should know that I am seeing a therapist. I need to work on myself before I can wrap my head around your affair with Nina."

Derek nodded his head.

"You might want to do the same because if there is no hope of our marriage surviving your infidelity, then we have to do what is best for the children. I don't have a clue how to make the transition easy for them. My father never cheated on my mother. I grew up with two loving parents."

"No one knows what goes on behind closed doors."

"I'm offended by your comment. My father would never cheat on my mother. He's a man that can be trusted unlike yourself. It's obvious you have a dark side, something you've kept from me. You've always been somewhat controlling when we made love. I'm sure these other women filled your needs."

"There are no other women. And if you thought I was too rough with you, why didn't you say something?"

"I don't feel comfortable talking with you about our sex life."

"We've known each other since college—twenty-four years to be exact. During that time, I assumed we both enjoyed the toys you brought into our bed. Was I wrong?"

"Obviously, the toys weren't enough for you. I'm guessing you're into whips and chains."

"I had an affair. It was wrong. There were no whips or chains involved."

Kathy screamed, "Then why did you fuck another woman?"

"I crossed the line. It happened. I wish I could go back in time, but I can't. I know you're hurting, and I'm truly sorry for hurting you. If I need therapy to figure out why I cheated on you, then I'll sign up tomorrow. I need you to know that I love you. I'll never stop loving you. You are the last person in this world I've ever wanted to hurt. You, the kids, this house, the love we shared were precious to me. Knowing that I can lose it all because I made a mistake is killing me. But if I have to lose it all because that will make you happy, then I'll have to lose it all. All I want or I've ever wanted is to make you happy."

"Words, they're just words. They go in one ear and out the other. I won't be fooled by your words. We have the children to think of. As I stand before you, I don't give a shit if this marriage survives or crashes down around our heads. It's going to be difficult lying next to you in the same bed, not because I desire you, because I don't. After I heard what you did to Lauren, I lost a lot of sleep with images of you and Lauren lying naked. To my surprise, I haven't had one dream of you and Nina lying naked. You know why, Derek? She can have you because I'm done with you."

Kathy slammed the door behind her. Derek sat with his head in his hands. There was no coming back from the hurt Kathy was feeling. He'd lost it all because of the thrill and power he felt when his sexual demands were met.

*****

Lauren retrieved her cell phone and dialed Jake's number. Three weeks had gone by, and she hadn't heard from Josh or Jake. Kelly did text Lauren to say she was back in Paris. A friend, whose parents owned a home in Monaco, had invited her to stay. A letter arrived two days after Kelly's text.

> Mom, I wish I can say I've accepted your life choice, but I haven't. Mostly, I've been dealing with how this situation has affected Josh. He and I made a decision to return to our lives. Time away from the family, I hope will give us time to figure out our true feelings. You are and will always be my mom.
>
> Love, Kelly

Lauren had to speak with Jake. He answered on the first ring.
"Lauren."
"Hi, Jake. Thanks for taking my call. Do you have time to talk?"
"I have a meeting in ten minutes."
"I haven't heard from Josh. Have you spoken with him?"
"I have."
"How is he?"

"He's fine. He got a job and is looking forward to returning to school."

"I've left a thousand messages, but he hasn't returned my calls."

"I can't make him return your calls, Lauren."

"Does he ask about me?"

Jake didn't respond.

"He hasn't asked about me, has he?"

"He made it clear that I'm not to bring you up when we talk. I can't go against his wishes, Lauren. I'm not going to lose my son."

"Can you at least share with me their feelings?"

"You know how Josh feels. Kelly texted you, and she said she wrote you a letter."

"She did. She said, I will always be her mom." Lauren began to choke up.

"I'm happy for you."

"You're happy for me. My son won't even text me."

"You have to respect his feelings. He doesn't want to accept your relationship with this woman."

"I bet you had something to do with that."

"Are you accusing me of swaying the children? Well, you're wrong. I had time to think, and I've decided not to waste time wondering if our marriage was a farce. I have a good life with Michelle, and I'm happy to put the past behind me. You made your choice, Lauren. You chose this woman. If I were working to destroy your relationship with our children, Kelly wouldn't be texting and writing. Josh is a grown man, and you're asking him to sway to your way of thinking. You're in love, and you want him to accept your choice. He's not there yet, and I don't know if he will ever be."

"I just miss him so much. You were right. I shouldn't have told them. I should have ended it with Shelby."

"Don't beat yourself up, Lauren. I've gotten over judging you. If you truly love this woman, then who am I or anyone to deny you your happiness. When I fell in love with Michelle, I was sure I was going to lose the kids' love, but I didn't because you supported our relationship. I have spoken to the children. I've asked them not to judge, to accept that this woman makes you happy, but Josh isn't buying it. He's ashamed of you. Feels that your relationship with this woman is going to affect his life. He believes your notoriety as an author and your relationship with this woman will be found out by the tabloids. I can't deny I haven't had the same concerns. I think we have to let him figure things out on his own. He loves you, Lauren. That hasn't changed."

Lauren disconnected with Jake and dialed Josh's number. The call went to voice mail. She left the same message, ending with "I love you, and I miss you. Please call me."

*****

Kathy and Derek arrived at the hotel in DC. "I didn't have time to book a room, I hope there is one available."

"Elle booked a room for us. I requested double beds."

Derek wasn't surprised that Kathy had shared his infidelities with Lauren, and Elle. "Does Jake know that I—"

"If you don't want Jake to know, that's your business. He won't hear it from Lauren, Elle, or me. If the marriage doesn't survive, you can tell him whatever lie you want. You seem to have a knack for lying."

*****

Lauren met Michelle and Jake in the lobby. The meeting at first was uncomfortable. Michelle broke the ice. "Have you heard from Elle?"

"They're at the bar. Jacques's whole family flew in for the wedding."

"She told me. Originally, she thought only the immediate family."

"I guess the Pascal family are close. Hi, Jake."

"Hi, Lauren."

Lauren's phone buzzed. "It's Kathy. Derek and she arrived at eight." Lauren texted back:

We are at the bar.

Trudy greeted Lauren, Michelle, and Jake. "Where's Kathy?"

"They're on their way down."

"Alice is at the bar talking with my brother, Charles. There's the handsome couple."

Lauren turned. Kathy walked toward her, leaving Derek several paces behind.

Kathy hugged Lauren. Lauren glanced at Jake. Last time she and Jake spoke, she was concerned about Jose. Kathy and her reconciliation was farthest from her mind.

Derek shook Jake's hand and kissed Michelle on the cheek.

Lauren smiled at Derek. She placed her hand on his arm to assure him there were no hard feelings.

He covered his hand over hers and mouth, "Thank you, Lauren."

Alice came to hug her friends and to introduce her new friend. "And this beautiful lady is Rita."

Lauren gave Alice a glance of approval. "It's a pleasure to meet you, Rita."

Elle joyfully joined her friends. "You all look marvelous. I want to introduce you to Jacques's family. There are fifty of them, and it's impossible for me to remember all their names."

When the uncomfortable feelings among friends subsided, they were able to have an enjoyable evening with the happy couple.

*****

"I'm exhausted. I thought this was going to be a small affair. I didn't know Elle had these many friends."

"I think Uncle Charlie's a hoot. If I leave Derek, I'm hooking up with him."

"He's handsome and rich."

"I have handsome and rich. I'm looking for faithful."

"I don't think Uncle Charlie is the faithful type."

"Where is Shelby?"

"She was busy, and truth be told, I'm happy she's not here. I'm not ready to deal with Jake's reaction to Shelby's playful kisses."

*****

"This is a really nice room."

"As a gift to Elle and Jacques, the network blocked out the entire floor for family and friends."

"Elle's worth it."

Derek's heart leaped when Kathy appeared before him dressed in a beautiful dark-blue satin dress. She was wearing the necklace he had given her not so long ago.

"I hate to ask, but can you help with the zipper?"

Derek came behind Kathy and slowly zipped her dress. When his thumb touched her skin, she felt warm. She immediately stepped away from him.

He sat on the bed and watched as she filled her evening bag. "I don't have any room for my phone."

"I have my phone."

"I like to carry my phone, just in case Fanny calls."

"If she can't reach you, she'll call me."

"Whatever. Lauren was pleasant with you last night. Did she surprise you?"

"I didn't give it much thought."

"How could you not? Your little secret was out of the bag. Three people at the table know what you did to her. The only person that isn't privy to your bad behavior is Jake."

Derek didn't answer.

Lauren's knock on the door put an end to an uncomfortable situation.

"It's Lauren, I'll get it."

Kathy opened the door, and Lauren whistled, "Wow, that dress looks great on you."

"You don't look to shabby."

"Do you like? This dress cost me more than what Elle paid for her wedding dress."

Kathy yelled back at Derek. "Lauren and I are going to help Elle, see you later."

*****

Elle's hairdresser was finishing up her coiffure. The tiniest of pearls were scattered throughout Elle's hair.

"The pearls are a nice touch," said Lauren.

Elle smiled. "They cost me a small fortune." Elle removed her robe. "It's time, ladies."

Kathy and Lauren helped Elle into her wedding dress.

When she turned to face them, she asked, "Well?"

The dress Elle chose was a classic—a strapless full-length dress in ivory crepe with a sweep brush train. The bodice was slightly gathered and a wedding sash of blush rhinestones and baby pearls surrounded her waist. A sensible addition to camouflage the beginning of a baby bump. A long circular sheer veil was placed at the nape of her neck. The veil was trimmed with the same embellishment as the wedding sash. The bride chose a small bouquet of pale-yellow roses and white calla lilies. The yellow roses were a remembrance of her dear friend Casey.

Tears welled in Kathy's eyes. "Elle, you look stunning."

"Amazing, Elle."

There was a knock on the door, and Uncle Charlie opened the door slowly. "Is everyone decent?"

"Come in, Uncle Charlie."

"Your mother is going berserk."

"Charles, stop being so dramatic." When Trudy stepped into the room and saw her daughter, her eyes began to well. "Elle, you look beautiful."

"Are you sure, Mom?"

Trudy smiled. "Yes. You're glowing, sweetheart. We do have a slight problem. Some of Jacques's family members are running a little late. Jacques's mom asked that we delay the wedding by twenty minutes. Jacques's language has been harsh because the minister has another wedding this afternoon, and he must leave no later than five. He's really upset, Elle."

Uncle Charlie chimed in. "The truth is your future father-in-law tied one on with his brother at last night's dinner. You might have that baby before papa can pull himself together."

Elle chuckled. "Mom, French people curse to release stress. Tell the minister to cut out the fluff and get right to the I-dos. Uncle Charlie has a point. I'd like to be married before I deliver this child."

Fifteen minutes later, Jacques's father was placed in the front row. Once papa was settled, Jacques and his brother stood beside the minister. The procession began when the pianist began to play the Christmas Canon. Kathy and Lauren walked side by side. When all were in place, Elle placed her arm through Uncle Charlie's arm, and they began to walk down the aisle. When she reached Jacques, he leaned in and whispered in Elle's ear, "Vous etes belle, mon amour."

Hearing Jacques speak words of love to Elle caused Kathy to glance at Derek. His eyes were fixed on the couple. When he glanced in Kathy's direction, she looked away.

Elle and Jacques wrote their own vows. There might have been twist and turns along the way to getting to this day, but no one could deny the couple had found their fairy-tale ending.

The wedding guests were served a five-course dinner. Dessert consisted of a three-tier lemon cake layered with French cream, covered with fondant icing. Inserted into the fondant icing were candy rhinestones and pearls. The couple playfully placed a smudge of cake on each other's lips. Jacques asked that the music begin. He offered his hand to his bride and escorted her to the dance floor. Several minutes later, he asked their guests to join them.

Lauren's mood shifted as she watched Jake, Michelle, Alice, Rita, and the happy couple cruise along the dance floor. Kathy immediately excused herself saying, she had to use the bathroom to avoid dancing with Derek.

"I can use a little fresh air, care to join me?"

Derek stood.

"It's a beautiful night."

"It is."

"How are things going?"

"I wish I could say, great! As you know, we are seeing therapists."

"I know."

"Lauren, I owe you a long overdue apology. I'm so sorry. There are no excuses or words I can offer to make what happened between us in college right."

"I never meant to tell Kathy. Things got heated that night, and I blurted it out."

"I'm not upset with you, Lauren. I'm upset with myself. I took it for granted that when we agreed not to tell Kathy, that put an end to it. I never considered your feelings. There is no excuse except I was only thinking of myself. I wish Casey were here, so I could apologize to her."

Lauren sighed. "She would have been over the moon to see Elle happy." Lauren paused. "I didn't much like you back in college, and I sure as hell didn't trust you. I thought Kathy was setting herself up to have her heart broken. You proved me wrong until now. Why, Derek?"

"I screwed up. I don't think Kathy will ever forgive me. I'm just biding my time."

"I hope that isn't so. I want to kill you for hurting that beautiful woman, but I'm hoping she finds it in her heart to forgive you. Maybe Nina was a mistake. In the heat of the moment, you forgot you were married and the father of five children. I know you love our girl, so I'm going to hope Nina was the first and last. I don't have to tell you when a man cheats, it sends a message to the woman that she isn't worth the ground she walks on."

*****

Elle and Jacques spent a glorious week in St. Bart's, relaxing on the beach, where Elle slept half the day away. The other half, they were playful in the ocean, and at night, they made love under the stars.

CHAPTER 19

Since Derek moved back into their bedroom, both tossed and turned the entire night. Kathy knew that Derek wished things could be as they were, and she hated herself for sharing the same feelings. But if he did attempt to touch her, she wasn't sure how she would react. Of course, she'd have to turn him away.

Her therapist harped on Kathy and Derek's sex life prior to the affair.

"You said your sex life took a turn after Lauren told you about the threesome. Have you had sex since hearing of Derek's affair with Nina?"

"No."

"Prior to the affair, did you enjoy a healthy sex life with your husband?"

"Yes."

"Did he satisfy you, and were there times you had to fake an orgasm just to please him?"

Kathy thought the questions ridiculous. "I never faked an orgasm. If I had to rate my husband as a lover from one to ten, he'd score a twenty."

"Did your friend Lauren and you ever discuss her sexual relationship with your husband?"

"Are you asking if Lauren and I ever compared notes? The answer is no."

"Are you curious to know how she would rate your husband as a lover?"

"Never crossed my mind."

"You said, after hearing of Lauren's encounter with Derek, your sex life was affected by images of your husband and your friend lying naked together."

"Yes. But I haven't thought of them together for a while."

"What changed?"

"What happened between Derek and Lauren was—"

Dr. Hunter waited for Kathy to finish her sentence. "What are you thinking right now?"

"Derek said he never thought Lauren and Casey would go through with the threesome. He said if they would have said no, he had no intentions of spreading rumors about Lauren."

"Do you believe him?"

"Lauren said at first Derek didn't participate."

"Was he turned on by watching the two?"

"Lauren said he looked embarrassed. She said Casey had to ask him several times to join them."

Kathy closed her eyes and gathered her thoughts. "Derek said he was just being a guy. Elle and Lauren don't believe what transpired in college makes Derek a perverted monster."

"Yet you've accused him of being perverted. I believe the issue here is that you are finding it hard to separate the actions of a twenty-year-old male from the man he is today. You've forgiven Lauren, why?"

"Lauren was a victim, and Derek placed her in that position. If he was capable of threatening two women at twenty years of age, what makes you think he isn't capable of doing it today? We had a good sex life, yet he cheated on me. Something doesn't add up."

"Was he forceful with you during sex?"

"After hearing about his encounter in college, I did concentrate on his treatment of me during sex."

"Did he make demands of you that were unbearable?"

Dr. Hunter waited for Kathy to answer, but she didn't.

"I'm assuming after hearing of the affair, you've abstained from having sex with your husband?"

"Of course. He's lost that privilege."

"You've described your sex life saying it wasn't uncommon for you and him to indulge any time during the day or night, if the time was right. You allowed him back into your bed. How do you manage to control the urge? Are you masturbating? Do you think Derek is satisfied with masturbation?"

"He just spent two weeks in Hawaii with Nina. I'm sure masturbating was off the table."

"You don't believe he ended it with Nina. You believe there were a number of affairs, and he won't stop his bad behavior. You believe there were signs based on his encounter with your friend Lauren. You've admitted you've hired a private investigator, and nothing so far."

"So if he comes up smelling like a rose, I should forgive him for screwing Nina and move on? Is that your advice?"

"I'll ask you the same question. If you find nothing to prove that your husband has a dark side, then what? Your husband had an affair, and that hurts like hell. You're a beautiful woman. Sex wasn't an issue. You say you were blindsided because you never doubted how much Derek loved you, still loves you. So the question is, can you live with a man who cheated? If the answer is no, should you tell him it's over? If you're still in love with the man, can you envision life without him? How can you trust a man who cheated on you? Are you afraid if you allow yourself to love him, he'll hurt you again? Does he deserve your love? I know you've asked yourself these same questions, a million times. And you've answered them a million times and changed your mind a million times. What we have to do is get to the answer that is right for you."

After her appointment with Dr. Hunter, Kathy sat in the car and sobbed. She couldn't admit to Dr. Hunter that lying next to her husband and not being able to touch him was exhausting. But she had spent many sleepless nights asking, why Nina? She could hound Derek for an answer, but the answer would be the same. He didn't know why Nina; it just happened. It was a mistake he wished he could go back and change.

*****

Life in the Wilson house went on as usual. Kathy was pleasant to Derek when the children or Fanny were nearby. Derek returned the same pleasantries. Derek sought counseling as Kathy had suggested, not because Kathy had suggested counseling, but because he needed to know what made him tick. It was a first in their marriage—working on a problem not as a couple but individually.

*****

Derek waited for Dr. Cooper to return. When Derek first met with Dr. Cooper, he felt uncomfortable. He would have preferred a therapist who didn't know him. To find one who didn't, he'd have to move to Madagascar.

The door to the office opened, and Dr. Cooper expressed his apologies.

"Sorry for the interruption."

"Is everything all right?"

"Yes."

Derek smiled. If Hank Cooper went on to explain why he was called away, the conversation would be casual doctor to doctor. Derek respected the man's values as a professional. He was the patient, and Hank's role was to find out what made Derek tick and fix him.

"Last time we spoke, you said that Kathy asked you to move back to your bedroom, so the children wouldn't become confused. Do you think that was her only reason, or was it a sign that she might be willing to work things out?"

"Kathy is a mama bear when it comes to her cubs. She doesn't want to upset the children until she can figure out if she wants me to stay or leave. We also have a live-in nanny, Fanny. Kathy's very protective of her as well."

"You're sleeping in the same bed, correct?"

"Yes."

"Has there been physical contact?"

"No."

"Was sex with your wife satisfying?"

"Hell yes. We never had a problem in the bedroom. Sex with Kathy is amazing. If your next question is, how often? Didn't matter what time of the day. If the opportunity presented itself, we made love. After our first two were born, and my work schedule at the hospital, making love was often in the afternoon or early mornings. Once we hired Fanny, things got easier, and we were able to sneak off whenever the urge hit."

"How are you handling abstinence?"

"Like every other guy, I masturbate."

"If you had a healthy sex life with your wife, what excited you about this other woman that caused you to be unfaithful to your wife? Was alcohol or drugs involved?"

"No."

"Dr. Wilson, for me to understand and help you, you need to be truthful. You stated that Nina was your first and only affair, correct?"

Derek began to sweat. The first time Dr. Cooper asked this question, Derek lied. Then and now, he was embarrassed to say, one other time. Should he also confess to threatening Lauren and Casey into a threesome? His encounter with Lauren and Casey might have been the start to his bad behavior. The angel on his shoulder was telling him to fess up, tell the truth.

"There are two other times in my life that I'm not proud of. That is why I neglected to tell you the truth."

Derek confessed to the first time he cheated. With great anxiety, he spoke about the encounter in college.

"I never thought my friends would agree. I was sure they wouldn't show. I had no intentions of spreading rumors about Lauren. My plan was to call them out when our paths crossed by saying, 'I knew you wouldn't show,' and leave it at that. After the first time I got a call from Casey, she wanted to know when we could meet again. We were together a handful of times. Out of the blue, Kathy accepted my offer to a movie and a burger afterward. I knew the girls were friends, so I begged them not to tell. Two years ago, while the girls were vacationing together, Lauren told my wife the truth. Kathy and Lauren got into a heated argument, and Lauren said she wouldn't be surprised if I had been unfaithful. Lauren's words caused Kathy to end her relationship with her. They didn't speak for two years. When Kathy found out about the affair, she reconciled with Lauren."

Humiliated, Derek said, "Kathy doesn't know about the nurse. I know she's been looking under very rock, and I swear, she isn't going to find anything. The affair with the nurse ended when her husband was transferred to Seattle. One time, she hinted that her marriage was on shaky grounds. She might have divorced her husband and moved away or remarried. Anyway, we weren't together long enough for any of our coworkers to suspect there was something going on. Now you know everything. Two affairs and an encounter I thought was dead and buried but has come back to haunt me."

"How did your wife handle hearing of your encounter in college?"

"She was appalled."

"Your marriage was in trouble before Kathy discovered you had cheated on her."

"She never told me she found out about the threesome. She acted a little strange when she returned home from the trip, but a few months later, everything was back to normal."

"Did you question why she wasn't speaking with Lauren?"

"Yes. But Lauren has a way of being condescending toward Kathy. Kathy said Lauren treated her badly, and she felt it was time to end their friendship. She asked me not to get involved. She said I should respect her decision, and I did. Never in my wildest dreams did I think that Lauren had told her the truth."

"So Kathy is dealing with the affair and that you were intimate with her best friend, correct?"

"Yes. She keeps saying I have a dark side. Kathy said I never considered how my treatment of Lauren might have affected her. She's right. The shame and humiliation I put Lauren through might have caused her enormous pain. I have two daughters, Dr. Cooper. I now know how wrong I was."

"Has Casey shared the same feelings as Lauren?"

"Casey died four years ago, cancer."

After leaving Dr. Cooper's office, Derek drove to the hospital. He sat in his car for twenty minutes. He could have gone home, but the session with Dr. Cooper left him feeling like shit. Having to admit you're not an upright guy caused Derek to wonder if he had a soul.

*****

Derek froze when Dr. Cooper asked, "Do you intend to tell Kathy about the first time you cheated on her?"

"I do not. Does it matter if I cheated on her once or twice? I cheated. She's in so much pain. I don't think hurting her more than I have is fair. It won't change anything, except the fact that she'll hate me more than she already does. I want to save my marriage, not end it. I swear on my children's lives, it will never happen again."

Dr. Cooper took a moment before speaking. "Honesty is the best policy in my book, but it's not my truth to tell. Let's work on the two times you were unfaithful. Why the nurse?"

Derek went on to explain how the affair began.

"It was your first difficult and successful surgery. You must have been walking on air. This woman, the nurse, she was impressed. What did Kathy say when you told her?"

"She was happy for me. She knew how hard I worked to prove to my colleagues and myself that I had what it takes to be a damn good surgeon. But Kathy, well—I know she's proud of me."

"What was the nurse's reaction?"

"She was impressed."

"It was an innocent encounter. You were on your way home. She stopped you and congratulated you, and then offered to buy you a drink."

"Yes."

"Why didn't you refuse the drink?"

"It was late. I knew Kathy would be sound asleep. As you said, I was walking on air, so I made the mistake of accepting."

"While you were at the bar, what was the topic of conversation?"

"It was so long ago. Obviously, we talked about the surgery."

"Can you remember anything she might have said?"

"I do. She went on about how wonderful it was to see me in action. She said, when the word got out that I was a miracle worker in scrubs, the top surgeons would be shaking in their shoes."

"Amazing, you remembered every word."

"You don't forget words as powerful as those."

"Did you enjoy making love to this woman?"

Derek's face began to flush. "The sex was good."

"Equal to or better than sex with your wife?"

"I told you, sex with Kathy is amazing. Sex with this woman was different."

"In what way?"

"This is very embarrassing."

"We're just two guys having a conversation."

Derek smiled. "We are. Well, if we are two guys having a conversation, then she pretty much did whatever I asked. Let's say, nothing was off the table."

"Such as?"

"There were no chains or whips if that's what you're asking, but she did like it rough."

"Are you rough with your wife?"

"I see where you're going with this line of question. Do I like it rough? I like to be in control."

The timer went off announcing the session had ended.

*****

Kathy wasn't in the mood to be grilled, but she was committed to finding out why her husband was unfaithful.

Dr. Hunter began the session by saying, "Most of our talks have been about Derek's cheating and the threesome with your friend in college. Today, I would like to talk about your childhood."

Kathy explained her childhood was perfect, two loving parents, and an older brother who had his younger sister's back.

"Max lives in England. He's a tech nerd. Great job, makes lots of money. My mom said he's seeing someone. He's a good-looking guy, but he didn't date much. The girls would stick around for a month or two, but lost interest when they couldn't compete with Steve Jobs."

"Were you popular in school?"

"I was a nerd like my brother, but that didn't stop me from having a great time in high school. But it wasn't until college that I truly felt I fit in."

"Can you explain why?"

"Well, I was always the prettiest girl in high school. I only had one true friend and two boyfriends. I got a lot of attention from the boys. The boys thought I was a dick tease. I don't know why. It wasn't like I came on to them and then dropped them like a hot potato. The other girls put up with me. Teenagers can be cruel. I was head cheerleader. I was captain of the soccer team and the debate team. I formed a science group to tutor kids that were struggling. I was class president my junior and senior year. As Lady Gaga sang, I was born this way."

"Why was college different?"

"I met three amazing women. They were beautiful and smart."

"They were your equals."

"I guess. College was different. I don't know why, but I didn't find that the women I met in college were intimidated by my looks. Going from high school to my freshman year in college shouldn't have made that big of a difference, but it did. I no longer felt like the most beautiful girl in the room."

"In high school—the girls who were intimidated by your looks and treated you unkind—did that have an adverse effect on you?"

"I didn't let it bother me. If you're asking if I struggled with depression in high school, no."

Dr. Hunter smiled.

"Are you questioning my sincerity?"

"Absolutely not. I admire you. Most of the teens I work with who are struggling in school find it hard to get out of bed in the morning."

Kathy sighed. "Yes. The rate of suicide among young people today is discouraging. Dr. Hunter, these questions about my looks, although at times were confusing to me as a teen, where are they leading?" Kathy didn't wait for an answer. "The reason I signed up for therapy was to see if my marriage was worth saving. Derek says his affair with Nina was a mistake. I hired a private investigator, and Nina is the only woman my husband crossed the line with. I don't think I'll ever get an answer to 'Why Nina?'"

The timer went off ending the session.

CHAPTER 20

November 15. Jake called to say that Josh was home for the Thanksgiving break. He had spoken with their son, and Josh had agreed to give Lauren a call.

Several days later, Lauren's cell buzzed.

She was sitting at her computer working when she reached for her cell phone. Josh's picture appeared on the screen.

"Josh."

"Hi, Mom."

"Your dad called to say you arrived at his home on Monday. Can I convince you to spend a few days at the cottage, of course, after Thanksgiving?"

"No. I thought we could meet in the city. We can meet for lunch."

"I'd love to meet you. Where, when, and what time?"

"What about Thursday, one o'clock, at Triumph?"

"Thursday works for me. I'll book a room at the Hilton for two days. Christmas is right around the corner. I can get some shopping done while I'm in the city. Maybe you and I can see a movie or a play or just hang out?" Josh didn't respond, and Lauren decided not to push him.

"I'll see you on Thursday," he said.

"I'm looking forward to seeing you. It's been a while."

*****

From the Cape to Boston, it was clear sailing. The second Lauren hit the city limits, traffic had crawled to a standstill. She checked the time—twelve fifteen. At this pace, she wasn't going to make it to the restaurant by one. She dialed Josh's cell. No answer. She left him a voice mail, saying she was stuck in traffic, not to leave, and she was on her way.

Arriving at the restaurant fifteen minutes late, she tossed her car keys at the attendant. Entering the restaurant, she glanced around the room, and seeing Josh, she walked toward the table.

"I'm so sorry. It was clear sailing until I hit the city." When Josh didn't stand to greet her, she leaned in and kissed his cheek. "Thank you for meeting me." Lauren sat across from him and smiled. "So how are things at your dad's? How's Michelle feeling, and your little baby sister, Grace? I love the name. It was one of the names your father and I were considering when we found out we were expecting a girl. Michelle was a week early, correct? Nice Thanksgiving gift for the family."

"Yes."

Lauren sighed, thinking, *This day is off to a great start.* "Aunt Elle and Michelle were due around the same time, but the doctors think Aunt Elle's baby won't arrive until after Thanksgiving. I was thinking of spending a few days with Aunt Elle, after Thanksgiving, of course. Can I talk you into driving down with me? I can sure use the company. Aunt Elle would love to see you. If we leave early Friday morning, I promise to have you back by Monday. Your flight isn't until Tuesday, correct?"

"Sorry, Mom. I have a lot of school work to catch up on before I head back."

Lauren decided to drop the subject. "What are your plans for Christmas?"

"Christmas is a long way off."

The waitress interrupted Lauren's next question, by asking, "Can I get you something to drink?"

"I'll have a glass of Riesling and a glass of ice water with lemon."

"I'll have a Coke, lots of ice, please."

"I'll give you a chance to look over the menu."

Lauren glanced at the menu. "What looks good?"

"I'm having a New York cheese steak sandwich."

"That's brave of you, a New York cheese steak sandwich at a Boston pub." Josh didn't laugh at Lauren's joke. "The cheese steak sandwich does sound good."

When the waitress returned with their drinks, Lauren placed the order for two New York cheese steaks and a large order of fries smothered with cheese. Josh's favorite.

"I don't want fries, Mom." Talking directly to the waitress, Josh asked for a side salad.

"Do you still want the fries?"

Lauren answered, "Yes, but can you place the cheese on the side and not on the fries? Thank you."

"If you're considering having the chocolate soufflé, it takes thirty minutes to prepare and should be placed with your order. Will you be having dessert?"

"I would love to try the chocolate soufflé," said Lauren. "Can you place a scoop of salted caramel vanilla ice cream on the side?" Another of Josh's favorites.

"That can be arranged."

"Thanks." When the waitress left, Lauren asked, "So how are things at school? How's the calculus class going? I hated calculus. Aunt Kathy tutored me the entire two years. Have you met anyone special?"

"School is good. I hired a tutor. Last marking period, I got a B in calculus. I date, but nothing serious."

"Great."

The waitress placed the cheese steaks before them, a plate of fries between them, and the side salad next to Josh's plate. They ate in silence. The tension between them caused Lauren to devour the fries, while Josh ate his side salad and didn't touch one fry.

When the plates were removed, Lauren asked, "Why haven't you returned my phone calls?"

"I wasn't ready to talk."

"Is that why you invited me to lunch? Are you ready to talk?"

"We've talked about school. There isn't anything more to talk about."

"Your sister calls once a week. We don't discuss my life, but at least I know she's alive."

"If something happened to me, I'm sure you'd be notified."

"Let's cut to the chase. I would never discuss my private life with you, Josh, I know how uncomfortable that makes you feel, but you can bring me up to date on what's going on in your life and school. I can tell you how my latest novel is going. We can talk about the family and our friends. Not returning one's calls is disrespectful."

"I knew this was a bad idea. I don't want to hurt you, Mom. You had my respect until you tore my world apart."

The waitress interrupted, asking if they would like coffee with their dessert.

"I'll have a cup of black coffee, please," said Lauren.

"Nothing for me."

"It does hurt to hear that you've lost all respect for me because I don't live up to your expectations of me."

"I wanted you to be happy. I was hoping you'd find a nice guy and settle down."

"Even if I found a nice guy, I don't want to marry. My being away from home so often was a problem for your father."

"You said you were in love with this woman. I think you would want to live under one roof."

"Her name is Shelby. Her career is in Manhattan. She also does some traveling. We haven't discussed what the future will bring." Lauren was lying to her son. On several occasions, Shelby had hinted that Lauren and she should move in together.

"If you were just going to screw this woman, then why come out? Why mess with my head?"

"I wanted you to hear the truth from me and not some stranger."

"I didn't want to hear the truth from you or a stranger. You should have considered me and Kelly's feelings before you got involved with this person. No, you should have considered how your being gay was going to affect me, your son."

The waitress placed the dessert between Lauren and Josh. "Coffee, black, correct?"

"Yes."

"Enjoy."

Lauren reached for the spoon and dug into the soufflé and then scooped up a large amount of ice cream. After swallowing another three spoons of soufflé, she felt sick. She dropped the spoon on the plate.

"I know this isn't easy for you, but we have to find a way to work this out. You can't ex me, your mother, from your life. I love you. I miss talking with you."

"I hope you don't allow this woman to spend time with you at the Cape. If you're floating around town with her, people are going to ask questions. Your face is plastered on book covers. If one person thinks there might be something between you and this woman, my life will be ruined."

"Why? You have friends with gay parents. This is the twenty-first century, Josh."

"I wasn't born into this situation. I had a father and a mother. Now I have a father, a stepmom, and a mother who recently announced she's gay. I can't deal with all the crap, Mom."

"All right. I understand, but if we find a way to communicate, we might be able to work through this. What about therapy?"

"My school is in Pennsylvania."

"We can do a virtual therapy session. Once a week, an hour of your time."

"You think therapy is going to help? It's not. It doesn't change the fact that you are gay and sleeping with a woman."

"I deserve to be happy. Don't you want me to be happy?"

"At this point, I don't care if you're happy or not. I only care about myself and my feelings. You're trying to find a way for us to be a family. Dad talked me into this lunch. I didn't want to meet you because I didn't want to have this conversation. I don't want to see a therapist with you. I want you to stop calling me and texting. I don't want to see you, and I don't want to meet your lover."

Josh rose and rushed from the restaurant. Lauren sat frozen staring at the empty chair across from her.

*****

Lauren was going to cancel her room at the Hilton. She changed her mind, realizing she was too upset to drive, so she checked into the hotel. Friday, she lay in bed the entire day and cried. There were several texts from Shelby, and ten voice mails asking her to call. Saturday, Lauren took a long walk around the Boston harbor. She ate a late lunch, returned to her room, and went back to bed. Sunday, she checked out of the hotel and headed home.

Her cell buzzed. Shelby's face appeared on the screen.

"Hello."

"Lauren, why haven't you returned my phone calls?"

"I can't talk, Shelby. I'm driving."

"By the sound of your voice, I'm assuming things didn't go well with Josh."

"Exactly."

"So why didn't you drive to Manhattan?"

"I need to go back to the Cape, Shelby. I hope you understand." Lauren disconnected the call.

*****

A week later, she arrived in Washington, DC, to have Thanksgiving dinner with Elle and her family. Shelby hadn't called, and Lauren didn't reach out to her. She assumed that Shelby would get the hint and move on with someone else. Lauren didn't feel she'd earned the right to be happy. She wouldn't find her fairy-tale ending. She called Kathy as soon as she arrived home and told her the words Josh had used to solidify the end of their relationship. Kathy asked if Lauren had reached out to Jake. She hadn't, but several days later, Jake had called to see how she was doing. She shared the same story with Jake. His reaction was to give Josh time. He was sure as the adult boy grew older, he would change his mind and reconsider reconciling with Lauren.

When Jacques answered the door, he embraced Lauren, kissing her on both cheeks.

"So good of you to come, Lauren. Elle has been counting down the days."

"Lauren."

Lauren smiled when she saw Elle sprawled out on the sofa. Her stomach was so large Lauren couldn't see her face.

"You're sure there's only one child in there?" Leaning down, she kissed her friend on the forehead. Elle raised her feet and asked Lauren to sit. She placed her feet on Lauren's lap. "Your ankles are swollen. You have to kick this kid out, Elle."

"I've tried everything. I take long walks with Jacques's help. I cruise the apartment three hours a day."

Trudy entered the apartment. "Lauren, when did you get in?"

"I just got here. Our girl is bursting at the seam."

Uncle Charlie and Elaine were behind Trudy, each holding several grocery bags. Jacques took the bags from Trudy and Elaine.

"We've tried everything, Lauren," said Jacques. "Nothing is working. This baby is happy right where it is."

"The doctor wanted to induce, but I wanted to spend Thanksgiving with Jacques. I'm so happy you're here, Lauren."

*****

Lauren slept in the baby's room. The correct word would be the baby's *suite*. Staring at all the baby things conjured up memories of when Lauren brought Josh home from the hospital. She and Jake were afraid to leave him alone, so Jake slept on the rocking chair for three nights. When Jake would bring Josh to her to feed, she and Jake would stare at him in disbelief. She began to cry. Losing Josh was destroying every fiber of her being.

Thanksgiving Day helped keep Lauren from thinking of Josh 24/7. Friday afternoon, Elle and Lauren took a walk to the park. Lauren supported Elle, who seemed to be favoring her right side.

"Are you all right?"

"Back pain. Started this morning."

"Elle, backaches are a sign of labor."

"I know, but I don't want Jacques and my mom to get their hopes up and then nothing."

"Better you should go into labor at the park?"

"You act like you never had a baby. Even if I'm starting labor, I'm a long way off from having this baby."

"You look like a whale. I don't think it's going to be a long delivery. I think we should go back."

"Let's just sit here for a little while. Fresh air is good for the baby. And I need to know what is going on with you? Yesterday, you were quiet, and the rims of your eyes are red from crying. What's up?"

"I had lunch with Josh."

"I'm guessing that didn't go well."

"He hates me, Elle. He said he didn't want to hurt me, but he did. He doesn't want me to call him or text. He doesn't want to see me ever again."

Elle reached for Lauren's hand. "I'm so sorry, Lauren."

"Why didn't I listen to Jake? I shouldn't have told the kids. I should have sent Shelby away, like I did Casey. What was I thinking?"

"You were thinking with your heart. Did you tell Shelby what Josh said?"

"I had a meltdown after speaking with Josh. I spent two days at the Hilton, in bed, mourning the loss of my son. I didn't answer Shelby's calls or texts. When she finally reached me, after I told her, I hung up on her. She hasn't called, and I haven't called her. It's over."

"I'm sorry. Maybe it's for the best. Shelby wants a life with you. She won't accept being placed on the back burner. It might be best to let this one go."

"You're right. I need to get away. I think I'll go visit Kelly, after the holidays."

"Sounds like a great idea."

*****

Elle knocked on Lauren's door. When there was no answer, she let herself in. "Lauren, wake up."

"What's wrong, Elle?"

"My water broke."

At six in the morning, Elle delivered a healthy baby boy, eight pounds, nine ounces. Jacques was passing out cigars to everyone—male, female, young, and old. Trudy had to take back the cigars he gave to the children. She came prepared. With their parents' permission, she offered the children a lollipop.

"*Mon amour*, he's beautiful."

Jacques and Elle stared at the child who was asleep in his mother's arms.

"He's amazing. He has ten fingers and ten toes. I checked. Did you call your parents?"

"My mother, how you say, 'Is over the moon.' What name did you decide on, Mama?"

"None of the ones we talked about. Don't be upset with me, but I already had a name in mind. I want to name him Liam James."

Jacques smiled. "It's a beautiful name."

*****

Elle was in love. Liam James was her world. Lauren and Trudy remained with her for two weeks. Liam was colic, and Lauren was ready to jump off the roof. Trudy graciously did all the things one does for a colic child. Jacques had scheduled to take three weeks off work. Elle sent him back after a week.

Once Trudy and Lauren had returned home, when her baby cried, which was every two hours, Elle went to him. She ran the dryer and placed his little body in the carrier and held it tight as he bounced up and down. In the day, she walked him around DC, showing him the points of interest. From all the walking she did, the baby weight was melting away. Elle tried to ease herself out of bed without waking Jacques, but Liam's screams woke him from a sound sleep.

"I'll warm a bottle."

"I'm going to try to breastfeed him. Stay in bed."

"It's never enough. I'll warm a bottle."

Although Liam's sucking at her breast was painful, Elle didn't mind. She sang to the child. Jacques would arrive with a warm bottle, which included sleeping drops. Liam would suck at the bottle, and drift off for another two hours. Elle found that Liam was quiet when she danced with him. She'd hum her favorite Bruce Springsteen song and gently sway back and forth. She loved being a mother and didn't find it one bit exhausting. The dark circles around her eyes told a different story.

Three months later, she woke, checked the time, and jumped from her bed. She ran to her son's room, where she found Liam asleep. Her baby had slept for five hours. Each night, he went down earlier and woke at six. Liam cried less, ate at the required time, and began to take longer naps. Life was good. Jacques spoke to his child in French and English, and Liam responded with a sound Jacques swore was a giggle.

After six months, Elle returned to work. She first spent two months with Liam's nanny, Jane. Reluctantly, she returned to work, leaving Liam in Jane's care. Jacques began to arrive at work at six thirty. Twice a week, he'd lunch at home and spend two hours with their son. Elle was jealous. When her work day ended, she'd return home to find Liam sleeping. Depression was setting in, but as Liam grew, his bedtime was extended to eight, so Elle could have two hours with her child. Weekends were entirely devoted to Liam. Jacques found a teenage girl, who lived in their building, who offered to babysit. Once Liam was down for the night, she and Jacques would have a romantic dinner at a fancy restaurant. Indulging in two glasses of wine, so the night would end with them lying naked, breathless.

CHAPTER 21

Ten months of therapy, and the couple were still in limbo. Kathy and Derek continued to share the same bed. Casual conversation was all they could muster up unless the children or Fanny were present. Derek was finished with book tours. The book was on the bestseller list for the second time in six months. He scheduled additional surgeries to keep out of the house.

The groundbreaking ceremony was March 28, followed by a black-tie dinner at eight that evening. Kathy wore a forest-green satin gown. Embellished along the breast line and at the bottom of the gown was an embroidery of imitation emerald-colored sequins. Her hair was pinned up, and several strands of loose curls surrounded her face. Kathy was the host and belle of the ball as she greeted the generous people who contributed not only their money but their time to a greater cause.

Derek couldn't stop staring at Kathy. He spotted Dr. Cooper and his wife entering the ballroom. He turned away not to make eye contact.

Dr. Cooper presented his hand to Kathy. Kathy smiled. "Dr. Cooper and Mrs. Cooper, it's a pleasure to finally meet you." The three chatted for a few moments.

Derek arrived just in time to hear the good doctor say, "Of course, a building of this magnitude took an enormous amount of hard work and intellect, which you possess, Mrs. Wilson."

"Thank you, Dr. Cooper." Kathy wondered if Dr. Cooper could read her mind. She wondered if he felt sorry for her. Knowing of her situation, did he feel a need to lift her spirits?

"Good evening, Mrs. Cooper. How are you doing, Hank?" said Derek.

"I'm doing well." Several people wanted to speak with Kathy, noticing Dr. Cooper and his wife had excused themselves. When the band began to play, Derek asked Kathy to dance. Refusing him in front of his colleagues and their friends would be a mistake. When Derek took Kathy's hand and placed his other hand around her waist, her skin warmed to his touch—a feeling she had avoided but longed for.

"It feels good to have you back in my arms," he said to her. "Did I tell you how amazing you look?"

"Several times."

"This is all possible because of you. You should be proud of yourself. Did I mention how proud I am of you?"

"Several times."

"I don't think we've spoken more than a thousand words in over a year."

Smiling to keep those from noticing the tension she was feeling in Derek's arms, she said, "This isn't the place or time to be discussing our private lives."

The music ended. Derek lingered before releasing his hold on Kathy.

Derek was asked to speak. He stood at the podium and spoke of his wife's accomplishments. Kathy smiled and blushed as one does when they are being honored. She wanted to jump up and tell the world her marriage was a farce. There was one other person in the room who wasn't buying the loving husband act. Dr. Cooper. Kathy wanted to scream for Derek to stop. On the drive home, she couldn't control her anger.

"I was humiliated by Dr. Cooper's praises."

"Why?"

"He knows our marriage is a farce. He felt sorry for me. I'm sure."

"Hank is a professional. He knows we are facing a crossroad in our marriage, and we're putting in the time to work things out because—"

"Because we have five children. I'm sure he realizes that is the only reason we are together."

"I love our children, but they aren't the reason why I've committed an hour a week to working on our marriage."

"Funny because I don't see a light at the end of this tunnel."

Derek didn't respond because he thought the conversation should end. Each time Kathy was in a mood, Derek had to answer the same questions she'd asked for over a year now. Why?

*****

Derek leaned on the shower wall with both hands. His head was submerged under the water. He wanted nothing more than for the shower door to open, and Kathy, naked, reaching for him. He didn't know how much long he could go without her touch. He masturbated with the thought of her in his arms. He knew where she kept the toys she used to pleasure herself. She had to miss what they shared, but not enough to forgive him. Two weeks ago, he found an answer to why he cheated with Nina and the nurse. He wanted to share his discovery with Kathy but couldn't because he knew she would never accept the reason. Tonight in the car, Derek was scared to tell Kathy that Dr. Cooper ended their therapy sessions.

Dr. Cooper thought it was time for couple's therapy. Derek accepted the list of marriage counselors and asked, "What if she refuses to go?"

"It would be wise to make the suggestion and then ask her to confer with her therapist. It may not be a matter of her refusing, she may not be ready for couple's therapy."

When Derek walked into the bedroom, he found Kathy seated at the dressing table. Derek approached her.

"Kathy, Hank said I'm ready for couple's therapy. He's not suggesting you are. He said I should tell you where I'm at, and you can discuss it with Dr. Hunter."

Kathy stared at Derek through the mirror. "You have an answer to why you're a cheat?"

"I don't have to tell you that cheating isn't something I do daily. I cheated, one time."

"You have your answer to why you cheated, a handful of times, with Nina?"

"An answer, I believe you won't accept, but one that makes sense to me."

"So tell me."

"Someday when we both understand how we got here."

"We got here because you chose to screw another woman."

"I did. And nothing is going to change what I did. I know you agree, we can't go on like this."

"And couple's therapy is the answer?"

"I want you to be happy. Are you happy with the way things are today because I don't know how much longer I can live like this," Derek stated bluntly.

"Masturbation can get boring. I'm sure you'd like to move on with your life, so would I."

Derek's stomach dropped. Kathy was going to ask him to leave. He would be gracious, pack his things, and move into a hotel.

"I'll talk with Dr. Hunter."

CHAPTER 22

Lauren exited Paris's Charles de Gaulle airport. Seeing her daughter, her heart leaped in her chest. Kelly looked different. When Lauren approached her, she noticed Kelly had cut her hair. Lauren didn't want to make the first move, she waited. Kelly embraced her.

"Hi, Mom."

It felt good to hold her daughter. "You cut your hair, sweetheart. Why didn't you tell me?"

"I did. Do you like it?"

"It looks great on you. Is it easy to manage?"

"No. I have to spend more time blow-drying it. I want you to meet someone."

Lauren looked past Kelly and hoped the wise-ass leaning on the pole wasn't a friend of Kelly's.

"Mom, this is Franco."

Kelly put her arm around Franco. He wrapped his arm around her waist.

"Nice to meet you, Franco. Franco, is that a French name?"

"No. Spanish. I'm from Spain. Nice to finally meet Kelly's mom."

Finally? thought Lauren. *How long has Kelly and this train wreck been dating?*

"Only one bag, Mom?"

"Yes."

"Hail us a cab, sweetie."

Franco did as Kelly asked.

Lauren said, "You never told me you were dating. How long have you guys been together?"

"Eight months."

"Eight months, and you never said a word?"

The cab pulled to the curb. Franco placed Lauren's luggage in the trunk, and the three squeezed into the back of the cab.

Arriving at Kelly's apartment, Kelly told Lauren to put her things in her bedroom. Kelly had asked Jake for money to purchase a sofa bed, and Kelly said she and Franco would sleep in the living room.

Lauren was appalled. "I need to use the bathroom." Kelly pointed to the room across from her bedroom.

"Franco and I haven't had breakfast. There's a bakery down the street. Can I get you an almond croissant?"

"That's great, honey." Lauren retrieved twenty dollars from her purse.

"My treat, Mom."

When the couple left the apartment, Lauren dialed Jake's cell. He answered on the second ring.

"Lauren?"

"Jake, did you know that Kelly is seeing someone?"

"I thought they broke up."

"Who?"

"She said she was seeing a boy from school, but they broke up."

"She's been dating this guy for eight months. And he isn't French. He's from Spain."

"Okay."

"She offered me her room. She and Franco are going to sleep on the sofa bed. The sofa bed you gave her money to purchase."

"Are you upset with me for buying her a sofa bed?"

"No, of course not. Should I remind you that Kelly is only eighteen and is shacking up with a guy who is going to share the sofa bed with her, with me in the next room?"

"Almost nineteen, Lauren. Did you tell Kelly you don't feel comfortable having Franco staying at the apartment?"

"I can't. I don't want to lose her again."

"Lauren, if you feel uncomfortable, you're going to have to tell your daughter."

"You don't seem upset that our daughter is sleeping with a guy?"

Jake chuckled. "What were you doing at eighteen, Lauren? If you want the guy to move out, tell your daughter how uncomfortable his being there makes you feel. If you're afraid of losing her, might I suggest a sleeping pill to get you through the night?"

Lauren couldn't believe how flippant and accepting Jake was regarding his daughter's behavior.

She should have listened to Jake's advice and taken a sleeping pill. She tossed and turned the entire night listening for sounds one makes when making love. Thank God, there wasn't a sound coming from the living room.

The following morning, she entered the living room and stared at the young bodies meshed together as they slept. She went into the kitchen and prepared coffee. She leaned over the counter and stared. Her daughter stirred. Seconds later, she rose and headed for the bathroom. Franco pushed the covers aside and stood before her, in his boxer shorts. He turned in her direction and smiled.

"*Perfecto*, you made coffee. Gracias, Mom."

Franco walked toward the counter and sat. Staring at Lauren, he smiled. She returned the gesture. "How long have you been living in Paris?"

"A year."

"Did you and Kelly meet at school?"

"No. I go to school in Spain."

"That's a long commute."

Franco chuckled. "I told my father I needed a break from school. He sent me to Paris."

"I see. Do you work?"

"Yes. I work at the pub on the Champs-Élysées. That's where I met Kelly."

"I see. What is the age limit for drinking in France?"

"In Europe, children taste the wine at the age of three. I had my first glass of wine at the age of five. My grandmother gave it to me because my teeth were hurting. Only in your country is it frowned upon giving a child a little wine with dinner."

"Good morning, Mom. Did you sleep?"

"I got about three hours. The time change doesn't help. Franco and I were just chatting. He told me his father is letting him take a little time away from school. Franco, you said you're living in Paris for a year. I'm assuming you'll be returning home soon to attend school?"

Lauren kept a close watch on Kelly, who seemed frozen in time.

"No, no. My father told me to take my time. School will always be there." Kelly smiled. Franco stood and was off to use the restroom.

"I thought your apartment would be filled with paintings. Do you keep your work at school?"

"Yes. The apartment is too small to have canvases all around. Mom, I know it's your first day in Paris, but since you haven't gotten any sleep, I was hoping you wouldn't mind if Franco and I left for the day. These plans with our friends were made before I knew you were coming."

"I don't mind, but you knew I was coming for a visit when we spoke in January."

"Yes, but then your plans changed, and this date was scheduled a while ago."

"No problem. When will you be home?"

"I'll be back late tomorrow night."

"You're spending the night out?"

"As I said, these plans were made long ago. It's only two days, and you're here for two weeks."

Monday, Kelly and Franco were gone before Lauren woke. The entire week, Kelly and Franco used the apartment like a revolving door. She wanted to call Jake to complain, but he was right. She had to work things out with her daughter. She questioned Franco whenever she got a chance. Unfortunately, she didn't much care for his answers. At the end of the week, on Saturday, Lauren rose early. Leaning over the counter, she kept a close watch on Franco's hand, which was cupping her daughter's breast. When they woke, she informed Franco that she wanted to spend the day with her daughter.

The Palm Reader

Kelly objected. "Mom, Franco and I were driving out to the countryside. I like to paint the scenery this time of year. I'd invite you, but the car only sits two."

"I'm sorry, sweetie, but I leave on Friday, and you and I haven't had one moment alone. I'm sure you understand, Franco. One day apart isn't going to kill you."

Franco smiled. "Fine. I'll work the lunch shift at the pub. I can use the extra cash. Go have fun with your mama."

Franco stood, but Kelly pulled him down. "What time will you be home?"

Strange question, thought Lauren.

"It's a Saturday, probably not until two."

"Two in the morning?" asked Kelly.

"Of course." Franco loosened Kelly's grip on his hand. Fifteen minutes later, he exited the bathroom, grabbed his jacket, and left.

Kelly ran after him. When she returned, she locked herself in the bathroom. Lauren waited patiently for her to emerge.

"Good, you're ready. I thought we could stroll the streets of Paris, check out a few museums, shop, and eat a late lunch or early dinner. Maybe we can get tickets to see a show?"

"Whatever."

Kelly walked several paces in front of Lauren. The conversation between them was next to none. Lauren bought tickets for the Museum d'Orsay. Afterward, she suggested they eat. Kelly suggested they visit Franco at the pub. Lauren declined.

Lauren spotted a quaint café. "This place is perfect." Kelly frowned. Lauren requested a table outside. The two sat. When Kelly showed no interest in food, Lauren ordered for both of them. "Wine sounds nice. Would you like a glass?"

"I don't drink."

"What is the drinking age in France?"

Kelly shouted, "Didn't you hear me? I don't drink!"

Lauren informed the waiter, "I'll have a glass of your best white wine. Merci."

The silence between her and her daughter was foolish. "How is school?"

"It's good."

"Do you plan on coming home at the end of April?"

"I don't think so."

"You're remaining in Paris because you're in love with Franco."

"Yes. I love him."

"But does he love you?"

"Why are you here, Mom? If you think I've forgiven you, I haven't."

"Doesn't matter if you've forgiven me or not. I know what's going on, Kelly."

"What do you think you know?"

"I asked you if Franco loved you. You didn't answer. I'll answer for you. He doesn't love you. He's a player, and you're his latest victim."

"He loves me. I know he does."

"If he loves you, why were you afraid to let him leave today? If I weren't here, would he be working at the pub, or would you have planned his entire day to keep him away from the other girls?"

"Do I question what you do with your girlfriend, Mom? Then butt out of my business. Franco and I are in love, and you can't do a thing about it. I'm old enough to take care of myself."

"True. You can get a job and support yourself. With your income and Franco's income, you might be able to cover the rent, nothing more. The deal was, your father and I would pay for your education. Since you've quit school, we are no longer responsible for you."

"I'm going to go back to school in the fall."

"Not on my dime or your father's."

"Dad doesn't have to listen to you!"

"Dad and I are in agreement when it comes to you and Josh. He won't go against me, not when he knows the truth."

"Can't you just go back home and let me figure this out on my own?"

"I can't drag you back to the States, so let's talk, not as mother and daughter but as friends. Does Franco have an apartment of his own? I'm guessing, no. Does he have intentions of going back to Spain and school? I'm guessing his parents wrote him off a while ago.

Does Franco cheat on you? I'm guessing you've caught him a few times. He's convinced you the other girls meant nothing to him, and you believe him. I think you realized a long time ago that Franco is not the right man for you. You probably tried to break up with him, but he begged you to forgive him. He'll change because he loves you. You know, he doesn't love you, Kelly. He's using you. He needs your money to survive. On Saturday, I'm getting on that plane. For your own good, I hope you'll be sitting next to me. We have five days to get your things packed. The rent is paid till May. You haven't signed another lease. I'm sure the landlord will agree a furnished apartment will earn him a higher rent. If you intend to stay, I'll pray it all works out for you. A parent wants nothing more than for their child to be happy."

On Saturday, mother and daughter boarded a flight for home.

*****

Josh transferred to Stanford in his junior year. He was dating a girl named Cindy, and they were flying back for the Labor Day weekend to introduce Cindy to the family. Jake and Lauren assumed that Josh had fallen in love.

*****

"Kelly, did you place fresh linens on all the beds? I don't know how we are going to manage. Your father and Michelle are going to sleep in your room. Michelle has a sleeper for Grace, and I set up the cot for Jack. It's a little tight, but I think they can manage. You'll sleep with me. Cindy will be in Josh's room, and Josh can sleep on the sofa bed."

"Settle down, Mom."

"I hope Josh wasn't upset when your dad told him Michelle's parents were going to be in town Friday and Saturday?"

"Mom, you have to calm down."

Lauren smiled. "Do you think he's forgiven me, Kelly?"

"You didn't commit murder, Mom. You had an affair with a woman."

"Are you forgetting that you weren't so forgiving a while back?"

"We all make mistakes, right?"

Lauren smiled. "Last Saturday, when you were at the movies with Jordan, I was invited to dinner at the Carlton's to meet their friend, Bruce Hollis."

"He took one look at you, fell head over heels in love with you, and asked you out."

"No. He asked, if after the holiday, if I was free, can I show him around town?"

"You said you were free. I hope."

"I did."

"You go, Mom."

Lauren didn't tell her daughter that the evening went better than she said. Bruce was handsome and well built. He introduced himself, and Lauren was overwhelmed by his good looks, and when he asked her a question, she giggled liked a school girl. At the end of the evening, Bruce asked her to dinner the following Friday. Since that night, she couldn't stop thinking of Bruce.

Lauren was elated that Josh had agreed to the visit, grateful that Josh hadn't change his plans finding out his father and Michelle weren't arriving until Sunday.

Lauren rushed to the door when she heard the car approaching. Josh got out of the car but didn't acknowledge Lauren. Instead, he went to help Cindy from the car. When the girl emerged, she smiled at Lauren. Coming toward her, Cindy said, "It's a pleasure to meet you, Mrs. Croft."

"It's a pleasure to meet you, Cindy."

"No. It's really a pleasure to meet you. I've read all your novels, and I'm happy to say, you're one of my favorite writers."

"You're too kind."

Josh stood behind Cindy. Lauren smiled at her son.

"Hi, Mom."

Lauren was so happy to see Josh and ignored that he didn't offer an embrace.

The two days she spent with her children and Cindy were a delight.

On Sunday, Jake and Michelle arrived.

Kelly, Cindy, and Josh were playing with Jack by the ocean. Michelle stood close by with Grace in her arms.

Jake walked toward her. "I didn't think Kelly and Josh would take a liking to the little ones, but they can't get enough of them."

"Doesn't matter what the age, they are related by blood."

"Cindy's a sweet girl. Josh is crazy about her."

"She's very sweet. Did Josh explain why he changed his mind and agreed to visit with me?"

"He said he talked it over with Cindy, and she insisted on meeting his parents. She probably wanted to meet the famous Lauren Hicks Croft. She might be the one to fix what's broken between you and Josh."

"I hope so."

The family enjoyed a full day of fun and sun. Jake barbequed while Lauren and Michelle set the table and prepped the side dishes. The older children kept a close watch on Jack while Grace napped. After the fireworks on the beach, everyone retired to bed. Lauren left the comfort of her bed and went down to the kitchen to get a bottle of water. Noticing that the front door was open, she smiled, then went outside to find Josh reclining on one of the patio chairs. Lauren leaned on the railing, opened the bottle of water, and offered it to Josh. He declined.

"I like your choice in women. Cindy is a lovely girl."

"She speaks highly of you. After we dated for a while, she asked about my parents. When I told her who you were, she couldn't stop talking about your books."

"You must have been bored out of your mind."

"No. I know you love to write, and you're good at it."

"Thanks." Mother and son were silent, enjoying the night sky. "When you were little, you'd sneak out of your room, and in the morning, we'd find you out here nestled tight in your Spiderman sleeping bag."

"I miss those days."

"You don't have to. The house isn't going anywhere."

"I guess you're wondering why I agreed to come? It isn't because Dad said you broke up with that woman. Cindy wanted to meet my parents, and I didn't have the guts to tell her you and I aren't on speaking terms."

"Correction, you aren't speaking to me. I miss talking with you."

"Are you dating?" Josh asked.

"If you're asking if I'm seeing another woman, no. Do you remember the Carltons? They invited me to dinner last Friday. Duke wanted to introduce me to his buddy, who just moved to the Cape, Bruce Hollis. He and Duke served together in the Navy. Bruce asked me to dinner this Friday, and I accepted."

"So you're back to dating guys, and you're hoping by telling me you're dating a guy, my feelings will change toward you."

"I never thought of you as a hard-ass, Josh. I guess the apple doesn't fall far from the tree. In college, my BFFs thought I was a hard-ass, still do."

"It doesn't make it any easier to hear your mom swings both ways, Mom."

"It's a date, Josh. I'm not shacking up with the guy."

"It's your life. You can do with it as you please."

"True, but I'd really wish you'd cut me a break. I'm sorry to have destroyed the perfect image you had of me. If the shoe were on the other foot, I wouldn't toss you aside."

"When I think of you and whomever doing whatever, it makes me sick."

"I do understand. Children expect their mothers to be as pure as the driven snow. When you don't fit the image they have of you, they forget the good and only remember the bad."

"You're right. That image is hard to erase."

"Is there any hope for us, son?"

"I'm afraid, if I let you in, you'll only hurt me again. You're not dating a woman now, but there could be another in your future, and that's what I can't live with. I don't want to have to explain to my children why Grandma has a girlfriend. It's bad enough that I have to explain why my mother and father are divorced."

"Even if I found happiness with a man, I don't think you will ever forgive me."

Lauren couldn't find the words to make things right between her and her son. She would let him grow older, and maybe, in time, he might come to accept her.

"I love you, Josh. If you decide to sleep outside, the bug spray is in the lower left side of the TV console. Good night."

*****

"Why did you decide to move to the Cape?"

"After thirty years in the service, it was time for a change."

"You left the Navy where you sailed the seven seas for thirty years to wind up in a cottage near the ocean."

"The last ten years, I'd been stationed at an office in South Carolina. The last time I was sailing on an ocean, I took a cruise to Bermuda. I fell in love with this area when Duke invited me to spend two weeks with his family last year. He told me the cottage was being placed on the market, and I offered the Santoris the asking price."

"It is a beautiful cottage. Larger than mine. I believe it has four bedrooms."

"Yes."

"Are you expecting a lot of visitors, such as family, friends, and exes?"

Bruce laughed. "I've never been married. I came close, but the girl decided that a military life wasn't for her. Since then, I've had several long-term relationships, which never materialized into marriage. I have one sister, Carol. She lives in upstate New York."

"Are you and Carol close?"

"We are. My father left when Carol was two. My mother had to find a job, and at the age of six, I became the man of the family. My mother couldn't afford to send me to college, so the Navy was the answer to me earning a college degree and then a master's degree in criminal justice. I was an attorney for the military."

"Interesting. Are you going to miss practicing law?"

"Duke is speaking with Louis Gerson. I might be able to work as a paralegal at the Gerson Law Office in town."

"You want to work with Louis Gerson? I hear he's tough on his employees."

"I think I can handle Mr. Gerson, two days a week. How was your Labor Day weekend?"

"Labored."

"In what way?"

"My son and I are having issues. We used to be so close, but lately, we can't see eye to eye."

"Little kids, little problems, big kids, big problems. My friends say I'm lucky I didn't have kids."

"Do you miss not having children?"

"I do. It would have been nice to have a little girl to spoil or a boy to play catch with."

"It's not too late. Men can have children way into their eighties."

"As the saying goes, that ship has sailed."

Lauren smiled. Duke had informed Bruce that Lauren was divorced with two grown children, prior to them meeting.

"Did Duke tell you that he and Jake are friends?"

"He did mention he was friends with Jake."

"I guess you're wondering why this wonderful man, Jake, and I divorced?"

"I didn't give it much thought, and I don't think Duke has a clue why you guys are divorced."

"Jake and I met in college. We were happily married and have two beautiful children. The marriage began to collapse when I wanted to spend my days writing, and he wanted me to write less. I knew he was unhappy, so we separated and divorced. Today, Jake is happily married to Michelle, who presented him with two beautiful children, Jack and Grace. My novels are selling, and life is pretty good, most times."

"Everyone loves a happy ending. A beautiful woman, like yourself, must have a date every night of the week."

"I've been out with friends, both male and female. But I haven't been out on a real date in six months until you came along."

Bruce chuckled. "Well, now that we know all there is to know about each other, where do we go from here?"

"Wherever our hearts desire."

Lauren had a wonderful time with Bruce, and when he dropped her off at the cottage, Lauren was hoping for more than just a kiss. But a kiss on the cheek was all she received. Two days later, she called Bruce to ask if he were busy on Saturday night. If not, was he up for a movie and a burger. Bruce accepted. The night ended with Bruce and Lauren sipping wine in front of a fire at her cottage. When he left, he placed another kiss on her cheek. Frustrated, Lauren wondered if she was losing her charm. There were two more dates ending with a kiss on the cheek.

Their fifth date, Lauren had invited Bruce to dinner. After dinner, they moved to the sofa to share a port wine Bruce had purchased. When Bruce rose to leave, Lauren had to ask, "Which cheek would you prefer to kiss this time, before you leave?"

Bruce sat down. "I prefer to kiss your lips, but there is something we need to discuss."

"And what is that?"

"When we met at Duke's home, it wasn't the first time I saw you. Actually, I was dining with the realtor a year ago, and I couldn't take my eyes off this beautiful woman. The beautiful woman was you, and you were dining with a lovely woman. I couldn't help but notice the intimate gestures."

"What you saw were two women being intimate. I was involved with this woman, but it's over."

"I see."

Lauren confessed, "I've been with both men and women. I know our friendship is new, and I hope what I've shared with you can remain between us."

"Of course."

Lauren smiled.

"So your relationship with this woman is over?" asked Bruce.

"Yes. I put an end to it because my son wasn't comfortable with the situation. It is also the reason why my son and I don't see eye to eye."

"I appreciate your honesty, Lauren."

"I'm a firm believer that one should always be honest. But being honest destroyed my relationship with my son and daughter. My daughter, Kelly, and I managed to get through the rough patch, but Josh isn't as forgiving."

"In time, he might come around to seeing things your way," said Bruce.

"I can only hope."

Bruce stood. "Well, it's getting late. I should be going."

Lauren walked Bruce to the door. When they were face-to-face, Bruce leaned in and kissed Lauren on the lips. When they parted, Bruce said, "I really like you, Lauren, but I need time to think things over."

"I understand. While you're thinking things over, please know that I'm pretty loyal to the people I become involved with."

Bruce placed a kiss on top of Lauren's head before saying good night.

Lauren leaned against the door; after a few minutes, she retrieved the wine glasses from the coffee table. Placing them in the sink, she was startled by a knock on the door.

She ran to the front door knowing it could only be Bruce on the other side. When she opened the door, Bruce was leaning on the doorjamb.

"Hi. Would it be to forward of me to ask if I can spend the night?"

Lauren rushed into Bruce's arms.

Bruce followed Lauren to her bedroom.

Exhausted after tossing and turning to be in control during their sexual encounter, they lay side by side.

"I've been less exhausted after an hour of cardio," said Lauren.

"Whatever it was, it was great."

"I was pretty good, wasn't I?"

Bruce laughed. He took Lauren into his arms. They kissed. Within seconds, he was once again inside her.

CHAPTER 23

Kathy tapped her foot waiting for Dr. Hunter to open the door to her office. The young lady sitting at the reception desk was typing away.

"How much longer will the doctor be?" asked Kathy.

As soon as the girl looked up, Dr. Hunter opened the office door and greeted Kathy.

"Sorry to keep you waiting, Mrs. Wilson."

Kathy rushed into the office, removed her coat, and sat in the same seat she had sat in for close to two years.

Dr. Hunter placed her notepad on her lap. "I would start by asking how you are, Kathy, but we've been down that road for close to two years. You might want to find another therapist because I don't think I can help you."

"You're kidding, right?"

"Actually, I am not."

"Doctors just don't give up on their patients."

"I've tried everything to get you to move forward, but you won't budge. How many times have we gone over the fact that you have to make a decision? Do you want to remain married to Derek or not? If the answer is yes, then what have you done to fix it? I'm guessing not a thing. You won't agree to couple's therapy. So Derek remains in limbo wondering if he is wasting his time."

"Did you forget he cheated on me?"

"No, I have not, and I don't expect you ever will be able to forgive him. It surprises me you haven't asked the man to move out of your home."

"I have five children, Doctor. I just can't toss their father to the curb."

"Why not? Or is it you who doesn't want to toss your husband to the curb? Kathy, it's obvious to me that you are still in love with your husband."

Tears began to well in Kathy's eyes. She lowered her head. "I love him so much it hurts."

"I know you do, and couple's therapy is the next step."

*****

Several days had passed since Kathy and Dr. Hunter's therapy session. She hadn't mentioned couple's therapy to Derek. During the day, the kids occupied her mind, but at night, she lay awake thinking how to approach the subject with Derek. Kathy needed to get out of the house, so she told Fanny she was going to Bloomingdale's. She bought clothes for the children and a few things for herself. Her stomach began to growl. She went to the café and ordered a salad and a bottle of water. While she ate, she glanced at the line of people placing orders and gasped. Rising from her seat, she approached the person standing in line.

"Nina."

Nina's face went white. "Kathy."

"Are you getting a bite to eat?"

"Yes. I'll take it to go."

"No. Why don't you join me for lunch?"

"I'm not comfortable—"

"I'm not going to bite your head off. Please I hate eating alone."

Nina ordered her food and sat across from Kathy. For a moment, the two felt awkward, and Kathy thought inviting Nina to lunch might have been a mistake.

"Kathy, I owe you an apology. I've wanted to call you, but then I lost the courage. I am truly sorry for the pain I've caused you. I regret lying to you. I regret the affair."

"It takes two to tango."

The Palm Reader

"Derek knew what he did was wrong, and he ended it. I hope you guys are still together."

"Learning that my husband slept with another woman was painful. Knowing the one person in this entire world that I trusted cannot be trusted hurts a hell of a lot worse."

"I'm sure it does, and I'm sorry I was the cause."

"I could call you a home-wrecker and the names associated with a woman who sleeps with a married man, but I know you're a decent woman, Nina. On the book tour, I watched women who wanted nothing more than to sleep with my husband, but Derek never crossed the line. I know this for a fact, and so do you. The question that keeps me up at night is, why you, Nina?"

"I don't know, Kathy. I knew how much Derek loved you and the children. Yet I allowed myself to fall in love with him. It didn't take me long to figure out that I was just a roll in the hay that meant nothing to him. He actually used those same words the night you walked out on him. He wasn't being vicious. He spoke his true feelings, and that's when I realized, I made a terrible mistake."

Kathy felt empathy for Nina. "Are you over the entire ordeal?"

"Therapy helped, and I met an unmarried man. I've been married for eight months, and two weeks ago, we found out we are expecting our first child."

"I'm happy for you, Nina. Are you living in this area?"

"No. We live in California. My husband, Max, had business in Boston, so I tagged along."

"Are you working?"

"Yes. I work for a small publishing firm."

Nina glanced at her watch. Standing, she said, "I'm meeting Max at three. Thank you for inviting me to lunch. Goodbye, Kathy."

*****

Kathy leaned on the wall outside her daughter Peggy's room. Derek was reading a story to Peggy and Eric. Peggy begged her daddy to read the story one more time. Derek sighed. "One more time, then it's lights out."

Kathy listened while Derek read their children the story for a second time. Silently she walked off to check on her other children, who were sound asleep. Making her way down the stairs, she went into the den and switched on the gas fireplace. She retrieved the leftover white wine in the refrigerator and poured herself a glass. She took the bottle with her back to the den and sat on the sofa. Sipping the wine, she stared into the fireplace. She heard Derek descend the stairs. Seconds later, he was standing next to her.

"I'm going to call it a night. It's been a long day."

Kathy turned toward Derek and noticed he did look tired. "Can we talk?"

"Sure."

"Would you like a glass of wine?"

Derek's stomach was in knots. He'd had a rough day at the hospital, two difficult surgeries. He was sure Kathy wanted to talk about separating. He wouldn't fight her. He refused a glass of wine. Collapsing into the armchair near the fireplace, he waited for his world to fall apart.

"You're never going to believe who I met today."

It wasn't what he was excepting to hear, but he asked, "Who?"

"Aren't you even going to try to guess?"

"I have no idea."

"Nina."

Derek's eyes widened. "Nina? Last I heard, Nina was living in California."

"Were you keeping track of her?"

"Absolutely not. The person who replaced her at the publishing firm told me she moved to California."

"I was having lunch at Bloomingdale's café when she walked in. I invited her to lunch."

"You invited Nina to lunch, why?"

"I was curious to hear what she had to say. She's married. She and her husband live in California, and they are expecting their first child in the fall."

Derek frowned.

"If you're wondering if you might be the father, you're not."

"I can assure you, I'm not. You didn't cause a scene in Bloomingdale's, did you?"

"No. We were civil. I'm happy for her. She was able to move on with her life, and we are stuck in limbo."

"Is that what we're calling it these days, limbo? The question is, how do we get from limbo to a normal existence?"

"You confessing that Nina wasn't your only affair might work."

"Really, then I had an affair with Pauline, our neighbor, and the checkout girl at the supermarket."

Kathy swallowed a hefty amount of wine and said, "It wouldn't surprise me."

Derek sighed. "So what did Nina have to say?"

"Nothing much, except that sleeping with you was a mistake. She's happy with her husband, and hopefully, he never causes her the pain you've caused me."

Frustrated, Derek asked, "Are we finished talking?"

"I thought you'd be happy to hear, I'm finished with individual therapy according to Dr. Hunter. I've made a decision."

Derek held his breath.

"I've decided to give couple's therapy a try."

Shocked and bewildered to hear his world wasn't coming to an end, Derek held back the joy he was feeling. "Hank gave me a few names to call when and if we got to this point. Do you want me to reach out, or would you rather choose the therapist?"

"Give me a couple of days to look over the list of names. When I've made a decision, I'll call for an appointment."

Derek nodded his head in agreement. He wanted to take Kathy into his arms and shower her with kisses; instead, he stood and said, "I'll leave the list on your desk. Good night."

*****

Kathy sat with her head down staring at her hands. Derek stared at the wall in front of him where a very expensive painting hung. The couple had been in therapy for two months.

The door opened, and in walked Dr. Leach, a marriage counselor and psychologist. He sat.

"Good morning."

Kathy smiled. Derek grunted. Dr. Leach acknowledged the grunt. "Having a bad day, Derek?"

"Same shit, different day."

Kathy apologized for Derek's crude remark.

"You don't have to apologize for me. The man asked me a question. I told him the truth."

Kathy turned her head away from Derek, and the good doctor and mumbled, "You're such an ass."

"I sense tension between the two of you. Should we discuss what's going on?"

"I'm fine. Did you forget, Dr. Leach, he's the one with the problem?"

Dr. Leach interjected, "Obviously, there is something going on. Do you want to share, or should we move on?"

The couple didn't respond.

"Then I'll continue. The last time we met, I made a few suggestions—one being a touching exercise."

"I was busy," said Kathy.

"Did either of you try to make an effort?"

"As she said, we were busy. Somewhere in your notes, I'm sure it says we have five kids. They take up most of our time."

"Yes. It also states in my notes that before Kathy found out about the affair, you had a healthy sex life." Dr. Leach placed his notepad and pen down. Moving forward in his chair, he asked, "Are you two committed to saving your marriage?"

"I'm totally committed to saving my marriage, but I don't think Kathy is or wants to."

Dr. Leach waited for Kathy to respond. "Kathy, have you made up your mind to end your marriage?"

Kathy drew a deep breath. "I can't go on week after week being asked the same questions. We had a good marriage, and I thought a healthy sex life, but I wasn't enough for him."

Derek shouted, "That's not true! I love you."

The Palm Reader

"Don't you miss each other?"

Kathy lowered her head. "Ever since you suggested the touching exercise, I've lived in fear that Derek might reach for me, and I didn't know if I—"

"Please finish."

"If I could stand him touching me."

Derek slumped in his chair.

Kathy made eye contact with Dr. Leach. "I've checked, and nothing, so I guess he's telling the truth. This was his only affair, but I can't shake the feeling that he's had more than one affair."

"There are no other women. I made a mistake. One that I wish I could go back and change, but I can't."

"Trust is the cornerstone to a good marriage, and Derek, you broke that trust. Kathy, Derek swore on his children's lives that he will never hurt you again, but you don't believe him. Why?"

Kathy didn't answer.

"Do you believe that Derek is truly sorry for hurting you? Do you believe him when he says it will never happen again? I can't promise you that Derek is not going to hurt you again, but I do believe he's sincere when he says he loves you and wants to work on saving the marriage."

Kathy didn't respond. Dr. Leach made a professional decision. "I think that's all for today."

*****

The couple drove in silence. When they arrived home, Derek went to their bedroom, and Kathy went to find Fanny and her little ones. An hour later, Kathy wondered what Derek was doing, and she went to find him. When she entered their bedroom, she found him stuffing clothes into his duffel bag.

"Where are you going?"

"I have two early surgeries in the morning. I'm going to stay at the hospital."

Kathy remained frozen. "You've never slept at the hospital when you had an early surgery."

"I think we both can use a break."

Kathy exhaled. "You might be right."

"I'll be home early on Thursday. Why don't you take the day off? I promised the kids a movie night."

"Would you mind if I spent a few days at the Cape with Lauren?"

Standing in front of Kathy with his suitcase in hand, Derek said, "I think that's a great idea. Text me when you arrive at Lauren's."

"I will."

When the door closed behind her, Kathy's eyes began to well.

*****

Derek placed the empty duffel bag at the bottom of the closet. Walking toward the window, he looked out. When the hospital was being renovated, Derek suggested to the board that several small apartments should be added for doctors to use in cases of emergency. His emergency was leaving behind a wife and children he loved and adored. He collapsed on the bed and switched on the flat-screen TV. Realizing he hadn't eaten since yesterday, he ordered dinner, snacks, and three bottles of water from the hospital cafeteria. While he waited for dinner to arrive, he tried to clear his mind of today's occurrences.

His marriage was over. He did the right thing by moving out. It was only a matter of time before Kathy could admit the marriage was over. He would return home to care for the children, and when Kathy returned, he'd make arrangements to move into a Residence Inn.

Today, if he thought it would help Kathy to move on, he would have confessed to cheating on her one other time during their marriage. What good would it have done to confess an affair that would only cause her more pain? No, he was done hurting her. Kathy wasn't in therapy to save their marriage. She agreed because she didn't have the heart to hurt their children.

He loved his children, but it was the mother of his children that he loved more than life itself. Losing Kathy would break him, but he couldn't watch her suffer in a marriage with a man she didn't trust or love. Couples remained together for the sake of the children. He would have gladly remained for his children's sake if it meant he'd been able to spend the rest of his life with Kathy.

*****

Kathy called out, "Hi."
"I'm in the kitchen."
When Kathy entered the kitchen, she found Lauren under the sink.
"What are you doing?"
"Tightening the cold-water pipe."
"Why didn't you call a plumber?"
Lauren rolled out from under the sink. "Are you insane? Do you know what a plumber would charge to tighten a loose pipe?"
"You can afford it."
Lauren smiled. "I'm so happy to see you. I can't believe Derek gave you the weekend off, but I'm happy he did. I can't wait to introduce you to Bruce. He's coming over to grill the fish. I hope you don't mind."
"I was hoping to meet him. Should I place my bag in Kelly's room?"
"Sure. Bruce will be here at five." Lauren raised herself off the floor. "Come here, give your BFF a big hug."
The ladies embraced. When they parted, Lauren smelled her armpit. "I need a shower. I'll be quick."
"Let me know when you're out of the shower. I'd like to freshen up."
"Will do, pretty lady. There's beer, water, wine, and soda in the fridge. Grab yourself something to drink. There's crackers in the cabinet if you're hungry."
Kathy chose wine. She poured herself a full glass. Retrieving her phone, she texted Derek to let him know she arrived safely. Avoiding an uncomfortable situation, she left before Derek arrived home that morning. Kathy collapsed onto the sofa in the living room. She drank a hefty amount of wine and swallowed. The burning in her throat felt good. Wine was becoming addictive. It had helped her through the

three restless nights she spent without Derek lying next to her. She wondered why Derek had made such a bold move. Moving out was the last thing she'd expected him to do. The therapy sessions were not going well. She assumed that Derek moving out was due to the fact that she confessed she didn't want him to touch her, but she lied. She lied to hurt him. She wanted to crush him, the way he had crushed her. Saying she didn't want him to touch her would do the trick, and it did. Over two years, and they weren't back to having a normal life, less the trust. She was sure Derek was ready to throw in the towel. How could she admit to him that she was weak, and she longed for his touch? When she returned home, she was sure Derek would say it was time for them to separate. They would figure out what days would work for Derek to visit with the children. Her children would suffer the most from their split, or would it be her? She loved her husband, and he professed his love a million times over, promising he would never hurt her again. If their love was strong, why couldn't she allow him back into her life?

Lauren shouted, "The bathroom is all yours."

Kathy cleared her mind of questions. She finished the wine in her glass and ran up the stairs to make herself presentable for Lauren's latest conquest.

*****

"Kathy, this is Bruce. Bruce, this is Kathy. I told you she's knock-dead gorgeous."

"It's a pleasure to meet you, Kathy."

"The pleasure's all mine."

"Now that introductions are out of the way, Bruce, you know where the grill is. I'm famished."

The three spent a lovely evening getting to know one another. Kathy was amazed by Bruce's adventures during his time in the Navy. The night ended around twelve. Kathy left Bruce and Lauren alone, saying she was exhausted.

The following morning, she and Lauren ate breakfast outdoors.

"So what did you think of Bruce? He's a ten, right?"

"He's very handsome and interesting. You seem happy."

"I'm in love. I know I've said those words before, but if he asked me to marry him, I'd do it in a heartbeat. The time we've spent together has been amazing. I see myself spending the rest of my life with the guy."

"Have the kids met him?"

"Kelly's met him. She likes him. Josh hasn't been home in a while, but he's not interested in meeting anyone I date."

"You said Josh calls twice a month. Are things getting better between you?"

"He does call twice a month like clockwork. I have Cindy to thank. She enjoys being with our family, so as long as Cindy is in Josh's life, he'll keep in touch. I can't live each day wondering if Josh will ever forgive me. Life is too short. I raised them to make their own decisions, and Josh has decided he's uncomfortable with me. Children grow up, and you're left wondering what's next. Well, I hope to spend the rest of my life humping Bruce." Lauren laughed and took notice Kathy didn't. "Kelly and Jonathan are still together. I think he might be the one. She's enjoying her second year at the university. So how's couple's therapy going?"

"It's not going well. Derek moved out."

Lauren dropped the muffin she was about to stuff in her mouth. "Derek moved out?"

"He didn't move out permanently. He moved into the hospital apartment for two days and three nights."

"What's going on with you two?"

"Dr. Leach, our therapist, gave us an assignment. Touching exercises."

"That shouldn't have been a problem for the two of you. From what I remember, you can hardly keep your hands off each other."

"For over two years, my lover has been a dildo and sex toys. I'm sure Derek has developed carpal tunnel masturbating."

"I'm guessing the touching exercises didn't go well."

"Monday, during our therapy session I said that I didn't want Derek to touch me."

"You made a decision to end your marriage?"

"No. I'm sure when I return home, a separation is going to be the topic of discussion."

"If you don't want to end your marriage, then what do you want?"

"I want to forget everything that's happened and go back to the way things were."

"You know that's impossible."

"I know. The fate of our marriage lies solely in my hands."

"Do you love him?"

"You know I do. I hate myself for loving him as much as I do."

"You know my feelings. The man made a mistake. Punishing him and yourself isn't working. Let the man touch you for heaven's sake. If you're grossed out by his touch, then your marriage is over. Finally, the two of you can move on."

The ladies spent the remaining time together enjoying each other's company, minus discussions of infidelity and marriage.

*****

Kathy entered the house and found the quietness strange. She went into the kitchen to find Derek reading the newspaper.

"Where are the kids?"

Confused, he said, "Eric and Peggy are at school, and Fanny took the little ones to the park."

"I forgot it's Monday."

"Did you have a nice time with Lauren?"

"I did. We have a therapy session at two, right?"

"I canceled. I thought we could use a break."

"Are you staying or going?"

"I thought I'd go back to the hospital. I won't leave until the kids are down for the night. If that's all right with you?"

"Whatever." Kathy turned her back on Derek. As she walked away, she asked herself, *What are you doing?*

The family ate dinner together. The parents attended to the children's baths. Kathy settled the little ones for the night. Derek read to Eric and Peggy. Kathy waited for him in their bedroom. She heard him descending the stairs and rushed out of the room, afraid he might be leaving. When she found him in the den, she said, "I thought you had left before we got a chance to talk."

"I washed a few things. There's ten minutes left on the dryer. I'll lock up before I leave."

Exhausted, Kathy collapsed into a chair. "Are you comfortable at the hospital?"

"I'll only be there for a few more days. I rented a place at the Residence Inn."

"So this is it. We're separating?"

"Living under the same roof is hurting you, and I don't want to hurt you ever again. Whatever it takes to make this easier on you and the children, I'll do. All I ask is that you don't cut me off from the kids. I don't want to be the every-other-weekend dad. I want to see the children during the week and maybe one day on the weekends. I know down the road you might, you know, go on with your life. I'm sure after I get settled, I'll hire help. I think we can amicably work out all the details. Whatever you want, I won't fight you. I want you to be happy. That's all I've ever wanted."

"Derek, I don't want you to leave. I don't want our marriage to end. I want to do whatever it takes to put our lives back on track. If that means we have to do those stupid touching exercises, so be it."

Derek had to hold on to the mantel to stop himself from falling. "Are you serious?"

"Yes. We both agree the marriage was good before—I'll admit I've been holding back, but I am committed to saving the marriage. If we work hard at it, I think we can be happy again. I do believe you love me, but I swear if this ever happens again, I'm going to—"

Before Kathy could finish her sentence, Derek lifted her from the chair and into his arms. Kissing her firmly on her lips. She wrapped her legs around his waist. They ascended the stairs locked together until they reached their bedroom, where they began to undress each other. When he entered her, the two and half years they had been apart became a distant memory.

CHAPTER 24

"He's beautiful, Elle," said Lauren. "I never thought I could love another child as much as I love Liam, but I took to this little guy like a duck to water."

"Ethan, you're one lucky boy," said Alice.

"He's a good baby. Thank God, he's not colic like his brother."

Elle smiled at her little boy. "He's so sweet, hardly ever cries. He's going to miss his grandma."

"I'm going to miss my little guys more."

"Trudy, you deserve a night out. Elle, is Jacques ready to handle the two boys on his own?"

"He doesn't have a choice, Kathy. Mama deserves a night out."

"Then let's get this show on the road." The ladies waved goodbye to Jacques, who was wrestling with Liam on the living room floor.

"Have a good time, ladies."

"Jacques, if you need me, I'm a phone call away. Mama's going to have herself a grand old time tonight."

*****

"This place is amazing, Elle. How far in advance do you have to call to get a reservation?"

"Three weeks," said Elle.

"Lauren, you look over the wine list and don't worry about the cost. Derek is picking up the check. His gift to Elle."

"I'm happy you and Derek were able to work things out."

The Palm Reader

Kathy smiled. "We're doing well. There was a time that I thought my marriage was over, but here I am back to being happy 24/7."

Lauren opened her mouth and pointed her index finger inside. "And she's back."

"You know you're happy for me, Lauren. You're the one that said, 'Let the man touch you for heaven's sake.' Sorry, Trudy, if the conversation is getting a little out of hand."

"Not at all. Obviously, Lauren's advice worked."

"Actually, Dr. Leach, our therapist suggested the touching exercises."

"I'm sure one session with Dr. Leach costs two hundred dollars or more, and the man came up with touching exercises as a fix. I'm in the wrong business," said Alice.

"Don't knock it. It worked."

"I'm happy it did."

"If it weren't for the support of my BFFs, which includes you Alice, Derek and I would be history."

Changing the subject, Lauren asked. "So what's new in your world, Alice?"

"I met someone."

"We talk twice a month, and you never mentioned you were seeing someone."

"Her name is Nancy. We've been dating for ten months. I might ask her to move in with me."

"Ten months, and you're ready to have her to move in with you? Are you sure?"

"I am, Kathy. I'm not getting any younger, and Nancy and I share the same interests. We enjoy each other's company, and I'm happy."

"If you're happy, then go for it. Elle, are you and Jacques thinking of adding to the family?"

"The baby shop is closed. Work and family is hard. I might ask the network for an easier gig."

"You'd be great with a morning talk show, Elle."

"I was thinking along those lines, Alice. I have three years to convince the network."

"You can always go back to Wildwood to find out what that scary woman thinks. Trudy, did Elle ever tell you we went to visit a palm reader a while back?"

"She did, Kathy. That scary woman was the answer to my prayers. My daughter is back in my life. I'd love to meet her one day, so I can thank her."

Elle smiled.

"Not only did she help with my mom and I reconciling, she gave me the strength to accept Jacques's proposal and a joy I never thought was in my future, my sons."

"She made me face that I'm bi."

The ladies laughed at Lauren's joke. "Well, I was bi, now I just want to spend the rest of my life with Bruce."

"She shook my perfect world. She told me to look past the clouds, and I found out my husband was cheating on me."

Lauren cheerfully said, "If dying is hard, then living isn't much easier. One day, you're up; next day, your balloon burst, and you're heading head first for the ground. You have to thank your lucky stars if you're able to get past the down days."

"Speaking of down, how are things going with Josh, Lauren?" asked Kathy.

"The same."

"I never found Josh to be this stubborn."

"He's not stubborn, Kathy. He's upset that I slept with a woman. I wish I could go back and change everything, but it's too late to right the wrong."

Kathy half listened to Lauren. Since the day Lauren had told her about her affair with Casey and then Shelby, Kathy was curious to know the difference between being touched by a man versus a woman. To stop herself from fantasizing, she said, "Let's order a round of drinks."

CHAPTER 25

Kathy lay back in bed and sighed. Derek was in the shower, and she was totally relaxed from making love with her husband. She pulled the sheets up to her chin and smiled. The gesture reminded her of Scarlett O'Hara after Rhett had forced her to make love to him.

They were celebrating their fifteenth anniversary in Vermont. Of course, there were gifts, and Kathy's gift to Derek would rock their world.

Derek with a towel wrapped around his waist lay next to her on the bed. Kathy smiled. He loved a hot shower, and Kathy could feel the heat radiating off his body.

"You look relaxed, Mrs. Wilson."

"I am. Thanks for remembering that Vermont was where you took me for the first time."

"I hope you're not disappointed that it is only for four days. I had to reschedule several surgeries to get four consecutive days off."

"I'm happy we're celebrating our anniversary and not signing divorce papers."

"I hate to think this could have all ended. I'm so grateful you gave me a second chance to prove how much you mean to me. I don't know what life would have been like for me without you and the children."

"I don't think you would have been single for too long. Women are drawn to you like a fly is to fly paper. I can name a few if you'd like."

"Not interested."

Derek gently slapped Kathy's behind.

"So should we start our day with a hike through the woods?"

"Sounds great."

"Later today, I've arranged a tee time. The Pro Shop hooked us up with another couple. If it goes well, we can have dinner together."

"This is our anniversary, remember—sun, fun, food, and sex? Just you and me, babe. No kids and no golf partners."

Kathy smiled.

*****

After a romantic dinner, the couple returned to their hotel room and made love. Lying together, Kathy said, "I can't wait to give you my gift."

Derek jumped from the bed and retrieved an envelope from the nightstand. Kathy did the same.

Returning to bed, she said, "We think alike."

"What's in your envelope?" asked Derek.

Kathy grabbed the envelope from Derek's hand and tore it open. "Derek, you didn't."

"I did. The sporty red Porsche you had your eye on. No room for kids. You and I cruising around the neighborhood in our car for two."

"You mean, me driving us around in my new sporty red Porsche? If you're a good boy, I'll let you drive it." Kathy flew into Derek's arms. "I love it. You spoil me, and I love being spoiled by you." She showered him with kisses. "Your turn." Kathy handed Derek her envelope.

Derek tore it open and frowned. "What is this?"

"I know it's unconventional, but I thought it was time we step out of our comfort zone."

"Is this what I think it is?"

"If you're thinking a night filled with erotic sex, then yes."

"Where did you find this?"

"Online, dummy. It isn't hard. I googled gifts of pleasure, and this came up."

Derek read. "Give the gift of erotic love to that special someone. Choose from our list of fantasies."

"I chose the threesome. You, me, and someone else. I arranged for a getaway weekend."

"In two months."

"Yes, I would have planned it for this weekend, but apple picking, bike riding, and erotic sex didn't go together. A fancy dinner at the Hilton, drinks in the room, and then whatever comes next works."

"A threesome. Is this a gift or payback?"

"Are you upset?"

"We just spent years in therapy, and you thought this gift would please me?"

"We have spent a lot of time in therapy, and I think we are strong enough to step out of our comfort zone."

"If this is a joke, it isn't funny." Derek tossed the card on the bed.

"When we reconciled, you said there wasn't anything you wouldn't do to please me."

"This is payback for what I did in college. You're not over it, are you?"

Kathy reached for Derek. "This isn't payback. I swear. I've been curious, and I want to satisfy my curiosity."

"What are you curious about?"

"Derek, please don't be upset. Maybe, I should have brought up the subject instead of trying to surprise you. Ever since I've known about the threesome, I've fantasized about you, me, and someone else."

"You have to be joking?"

"It's not a joke. I've arranged for someone to meet us in two months. As I said, I want this."

"And if I'm not on board, you're still going to go through with this? You'd sleep with another man, and I assume a woman, just to satisfy your curiosity? If this isn't payback, then what would you call it? I guess it isn't cheating if your wife tells you up front it's going to happen."

Placing her arms around Derek's neck, she said, "I want it to be you, me, and of course, another woman. I swear on our children's lives, there will never be any other man in my bed other than you. Please say yes. It can be fun, or it can be a bust. Come along on my fantasy ride. I love the Porsche, but if you really want to please me, one night, that's all I'm asking for." Kathy crossed her heart.

When Derek realized Kathy wasn't joking, he felt the bile in his stomach rise. If he didn't agree to Kathy's wish, she might consider going through with her plans without him. Derek detested another man touching his wife, and because of his fear, he said, "I'll consider it."

Kathy smiled.

*****

"So how was Vermont?"

"Fabulous."

"Was the motel still standing?"

"No. It was torn down and replaced with the Ski-Lift Hotel and Spa."

Lauren laughed.

"We golfed. I told you I was taking golf lessons. I'm not bad. We biked, hiked, swam, and—"

"You screwed like dogs in heat."

"How's Bruce?"

"He's good."

"Has he brought up shacking up together?"

"No, and I'm furious."

"Why don't you just ask him?"

"I'd rather be asked."

"This is the twenty-first century, Lauren, and Gloria Steinem is your idol."

"What if I ask, and he refuses me? I want to save myself the embarrassment of being rejected."

"True, you can't handle rejection. Bruce has been living on his own for so long he might not like living with someone 24/7. You can take the bull by the horns or wait to be asked—your choice."

"Lauren, this question might seem strange, but you've slept with both men and women. Is there a difference?"

"You're kidding me, right?"

"I know the difference between a man and a woman, girlfriend. A woman is soft, and a man is a man. Which one is more pleasing?"

"Haven't you ever had fantasies about being with a woman?"

Kathy chuckled. "Everyone has fantasies, Lauren."

CHAPTER 26

Elle entered the apartment and found Jacques alone in the kitchen. "You're home." He came to greet her with a hug and kiss. "How was your day?"

"Stressful. I'm sure the boys are down for the night."

"They too had a stressful day. Liam fell off the round-wheel thingy at the park and scraped his knee. Julie said he cried on the way home but went down for his nap easily. Ethan has a runny nose. I called the pediatrician. We have an appointment at nine tomorrow. I don't have anything pressing at the office in the morning. I told Julie to arrive at ten tomorrow."

Elle's eyes began to well up with tears.

"What is wrong, *mon amour*?"

"Nothing. I'm going to check on the boys."

"I'll warm your plate of food."

Elle stared at her boys while they slept. She loved her job, but on late nights like this, she felt the pain of not spending precious time with her children. Liam's breathing was steady and slow. Ethan's breathing was rapid and wheezy. She felt Ethan's head; it was cool to the touch. She sighed. Elle touched his thick head of blond hair, so different from Liam's whose hair was brown and wavy. Both had striking blue eyes. She smiled. Before she left the room, she looked under the blanket to take a peek at Liam's knee. It was covered with a large Band-Aid. She noticed the surrounding skin, not covered by the Band-Aid, was red. Elle gently lowered the blanket and left the room.

Jacques was in the kitchen loading the dishwasher.

She sat at the counter and uncovered the plate of food in front of her. "This looks good, but I'd rather have tea and a few cookies."

Jacques removed the plate. Elle rose and filled the teapot with water. "I want the doctor to take a look at Liam's knee to make sure it's not infected. Ethan's breathing is wheezy."

"I'm sure it's only a cold," said Jacques. "I'll have the doctor check Liam's knee. Elle, did you get a chance to speak with the producers?"

"I did. They weren't crazy about the idea. Seems I'm really good at anchoring the six o'clock news."

"I know your career means a lot to you, but you can leave if you want. We have enough to purchase a nice-sized home with a backyard. We can get Liam the puppy he's been wishing for. You don't have to work, Elle. I earn enough to support us. If you wish to return to work when the boys are in school full-time, you can."

"I love my job, but it's the time I'm not spending with the boys during the week that hurts. I look forward to the weekends just to spend quality time with them. Life was easier in Paris."

"We Parisians don't handle stress very well. We need time to relax, drink wine, make love, and enjoy the family."

"Are you enjoying life here in the States, Jacques?"

"I do. My job isn't as stressful as yours. At least twice a week I come home for lunch and spend two hours with the boys. I don't have a problem getting home before my wife and cooking her dinner. Nights, when you're working late, I don't mind bath time or bedtime with the boys."

"And I'm jealous that you get to spend more time with them than I do. If I get to spend thirty minutes with Ethan daily, it's a lot. Liam doesn't make it through one page of the book we read together at bedtime before he nods off. I fear that one day, I'm going to regret not being here for their formative years."

"The boys love you, Elle. Liam is so proud that his mommy gets to be on TV. He tells everyone he meets that his mommy is in the TV every night."

Elle smiled.

"You have to stop beating yourself up and make a decision that is right for you."

After hearing that Ethan was going to be fine and Liam's knee would heal nicely, Elle went back to work confident that she was doing a good job as a mother and as the anchorwoman of the six o'clock news. She couldn't deny that her life in Paris was good. The stress was minimal, and she always had enough time to be with Jacques, their friends, and his family. She wondered if she had made the right decision to return to the States. If she would have remained in Paris, her children would have spoken more than one language. Friends of Jacques spoke a total of four to five languages. It was common for people living in Europe to speak more than one language, and that was what she wanted for her boys. She worried that living in the States, where it was instilled in young immigrants to learn to speak English and rid themselves of their native language, her boys would grow soft and cast off speaking more than two languages, French and English. Jacques had kept his promise. He spoke to the boys in French, and they understood. English it's a *truck*, and in French it is *un camion*. Elle's phone buzzed.

"Hi, Kathy."

"I didn't think you would answer. I was going to leave a message. I won't keep you. I was just wondering what you guys were doing for Thanksgiving this year?"

"I guess spending it with you."

"Is Trudy spending Thanksgiving with you?"

"No. Mom and Uncle Charlie are spending Thanksgiving with Elaine's family and then heading to us for the entire month of December."

"Great. Lauren will be thrilled to hear you guys are coming. Have you spoken to Lauren?"

"Just last week. She's still head over heels in love with Bruce."

"Isn't it wonderful? I'm glad she has Bruce to take her mind off Josh."

"I'd like to ring that boy's neck. He negligent on calling."

"He's probably busy studying. Can you believe he's graduating college in May? Did Lauren mention that he knew the date of graduation and didn't bother to tell her? Jake called and gave her the details. She isn't sure Josh wants her there."

"She has to go whether he wants her there or not. Together, we can convince her to attend her son's graduation. How are the kids? Are you and Derek still humping like rabbits?"

Kathy laughed. She wanted to tell Elle her little secret but decided against it. "Of course. I know you're busy. I called to confirm you're spending Thanksgiving with us. Alice, Nancy, Lauren, Bruce, Michelle, and Jake are coming. Kelly, of course. Did I forget anyone? Oh yes, Derek's family. Should I make a reservation for you at the same hotel as the others?"

"I'll have my assistant make the arrangement. The Hilton, correct?"

"Yes. Wow, your own assistant. Girl, you sure have come a long way from waitressing in Cape May."

Elle chuckled. "I've got to go. Kiss the family for me."

*****

Kathy disconnected. Placing the pad and pencil that were in her hands on the kitchen counter, she thought about the upcoming weekend and smiled. She had purchased sexy undergarments for the occasion. She wanted to look her best for Derek and their guest. Grinning ear to ear, Kathy wondered what the woman would look like. She had requested an exotic-looking woman, one with dark hair and complexion. Derek hadn't fully committed to her request, but he was mindful that three days from now, their lives were about to change. They only discussed the upcoming event one other time.

Two weeks ago, after making love, Derek moved onto his side and asked, "Kathy, I've given your fancy request a lot of thought. I've been hoping you'd tell me this is all a joke, but I think you might be serious about—"

Kathy nodded her head in agreement.

"You know how truly sorry I am for hurting you. I swear on our children's lives that I will never hurt you again. So I'm asking—no, I'm begging, please let's not do this."

"What are you afraid of, Derek?"

"Kathy, you said you're curious about what it would feel like to be with a woman. I'm curious why this is so important to you."

"Are you changing your mind?"

"I never said I was going through with it."

"You never said you weren't."

"I'm concerned. We just got over a huge hurdle as a couple. The affair, you discovering what transpired in college—it almost destroyed us. This could change everything."

"How?"

"Sexual encounters, such as these can become addictive. I'm not sure this is what I want for myself. I like my life just as it is—you and me and the kids."

Kathy laughed. "You can't become addicted to something that will only happen once."

"How can you be so sure?"

"Do you trust me, Derek?"

Derek didn't answer.

"I'm curious, and I need to scratch the itch. One night."

They didn't bring up the subject since that night. Kathy couldn't understand why Derek wasn't as excited as she. Most men would be thrilled to have a wife who wanted to spice things up in the bedroom. She and Derek had a solid sexual relationship, but he feared this encounter would change them. One does not become addicted from one encounter. One night, and all that would remain were the memories they would share on their anniversary.

*****

Derek sat behind the desk in his office and tried to concentrate on the file in his hands. Placing the file on the desk, he ran his fingers through his hair. In three days, he would be confronted with a choice to go through with Kathy's request or say no. Derek was sure that a threesome was never going to happen. But as the time drew near, he feared Kathy's curiosity might come to fruition.

Wasn't this every man's dream to make love to two women? The encounter in college had turned him on, but he was young and inexperienced. Casey directed the entire show. She knew what would excite him and how to excite Lauren. They met several times before Derek put a stop to it once Kathy had agreed to a movie and a burger. He remembered the night well when he confessed to Lauren and Casey that this was a mistake. Lauren seemed relieved. Casey questioned how could they be sure he wouldn't go through with his threat? He confessed that Kathy had agreed to go out with him. If Kathy found out, it could hurt his chances with her. Casey laughed saying, "What makes you think we would keep something like this from our best friend?" Derek begged and pleaded. When Casey wasn't buying it, he went in for the kill saying, if they told Kathy the truth, he would make good on his threat. At first, it was difficult being in Lauren and Casey's company with Kathy at his side, but in time, all seemed to be forgotten, and the five, along with Jake, became inseparable.

This time, it was different. The threesome included a complete stranger, who was hired by his wife. There would be no deceit involved. He could sit back and enjoy the ride, but he didn't want to. He didn't want another person pleasuring his wife. He was jealous and envious that Kathy might enjoy another.

Up until now, his wife was faithful to him, but this weekend would change everything. Kathy wasn't being unfaithful to him if the parties involved agreed, except Derek wasn't in agreement and wondered what would happen if he disagreed. He'd put Kathy through the wringer when he cheated on her with Nina, and she forgave him. Was this his penance, and now it was his turn to pay the piper?

This was happening, and he was sure of it. His only hope was that it was a trick. He deserved this long two months of anguish he was experiencing since receiving this ridiculous gift. Deep down, he prayed before anything happened, Kathy's laughter would fill the room, saying, "*April Fools*," in September.

His subconscious was also playing tricks on him. There were many nights while Kathy's breathing was slow from a state of deep sleep. He imagined her breathing growing louder, envisioning Kathy being pleasured by the woman, with him behind his wife, her breasts cupped in his hands, nibbling and kissing them angrily, hungrily kissing her mouth while he searched for her tongue, her whining with pleasure and asking them not to stop. Becoming aroused, he rose and went into the bathroom to satisfy his erection. Returning to bed, he tried hard to put the thought out of his mind, but time after time, he was unsuccessful.

Derek wondered, *If I go through with Kathy's wishes, what will be the outcome? Will I desire more of the same, or will I feel betrayed and hurt?* Finally, he now knew the pain his wife had felt when he betrayed her. In three days, he would have his answer.

*****

Kathy was at the dressing table applying ruby-red lipstick to her lips. Derek was showering. Life as she knew it had changed. She didn't beat herself up about leaving the children with Fanny. It was only for one night. And she was hoping this would be a night she wouldn't soon forget.

Derek entered the room. He had been silent on the drive to the hotel. They went for a swim after checking into the room. Usually, they would have made love as soon as they entered their hotel room. A swim in the pool, relaxing in the Jacuzzi, cocktails at the bar.

"Good shower?"

"It was okay."

"Derek, what's wrong? Are you nervous about this evening?"

"Am I nervous about this evening? What do you think?"

Kathy smiled. "I think you're being ridiculous. It's not like you haven't made love to more than one woman at a time."

Derek frowned. "I'm convinced you still haven't forgiven me for Lauren and Nina."

"Lauren, Nina, and Casey. How easily you forget."

"How could I forget with you reminding me every so often?"

"Derek, I'm only kidding with you. That is our past. Tonight is our future."

"Future? This isn't the future I've planned for us. As far as I'm concerned, this is a one-time experience for you. Remember, I only agreed to put an end to your curiosity."

Kathy laughed.

"I don't see the humor in any of this."

"You know what you need, a few bottles of vodka from the mini bar."

"I can't believe you think tonight is a good idea. After two years of therapy to try to work through me cheating on you, you want to hook up with another woman."

"I want *us* to hook up with another woman." Kathy rose. "I'm going to get ready. We are meeting Patty at seven."

"She has a name?"

"Of course, she has a name, silly."

Derek collapsed in a chair asking himself how he could put a stop to this evening.

Kathy entered the room, naked. Derek stared at her as she stepped into a thong panty and a sexy bra. He couldn't take his eyes off her. When she walked toward him, he wondered if she would spread her legs and place herself on his lap, but instead, she reached into the closet and retrieved the dress she would wear that night. Of course, the dress was red and sexy. She slipped her feet into four-inch heels that laced around her ankles. She swung her hair to the left when she retrieved a small purse and then to the right as she filled it with several items.

She twirled around asking, "How do I look?"

He answered, "Beautiful. I don't know how you do it. You can wrap a sheet around you and still look like a million bucks."

"This dress might not have cost a million, but it wasn't cheap."

"By the looks of those shoes, the dress was probably a bargain."

"And you would be right. It is six forty-five. We should go."

When the couple entered the restaurant, heads turned. The attention went unnoticed by the couple. The waiter informed them that their guest had not yet arrived. Kathy whispered to Derek, "She hasn't arrived."

Derek answered, "Maybe she isn't coming."

Kathy slapped Derek's arm.

Kathy and Derek waited twenty minutes before Patty arrived. She was directed to the table. She introduced herself. Patty was five nine with shoulder-length wavy brown hair, eyes the color of night, her body curvy, and ample breasts. Kathy was impressed with the choice the service had provided. Derek became uncomfortable by the looks of the woman standing before him.

Light conversation transpired between Kathy and Patty while they ordered dinner and drinks. Derek only spoke when spoken to.

Kathy commented on the wine. "This is really good. It's a German wine, correct?"

"Most prefer a French wine, but I prefer a German Riesling," said Patty.

"I agree. Derek, I don't think we've had this brand before, do you?"

"All wines taste the same to me."

Kathy needed to address the elephant in the room. Speaking directly to Patty, Kathy confessed, "You have to excuse my husband, Patty. He's really quite charming. He's just uncomfortable with this arrangement. Can I start by asking how long you've been in this profession, and what health precautions are required of you?"

"Kathy," said Derek.

"You're a doctor. Of course, the latter question is necessary."

"I'm not offended. I graduated cum laude as a sex therapist. Of course, I am required to meet all the state health requirements. You should have received a copy of my recent tests. It's sent via email."

"Yes, of course, I did receive the email."

Derek asked, "You're a sex therapist?"

"Yes."

"We aren't in need of a sex therapist. We have no issues in that department. My wife would agree we have a healthy and happy sex life."

"Kathy, might I ask why you requested my services?"

"My best friend recently informed me she's bi. I've never been with a woman, and I wanted to test the waters. I asked my husband to be a part of the experience. I wasn't expecting a sex therapist, more along the lines of a call girl. I hope that wasn't offensive."

"None taken. It might shock you, but I've dealt with your situation a number of times. Dr. Wilson, correct me if I'm wrong, but I don't think you're fully on board with your wife's request."

"And you would be right. I don't feel comfortable with this conversation."

The Palm Reader

"I agree it is a difficult conversation, but you're here, and now, I'm curious to know why you went along with your wife's request."

"I get the feeling that Kathy will satisfy her curiosity, with or without me. I like it to be with me."

"I see. I rather a couple be in agreement." Patty paused. "You've already paid for the evening. Why don't we enjoy the dinner and drinks and then call it an evening?"

"Derek, you agreed. I don't want Patty to leave."

Derek bowed to Kathy's request. "Let's enjoy dinner and have dessert sent to the room."

Derek reached for Kathy's hand and gently squeezed it.

*****

When the trio entered the hotel room, Derek poured himself a stiff drink. Kathy offered Patty a glass of wine, and she accepted. With a glass of wine in hand, Patty walked toward the sofa in the room and sat. Sipping her wine, she kept a close watch on the couple. In her professional opinion, the woman would easily accept her advances, and the man could be easily persuaded to join in.

Kathy sat next to Patty on the sofa. She gulped the wine in her glass. She was excited about what would happen next. She glanced in Derek's direction and smiled before refilling her glass with wine. Derek sat stoic in the chair across from them.

Kathy, again, reached for the wine bottle. Patty stopped her and placed the bottle down. She rested her right hand on Kathy's knee. Derek's eyes immediately went to Kathy's knee. Patty moved her hand further up Kathy's leg. Kathy moved closer to Patty. She placed her hand on the woman's hair and stroked it.

"Your hair is beautiful." Patty smiled, placed her left hand on Kathy's cheek, and leaned in for a kiss.

Kathy's mouth opened easily. Patty enjoyed the soft feel of Kathy's lips. She was a beautiful woman. From the corner of her eyes, she took notice of the husband watching. He seemed uncomfortable with how easily his wife responded to Patty's kisses. Patty pulled away. Kathy stared into her eyes. "Did I do something wrong?"

"No. I thought you might want to remove your dress."

Kathy didn't hesitate. She stood and turned her back to Patty. Patty stood and slowly lowered the zipper on the dress, which fell from Kathy's body. Now she turned toward Patty, who became aroused seeing Kathy's half-naked body. She reached in and took Kathy into her arms, kissing her gently on the lips, while she unhooked the strapless bra. When Kathy's breasts were free, she cupped them in her hands. Every so often keeping a close eye on the husband. Derek rose and pushed the coffee table to the side. When he was at Patty's side, she removed her lips from Kathy and placed them on Derek's mouth. His response to her touch was instant. Feeling guilty, he removed his lips from hers and began to kiss his wife.

She whispered, "Let's move this to the bed."

Patty removed Kathy's panties and began to pleasure her. Derek stood beside the bed.

Kathy pleaded, "Derek, please."

Derek lay with them. After making love a second time, the threesome went into the shower. The night was wild and exciting.

When morning came, Derek and Kathy rose to find Patty gone. They knew they had crossed the forbidden line. Neither felt any guilt, remorse, or pain for inviting Patty into their bed. Derek noticed a note on the nightstand. Retrieving it, he read, "Thanks for an erotic evening." Derek passed the note to Kathy. "She left her business card." Kathy read it and smiled.

Their marriage only grew stronger after the night they spent with Patty. Derek and she were united, not only by the deep love they felt for each other, but by a secret that they would take to their graves. Kathy and Derek made love often, each thinking of the night they had spent with Patty. The pleasure they felt from Patty's touch and her soft and silky body made their pleasure for each other intensify. This was not something one came back from easily. Months later, Kathy confronted Derek and informed him that not Patty, but another woman would be joining them on their next getaway weekend. Derek did not protest. They would enjoy others during their marriage. It wasn't a constant in their lives, but when the heat was cooling in the bedroom, they made arrangements to rekindle the fire.

CHAPTER 27

Lauren woke early on Thursday. She wanted to get to the supermarket before the Labor Day crowd started pouring in. Labor Day, the summer had gone by in a flash. In May, she and Bruce had attended Josh's graduation. Josh was cool to Lauren but took an instant liking to Bruce. Jonathan and Kelly were spending time at the Cape, so Josh, with Cindy, had agreed to come for a visit. She left her children sleeping when she left for the supermarket.

In June, Josh presented Cindy with an engagement ring. Lauren loved the girl and thought Josh had made the right choice. This picnic was a small celebration of the upcoming nuptials.

Lauren entered the supermarket smiling from ear to ear. While strolling from one aisle to the next, she hummed her favorite Adele song, "Rumors." Adding her own version, she sang, "Rumor has it, you might want to make me your wife." After a night of sex, Bruce brought up their living arrangements. He was ready to share a home with Lauren. His house, of course, was larger than hers, but they both agreed the cottage was cozy and warm. More than enough room for two people, but not large enough for grandchildren. She would cross that bridge when she came to it. She considered many times adding on an extension to the house. It might be time to talk with a contractor. She ran her thoughts by Bruce later in the month.

"Hello, Lauren."

Lauren turned toward the familiar voice. "Shelby."

"Shopping for the Labor Day weekend?"

"Yes. I thought your run with the gallery had come to an end?"

"It did."

At that moment, a beautiful girl several years younger than Shelby stood beside her.

"I can't believe it's you, Lauren Hicks Croft. It's a pleasure to meet you." The young girl extended her hand, and Lauren shook it. "When Shelby found out that I'm a fan, she told me you and she were friends. When I heard we were spending a few days at the Cape, I asked her to give you call. It would be great if we could have lunch together."

"Sweetie, I told you Lauren spends the holidays with her family. How are Josh and Kelly?"

"Kelly is teaching art at the Winchendon School."

"And Josh?"

"Josh is living in California, has a great job, and is engaged to an amazing girl. Her name is Cindy, and I adore her."

"So things are going well with the children."

Shelby was dying to know if Josh and Lauren had worked out their differences. Lauren wanted to put the girl at ease since Shelby blamed herself for coming between them.

"Yes, we are all good. Josh and Cindy are here for the long and much-needed relaxing weekend. Kelly has been dating Jonathan for several years. How long are you staying?"

"We leave on Wednesday."

"I might not be able to swing a lunch, but breakfast might work."

Shelby interjected, "I want to be on the road by seven on Wednesday."

Lauren got the hint that Shelby wasn't interested in catching up. "Well, maybe next time you're in town, we can have lunch."

"Shelby, does it make a difference if we get on the road by twelve on Wednesday? What about an early breakfast on Wednesday. I want to hear what Lauren has planned for the *Millennium Agent*."

Lauren asked, "I'm sorry, I didn't get your name."

"Constance, but you can call me Connie."

"Connie, a writer takes an oath never to give away the plot."

Connie begged, "Not even a little hint?"

Lauren chuckled. "If you want to know if she's going to marry the hunk, no. A mysterious woman will enter the picture, and our girl will have second thoughts about marrying."

Lauren spoke without thinking. She could sense how uncomfortable Shelby had become by what was said.

Connie said, "I can't wait for the next book. Do you know how long it will be before I can purchase a copy?"

"I'll send Shelby a copy. Are you still living at the same address?"

"Yes. Connie, you didn't forget to get toothpaste and a bar of soap, did you?"

"I did forget. I'll leave you two time to catch up while I finish shopping. It was nice meeting you, Lauren. I'm going to work on changing Shelby's mind about an early breakfast on Wednesday."

Lauren smiled.

"She's lovely. How long have you been dating?"

"Six months. She is lovely, but a little too young for me. Are you still with Bruce?"

"Yes. It's going well."

"I'm happy for you, Lauren. I'm glad we have a few minutes alone so I can ask. Were you able to mend the fences with Josh? I've always felt awful about coming between you and your son."

"You shouldn't be. Josh and I are fine," Lauren lied. "He just needed a little time."

"I guess he's happy you're with Bruce?"

"He never really says how he feels about Bruce, or what happened between you and me. My guess is, he'd rather I keep my private life to myself."

Shelby nodded her head. "I'm sure you can understand that breakfast is out of the question."

"I understand. I should be going, I have to pick up my order from the butcher. It was good seeing you, Shelby."

*****

While lying together on the cot staring at the stars, Lauren said, "I met Shelby at the supermarket today. She's in town for a few days."

Bruce didn't respond. Lauren turned toward him. "She's dating a very young and attractive woman. Her name is Connie, and I'm her favorite author. Connie wanted to have breakfast on Wednesday, but Shelby put a stop to it."

"Why? I hope she didn't think I'd be jealous if you had breakfast with an old flame."

"So you wouldn't be jealous if an old flame asked me out?"

"No."

Lauren rose to face Bruce. "You're kidding, right? I thought we had something special. I guess I was wrong."

Bruce laughed. "If an old flame came on to you, I'd knock his or her lights out."

"I don't believe you. Anyway, I made you a promise that if you and I connected, you'd be my one and only."

Bruce laughed. "And, Ms. Hicks, since you kept that promise, I have something for you." Bruce pulled a little velvet box from behind his back.

"Is that what I think it is?" Lauren reached for the box. "Wait, are you asking me to marry you?"

Bruce opened the box and presented Lauren with a sizable solitaire diamond ring.

"Bruce, it's beautiful."

"Lauren, I might have overstepped. I'm not sure you even want to marry. This ring can be whatever you want it to be. I'm committed to this relationship."

Lauren hugged Bruce, then whispered in his ear, "Are you sure you want to spend the rest of your life with me? I can be a little difficult at times. I don't want to be responsible for making another person unhappy."

Bruce kissed Lauren to keep her quiet. "You think a Navy man can't handle a few difficult situations? Your mood swings don't change how I feel about you."

"I don't have mood swings."

"You don't? I agree to disagree."

"Do you think you're perfect? Don't answer because you are perfect. It sickens me how perfect you are."

"Then it's a yes. Whatever this ring represents, we are committing ourselves to a life of happiness."

"I do see myself married to you, but can we keep the ring between you and me for now? Josh just announced his engagement to Cindy, and I don't want to upstage them."

"As I said, pretty lady, I'm not going anywhere. If one day, you wake up and decide to visit a Justice of the Peace, I'm on board."

*****

In the morning, Lauren watched Bruce as he slept. She glanced at the ring on her finger and smiled. Slipping out of bed, she placed the ring in her jewelry box and descended the stairs. Opening the front door, she went outside and sat on the porch swing to watch the sunrise, thinking about her life and the changes that had occurred over the past five years, thanking the heavens that her friendship with Kathy had remained intact; her son was able to spend time with her after her affair with Shelby had placed a crack in their relationship; that her daughter was a forgiving soul; and Bruce entering her life was more than she could have hoped for.

"You're up early."

"Josh. Come sit. It's a beautiful sunrise. Looks like another fabulous day."

Mother and son sat in silence watching the sunrise. As the sun reached its peak, Josh asked, "Did Bruce stay the night?"

Lauren wondered if it was a bad idea having Bruce stay the night with her children in the house. "He did. Does that bother you? Of course, it does. I should have been considerate of your feelings."

"It's your house."

"Yes, but I owed you the courtesy of asking."

"I like Bruce. It doesn't upset me that he spent the night."

Lauren smiled.

"I'm happy you like Bruce. He might be around for a very long time."

"Do you love him?"

"I do."

"Two years ago, you wanted to spend the rest of your life with that woman."

Lauren sighed. "You don't trust that I know my own feelings?"

"I guess I'm trying to figure out how you go from loving a woman back to loving a man and maybe back to loving a woman."

"It isn't uncommon for a woman to test the waters with another woman. To you, I might seem fickle, but I can assure you, I'm not. I am in love with Bruce, and I want to spend the rest of my life with him."

"I hope you didn't break it off with your girlfriend and hook up with Bruce because you thought my feelings toward you might change?"

Lauren became furious with her son. "You think I'd stoop that low just to win back your love? You are gravely mistaken, young man. I'm not walking on shells with you any longer, Josh. I think your treatment of me is disrespectful and unwarranted. The world isn't a perfect place, and neither are the people that walk this earth. It's time you grew up, Josh."

Lauren rose and left Josh with his thoughts. Suddenly, the black cloud that had followed her for years had lifted. She didn't need Josh's or anyone's approval to live her own damn life.

Lauren thought of the gypsy woman; she would be proud to know she no longer hid behind the character in her novels.

CHAPTER 28

"You're engaged?"

"I wasn't going to tell anyone, but I can't keep something like this from you and Elle. By the way, I've been calling Elle, but she hasn't returned my calls."

"She's in Disney World. Did you set a date? Are you going to change your name to Hamilton?"

"A date?"

"A wedding date."

"As I said, we are not telling anyone, and no, if I marry, I'm not changing my name."

"I don't get it. You accepted the man's ring, but there won't be a wedding?"

"Maybe one day."

"Kids today. They like to milk the cow, but don't want to pay for the cream."

"You just made that up, didn't you?"

"No, actually I forgot how the saying goes. I'm happy for you, Lauren. How big is the stone?"

"A little over two karats."

"Perfect. Clear cut? Good color?"

"I'm not a jeweler, but it's impressive."

"Great."

"What is Elle doing in Disney World?"

"Spending time with the boys and Jacques."

"Oh, I thought she was on assignment."

"No. I think the job is getting to her."

"She's mentioned to me that she'd like to slow down and spend more time with the boys. Maybe she should give up working."

"I'm proud of you, Lauren. You can finally admit that having a career isn't all it's cracked up to be."

"I'm going soft. I cry more now than I ever did in the past. I'm getting old."

"Speak for yourself. I've never felt better."

Kathy wanted to tell Lauren about the erotic weekends with Derek, and the two fabulous women that had rocked their world.

She thought of the gypsy woman and questioned her powers. The woman never saw Kathy as the promiscuous woman. The new role her life had taken gave her overwhelming pleasure and happiness. Whoever said you can't be happy 24/7 should try living her life.

*****

Elle sat under a shaded tree waiting for Jacques to return with the boys. She had just spoken with Lauren and was grinning from ear to ear. Elle loved how Lauren put her own spin on receiving an engagement ring.

"It's a commitment ring, Elle, for now."

Only Lauren, being the pillar of strength, could accept an engagement ring and want nothing more than to live happily ever after.

"So you don't want to get married?"

"I don't want to talk weddings with Josh just getting engaged. Anyway, we are not children. We don't need a piece of paper to commit."

"My feelings exactly. How did the weekend go with Josh?"

"Great. I told him to grow up, and it felt good."

"Good for you."

"How's Disney World?"

"I'm over the long lines, the sweltering heat, Mickey, and Minnie."

Lauren laughed. "Are the kids having a good time?"

"They are loving it."

"You're loving every minute being with your family, aren't you?"

"I am, but all good things must come to an end."

Lauren didn't push discussing Elle's job. They talked for ten minutes longer before they disconnected.

Tomorrow, she and her family would board the red-eye for home. Elle didn't want her time with the boys to end. Waiting for her family to return, she reflected on her last conversation with the network producers. She made a plug to give her a shot as a talk show host. Her work hours would be conducive to the boys' time away from home. They didn't shoot down the idea but didn't think the time was right for another talk show host. The news had taken on most of the daytime slots, and game shows were popular with the nighttime audiences.

Elle thought there was too much news time and not enough "lie back and enjoy" time. She could see herself having a blast interviewing pop stars, actors, and actresses. When the viewers tired of the Hollywood scene, she'd slam dunk an interview with the latest politicians or a world leader.

She'd give it another six months before approaching the producers again. If they weren't receptive to her idea, she would send out feelers to other networks. If all her efforts to reduce her working hours failed, she might consider hanging up the towel.

The gypsy woman told her to face her demons. Her job was her latest demon. She needed to find a way to control the demon before it took control of her.

*****

Derek sat staring at the computer. He was about to research the latest heart valves, but his mind was consumed with thoughts of their latest hookup, Janice, another beauty but not as beautiful as his wife. He couldn't get the image of Kathy and Janice out of his mind. Kathy seemed too implored while the woman did her magic. He didn't feel threatened or jealous, and that upset him. He didn't like the path their lives had taken.

Kathy had said it would be a one-time experience. Janice was their third experience, and Derek wanted out. The conversation and action that transpired after Janice left that day convinced him that convincing Kathy enough was enough wasn't going to be easy.

Kathy was seated in a chair her robe hanging loosely off her shoulders, totally naked underneath. She was brushing her hair. Janice had just left, and Derek was lying naked on the bed.

"Kathy, we need to talk."

"Talk about what?"

"I think we have to put a stop to this. You said this would be a one-time experience, and Janice is the third woman we've slept with."

Kathy lowered her head, placed the brush on the table, stood up, and began to walk toward Derek. Pulling the sheet back from his body, she straddled him. "Didn't you enjoy yourself?"

"That's not the point. You know I wasn't in total agreement with this arrangement. I don't think it's healthy or good—"

Kathy let the robe slip from her body. She placed her hands on Derek's chest and lowered herself, placing her lips upon his. "You're right. It's not good. It's great."

"Kathy."

"Derek, why do you want to ruin a good thing? I thought you were really into Janice. I thought this might be the time that you took her for yourself. Is that what you're worried about? You're afraid if you had sex with her, I'd be jealous, or worse, I wouldn't be able to handle it? Well, you're wrong. Or are you jealous of my having sex with someone else?"

"I don't want to have sex with any other woman but you. And yes, I am feeling a little jealous. You seem to be enjoying this more than I thought you would."

Kathy laughed. "I'm not going to lie to you. I look forward to our special weekends. Don't look so sad. You know that I love making love to you, and we have a fantastic love life, but the women are the icing on the cake."

"Kathy, I want us to take a break."

"I can handle a break. I promise not to hire another girl until after the holidays. Although holidays can be stressful, and an erotic night of sex might be just what a doctor would suggest."

"This isn't funny, Kathy. For this to work, we have to be in agreement, and I'm becoming uncomfortable."

Kathy leaned in with another kiss. She forced Derek's mouth open and placed her tongue deep inside his mouth. She had accomplished what she was after; Derek was hard.

When she released him from the kiss, she whispered into his ear, "You have to let go. If you need to enter the woman, I can help with that."

The warmth of Kathy's breath on his ear and the offer of intercourse with another woman aroused him further. He ran his fingers through her hair. He pulled her hair so hard her head fell back, and she moaned. He tossed her down and turned her on all fours. He took her from behind and didn't release the hold he had on her hair. Kathy didn't cry out in pain. The sound coming from her was sheer pleasure.

When they were finished, Derek lay exhausted on the bed. Kathy rose up, looked down upon him, and said, "We'll hold off until after the holidays." As she sashayed away, *triumphant* was the word Derek would use to describe the look on her face.

He ran his fingers through his hair. He considered himself an equal to Kathy, but lately, he felt she held all the cards. Leaning back in his chair, he stared at the ceiling and sighed. He wanted back the life he and Kathy had before the affair with Nina. But what man wouldn't want the woman Kathy had become? She was sexy as hell before their weekend encounters, but now she was even sexier and more erotic. She went down on both him and the women, like a pro. Nothing was out of the question when it came to sexual pleasure. They'd never locked the bedroom door when they made love. Now Derek made sure the door was locked and secure because he never knew what tricks Kathy had up her sleeve.

It was like being married to Dr. Jekyll and Mrs. Hyde. During the day, she was Jekyll, the sweet and loving mom. At night, Mrs. Hyde found her way into their bedroom.

He wasn't complaining, but how far does one go for pleasure? He slapped the back of his head to stop his thoughts from escalating. He was sure, in time, the thrill would run its course, and then they would find a way back to a normal life. Would their marriage take a downward turn when the thrill was gone?

He had to find a way to convince Kathy that they didn't need a third person to enrich their already enriched sex life.

CHAPTER 29

The girls shouted cheers of joy when they arrived at Kathy's house to celebrate Thanksgiving dinner.

"Alice, it's so good to see you."

"We talk every week, Lauren."

"Yes, but not in person. How are you?"

"Good."

"Nancy, how are you? Still dating this one, I see."

Alice draped her arm around Nancy's shoulder. Nancy blushed to her touch.

"Liam, the boys are in the playroom," said Kathy.

Liam ran off, and Ethan followed his brother.

Derek almost collided with Liam and Ethan.

"Wow, the boys have grown." Derek extended his hand, "Happy Thanksgiving, Jacques. Where is Bruce?"

"He had to use the little boy's room," said Lauren. Lauren turned to see Bruce heading toward her. "Here's my handsome man."

"Happy Thanksgiving, Derek."

"Bruce. My apologies, man. Good luck with this one."

Lauren slapped Derek's arm. "He's lucky to have me."

Elle kissed and hugged Bruce. "Congratulations. She's a keeper."

"I agree with Derek," said Alice. "Are you sure you want to tie yourself down with this woman, Bruce?"

"As I told Lauren, I'm in for the long haul."

"Hey, I thought we were friends," said Lauren.

Alice smiled. "We are, but you can be difficult."

"Exactly what I said, but he didn't seem to care."

The friends had a good laugh at Lauren's expense.

When Jake and Michelle arrived, the party was in full swing. The children entertained themselves in the playroom with Kelly and Jonathan's supervision.

At the end of the day, the ladies gathered around the island in the kitchen, leaving the men to their football games while the children napped nearby.

"Grab that bottle of wine, Lauren. The firepit is ablaze in the backyard. Let's take advantage of the quiet," said Kathy.

Surrounding the firepit with their wine glasses filled to the brim, they began a casual conversation.

"News alert. I'm adding an addition to the cottage. Bruce is putting his home up for sale and moving in with me."

Joking, Elle asked, "To accommodate the grandkids when they visit?"

"I hope so."

"When are you starting construction, Lauren?"

"Sometime in March, Alice. I already started to clear out the attic to house some of Bruce's things."

Kathy chuckled.

"What so funny, girlfriend?

"You, my friend. You're over the moon about your new beau."

"I get butterflies in my stomach just thinking about him, and the sex is amazing."

"Sexually, we are at our peak," said Kathy.

"I thought the new peak was sixty," said Alice.

"Life isn't fair," said Elle.

"Why, Elle?"

"Men are always ready, willing, and able. Women have to deal with menopause, vaginal dryness, and gravity."

Alice laughed at Elle's comment. "I never heard my mother complain about menopause, vaginal dryness, or gravity. The women of the past were pioneers. They suffered in silence. On a lighter note, when are you ladies going to pay me a visit? I've been out to the Cape every summer for five years. Washington three times a year. Connecticut twice a year."

"The only good memories I have of Cape May are the summers we spent there during college," said Lauren.

"I would love to visit the gypsy woman. Is she still there, Alice?"

"She is, Elle."

"That woman scared the crap out of me. What about you, Lauren?"

"I wasn't her favorite client, Kathy. Heck, I called the woman a fraud right to her face."

"I don't know if she is a fraud. All I know is that she was right when she said I had to look beyond the happiness to find the truth. I had no freaking idea what she was talking about. When I figured it out, the truth nearly destroyed me and my marriage."

"She told me I lived vicariously through my writings. When I created the character Millennium Agent I didn't have a clue that I was writing about myself. The old woman saw right through me."

Kathy said, "I think it's a great idea. I'll even visit the old woman if everyone is on board. How does next September sound—the week after Labor Day? The kids will be back in school, which will make Fanny's life easier. What do you say?"

"I don't know if I can get the time off work. To hell with work, I won't ask. I'll tell them I'm taking that week off."

Lauren laughed. "Good for you, Elle. Put those suits in their places. I'm good. No book tours scheduled."

"Okay, then it's settled. The week after Labor Day, my place. How does that sound, babe?"

Nancy nodded her head in agreement.

CHAPTER 30

Lauren planned to be on the road by six. At five thirty, she kissed Bruce on the cheek while he slept. He grunted, "I love you."

On long drives, in the past, Lauren created a mental script of her next novel. Today, she thought of her mother. She once asked her mother, "How did you know Dad was the one?"

Her mother's response was "A man who truly loves a woman sees her as an equal, not an object. Your father saw me as his equal." *Equal,* pondered Lauren. She felt herself superior to men until Bruce. So she thought, *This must be love.*

She stared at the ring on her left hand. Her confessing that she and Bruce didn't need a piece of paper to solidify their relationship was a lie. She wanted to be Bruce Hamilton's wife. While lying in his arms last night, she came close to telling him but didn't. She smiled. When she returned home, she would ask Bruce to marry her.

*****

Arriving at Kathy's home, Lauren leaned on the bell. Derek answered the door, shirtless.

"You're annoying."

"I take pleasure at being annoying, and again, you're shirtless. Do you even own a shirt?"

Derek smiled. "Come in, Lauren."

When Lauren entered the kitchen, she gasped. The children were planted quietly at the kitchen counter. Smiling, they greeted her, "Hello, Aunt Lauren."

"Hello. My, how you have grown."

The older children asked to be excused, but Gabe, the youngest, continue to color in his Spiderman coloring book.

"Hey, sweetie, is that a Spiderman coloring book? Do you know Spiderman was Josh's favorite superhero?"

"I do, Aunt Lauren. Josh told me."

Lauren glanced at Derek and mouthed, "He's all grown up."

"Aunt Lauren, thank you for the birthday card and gift."

"Did you have a good time with your friends? You celebrated at Chuck E. Cheese, right?" Lauren glanced at Derek and stuck her finger down her throat to create an image of her causing herself to vomit. "Sorry I couldn't be there, sweetie."

"It was fun. Mommy got me a *Star Wars* cake, with the word *six* printed on Darth Vader's face."

"Wow. Did you save me a piece?"

Gabe laughed. "No. It was all gone. Daddy, can I be excused?"

"Of course, buddy."

After Gabe was out of hearing, Lauren said, "'Can I be excused, Daddy?' I can't believe I'm going to say this, but I miss the runny-nose-screaming-at-the-top-of-his-lungs Gabe."

Derek smiled. "Looking forward to the trip?"

"Yes, but I hope it turns out better than our last trip to Cape May. How's the new book going?"

"It's going. Kathy has two more chapters to edit, before I turn it over to the publisher."

"She told me. Said she had to spice it up a little. Your writing was a little wishy-washy in the sex department. Doesn't sound like the Derek I know?"

Derek didn't respond. Lauren found his change in mood and expression strange. "Speaking of your wife, where is she?"

"Right behind you." Kathy hugged Lauren from behind. "I missed you, girlfriend."

Gabe entered the kitchen. "Mommy, how long are you going to be away?"

Kathy lowered herself to her son's level. "A week, sweetheart."

The Palm Reader

"When is your weekend away with Daddy because I have a soccer game next weekend, and I wanted the both of you to be there?"

Kathy glanced at Derek. His look said it all, "Cancel the damn weekend."

Looking back at her son, Kathy said, "Daddy and I will be at your game. I promise."

Satisfied, Gabe kissed Kathy goodbye.

Kathy said her goodbyes to her children, and when she and Derek embraced, Lauren couldn't help but noticed that she whispered something in his ear. Derek smiled. Turning to Lauren, Kathy said, "Let's get this show on the road." Kathy kissed Derek one more time before leaving the house.

"Well, your departure went a hell of a lot better than it did the last time we took this trip."

"The kids are growing up. They don't need my attention 24/7. Now that Gabe is in school full-time, I might consider finding a job."

"Your job isn't quite finished. I remember you saying, you'd consider going back to work when your last child went off to college."

"I was young and naive. Fanny isn't moving out West any time soon. I should take advantage of finding a job while she's still with us. I don't want a permanent job, but one that would work around my children's schedule. Between Derek and me, I'm sure with our connections, I can find something that works."

"You did a great job on the family care facility. What about something along those lines?"

"I haven't ruled it out. How's Bruce?"

"He's good."

The conversation went silent for a few moments. "I saw you whisper something in Derek's ear. Was it something he could reflect on when he's alone in your bedroom?"

Kathy turned toward Lauren and smiled. "Something like that."

"Is it too hot to share?"

"It's enough to keep him happy while I'm away."

"I'm happy you were able to work things out. I don't think I could handle seeing you in the arms of another man."

"You gave me hell when I said I couldn't see Jake with any other woman but you."

"True."

Kathy half listened as Lauren went on about how devoted Derek was to her. Things between Derek and she weren't as rosy as Lauren was describing. Derek had told Kathy flat out that he was through with this little game they were playing. She knew the excitement would not be the same if Derek wasn't in the mix. She didn't mind the women they slept with, but having another man who wasn't Derek didn't appeal to her.

Then there were the children. They seemed to resent the weekends Mom and Dad were away. Kathy kept the calendar free of crossovers. When she planned her special weekends with Derek, she made sure there was nothing coming up regarding the children that she and Derek should attend except when a storm had interrupted Peggy's music recital. Stacey was booked and paid for. When Derek insisted Kathy cancel, she argued the hotel was booked, and she had already paid for the service. When she stated that there would be other music recitals, she'll never forget how furious Derek had become.

"Do you hear yourself? You'd dismiss our daughter's music recital for your own pleasure? I don't give two shits about the money or this woman. Our daughter should be our main priority."

Kathy lowered her head while Derek went on.

Derek scolded, "I told you this wasn't going to be easy to walk away from once we crossed the line. I'm no saint. I enjoy those weekends as much as you do, but we have five children who need us. Kathy, can't you see what this is doing to our family?"

"I've been extremely careful with the calendar. Forgive me for not predicting a storm was brewing, and the concert would be canceled."

"Stop making excuses for wanting to keep your appointment with whomever her name is. I'm going to our daughter's recital. If you wish to continue on this path, don't include me."

"I would never think of doing this without you."

"Are you sure about that? You seem to be enjoying these weekends more than me. My fear of losing you or the fear of having another man touch you is why I agreed. Now we are truly fucked. I'm finished with the game, but I don't think it's going to be that easy for you."

Kathy canceled that weekend to attend her daughter's recital with Derek. Without the excitement of an upcoming getaway weekend, Kathy conjured up exotic dreams. Often, her cries of ecstasy woke her from a deep sleep. While making love to Derek, she had to envision their past experiences with these women to climax. Derek was right. Crossing the line had caused her to lose her precious love life with Derek. She couldn't allow that to happen. So before leaving her husband, she whispered, "You're my life and my only love. We can overcome anything, but I might need a little help."

It would mean going back to therapy, but this time, she wouldn't resent the hour.

CHAPTER 31

The week was moving along nicely. The weather was perfect—sunny, low eighties. On Thursday, the ladies were forced off the beach by a fast-moving rain shower, so they decided to pay a visit to the palm reader.

The sun had returned as they drove to the boardwalk. Strolling along the boardwalk, Lauren thought it would be a great idea to indulge in a Kohr's ice cream cone before entering the woman's establishment. They sat across from the entrance to the woman's home. As they stared from within, Bella stepped out. The women gasped.

"Elle, is that the granddaughter? Do you remember her name?" asked Lauren.

"Her name is Bella." A boy came to greet Bella. He kissed her on the lips.

"She's not a little girl anymore. She grown into an exotic beauty."

"Before long, my Peggy will be sneaking out and kissing boys."

"I can't wait to see how Derek handles his daughter running off with some boy behind the rose bush to smooch a kiss."

"It gives me the creeps thinking of my precious baby being manhandled," said Kathy.

"I wonder if Grandma foresaw her granddaughter running off and smooching with this boy."

The women glanced at Lauren. After a few seconds, the four began to laugh.

*****

The ladies made their way toward the entrance. Pulling aside the curtain that covered the front entrance, they entered the room. It took a few moments for their vision to adjust to the darkness.

"Hello," called Elle. They slowly made their way into the room.

Alice touched Lauren's elbow. "This place gives me the creeps."

Lauren didn't respond.

Elle raised her voice higher. "Hello."

The woman stepped out from the kitchen. She glanced in the ladies' direction.

"Hello. Do you remember me?" asked Elle.

The woman walked toward them. "I remember you."

Elle smiled. "We were in the area and thought it would be nice to stop in and say hi."

"Why?"

Lauren mumbled, "I see she hasn't lost her charm." Frightened of being heard, Lauren asked, "Do you remember me? I'm the writer."

"You, I remember."

A boy around the age of eight came to stand beside the woman. "This is my grandson Rile. Rile, say hello to the nice ladies."

Rile whispered a greeting.

"Hello, Rile. My name is Elle. These are my friends Lauren, Kathy, and Alice. Your grandmother is an old friend of ours."

Rile shrugged. "Your lunch is getting cold, go eat." Rile did as the woman told him. The woman motioned for them to sit.

It was a little tight on the sofa, but Lauren, Kathy, and Alice managed to squeeze together. Elle sat in the armchair. The woman retrieved a chair from the kitchen.

"So why are you here?"

Elle smiled. "I wanted to thank you."

"Thank me?"

"Yes. You told me to face my demons, and I did. I'm married. I have two sons, Liam and Ethan. I have a good life, and you to thank."

The woman asked, "And your mother? How is she?"

The question caught Elle off guard. She had never discussed her turmoil relationship with the woman. "She's good. We're good."

The woman nodded her head. Turning toward Lauren, she asked, "And you, still writing those girly books?"

"Of course, it pays the bills."

"How's your love life?"

"It's funny you should ask. My love life took a few turns before I met the love of my life."

"Male or female?"

"Male. But I guess you already knew that."

The woman didn't respond.

Kathy didn't wait for the woman to speak to her. "Remember me? You told me to look beyond the clouds for the truth. At first, I didn't know what the hell you were talking about. But it didn't take long for me to figure it out. My husband was cheating on me. I quickly found out that no one is happy 24/7."

Lauren was about to interrupt, but Kathy quickly placed her hand in the air and stopped her. "Thank God it was only with one woman and one time. We got past the mess. My marriage is back on track."

The woman listened intently as Kathy spoke. Not wanting to make Kathy feel uncomfortable, she directed her attention to Alice.

"There is a new love in your life. This is good."

"How did you know?"

"I saw the two of you walking hand in hand along the boardwalk a few months ago. From the way she looked at you, it was obvious to me, she loves you."

Alice smiled.

Bella entered the room.

"You're back. You promised to spend time with your brother. And you don't fool me. I know you snuck off to see that boy."

The ladies weren't facing Bella but sensed that a girl of Bella's age, at that moment, was rolling her eyes.

"You're going to get your heart broken. Once his family knows he's hanging around with a gypsy girl, he'll drop you like a hot potato."

"We all have to get along, Grandma."

"Yes. Whites with whites. Black with blacks. Whites with blacks. White, black, and Asian. But no one wants their children marrying a gypsy."

"You're living in the Dark Ages, Grandma. Today, you can marry whomever you want." Bella called to her brother, "Come on, Rile, Grandma is in one of her moods."

"Please don't take this the wrong way, but I have to agree with your granddaughter. This isn't the Dark Ages. Today, one has a right to marry the person they love whatever their ethnicity," said Lauren.

"His parents will never accept her."

"I don't know," said Kathy. "I do agree with Lauren. This isn't the Dark Ages. And before stepping into your establishment, we caught a glimpse of Bella and the young man holding hands. He seems quite smitten with her. If his parents object to him loving Bella, I'm sure he would defy them and continue to see her."

"They are kids. What do they know about love?"

"I agree, they are young," said Kathy. "Tomorrow, this relationship can be over, but forcing them to see it your way will only bring them closer. Don't you agree?"

"You're of the belief that racism does not exist, but it does. I only want to protect Bella from the cruelty of those who think we are no better than a swine."

Kathy said no more. Racism still existed in the good old USA, and the woman was right to want to protect her own.

"Does your husband agree with you?" asked Elle.

"My husband is gone."

Lauren said, "Gone, like he left you or gone for good?"

"Passed three years ago. Rotting of the stomach."

"Cancer. I'm so sorry," said Elle.

"Please don't take this the wrong way, but I have to ask," said Lauren. "Did you see your husband's demise before his doctor?"

Elle shouted, "Lauren!"

"I'm curious, Elle."

Kathy chuckled. "Forgive our friend. As you can see, she has absolutely no filters. Says whatever pops into that gorgeous head of hers."

Elle nodded in agreement, but that was what she loved most about her friend Lauren. She asked the questions Elle was too embarrassed to ask. Elle could see that the woman was growing tired of her and her friends. But she didn't want to leave without letting the woman know how grateful she was to have stepped through that door all those years ago.

"I don't know what you possess, but I do believe that you are the real deal. If it weren't for you telling me to face my demons, I would have gone on keeping my guilt bottled up inside. I don't think I would have had the strength to marry or have children. I just want you to know that I don't think you're a fraud."

The woman showed no emotion to Elle's words of respect, but Elle did see a glimmer of thanks in the woman's eyes.

Two women entered the establishment. Seeing them, the woman called to them, "Have a seat at the table. I'll be right with you. Well, it's been a nice visit, but it's time for you to go. I have customers."

The woman kept a close watch as the ladies existed her establishment. The pretty one, Kathy, turned and smiled at the woman. *Such a beauty,* thought the woman. The hairs on the back of the woman's neck tingled, and a chill invaded her entire body as she watched the pretty one interlock arms with her friend the author.

*****

To celebrate the end of their vacation, Alice made a reservation at the Mud Hen restaurant in Wildwood.

Arriving at the restaurant, the hostess informed them the wait was forty minutes. Making their way to the bar, they ordered drinks. The band was in full swing. When seated, they were placed close to the band. It made it hard to talk, but the music was uplifting. So they shouted as they spoke.

"This band is pretty good," said Lauren. "Too bad Nancy couldn't make it."

"Her friend is having a rough go of it. She and her husband were close. His passing was a shock. They were enjoying breakfast, and without warning, he clutched his chest, and his head hit the table. Massive heart attack."

"Being married to a heart surgeon, I can say, heart attacks most often don't come with a warning."

Thankful that the waitress had interrupted an uncomfortable conversation, the ladies ordered burgers and fries. Since the restaurant's specialty was their own brewed beers, they ordered a pitcher of the day's brew. The beer and food arrived at the same time.

The band asked for requests. Of course, the ladies called out, "Bruce Springsteen." Bruce being the fourth messiah—after Jesus, Sinatra, and Frankie Valli to those who were born in New Jersey—received an overwhelming applause from the patrons.

Kathy sang the loudest to "Born in the USA," and after several verses, she stood and began to dance. Elle joined Kathy seconds later, gesturing for Lauren and Alice to join them. When the band played "Jersey Girl," everyone, including the ladies, swayed to the song.

"I might not be from Jersey, but I think Springsteen wrote that song with me in mind," said Kathy.

"If Casey were here, she'd disagree," said Alice.

When the band took a break, so did the ladies. Sweat beaded their brows as they fanned themselves cool with their napkins.

"I'm getting too old to act like a fool," said Lauren.

Kathy placed an arm around Lauren. "I have to agree with you, Lauren. You are looking a little piqued. Maybe you should get your ass off your writing stool and get yourself to the gym."

"You would think with all that humping you and Bruce are doing, you'd be in better shape."

"I thought you and I were over poking fun at each other, Alice?"

"I'm only pulling your chain, Lauren. You look great. Your man has put a spring in your step. And I'm delighted for you, and happy you're back to loving dicks, which means I don't have to worry about you hitting on my girl."

"Have no fear, Alice. This gal is off the market unless Bruce has a change of heart. Then watch out, Alice, because I'll be coming for you. Don't you think Alice and I would make a lovely couple, ladies?"

Alice smiled. "Never. We're both too strong-minded."

"I think you and Alice would make a lovely couple. Don't you think they'd make a lovely couple, Elle?"

"No, Kathy. I think Alice is right. They are both hard heads. For a relationship to work, you have to compromise."

"Well, we will never know because I am madly in love with Bruce. Bruce Hamilton, not Springsteen. I'm convinced Bruce Hamilton and I will share a long and happy life till death do us part, at the ripe old age of one-hundred-plus."

Hearing Lauren speak fondly of Bruce caused Kathy to think of Derek. Surrounded by her friends, she watched as Alice lovingly spoke of her relationship with Nancy. Lauren talking marriage. Elle, once again, praising Jacques for never giving up on them.

Kathy never saw children in Elle's future, and now she had two boys to love and Lauren content to spend the rest of her life with a man that was her equal. Jake would always have a special place in Kathy's heart, but Lauren was right. She and Jake didn't belong together. He was happily married and in love with Michelle. Everyone was happy, except for Derek. Derek wanted out of the three-ring circus Kathy had placed them in. Whether curiosity or payback was Kathy's ulterior motive, enough was enough. She enjoyed making love to a woman, but it was her husband she'd seek out during the act. The threesome would be placed on the back burner of her mind, never to show its ugly head again.

When she got back to the hotel, she would call Derek and inform him that the threesome weekends were no more. She'd assure him that all she wanted in her bed was him and only him.

"I want to make a toast," said Kathy. "Everyone lift your glasses."

The ladies did as Kathy requested. "This has been the best week ever in the history of girl vacations. I want to thank you for being my besties. The only thing that could make this night perfect is if Casey were here with us. RIP, girlfriend. BFFs forever!" shouted Kathy.

*****

Lauren opened the car roof and let in the night air. She glanced at the stars that gave light to the darkness of night. She sighed. *Isn't it great to be alive?* thought Lauren. She looked over at Kathy who was checking her phone for text messages from Derek. Lauren smiled. She placed an Adele CD into her car radio. Raising the volume on the car radio, she sang alone with Adele to her favorite song, "Rumors." She never heard Kathy scream her name. "Lauren!"

Lauren tried to open her eyes. Flashes of light crossed over her eyelids, repeating colors of white and red. Slowly, she willed her eyes to open. Dark figures moved quickly from one side to another. Had she dozed off while watching a science fiction movie with Bruce? She tried to move her head to find him but found it difficult. One of the dark figures knelt before her and flashed a light into her eyes. The light blinded her for a moment. The figure began to speak, but Lauren couldn't make out what was being said. Another dark figure approached. The two began to speak to each other. Lauren willed her head to move toward the right. A glossy dark liquid lay beside her. A white light passed over the liquid; seeing the redness of its color, she gasped. Without asking, she wondered if the liquid was blood. Looking past the red liquid, she noticed that entwined in the dark liquid were strands of gold. The flashing lights caused the gold to shine even brighter. There was a familiarity to the golden color. It reminded her of Kathy's hair. Excruciating pain ripped through her; she screamed before everything went black.

CHAPTER 32

Alice lay on the side of the road. Suddenly without warning, she felt herself being lifted onto a gurney.

A woman leaned in and spoke but not to her. "This one has a broken collarbone and arm. Nasty cut. It's deep. Starts at the brow, along the right ear, ending at the back of the scalp. Cape May General is expecting her. I administered a sedative to cut down on the pain. The chart is updated. Let's get her into the ambulance.

Alice was placed in the ambulance. Her vision was impaired, but she forced herself to focus. A young woman worked diligently, monitoring her vitals.

"What is your name?" asked Alice.

"You're awake. That's a good sign. We are taking you to Cape May General."

"What is your name?"

The young woman smiled. "My name is Stella, and I'm going to take good care of you. Just relax. It will just be a few minutes, and we'll be on our way."

Alice heard helicopters above. "Helicopters. Why?"

Stella avoided the question by checking Alice's vitals.

"There is more than one helicopter."

Stella knocked on the window to get the driver's attention. "What's the holdup, Max?"

"How are my friends?" asked Alice.

Stella, the professional, knew it was wise not to agitate a patient. "They are alive."

"How bad?"

The Palm Reader

"They are being transported to the Philadelphia Trauma Unit."

"Philadelphia!" Alice began to stir.

Stella knocked on the window again. The ambulance began to move. "Your friend is waiting at the hospital."

"My friend?"

"Nancy Sullivan. We found an emergency card in your purse."

"How bad was the accident?"

"I don't have all the details. Your car collided with a tractor trailer. That's all I know."

"Tractor trailers aren't allowed on this road."

The siren on the ambulance began to sound, and the vehicle began to move.

"I want to be taken to the hospital in Philadelphia."

Stella paid no attention to Alice's request. Stella injected the IV. Alice began to drift off.

*****

A light flashed across Alice's eyes forcing them to open.

"Hi, there. Are you in pain?"

"Where am I?"

"You're at Cape May General. I'm Dr. Pitman. You've been in and out for two days. Broken collarbone and left arm. Both required surgeries. Several pins were placed in your shoulder to set it correctly. Let me check those stiches." Dr. Pitman leaned in and removed the bandage on Alice's forehead. She flinched. "Looks good. We had to shave the left side of your head. Your friend likes the punk look. I think it would look cool if you dyed your hair purple."

Dr. Pitman smiled. "One more time. Are you in pain?"

"No."

"Good."

"I was told my friends were taken to Philadelphia. How are they doing?"

"I don't have any information on your friends."

"They were transported to Philadelphia Trauma Unit."

"All I know is what I read in the newspaper. There were four of you in the car. Three were transported to the Philadelphia Trauma Unit. The driver of the tractor trailer didn't make it."

"I don't understand. What was a tractor trailer doing on that road?"

"He was inebriated. Way over the speed limit. In his condition, I'm sure he ignored the warning signs. 'No Trucks Allowed on This Road or the Bridge.' If he would have made it to the bridge, he might have figured it out."

"After I heard my friend scream, I looked up and saw the body of a truck coming toward us."

"At the speed he was going, he definitely lost control."

"Oh my god, where is Nancy? I have to get out of here."

"I sent your friend for coffee. She should be back soon."

"I need to get out of here." Alice tried to sit up. She felt nauseous and dizzy.

"You're not going anywhere for a few days. Concussion."

Nancy entered the room. "Alice, you're awake." Nancy sat on the bed.

"Nancy, have you heard anything about the girls' condition? They were taken to Philadelphia."

"I'm sorry, baby. I've called the hospital, but they won't give me any information. They will only speak with immediate family. They're alive. That's all I know."

"I've got to get out of here."

Nancy turned to the doctor for help.

"As I said, young lady, you're not going anywhere for at least three days. We wouldn't want anything to mess up the fabulous job I did on repairing that shoulder and arm. Also, that nasty cut on the head needs to be attended to."

"Sorry, babe."

"Do you have my phone?"

"It's at home."

"I have Kelly's contact information on my phone. Go! Get my phone."

The Palm Reader

"All right. I'll make the call. I don't want you getting yourself upset."

Nancy did as Alice requested. When she retrieved the phone, she entered Alice's pass code and found Kelly's contact information. She dialed Kelly's cell. Kelly answered after three rings.

"Hello."

"Kelly." Nancy paused. Kelly's voice was strained. "This is Alice's friend, Nancy."

"Yes, Nancy. How is Alice doing?"

Nancy was caught off guard by Kelly's concern for Alice. "Broken collarbone and left arm. Nasty cut on her head, but in time, she'll heal. Kelly, how—"

Kelly began to cry. "Not good. Not good at all. My mother is in surgery. She developed a clot behind her right ear. The surgeons took her to surgery to try to relieve the pressure on her brain."

"Kelly, I'm so sorry."

"Her leg was crushed. She might lose it." Kelly began to sob. Jake took the phone from Kelly.

"Nancy, this is Jake. Lauren's ex-husband."

"I'm so sorry to be a bother at this time, but Alice needed to know how they are doing?"

"It's bad. Lauren might lose her leg. It was crushed. She hit her head pretty bad. There's a clot. It could kill her. She's in surgery."

"Elle and Kathy?"

Jake lost it. "Elle has a severe spinal injury, and Kathy… Kathy…"

Nancy felt faint.

"She's alive, for now. She took the brunt of the impact."

"I won't keep you. Can I call again? After Lauren is out of surgery."

"Of course." Jake disconnected.

*****

When Nancy arrived at the hospital, Alice was asleep. She sat on the chair next to Alice's bed. Nancy was exhausted. Alice, she knew, would survive her injuries. Nancy didn't have the strength to tell Alice the news about the girls. How would she explain that by the end of day, one or two, might not survive?

*****

The old woman placed the newspaper on the kitchen table. Across from her sat Bella, reading a book. The old woman took notice of the author's picture on the back cover.

"What are you reading?"

Without looking up, Bella answered, "*Millennium Agent*."

"Is it good?"

"It is."

"Who's the author?"

"Lauren Croft Hicks. I love her books. I've read this book twice."

"So you really enjoy the way she writes?"

"Yes. Do you want to read it when I'm finished?"

The old woman sighed. "You like her so much, but you never noticed that she was here last week."

Placing the book down, Bella questioned, "What did you say?"

"If you didn't have your head in the clouds with that boy, you would have noticed. There were four women here last week. Lauren Hicks was one of them."

Bella took a few moments to search her memory of the past week. "Yes, I do remember the four women, and you think one of them was Lauren Hicks." Bella chuckled. "Lauren Hicks isn't the kind of woman that would have her palm read."

"Never surprises me how you think my profession is a farce. Palm reading puts food on the table and into your mouth."

"Grandma, I respect the way you earn a living, but you having special powers is questionable. Just because we are gypsies doesn't mean we can see into the future."

"So you think your grandmother is a fraud?"

"Grandma, I don't want to fight with you. I'll agree there are times when you guess a storm is brewing before the weatherman does. But these are everyday occurrences. It doesn't take a rocket scientist to figure out when customers come in all teary eyed and bewildered, that their lives suck. So they visit a palm reader in hopes you will assure them life isn't so bad, or it can be worse. I respect that you give them the hope they need to go on. No foul, no harm, right? But if you're asking if I believe gypsies have special powers, no."

"This woman you admire was here. She came back to thank me. Said I knew my stuff and was very helpful in helping her to find her way."

"I think you're confusing Lauren Hicks with someone else. First, Lauren Hicks resides in Cape Cod. Do you know how far that is from Cape May? North, Grandma. Way north."

"Lauren Hicks was here, and now she's in a hospital in Philadelphia." The old woman picked up the newspaper and opened it to the section that spoke about the accident. She handed the paper to her granddaughter. Bella read the article.

"Oh my god, it's her. It says she was involved in a terrible accident in Cape May. She's alive, but in serious condition along with two other women. Grandma, do you think they will survive?"

"Are you asking if I foresee their fate?"

Bella frowned continuing to read the article. "It says here the driver of the truck was pronounced dead at the scene. The three women are in the ICU."

Bella informed her grandmother of each woman's condition. "One of the women on the passenger's side sustained facial injuries. Says here, her face was a bloody mess."

The old woman lowered her head. The last time she saw the pretty one, Kathy, there was a darkness surrounding her. It explained why the woman had an overwhelming feeling of despair when Kathy departed her establishment. What the woman hated most about having the powers was when she didn't have a clear vision, only a strong sense of doom.

*****

Alice was dressed when Nancy entered their bedroom. Nancy gasped.

"Where are you going? How did you manage to dress yourself?"

"I'm going to Philadelphia, with or without you."

"You're only out of the hospital one day. The doctor said you shouldn't leave the house for at least a week. You have a concussion."

"I'm fine. I dressed without passing out. Are you driving me, or should I call a cab?"

"Alice, we're not family. They won't let you anywhere near the ICU."

Nancy stared into Alice's eyes. She knew she wasn't winning this fight.

"You're not going anywhere without me. I'll get the wheelchair."

*****

Nancy wheeled Alice into the hospital, and approached the front desk. Nancy hated hospitals. Her father had given her family a gift when he passed quietly in the night. Her mother lingered on, suffering until the good Lord decided enough was enough.

Before Nancy could inquire about the patients, Alice asked the attendant what floor the ICU was on.

"Do you have family in the ICU?"

"Yes."

"What is the name?"

"Croft, Kessler, and Wilson."

The man called Tom glanced up at Alice. His first thought by the looks of the woman's injuries was she should be a patient, not a visitor. "Are you saying, you're a relative to all three?"

"One. Lauren Croft."

"Alice," scolded Nancy.

Tom wasn't in the mood to argue with the women. "All right," he said. "I need to place a call to the ICU. Please take a seat."

Tom lowered his voice when he spoke into the phone. When he disconnected, he motioned to Nancy. "Ms. Croft's daughter is coming down."

*****

The Palm Reader

Jake and Kelly approached the women. Kelly gently leaned in and hugged Alice. "Alice, you shouldn't have come."

"Kelly is right, Alice. You don't look well."

"I had to come, Jake. Is there any chance I can see them?"

Jake lowered his head. "Alice, it's bad. The good news is they're still alive. Lauren drifts in and out. When she is awake, the pain is too unbearable. She's kept heavily sedated."

"How is the leg?"

"She was in surgery for six hours. We won't know if the surgery was a success for several days. If the blood flow and color doesn't return to the leg, they will need to amputate. I think she'll pull through. She's strong. Even if she loses the leg, she'll get through this."

Kelly began to cry. Alice squeezed her hand. "She's going to make it, Kelly. Your father's right. Your mother is a strong woman." Alice addressed the newspaper article with Jake. "The newspaper spoke of Kathy and Elle's injuries. Doesn't sound as promising."

"Elle's surgery lasted eleven hours. She is strapped in a contraption upside down." Jake paused. "Don't know if she'll ever walk again. She is heavily sedated for the pain. Kathy—I don't know where to start."

"How is Jacques and Derek?"

"Jacques takes a break every so often, but Derek hasn't left Kathy's side. Bruce is here. He's with Lauren now."

Alice realized the situation must be uncomfortable for the ex and the future husband fighting for time with Lauren. Jake and Lauren shared two children. Jake needed to be here to support his children. Bruce and Lauren were planning a life together. Both men had the right to be by Lauren's side.

"Is Josh here?"

"Yes, Josh spent most of the night by Lauren's side. Listen, I know how important it is for you to see them. Take our passes." Jake handed Alice his pass. Kelly extended hers to Nancy.

Kelly reassured Nancy, "You go with Alice, Nancy. My dad and I haven't eaten."

Nancy and Alice entered the elevator. Nancy pressed the button to the second floor. When the doors opened, on the wall in front of them were the letters *ICU*. Seeing the letters made Alice shiver. When they exited the elevator, they were met with the disinfected smells of a hospital. Nancy felt nauseated, but the feeling quickly subsided.

Nancy spotted the buzzer on the wall and pressed it. The doors opened, allowing the women to pass through. Approaching the front desk, Alice inquired the room numbers for her friends. She instructed Nancy, "Lauren's room first."

Bruce was sitting by Lauren's bed holding her hand. The sound of the door opening got Bruce's attention. He rose and went to greet them.

"Alice, what are you doing here?" Bruce extended his hand to Nancy. He gave her hand a gentle squeeze.

"I had to come. How is she doing?"

"She's sedated. It's best. When she's awake, she screams and shouts their names." Bruce lowered his head. Gaining his composure, he asked, "How are you doing?"

"I'll be fine."

Alice motioned for Nancy to push her closer to Lauren. With her good hand, she took Lauren's hand in her own and whispered, "You're going to get through this. You're the strongest lady I know. Now that I've discovered you're not such a bad person, I refuse to let you go. Besties forever, right?"

Alice stared at Lauren's legs, which were cast to her waist, both in a harness and elevated. Her eyes were swollen shut. The side of her head was extended and wrapped in bandages. Shades of black and blue surrounded her face, neck, and arms. Several deep cuts on her arms had been stitched. Alice motioned for Nancy to push her away.

"I need to see Elle and Kathy. If she wakes, will you tell her I was here? When I'm able to get out of this wheelchair, I'll come visit."

"I promise. Promise me, you'll listen to the doctors. You need to get healthy, Alice, because they will need you and Nancy to help them get through this."

*****

When Nancy approached Elle's door, Alice stopped her from entering. Elle was turned upside down in a contraption that housed her entire body. Alice needed a few moments. Elle's face was visible but unrecognizable. Obviously, Elle was heavily sedated. Jacques sat beside her with his head in his hands. Raising his head, he gently touched Elle's hand. It seemed by the gesture that Jacques didn't want to cause Elle any more pain. He began to speak to his wife. Alice didn't see Elle's mom but knew she wasn't far from her daughter's side.

Jacques seemed to be having a private conversation with his wife. "Let's give him a few moments," said Alice. They moved on to Kathy's room.

Alice entered Kathy's room. Derek turned. The rims of his eyes were scarlet and swollen from crying.

"Alice."

He walked toward her, then collapsed to his knees, and sobbed.

Alice's eyes began to well with tears. She looked beyond Derek to Kathy. A *mummy* was the only word to describe Kathy. She was covered in bandages. Her left eye was visible, severely bruised, and swollen shut.

Derek began to confess his sins to Alice. "I'm going to lose her, Alice. This is my punishment for all the wrong I did to her. He's going to take her from me. I keep praying, but no one is listening. She's in and out of surgery. Internal bleeding, and I can't do a damn thing to help her. Look what that bastard did to my beautiful girl."

Nancy's throat constricted. Alice choked but quickly found the strength to speak to a grieving husband. "I'm not a stranger to this pain, Derek. I know what you're going through, but you can't give up. She's alive. She's still with us. Kathy wouldn't want you to give up on her."

Derek raised his head staring into Alice's eyes. He said, "You're right. She's still with us." Derek rose. Patting Alice on the hand, he whispered, "She needs me, Alice. I promised her, I wouldn't leave her until—" Derek walked away without finishing his sentence. The man was clearly in shock.

Nancy noticed Kathy's mother and father sitting in the corner consoling each other. When Derek returned to Kathy, he placed his hand on her body and sobbed.

Alice left Derek to his grief, and now it was time to console Jacques.

CHAPTER 33

One month had passed since the accident. Lauren was moved from the ICU into a private room. She was waiting patiently for the doctor. If all went well, she would be granted her wish. She wanted desperately to be placed in a wheelchair, so she could visit with Elle and Kathy.

She checked her phone for the time. It was ten forty-five. Lauren began to tap her index finger on the bed railing. To calm herself, she inhaled eight times, releasing her breath slowly in hopes to calm her nerves. Clearly, the breathing exercises didn't help. When she was left alone, all see thought about was the accident. How many times do people have to be told don't drink and drive before they understand that innocent lives are affected by their bad decisions? She never considered herself a vicious person, but she was happy the driver had met his demise. The foolish man deserved what he got.

Bruce didn't share her feelings, telling her the man left behind two young children.

Lauren's response was cold. "Whatever! What about Kathy's children and Elle's?"

Lauren looked up at the ceiling. She couldn't take another minute in this white-washed room. Was it too much for the designers to think outside the box and come up with soothing pastel paint colors? "Where the hell are you, Bruce?" whispered Lauren.

Poor Bruce. She was trying her best not to be too awful to him. At the beginning, when the pain was unbearable, she freely used the F word. Bruce was the recipient of her foul mood. When her children or Jake were around, she managed to control her temper. The accident had secured her relationship with Josh. Jake and Bruce told her he never left her side. *An accident,* she thought, *was the solution to her regaining her son's love. Sad.* When Josh asked her to forgive him, she smiled and said, "I love you."

Using several F words in a row, she informed Bruce that if he thought sugarcoating Elle's and Kathy's condition was going to earn him brownie points, he was mistaken. If she found out that he thought it best to keep the truth from her, she would ex him from her life.

Being a man of honor, Bruce kept her up-to-date. Elle was still strapped in that awful contraption. When she was awake, she was in an enormous amount of pain. Jacques was concerned about the pain meds she was receiving. Of course, he was reassured that the meds were being cut back as time went on. Jacques saw by Elle's reaction to the pain that the pain medication was being reduced. There was still the question of her being able to walk again. As of this date, there were no signs of feeling in her feet or legs, but the doctors were hopeful. Trudy and Uncle Charlie were sent to care for the boys and visited on weekends.

When Lauren was able, she called Jacques's cell. He reported the same information as Bruce. Lauren asked to speak with Elle, but Jacques told her she didn't want to speak with anyone.

"Even me?" asked Lauren.

Jacques did his best to assure Lauren, Elle wasn't herself. Every time Lauren spoke with Jacques and was told Elle didn't want to speak, it set off a crying fit. Lauren was sure her friendship with Elle and Kathy was over. They would blame her for the accident. Nothing that Bruce, Jake, or her children said made Lauren feel the accident wasn't her fault.

Lauren didn't have the courage to call Derek's cell. No one questioned why she hadn't. Speaking with Kathy was out of the question, and Derek was holding on by a thread. Hearing her voice would only bring him additional pain.

Kathy, my poor beautiful Kathy, thought Lauren with tears in her eyes. She was rushed in and out of surgery. Today, the internal bleeding was under control. Thank God. She was placed in a semicoma,

The Palm Reader

awakened on and off several times a day. Her only form of communication was a moan. Her face was completely destroyed. Lauren placed her hands over her face and cupped her mouth screaming into her hands. The only saving grace was they were alive. Her leg was not amputated. Elle would survive her injuries, with or without a wheelchair. Kathy—what was in store for her was a life of plastic surgeries.

Kathy's mother and father never left their daughter's side. Derek's parents were sent to take care of the children. Then the parents' roles were reversed when Kathy's parents objected to Derek's decision.

Bruce informed Lauren, after speaking with Kathy's mother, that Derek had plans to move Kathy to Germany. With Derek's connections, he got Dr. Frankel, the top plastic surgeon in the world to work with Kathy.

Kathy's parents didn't agree with the move nor did Lauren. "She needs her family and friends to help her get through this, Bruce. Derek isn't thinking straight. He's not himself. He hasn't left this hospital since the accident. That is why I need to see him, convince him that he is making a mistake. I'm sure he can find as good a plastic surgeon as Dr. Frankel in the States."

Bruce had to remind Lauren on several occasions that Derek was Kathy's husband, and it was his legal right to do what he thought was best for his wife.

Lauren was convinced that once she made her case, Derek would see things her way.

The door to the room opened, and Lauren called out to Bruce. "Where have you been?"

"Hello, Lauren."

"Alice." Nancy entered behind Alice and smiled at Lauren. "Nancy, can you do me a favor? Ask the nurse in the red sweater where the hell is my doctor."

Alice gestured for Nancy to heed Lauren's request.

Alice pulled up a chair beside Lauren's bed. Lauren smiled.

"Your scars are healing nicely, Alice. You got your hair cut. Looks good." Lauren touched the scar over her right ear. "Guess I'll have to look into getting my locks cut off as well."

"I don't think so. You still have enough hair to cover up that side of your head."

Lauren smiled and reached for Alice's hand. "Every time I see you, I feel that I have to apologize to you."

"For what?"

"I'm so sorry. I never saw the truck coming at us. I was watching the road. I swear. Before I had a chance to react, the truck was there."

"Lauren, we're alive, so whatever you did was the right thing to do."

"But was it for Kathy? She took the brunt of the hit. She's never going to forgive me."

"You have to stop beating yourself up. It was an accident, which you didn't cause. I'm able to walk without passing out. My arm and collarbone are healing. You managed to keep your leg. Elle—I'm sure will walk again. And Kathy—well, her road won't be as easy, but I'm sure we haven't seen the last of her."

"Derek is taking Kathy to Germany. I think it's a mistake. What do you think?"

"Kathy hasn't been able to speak for herself. In time, as she improves, she might welcome going away to heal, or she might want to stay in the States."

"Derek isn't giving her enough time to make that decision. I think he'll move her before she has a say. It could take years for her to regain even a little of herself."

"Good morning. This young lady informed me that you are patiently waiting to speak with me."

Nancy and Bruce stood behind Lauren's orthopedic doctor.

"You said today's the day, Doc. I'm going to get my wheelchair, correct?"

"Is that what I said, Ms. Croft, or did I stay today is the day we are going to remove the harness?"

Lauren sighed.

Two days after her leg was removed from the harness, the doctor approved her long-awaited wheelchair. One-hour intervals, several times a day. After a week, Lauren became a pro at maneuvering herself around, without Bruce's help. She asked the doctor if she could visit with her friends. She was granted permission.

*****

Lauren exited the elevator to the ICU floor. Wheeling herself toward the doors to the ICU area, Bruce rushed behind. Reaching for the handles on the wheelchair, he said, "Slow down, lady."

Lauren inhaled deeply. "I've waited for this moment for so long. Now I'm not so sure—"

"Seeing for yourself that they are alive and fighting to remain alive is the hope you need."

Lauren looked through the glass door. Seeing Elle still housed in the contraption but right side up was a relief. The wires surrounding Elle reminded Lauren of a documentary on Auschwitz. Lauren remembered the emaciated faces of the men sitting Indian-style behind a sea of wires. These men were alive and close to regaining the lives they once knew. And so was Elle, alive and fighting to regain a life she treasured.

Bruce pushed open the door, and Lauren began to wheel herself toward Elle.

When Elle made eye contact with Lauren, their eyes began to well. "Lauren!" cried Elle.

Lauren angled the wheelchair to get as close to Elle's face as possible. From the corner of her eye, she saw Jacques make his way toward Bruce, leaving the ladies to their privacy. Lauren reached for Elle's hand; squeezing it gently, she said, "I love your outfit. Chains and wires are in."

Elle smirked. "They should have amputated your tongue."

"I love you, Elle. I'm so sorry." Tears began to roll down Lauren's cheeks.

"You didn't do this to us, Lauren. So stop the pity party."

"All right, Elle."

Elle squeezed her eyes shut. Opening them again, she glanced at Lauren. "I'm in so much fucking pain, Lauren. I'm sure you've had your share of pain. I'm happy you didn't lose the leg."

"Bruce gave me the good news yesterday. You have some feelings in your toes."

"Today, they pin pricked my legs, and I cursed at the doctor."

Lauren smiled. "I knew you'd walk again."

"My pain medication was cut back again. I can't stand the pain, Lauren. They have this hard-ass nurse who keeps saying, 'You have to learn to tolerate the pain, sweetie. It's only going to get worse when you begin therapy.' I hate the fucker."

"I start therapy next week. Not looking forward to it. In two days, they are moving me across the street. Three weeks of therapy. After, I'll be shipped home to a rehab center in town. I told Bruce, I'm not leaving until—"

"Until what, Lauren? Kathy's being shipped off to Germany? I've got another two months in this town once I start therapy. Then I'm shipped back home for more therapy. It could take me a year before I can walk on my own. One fucking year of hospitals."

"I know you're angry, Elle, but there is a light at the end of the tunnel."

"Maybe for you and me, but Kathy is another story. She hasn't been awake for more than five minutes every four hours. She still can die from her injuries, and if she lives, a life of plastic surgeries is ahead for her. Her face is gone. Derek's a mess. I hear him yelling at the doctors. He wants to know why she isn't conscious. Would you want to be awake in her condition? I want to scream at him to shut the fuck up. Let her sleep."

Lauren lowered her head. "I wish it was her driving and me in the passenger's seat."

"Why? Is Kathy's life worth more than yours? I'm sure Josh and Kelly are happy you were in the driver's seat."

"Do you think Derek is making the right decision taking Kathy to Germany?"

"Yes. Dr. Frankel, from what I hear, is the best."

Elle squeezed her eyes shut again. "You better go. I'm not at my best when the pain is at its worse. Good luck with therapy, Lauren."

Lauren didn't like that Elle was dismissing her. "Can I come visit again?"

"Sure. But now you have to leave."

Lauren did as she was told. Before leaving, she turned her wheelchair in Elle's direction and shouted, "This pain is your new demon, Elle. Remember what the gypsy woman told you. You have to face the demon head on."

*****

Lauren pushed open the door to Kathy's room, finding Derek at her bedside. Entering Kathy's room felt like a passage into hell. Machines surrounded her bed. She wondered how Derek was able to stand all the beeping. Wires exited every part of Kathy's body. Some were hooked to machines. Others were securing her broken body. Lauren didn't flinch seeing Kathy lying there bandaged from head to toe. Whenever she thought of Kathy, that was the vision she saw.

She wheeled herself behind Derek. His head was resting on Kathy's bed. He was holding her hand while he slept. Lauren gently called his name, several times.

"Derek."

He stirred. Raising his head, he turned toward her. "Is that you, Lauren?"

"Yes. It's me, Derek."

"How the hell—a wheelchair?"

Avoiding a response, Lauren said, "Derek, I've been so worried about you."

"It's not me you should be worried about. Look at her, Lauren. Look at what he did to my beautiful girl. I'm glad he's dead because I would have paid to have him killed."

"Has there been any change?"

"Nothing. She moans. She can't speak. Her mouth is wired. God knows what she looks like under all those bandages. I'm going to fix her. I'm taking her to Germany. The doctors want me to wait until she is fully conscious."

"That might be a wise decision. If Kathy does come to, she might object—"

"Don't, Lauren. I've heard it all before. It's wrong of me to take Kathy away from her family and friends. Do you really think she's going to want our children to see her in her condition? No. She needs to be somewhere far away from the pity stares. Two years, maybe less, and I'll bring Kathy home. Maybe not the perfection she once was but as perfect as possible."

"As her husband, I know you have Kathy's best interest at heart, but—"

"You know there isn't anything I wouldn't do for my sweet girl. I love her. I've been told that you have to love yourself in order to truly love someone else. But that's not true. I love her more than myself and, God forgive me, more than our children. I hurt her, Lauren. Maybe this is my punishment. If my prayers are answered and she lives, I'm going to spend every penny I have to get Kathy back to me and the kids. I swear."

Lauren swallowed hard. She might not have agreed with moving Kathy far from her family, but she also knew that Derek would keep his promise.

Lauren wheeled herself to the other side of Kathy's bed. She took Kathy's bandaged hand in hers. "Hey, beautiful, I hear you don't want to wake up. I don't blame you. But if you give it a try and let these doctors see that you're a fighter, you'll make this handsome man and me the happiest people on earth. Can you do that for me, beautiful?" Under her breath, she spoke privately to Kathy. "Sweetie, you're being taken far from Elle and me. What we think doesn't matter. I might not agree, but I have to trust Derek knows what's best. He loves you so much. I promised Elle I wouldn't blame myself for the accident, but when I see you lying here all broken, I wish I could have driven us out of harm's way."

Lauren glanced over at Derek. He was crying.

"Derek, I'm being transferred across the street in a week to start therapy. There is a beautiful hotel across from the rehab hospital. Why don't you get a room? We can have breakfast together in the morning and a late dinner at night. Sitting vigil isn't going to be good for Kathy or you. You need to get some rest."

"I'm not leaving until she's awake, until I know she can understand me. Anyway, I'm working on having her moved. I don't have time for breakfast or dinner."

"How can she travel in her condition, Derek?"

"Did you forget I'm a well-known surgeon, Lauren? I called in a few favors. American Airlines CEO was doomed until Dr. Wilson was called in to work his miracles. It was me who saved his life. Well, I got him to agree to have Kathy flown on a medical jet to Germany. Fully staffed with doctors and nurses who will make sure she arrives safely. Plus, I'll be there to make sure nothing goes wrong."

"Will the doctors here provide the clearance for you to move her?"

"I don't need their fucking permission."

"Derek, do I have to remind you, a doctor should never perform surgery on a family member? The reason is, because he or she might not be thinking clearly. Would you advise a doctor in your situation to override the decisions of the doctors that have cared for Kathy since she arrived at the hospital?"

"I want her to wake up, Lauren. I need her to wake up."

"She might not want to wake up, Derek, because when she's awake, the pain is too unbearable."

"She doesn't have a choice, Lauren. She's facing a good year or two of pain. She needs to wake up. Whatever way possible, I need her to communicate with me. I need to know she understands what I'm doing is for her benefit." Derek paused. "I'll give it a few more days."

"Will you promise me, if she wakes up and you can communicate with her, you'll check into a hotel and get some rest?"

The corners of Derek's mouth lifted slightly. "I will promise you this. I'm not letting her drift out of our lives. I'll bring your BFF back to you—beautiful and healthy."

Lauren couldn't ask more of the man she once hated. Derek, today, sealed Lauren's trust that although Derek had slipped up and broken Kathy's heart, his devotion and love was the medicine Kathy needed to heal.

CHAPTER 34

Lauren sat staring at the email she'd received three days ago. She wanted to laugh but couldn't even will a chuckle. The email was from Derek, a request for family and friends to join his family on Saturday, September 18, at Alice's home, of all places, Cape May. The accident had occurred two years prior on September 20.

Lauren had read the email several times for the past two days. Hearing the front door to the cottage open, she closed her computer.

Bruce walked into the kitchen and placed the grocery bags on the counter.

"Let me help you."

"I got it."

Lauren ignored Bruce and began to empty the bags.

"I left the supermarket just before the crowd started to roll in. Kelly and Carol decided to remain in town. Jonathan is on his way, so they will hitch a ride back with him."

"It's going to be a wet Labor Day. My leg is aching."

Bruce smiled. "What have you been up to while I was gone? I'm hoping you were working on chapter 1 of your latest novel?"

"No such luck. Did you forget, I have a bad case of writer's block?"

"I'm going to guess you were reading Derek's email for the hundredth time?"

"And you would be right. What the hell is he thinking? Why Cape May? I've avoided the area like the plague since the accident."

"Did you call Elle last night?"

"I did. She's going."

"On the ride to town, Kelly told me Jake also accepted the invite. He booked a flight to AC for himself, Michelle, and the kids. He's spending a few days in Wildwood Crest and taking the kids to the amusement park."

"I know. Elle's family is joining them."

"Up for a few days in Wildwood?"

"No. If I decide to go, I'm flying in and out the same day."

"Well, you'll need to make a decision soon, so I can book a flight."

"I still can't believe that Alice agreed to host this absurd event at her home."

Lauren had placed two calls in the past two days. One to Alice, and last night, she spoke with Elle.

Alice was jovial when she answered her cell. When she heard Lauren's voice, her mood changed.

"Hi, girlfriend."

"I guess you didn't take note of the number before answering?"

"What makes you say that?"

"Your voice changed once you knew it was me."

"Well, you might be right. I was going to call you, but the day got away from me. I knew you'd want an explanation on why I agreed to let Derek host at my home."

"Why did you agree to his request, Alice?"

"I will admit when I was asked, my first thought was to say no. I knew how you felt about visiting this area. After speaking with Derek, I realized it was Kathy who suggested—"

"Kathy?"

"Yes, Lauren, Kathy."

Lauren decided not to question Alice any further.

"Have you responded to the invite?" asked Alice.

"No. Not sure I'm going to attend."

"I'm sure Derek will be disappointed."

"I'm sure. I have to go. I hear Bruce calling. I'll let you know if I change my mind."

"I hope you do, Lauren."

Lauren's second call was to Elle. Elle would understand and agree with her decision.

"Hi, Lauren. I was sure I would hear from you once you received Derek's email."

"I needed time to digest this ridiculous request."

"I don't know. Maybe it's not so ridiculous."

"I heard you're going."

"Yes."

"I thought if you and I refused—"

"I couldn't refuse when I heard Kathy requested—"

"I don't believe that. Well, good luck. Let me know—never mind. I don't want to know. I'll respond by saying, 'I'd like to plan a private visit to the Wilson clan.'"

"Would it be too much, Lauren, to put your feelings aside for a friend?"

Since the accident, those involved could not say the tragedy didn't change them. Elle lost the gentle tone she would take with Lauren when they didn't agree. The accident had hardened her friend.

"What the hell is that supposed to mean?"

"I'm sure you'd rather be planted in front of your computer writing your next bestseller rather than spending a day in Cape May. I know what's got your goat. You're probably pissed that Derek didn't consult you before making his plans. Who the fuck do you think you are? The Queen of England? Even the tight-ass queen would make an appearance for a friend."

"Don't hold back, Elle. Say what's on your mind. You know I never was a fan of Cape May, and now since the accident, I'd rather stay clear of the place. That's why I don't want to go. How about you consider my feelings, Ms. High and Mighty?"

"Whatever, Lauren."

"Why this holier-than-thou attitude, Elle? How could you not have a problem with going back to the place that laid you up for two years?"

"It was a fucking accident, Lauren. It could have happened in my back door. No. I don't have a problem going back if that is what my friend requests."

"Well, say hi to everyone for me."

Lauren disconnected before Elle could respond. She lay awake the entire night. The thought of Kathy requesting to return to Cape May was nauseating. She had a good mind to call Derek and offer her opinion. She wouldn't and couldn't do such a thing. She needed to make a decision.

In the morning, she stared at the email once again and hit the respond button. Over breakfast, she told Bruce to reserve two seats on a flight to the AC airport.

*****

Elle stared at her sons as they slept. Jacques came up behind her. "Seems as if they grow an inch or two every other day."

"I love watching them sleep."

Jacques squeezed Elle's shoulders. "Can I convince my wife to come snuggle with me on the sofa?"

Elle rested her head on Jacques's chest. She reflected on her last visit with Lauren before Lauren returned home to rehab. Derek had held off for another week before moving Kathy. Kathy's parents visited with their daughter. Elle could hear the sounds of a heated conversation between the parents and Kathy's legal guardian, Derek.

She would begin therapy the day after Kathy was rushed off to Berlin.

The contraption that was her home for two months was removed. It had only been a week since she was able to deal with the pain, and a week since the pain was tolerable. She agreed to the pain medication in the morning and before bed. When offered at noon and at three o'clock, she refused. Jacques told Elle that Lauren was coming to visit before returning home. Bruce had purchased a mattress and placed it in the back of his SUV. Lauren's comfort was his top priority. Jacques said, Bruce was excited about returning to Cape Cod. Life would get easier for the couple. Elle was jealous. Her life was becoming more difficult with each passing day. The door to her room opened.

Lauren slid in on her wheelchair and said, "Watch this, Elle." She lowered the leg holders on the wheelchair. Bruce handed her crutches. Lauren placed them under her armpits and stood. With the help of her good leg, she slowly walked toward Elle. Handing Bruce the crutches, she collapsed into the chair next to Elle's bed.

"This will be you in a very short time."

Elle frowned.

"Why the long face?"

"Not looking forward to therapy."

"It isn't all it's cracked up to be, but it does the trick. One more demon to face before you can rid this place forever."

"Can you stop with the demon analogies?"

"Wow, you're in one crappy mood. I don't know how Jacques puts up with you."

"He doesn't have to for much longer. After my first week in therapy, he's returning home for the week. He'll come on weekends. Mom will tag along, so the boys can visit."

"That's great."

"I guess. I was told I wouldn't have a day to rest. Therapy seven days a week. Are they kidding me?"

"I'm sorry. I guess with the severity of your injuries, it's important they keep you moving."

"I guess. Did you get a chance to say goodbye to Kathy?"

"No. Derek arranged for the flight to leave at six this morning. I said my goodbyes last night. Kathy's parents expressed their concerns to me regarding Derek's decision to ship Kathy off to Berlin."

"Derek's her husband, and Kathy isn't capable of speaking for herself. Happy to be going home?"

"No. I was hoping you and I would be released together."

"There isn't a chance in hell that's going to happen."

"Elle, I know it's rough. It's going to be a long two to three months before you head home."

"I'm not going home, Lauren. After here, I'm shipped to a rehab hospital in Washington, DC."

"If I am not mistaken, you live in Washington, DC."

"Rehab is not home, Lauren."

"Of course not. But the boys will be able to visit more often. Your mom can stop by for lunch while the boys are at school. Being close to home will make you work harder to get back to a normal life."

"Easy for you to say. What's your schedule look like? Rehab several hours a day. Then you get to go home and sleep in your own bed."

Elle's words caused the guilt that Lauren was trying to put to rest work its ugly head back into her life.

"I'm sorry, Elle. If I could take your place, I'd do it in a heartbeat."

"I would agree in a heartbeat to trade places with you if it were possible."

*****

For three long and painful months, Elle worked her ass off to get through each therapy session without too many tears. The first week was the worst. Jim, who served in Iraq working with injured soldiers until the work was taking a toll on his own physical and mental health, was a gentle and caring man. Elle would scream out in pain not caring who heard or listened. By week 3, she replaced the screams with moaning when the pain was too much for her to bear. By week 6, she took the pain in stride. She was sent to DC after the eighth week.

In DC, she was put under the watchful eye of Sylvia, who said Jim was a pussy who should have had Elle walking with the help of a hydraulic walking device a month earlier. Elle hated Sylvia. She asked Jacques to get Sylvia off her case.

"I heard you requested to get rid of me?"

"I did. You're too hard on me."

"Do you want to walk again?"

"That's a ridiculous question."

"Then if I were you, I'd stick with me."

Sylvia was right. Within two months, Elle was able to walk with a walker for thirty minutes each day. Sylvia had promised Elle she would be home for Easter, and on Palm Sunday, Elle returned home.

She watched the fire dancing before them. Her head rose and fell with each breath Jacques took. She welcomed the smell of him. She longed for intercourse. Jacques was a generous lover and tended to Elle's needs, but the actual act of intercourse was off the table. Three days prior, Elle had questioned Sylvia about sex.

"So you're worried that your man might develop lockjaw? Hand jobs getting a little boring?"

"Were you raised by animals, Sylvia?"

"I'm joking with you. Here's a little exercise for you and your man. Gently, as I do, allow him to bend your legs and then straighten them in the air. If there isn't too much pain, and you're willing to give it a go, have him remain on his knees and enter you. Tell him not to put any pressure on your hips. If it's not too uncomfortable for you, then give it a go. It's not going to be sunshine and roses the first few times, but it's a start."

*****

"Sylvia thinks we should try, you know."

Jacques softly said, "I don't think you're ready, Elle."

"No. You're afraid of hurting me."

Facing him, she stared at him, forcing an answer.

"I am."

"I trust Sylvia. If she thinks we should give it a try, so do I."

"Are you sure, Elle?"

Placing her head back on Jacques's shoulder, she said, "I'm sure. I miss you, Jacques."

"If you're worried about my needs, please don't."

"Sylvia says hand jobs can get boring after a while. I agree."

Jacques chuckled. "I heard you speaking with Lauren, or should I say arguing with Lauren?"

"Both. Lauren is a selfish son of a bitch."

"Elle, what did she say that was so upsetting?"

"She's not going to Cape May. She thinks Derek was inconsiderate asking us to return to the place that brought us an enormous amount of pain."

"You felt no different than she when you read the email."

"We both had days to think about why it's important to show our support. Jake's family is going. We're going. Alice, I'm sure, wasn't crazy about the idea, but she agreed to support her friends."

The Palm Reader

"Have you told Lauren that we are considering moving back to Paris?"

The question hit Elle like a ton of bricks. The only person she hadn't told was Lauren. Alice, Jake, Michelle, and even Derek knew she was considering—no, considering was the past. Jacques had applied for a transfer, and there wasn't a doubt in their minds, it would be approved. Elle informed the producers when asked if she was returning to the anchor desk, that the likelihood was she was moving back to Paris. She had already made contact with her old boss in Paris. She wanted to work at the position she currently held, writing for the anchor and coanchor of the network news. There was no question in her mind that she would be offered a position.

The question of moving was brought on by her fear of traveling. Her Uber driver was weaving his way through the DC traffic trying to get her to her appointment on time with Sylvia. When a car came too close, she screamed for him to slow down, frightening the poor man to death. She wanted the calm of Paris. The ability to walk to and from work and the boys' school. She wanted her children to grow up in a city that frowned upon stress. She addressed the move with Jacques. He said, if she was serious, he'd move forward and request a transfer. She was serious and happy to be leaving the States.

"I haven't told Lauren we're moving. I'm sure she's going to blame the accident for my fleeing the States. And she would be right. I don't have the patience for her condescending tone."

"It would be easier coming from you than one of the others."

"Right. I'll tell her after we return from Cape May."

*****

Lauren called Alice after responding yes to Derek's email. Because of Elle's attitude toward her, she waited several days before calling Elle. The call went to voice mail. "Hi. I accepted Derek's invite."

*****

"The car is packed. I packed a thermos of coffee and muffins for the road. There's a chill in the air. You might need a light jacket."

Sitting on the bed, Lauren stared out her bedroom window and watched the high grass that sat on top of the dunes, blowing in the wind.

"Did you hear a word I said?"

Without looking at Bruce, she answered, "I did. Coffee, muffins, and a light jacket."

"What's wrong, Lauren?"

"I'm not looking forward to this day."

"You want to cancel?"

"I don't have a choice."

"You always have a choice, Lauren."

Lauren stood. "Do I?" Grabbing her jacket, she passed Bruce. Descending the steps, she exited the house and waited for Bruce in the car.

*****

At the airport, they parked in the long-term parking section and boarded the shuttle bus to Logan airport. Flight 516 Spirit Airline to AC airport was scheduled to leave on time. A rental car would be waiting. With an hour's ride to Alice's home, they should arrive at the expected time of 1:00 p.m.

In the terminal waiting area, Lauren sat close to the window and stared at the runway.

"Hi, girlfriend."

Michelle was standing in front of Lauren with Grace in her arms. The child had her arms tightly wrapped around her mother's neck. An oversized bag was hanging from Michelle's other arm, and Jack was holding onto his mother's pant leg.

"You can let go of Mommy's leg, Jack. Have a seat next to Auntie Lauren."

"Hi, Jack. Grace, come sit on Auntie Lauren's lap."

Michelle sat next to Lauren. "Thanks. I think I lost the flow of blood in my arms. Did you hit a lot of traffic?"

"Nothing. Clear sailing."

"Great. I bet you we hit more traffic than you guys, and we live right outside the city."

Lauren smiled. "Where's Jake?"

"With Bruce. There's a long line at Starbucks. I hope Jake remembers not to put cream in my coffee. I spotted Jonathan and Kelly. I think they stopped to give Jake an order. Thank God, this flight is less than two hours. I brought enough video games to last a lifetime."

Lauren smiled.

"Elle and Jacques are spending a few days with us in Wildwood. Alice offered to babysit, so the adults could enjoy a quiet dinner or two. The weather is going to be perfect. I'm sure the kids will enjoy the beach, the water park, and the rides. They'll be so exhausted they won't be a bother to Alice. Nancy offered to watch them one night, so Alice could join us for dinner."

Lauren nodded.

"Can I convince you and Bruce to spend a few days with us?"

"Sorry, we have plans."

"We'll miss you guys."

"Kelly says you're returning to work, part-time."

"Yes. I need to get back to having adult conversations."

"How does Jake feel about you returning to work?"

"He was a little reluctant at first, but I assured him, there's no traveling involved."

Lauren was sure Jake put his foot down when it came to traveling. She could hear him say, "I had enough of that shit with my first wife."

"Mom, you look great."

Kelly hugged Lauren. Jonathan placed a kiss on Lauren's cheek. Ever since the accident, Kelly never failed to tell Lauren how great she looked.

"You look pretty good yourself, kiddo."

Bruce handed Lauren his coffee, offering a sip. "No thanks, babe. I've had my share of caffeine for today."

Jake greeted Lauren with a kiss on the cheek. "How's the leg?"

"Good."

"That's great."

The announcement was made to board the plane, and Lauren's stomach filled with butterflies. Kelly put her arm through her mother's, and together, they entered the plane.

After forty-five minutes in flight, leaving Bruce asleep, Lauren rose and walked to the back of the plane, passing Michelle with a sleeping Grace on her lap, and a magazine in her hand. Jake made eye contact with Lauren. He placed Jack on his seat and whispered something to Michelle.

Joining Lauren in the back of the plane, he asked, "Is the leg bothering you?"

"No. I'm fine."

Lauren lingered, staring into Jake's green eyes. Without a word passing their lips, the man she had fallen in and out of love with was there to offer his support. Bruce didn't possess a jealous bone in his body. When Lauren was conscious and ready to hear how close she had come to dying and losing her leg, Bruce told her how Jake refused to leave her side or their children's side until he knew she had passed the critical stage. She regretted hurting the man her children adored and loved. She and Derek were lucky to have him in their lives. To Derek, there was no truer a friend. When the man needed a shoulder to cry on, Jake's was offered. He listened when Derek explained why it was imperative that Kathy be shipped off to Germany. The husband insisted it was the right decision. Lauren guessed, Jake agreed, even if he didn't think it was a wise decision. A good friend listens without offering his or her own opinion except when asked.

"Did Derek ever explain why Cape May?"

"He said it was Kathy's choice."

"I don't believe that."

"Why would he lie?"

Lauren couldn't think of a reason Derek would lie.

"I was surprised when you changed your mind and decided to come."

"Elle called me a selfish bitch. I've had enough of her foul moods. I intend to get to the bottom of her shitty attitude."

"She has a lot on her mind. Moving, being at the top of her list."

"Moving? Why, did she lose her job? I mean, as long as she's employed with the network, the apartment is a guarantee. Losing her job would answer the question why her mood has been so shitty."

Jake's brow furrowed.

By the look on Jake's face, that wasn't the reason for the move. "What? She didn't lose her job? Then why would they move out of the apartment? I'm guessing by the look on your face, you figured out Elle hasn't shared this important news with me."

"I said too much, Lauren. I'm sure Elle has her reasons for not telling you. I'll let her tell you."

"No. I want to hear it from you. Jake, tell me. Where are they moving to?" Lauren gasped, thinking she might have answered her own question. "Jake, don't tell me they are moving to Paris?"

"They are, Lauren. I'm sorry. I thought Elle would have told you before she told anyone else."

Lauren decided to play it cool. She didn't want Jake to see that his words had just torn her heart in two.

"I'm not surprised she didn't tell me. Things haven't been the same between us since the accident. Bruce and I went to visit her and Jacques in July. Jacques was a sweetheart, but Elle was cool toward us. I truly think she blames me for the accident."

"She doesn't blame you, Lauren. The accident was not your fault. You know that. She probably was afraid to tell you she had decided to move back to Paris."

"Whatever!"

*****

On the drive to Alice's home, Lauren told Bruce that Elle and Jacques were moving to Paris.

*****

Bruce held the car door for Lauren. Taking her arm, he helped her from the car. A rental car was parked on the road. Elle and her family were already there. Bruce opened the front door calling out to no one in particular.

"Hello."

"Bruce. Come in," replied Nancy.

She walked toward Bruce and placed a welcome kiss on his cheek. Bruce accepted the gesture with a smile. Stepping aside, he allowed Lauren to enter.

"Lauren, you look great. I see you're not favoring the leg. That's great."

"Where is your partner in crime?"

"Right here. Hello, Lauren." Alice hugged Lauren. Whispering in her ear, she said, "I'm so happy you decided to come. Elle's out back."

Lauren held onto Alice's arm while Bruce and Nancy walked arm in arm to the kitchen.

"Alice, did you know that Elle is moving to Paris?"

Alice frowned. "I did. She was going to tell you the day we received Derek's email."

Lauren shouted, "Then she changed her mind and decided to tell everyone else but me. So much for BFFs forever."

"Lauren, go easy on Elle. She's had a rough time of it. You and I have had this conversation. We both agree Elle is forever changed since the accident. After she received Derek's email, well, she didn't think it was the right time to tell you she was moving. I know how awful it is to have your best friend living on another continent, but I personally think this move will do her good. I'm asking that you put your feelings aside and wish her well."

"Are you forgetting since the accident, I've had a severe case of writer's block? One book in two years, and it was a flop. Elle is like a sister to me. We told each other everything before the accident. Deep down, I think she blames me. I have been strong and supportive for two years, trying to lift my BFF's spirits because I drew the short straw, which placed me in the driver's seat. What would make any of you think that I couldn't handle a fucking email or the shocking news that my best friend was running off to Paris."

"That's it right there, Lauren. If Elle would have told you she thought it was best for her and her family to move to Paris, you would have told her she was running away from her demons. You call that supporting a friend? Support would be letting Elle go in the hopes that she finds the gentle soul she once was before the accident. If you don't speak to her with compassion, you will drive a deeper wedge between you."

*****

When Lauren stepped out into the backyard, she was brought back to another time so long ago. There were tables draped in white linens, chairs adorned with yellow bows, and yellow roses in the center of each table. Six years ago, they met here to watch Casey's ashes take flight. That day, just like this day, she wanted to be anywhere but where she stood at this moment.

The sun reflecting on the ocean blinded Lauren. She raised her hand to cover her eyes. When she did, she spotted Elle and Jacques in conversation with Jake, Michelle, and Bruce. The children were playing near the shore. It was a warm day. The picture-perfect sky was the deepest color of blue and cloudless. The children's shoes were lying on the sand. The boys' pant legs were rolled up, and they used their feet to splash one another. Suddenly, Grace ran to her mother whining that Jack had gotten her pretty dress wet. Jack, Liam, and Ethan ignored Grace and continued to splash and run. Jonathan and Kelly stood nearby watching that no one ran deeper into the ocean.

Lauren couldn't face the adults, not yet, so she went and stood beside Jonathan and Kelly. After several minutes, she joined the boys and allowed them to splash her. The water felt warm against her skin. Raising her face to the sun, she relished the warm feeling on her face.

"Still a child at heart."

Lauren turned to see Elle standing behind her. She was still using a cane to support her right side.

"Elle, you're still using the cane. I thought—"

"That my doctor told me to shitcan the cane. It was my first plane ride. I knew I'd be standing for a long time today. I thought I might need this little guy for support."

Lauren searched the temporal lobe of her brain, and Alice's advice flashed before her.

"Whatever you need to feel comfortable, Elle."

Elle smiled and walked toward Lauren. Taking Lauren into her arms, Elle gave her a huge hug. Lauren relaxed into Elle's embrace. She rested her face next to Elle's and squeezed her eyes shut. She didn't want to let Elle go. Lauren wanted to hold on to her forever.

Still in a tight embrace, Elle confessed, "Jake apologized for letting the cat out of the bag." Elle released her hold on Lauren. She placed her hand on Lauren's face. Staring into her eyes, she said, "I didn't have the heart to tell you. I know what you're thinking. I'm running away. And you would be right. The only problem with me running is I'll be so far from you. But I need to go, Lauren. I need to find the old Elle. I know I've been a total bitch to you, and it isn't because I blame you for the accident. Lauren, I was so happy with my life, my family, and my friendships. I was ready to toss the job in the air and give my boys my full attention before that god-awful day. In a flash, I wasn't able to get down on the floor and rough it up with the boys. I couldn't make love to my husband. I didn't have the patience to deal with my friends' problems. The accident robbed me of two years of my life. I was bitter. I can't find a way to get me out of this funk. Remembering how much I loved living in Paris made me think Paris might be the answer. Who knows, I might regret the move. Jacques says, 'If it doesn't work out, we can always head back to the States.' He says, 'Happy *wife*. Happy *life*.'"

Lauren's eyes began to well. "I love you, Elle, but if Paris is the answer, then go, be happy. Heck, it's an eight-hour flight. Piece of cake. If you need me, I'll be there in a flash."

Elle and Lauren's private moment was interrupted by the sounds of welcome laughter. When Elle and Lauren turned to see what was going on, they saw the Wilson clan standing at the backyard door, and they gasped.

CHAPTER 35

Derek sent Fanny off to her place at three that afternoon. Satisfied the kitchen was spotless, he was ready to ignite the fireplace, crash on the sofa, and start that John Grisham novel he had been putting off. His cell phone began to buzz. "Shit," cursed Derek, until he realized it was his beautiful wife calling. Kathy's face appeared on the screen. He smiled. Overshadowing his wife's beautiful face was the date, September 18, time ten o'clock.

"Hey, babe."

"Derek, it's me, Kathy. Can you hear me? There's a lot of noise in here."

"Where are you?"

"I'm in the ladies' room at the restaurant."

"What's up, sweetie? Are you having a good time? Wait, if you're calling me, maybe you're having a lousy time? What did Lauren do this time?"

"You have to speak louder, so I can hear you. I was going to call when I got back to the hotel, but this couldn't wait."

Derek spoke louder. "You met someone, and you're leaving me?"

"No, of course not."

"You're checking in on me. The kids are fine. The five are down for the night. The house is spotless without Fanny's help. I gave her the afternoon and evening off. I'm sure you will agree I worked hard and should reward myself with two hours of relaxation."

Kathy chuckled. "When you hear what I have to say, I'm sure you will agree it will be the perfect ending to your long hard day."

"I'm all ears."

"Derek, I don't know why I went down that dark path. Curiosity or payback. Whatever! I called to tell you I agree with you. I don't want anyone in our bed other than you and me until death. The times we spent with other women, although exciting, in the end you were all I wanted and needed. Please forgive me."

Derek smiled. "I owe you one, so yes, I'd forgive you anything, my beauty. We tested the waters. Been there, done that. It's over."

"Derek, what do we do, if—"

"If we miss the thrill, and remembering isn't doing the trick? We'll cross that bridge when and if we come to it. Hopefully, we'll never have to. Kathy, baby, I love you. Love got us through the worst of times. As long as we are together, we can face whatever this world throws at us. Now go back to your BFFs, have fun, and I'll be here waiting for you tomorrow. I promise you a homecoming you won't forget. That is, after we bathe and bed down those brats."

Kathy laughed. "I can't wait. I love you, Derek, and only you. Kiss the kids for me." Kathy blew kisses into the phone before disconnecting.

*****

Two chapters into the John Grisham novel, Derek laid his exhausted body on the sofa and drifted off to sleep. His dreams were of Kathy. She was running and laughing. He didn't see himself, but he knew he was not far behind. Kathy was wearing a white dress, no shoes, and daisies in her hair, spinning round and round. Her beautiful hair whirled around her face. Her smile was illuminating. The brightness of the sun made his vision impaired. The blurry image of Kathy caused him to fear losing her.

His cell phone began to buzz, causing his arm to vibrate. Without opening his eyes, he answered. "Kathy, baby, where are you?"

Within seconds, he was conscious and running for the back door. He screamed Fanny's name in the yard. Seconds later, he was banging on her back door. The cottage light came on, and the door opened.

"Doc, what's wrong?"

Derek didn't respond. He reached for Fanny's arm and dragged her to the house. When they entered the house, Derek searched for a number on his phone and dialed. He yelled into the phone. "Jessy, I need the jet. It's an emergency. I'm heading out."

"Doc, what is it?"

"Fanny, it's Kathy. There's been an accident. I'm taking the jet to the Philadelphia Tamar Center."

"Ms. Kathy. What happened?"

Derek's cell buzzed. He grabbed the car keys and his jacket before answering. "Jake, hold on." Heading for the front door, he motioned to Fanny, "I'll call you." Before he stepped from the house, he checked to see if he had his wallet. He did. He entered the red Porsche and placed his cell phone in the phone holder and tapped the speaker button.

"Jake, are you there?"

"I'm here."

"What the fuck happened?"

"I don't know. Lauren had Kelly's contact information in her wallet. Thank God, I was with Kelly when she got the call. She said we had to get to the hospital immediately. Where are you, Derek?"

"I called for the hospital jet. I should be there in thirty minutes." Making his way onto the highway, Derek swayed to avoid hitting a car in the right lane. The driver, annoyed, blew the horn several times. Derek cursed, "Fuck you!"

"Derek, calm down. Did they say how bad the accident was?"

"No. Nothing. Just to get there as soon as we can. It doesn't sound good, Jake."

"I know."

"I'm getting off the exit. I'll be at the airport in ten minutes. I'm sorry, Jake, I can't wait. It will take you too long to get here. I'll call you once I know what's going on."

Derek disconnected before Jake had time to object. Arriving at the terminal provided for private flights, Derek paid the attendant, Chris, $200 to park his car. "I trust you, Chris, give the car ticket to Gus when he returns."

"You can trust me, Doc."

Derek spotted Gus standing by the plane idling on the tarmac. When Derek reached Gus, the two entered the plane. Gus had been called often in the middle of the night to get one of the top surgeons off to help save a life.

"I called ahead, Doc. I have clearance to land at the Philadelphia airport. I arranged for an ambulance to get you there ASAP."

Derek reached for Gus's arm. "It's my wife, Gus. Kathy. An accident."

Gus nodded.

*****

The emergency room attendants ran when the ambulance with its flashing lights pulled in. When the doors opened, Derek got out and pushed past the confusing looks. He ran to the front desk and asked what floor the ICU was on.

"Name please."

"Listen, I'm Dr. Wilson, I don't have time for this. What floor is the ICU on?"

The young lady knew the man standing before her wasn't going to answer her questions. She went against protocol and answered, "Second floor."

Exiting on the second floor, Derek found the buzzer to the ICU. The doors did not open, but a voice asked, "How can I help you?"

"Dr. Wilson. I'm Kathy Wilson's husband."

"Dr. Wilson, someone will be with you shortly."

"I need to see my wife, open the fucking door."

The phone went dead. Derek banged on the ICU door. When no one came, he began to pace. He spotted the waiting area, which was empty. How many times did families wait for him to find out if their loved one was alive or dead? Derek ran his hands through his hair. The ICU door opened, and a doctor stepped through.

"Dr. Wilson. I'm Dr. Walters."

"Where is my wife?"

"Your wife is in surgery."

"Surgery?"

"Yes. I'm sure you were informed there was an accident. Three women were traveling with your wife. Do you know these women?"

"I do. Lauren Hicks and Elle Kessler." Derek gave Elle's maiden name. "And Alice. I don't remember her last name."

"Only three arrived tonight, including your wife. Says here the other was taken to Cape May General. Hicks and Kessler are here. The other must be at Cape May."

"My wife, Doctor. You said she was in surgery, what for? Listen, I'm a doctor. Dr. Derek Wilson. Ring any bells?"

"The heart surgeon."

"Yes. So you know who I am. Can you take me to the operating room?"

"I can't do that, Dr. Wilson."

"I know, protocol. But I might be able to help."

"She's in good hands, Dr. Wilson."

Derek knew the doctor before him did not have the authority to allow him into the operating room. "Can you get the chief surgeon on the case on the phone and get me access?"

"Why don't we have a seat in the waiting area and talk?"

The doors to the ICU opened. Derek rushed through the doors causing the nurse who was exiting to crash against the wall. Dr. Walters ran behind Derek calling his name, "Dr. Wilson!"

When Derek was at the front desk of the ICU, he turned and through a glass door, he saw a room. He crashed through the glass door. He noticed that the bed was empty, and the sheets were splatted with blood. The floor was also covered in blood.

Dr. Walters entered the room.

"Who was in this room?" asked Derek.

Dr. Walters retrieved a chair. "Please, Dr. Wilson, have a seat."

Seeing the blood-soaked sheets and the floor splattered with blood, Derek's legs weakened. He fell into the chair provided by Dr. Walters.

"I can't provide that information, as you know, if you're not a family member."

"Who was in this room for Christ's sake?"

Antoinette Zam

"Ms. Kessler. That is all I will tell you."

"Ms. Kessler is a friend."

"Is Mr. Kessler on his way?"

"I have no fucking idea where he is. Where is my wife?"

Dr. Walters pulled up a chair. "She's in surgery."

"How bad?"

"From what was noted in the chart, the car was in an accident with a tractor trailer."

"A tractor trailer? What the fuck! Are they alive?"

"Yes. Surgery was needed in each of the cases."

"My wife, Doctor. What's her condition?"

"Your wife was in the passenger's seat in the front of the car. I'm sorry. The passenger's seat was hit hardest at impact."

Derek placed his hand on his head and cursed. "How bad?"

"She's in surgery for internal bleeding. Once the bleeding is under control, the doctors will tend to the other injuries."

"And they would be?"

"Facial. Her jaw, cheek, and left eye."

"Facial injuries. I'm sure the glass shattered."

"Yes. There are glass fragments on the upper part of the body. Her left eye was affected."

Derek screamed.

"Dr. Wilson. I know this isn't easy—"

Derek rose. "I need to get into that fucking operating room."

"Dr. Wilson." Before Dr. Walters could explain that was impossible, the door opened. The nurse announced that Ms. Kessler's husband had arrived.

Derek left the room and went to let Jacques into the ICU.

"Derek. Have you seen them?"

Derek lowered his head. Sensing that Dr. Walters was standing behind him, he said, "Jacques, this is Dr. Walters."

Jacques extended his hand. "Mr. Pascal, Elle's husband. How is my wife?"

Dr. Walters asked if they could step outside to the waiting area. Derek took Jacques's arm wanting to spare Jacques the room that once housed Elle.

When they were seated, Dr. Walters gave Jacques the bad news.

"Ms. Kessler is in surgery. Internal bleeding. Mr. Pascal, there isn't an easy way to say that your wife has sustained spinal injuries. I don't know to what degree. The surgeon will speak to you further about her injuries. I'm going to head back to the surgical area for an update."

Before Dr. Walters headed back, Derek reached for his arm. "Dr. Walters, what about Lauren Croft?"

"Dr. Wilson, let me know when the family arrives. She's alive and in surgery. That's all I can say."

Derek let go of Dr. Walters's arm.

He sat beside Jacques. "Derek, why aren't you in there with them?"

"Protocol, Jacques."

Jacques placed his hands on his head. "It doesn't sound good, Derek. Spinal injury. What if Elle losses the ability to walk? I can't believe this."

Derek glanced at Jacques, who was contemplating how he will break the news to Elle that she may never walk again.

According to the most recent report, Derek was told Kathy's face was damaged. He started to shake, and his eyes welled up with tears. To stop Jacques from seeing, he began to pace.

*****

Over a ten-day period, Derek held Kathy's hand as she was taken yet again to surgery. The update from the doctors wasn't promising. Kathy had lost the sight in her right eye. Her face was shattered. Years of plastic surgery, if she survived. His beautiful wife was broken, and her devoted husband was losing his mind. He wanted nothing more than to communicate with his wife. When Kathy showed signs of communication, it was to moan. The pain was too much. Derek feared that death was the only way to stop her pain. He sat vigil asking his wife to fight. He repeated over and over, "I can't live without you, Kathy. Please don't leave me."

Twenty days later, he reached out to Dr. Frankel in Germany. Kathy's facial injuries were severe, and she needed the best to make her whole again—that is, if she survived. He hadn't and couldn't speak with his children. He did speak with Fanny once since the accident. She assured him the children were fine. Kathy's parents sat vigil with Derek, but when he informed them of his plans to take Kathy to Germany, they disagreed. He couldn't understand why. Their persistence in trying to change his mind was overwhelming. The only answer was to send them away. He told them, he needed their help in caring for the children, made up an excuse that his mother and father had to get back home. Kathy's mother knew she was being sent away because she disagreed with her daughter being shipped off to a foreign country. Kathy's father agreed with his wife but assured her that their son-in-law was a well-known surgeon who dealt with these issues on a daily basis. Who would know better what's best for a patient than their son-in-law? The devoted love Derek bestowed on their daughter should dispose any doubt that he didn't know what was best.

Derek was growing tired. It was over a month, and he had not left Kathy's side. Clothes appeared and disappeared. Sundry items appeared and were replaced when needed. He had no hand in any of these things. He was sure it was Jake's doing. He showered each morning, ate one meal a day. The clothes on his body grew larger with each passing day. The rest of his day was sitting by his wife's bed and begging for her to wake.

The arrangements were made to move Kathy. In a week's time, for the next two years, they would reside in Berlin.

CHAPTER 36

The sound of the ocean crashing against the shore and the sand between her toes were soothing. Kathy was seated on a beach chair. Lauren was sitting next to her. Lauren's computer was on her lap, and her fingers were rapidly striking the keyboard. Kathy knew Lauren was working on her next bestseller. Kathy spied Elle on her phone. *Elle is always an arm's reach from her desk in Washington,* thought Kathy. Alice was on her right, reading a book. She wondered where Casey might be. Alice stood to adjust the umbrella on her beach chair. Kathy wanted to ask about Casey, but she found it difficult to speak.

She stared at the sky. Looking down, she was no longer at the beach. She was dressed in a beautiful red gown embroidered with the finest crystals. On impulse, she touched her hair that was pinned up to a knot at the nape of her neck. Suddenly, a bright light came toward her. Gathering the dress in both hands, she began to run. The bright light was gaining speed. She ran faster. A hand appeared. She knew this hand. Derek stepped out and wrapped her in his arms, where she felt safe from harm. Gently, he placed her on a red carpet and said, "You look beautiful. Are you ready?"

The quizzical look on her face asked, "Ready for what?"

"Silly girl, the grand ball." He motioned to the right. The family care facility building stood tall in the night sky. Of course, the grand ball to celebrate the opening of the facility. How could she forget such a fabulous event, which was planned entirely by her? Derek extended his arm. The expression on Derek's face said how proud he was of all she had accomplished. Together, they walked the red car-

Antoinette Zam

pet. The vision of them walking side by side was fading. The bright light has returned and was heading toward her. She feared the light was going to swallow her up. She screamed. The bright light vanished and was replaced by the darkness.

Once again, she was dreaming. She was enjoying a day at the park with her children. Eric was teasing his younger sister Mary, a sweet but timid child. Kathy called to Eric to come sit next to her. She wrapped her arms around him and said, "A big brother should protect his sisters."

He shrugged his shoulders. Peggy has taken on the task of pushing Gabe on the swing. Mary asked if Peggy would ride the seesaw with her. Peggy said yes, leaving Gabe on his own. Once Gabe realized Peggy was gone, he began to cry. Eric left the comfort of his mother's arms and rushed off to swing his brother. Kathy looked toward Scottie who was crouched down, staring at the dirt and watching the ants at work. When he lost interest, he ran toward the swings, found his favorite, and climbed in, asking Eric for a push. It warmed her heart to see her children so happy. She turned her face to the warmth of the sun, and without warning, the darkness appeared.

It was another dream. This time, there were no visions, only a strong sensation that her parents were close. She heard her mother and father talking to her. Her father was calling her by his favorite name for her—pumpkin. Her mother was whispering, but she could not understand what her mother was saying. It didn't matter; she knew her parents were near, and their presence brought comfort. Darkness.

She heard the drone of a plane engine. She was transported back to a time when she and Derek vacationed in Italy. Images of the places they visited flashed before her, each day ending with the couple naked in each other's arms.

Darkness. Something strange was happening. There were flashes of light, similar to the flashing of light from a camera. Darkness.

She heard voices. Everyone was speaking at once. *Excitement* was the only word to describe what she was hearing. Darkness.

Flashes of light. Her eyelids twitched. Voices. Excitement. Darkness.

She wanted to open her eyes, but something was stopping her from opening both eyes. She willed herself to open one eye. Voices. Light. Intensified pain. Darkness.

Someone was shouting. A blurry vision blocked the light. Her vision was impaired. She forced her eye open. The voices were becoming clearer.

"She's awake."

It's been two months since Kathy woke from the darkness and came to the realization that the darkness was a blessing to the hell she was facing.

One week after she entered the world of the living, she was told about the accident and why she was now residing in a hospital in Berlin.

Three months had gone by before she found her voice. She was able to speak three audible words at a time. With her jaw wired, it was hard to express her feelings. The cast was removed from her right arm, and Derek massaged the arm daily. She was now able to scribble two words at a time. Derek assured her, time and time again, that Dr. Frankel was the best in the field of face reconstruction. Dr. Frankel had asked her to think of him as a friend and to place her fate in his hands. She hated Dr. Frankel, the hospital, Berlin, and sorry to say, her beloved husband.

Since waking, at least two days of her miserable week were spent removing the bandages that surrounded her face and neck and taking more pictures.

The first time the bandages on her face and neck were removed, she felt excruciating pain. She cursed God for not allowing her to die that awful night.

Antidepressants were added to her excessive medications. Derek was exhausted from her constant complaining and her excessive writing of the word *home* on the notepad she was given to express her feelings.

She refused to meet with patients that Dr. Frankel had worked his magic on. The good doctor assured her it would help her to move forward with the first surgery. As the days dragged on, the couple argued often. The battle was one-sided. Derek expressed his frustration with her, and she responded with two words: "*Fuck you.*"

He'd shout, "Kathy, you have two choices. Dr. Frankel and reconstruction or—"

He could never bring himself to finish the sentence. It didn't take a rocket scientist to figure out that whatever was left of her face, in time, would heal and the outcome grotesque.

Of course, she had no way of confirming this since she was not granted her request for a mirror. She knew Derek was meeting privately with Dr. Frankel to study the images of the final results of the surgeries. She wasn't privy to the images of what she would look like two years from now. She was sure that was due to the fact that Derek wasn't pleased with the outcome.

Today, he was extremely agitated. She reached for the notepad and wrote as clearly as she could. "*What's wrong?*"

"Nothing" was his response. So she continued. "*How many scars?*"

"What?"

She pointed to her right arm that housed a number of scars.

"It depends. Down the road, there will be a number of skin grafts." Derek ran his fingers through his hair. His facial expression revealed his frustration. "You're asking questions that I can't answer, Kathy. At least not until the surgeries begin. And you've made it clear, you're not ready."

When she didn't respond, Derek collapsed in the chair and stared at the TV.

At night, when she was left alone and given time to think, the same questions plagued her. She had lost the sight in one eye. A glass eye would be implanted. She could live with that. Then the following questions haunted her constantly.

Her husband, the heart surgeon—who rips open one's chest on a daily basis and not shy to the sight of massive amounts of blood—was nowhere to be found when the bandages were removed. She didn't fault him. She wasn't sure she could handle it if the shoe was on the other foot. But she would be there to hold his hand and stare blankly into space.

The questions took over her night and deprived her of the sleep she longed for. After two years of surgery, could she live with her newly reconstructed face? How many scars would she have to deal with? Would people pity her by saying, "She once was a beautiful woman. Look at her now." Could she live with the stares? How would her children handle the change in Mommy's appearance? Would they be embarrassed to be seen with her?

Once while shopping at Bloomingdales, she collided with a woman. When she went to offer an apology, she gasped at the sight of the woman's face. The left side of her face and neck were scarred. Her hair was gone on that side, and where there once housed a healthy ear, just a small hole remained. She wanted to do the right thing—smile and offer another apology—but she said nothing. She rushed off with her tail between her legs.

Asking herself over and over if she was strong enough to be seen, like that brave woman, the answer was always the same—no. Putting aside her vanity, she thought about her extremely handsome husband, Derek. He married a beauty who would turn into a beast. Their marriage was doomed. Sex—nonexistent. Therapy was back on the table for years to come.

At the start of the fourth month, Dr. Frankel announced that the first surgery would be on Monday if she were in agreement. Of course, she gave Derek and Dr. Frankel the answer they were waiting for—yes.

The day prior, while Derek sat asleep in the chair, a lunch tray was brought in. The food was for Derek since her mouth was still wired and she was hooked up to a feeding tube. An object on the tray caught her eye, and she managed to retrieve it.

On Sunday, the TV was turned off the entire day, giving Derek time to reassure her that all would be well.

The hate she felt for her husband had ceased. Other than his fall from grace with Nina, he was a good husband and father, and she loved him dearly.

Taking her hand in his, he said, "Kathy, you know that I love you more than life itself. I thought it was the right decision for you and the children to come to Berlin. You know everyone tried to talk me out of taking you so far from home, but Dr. Frankel was the best, and you deserve nothing but the best. I need you, Kathy, and the children need you. I've been rough on you, and I know that you've come to hate me, but if the shoe was on the other foot, wouldn't you want me to fight like hell to live?"

She released her hand from his and asked for the notepad. Before writing her thoughts, she placed her hand on his cheek. He smiled. She scribbled this: "*You made the right decision.*"

He was elated by her words. His eyes began to well with tears. Taking her hand to his lips, he showered her hand with kisses.

During these months, she had heard her children's and parents' voices three times by phone. She refused to talk with her friends, and she knew that they were disappointed, Lauren especially. Knowing Lauren, she was blaming herself for the accident. Elle was going through her own hell, and Kathy was sure Elle thought of her less frequently.

Derek looked exhausted. "Thank you for loving me, Derek."

Derek smiled. "I love you, baby. There isn't anything I wouldn't do for you."

"The children need you."

"I know."

"Promise me if—"

"No. Stop. It's going to be fine. You're going to be fine."

She squeezed his hand. In a raspy voice, she said, "*Phone.*"

"Of course, is there someone special you want to call?"

"Everyone."

"Everyone, including Lauren and Elle?"

"Yes."

"Okay, let's start with the kids and your parents."

Placing the phone close to her ear, Derek said, "It's your mom."

"Mom," Kathy whispered.

"Yes, sweetheart, I can understand you." Her mother choked up but managed to tell her husband to gather the children. He did as his wife asked, and Kathy could hear and envision her children running down the circular staircase in her home.

"Mom." Her son Eric had grown since she last saw him. He said "Mom" instead of Mommy.

She managed to speak his name, "*Eric.*"

"Don't be afraid, Mom. Dad told us Dr. Frankel is the best. Right, Dad?"

"Nothing but the best for your mom!" shouted Derek.

Peggy takes the phone. "Hi, Mommy. Mary, stop. Mommy can't FaceTime. Mary wants to FaceTime, but Daddy said you need a few more months. Stop grabbing for the phone, Scottie. Mommy, Scottie wants to talk to you."

"Mommy, when are you coming home? I miss you."

If she could produce a tear, they would flow like a river. "As soon as I can."

Gabe called out "Mommy" several times. "Grandma, I want to talk to Mommy."

My mother handed Gabe the phone. "I love you, mommy. Come home."

"I love you, sweetheart."

"It's my turn, Gabe. Mommy, I love you," said Mary. "I'm saving my allowance to buy you flowers for when you come home."

"Yellow?" She asked.

"Yes, Mommy, yellow roses. Your favorite."

"Mary, Mom has to rest." My mother took the phone. "Sweetheart."

She heard her father whisper. "I'm right here, pumpkin."

"Your father and I would be there—"

"No. The children." Her mouth was dry, but she managed to say "I love you all" and motioned for Derek to remove the phone.

*****

Lauren shouted, "Kathy, how are you, my beauty? Your first surgery—how exciting. Kathy, don't give it much thought. Think of this as a day at the spa. Remember when the four of us got those awful facials? Your face blew up like a balloon. Who knew you'd have an allergic reaction to the cream?"

Her heart warmed to the sound of Lauren's voice. In the worst of situations, Lauren always found a way to make her laugh.

"All kidding aside. I love you, Kathy, and I'm praying that each surgery is a success. I'm so sorry—"

"No. Stop, Lau. I love you."

"BFFs forever. I don't want to end this call, but you need to rest." Lauren whispered, "Good luck, my dearest friend."

"Bye, Lau."

The accident had changed Elle; Kathy could hear it in her voice.

"First surgery, I bet you'd rather be any place but in that hospital."

"How are you, Elle?"

"Still the sweet and caring gal you've always been asking how I'm doing. I'm managing. Enough about me. All I have to offer in support is hopefully in two years, God willing, this will be behind us. I love you, Kathy. Good luck.

"I love you, Elle, goodbye."

In the remainder of the day, Derek and she talked about memorable moments they shared. They professed their love for one another often. The door to Kathy's room opened, and a nurse that she had not seen before entered.

"Dr. Wilson, it's time to say, 'Gute Nacht.' It's been a long day and a longer day for this young lady tomorrow." The nurse injected the IV bag with sleeping medication.

"Derek, go."

Derek stood, gathered a few things, and placed several kisses on her bandaged head as he had done hundreds of times since arriving in Berlin. They made eye contact, and Kathy took Derek's hand in hers. "I love you, never forget."

The tears welled in his eyes. With his free hand, he wiped his cheeks. "These are tears of happiness. This will be the last time we see each other before the surgery. The surgery will be at six. You won't be awake when I arrive, but I promise I'll be here before you're taken into surgery. I love you so much."

She whispered, "The memories we shared today, keep close to your heart. I love you."

The Palm Reader

When the door closed behind her beloved husband, Kathy stared at the IV bag. The sleeping medication would be working its magic shortly. She retrieved the object she had hidden in the cast on her left arm. She moved her right wrist close and hacked away at her wrist. The blood flowed easily onto the sheets.

Since the accident, her fate has been in the hands of others. That day, she took control over her own life. Derek often said she had two choices, but there was always a third and the one she decided on.

Staring at the ceiling, she begged for her children and Derek to forgive her. She knew a month ago that she didn't have the strength to go through years of surgery without a clear picture of the outcome.

She hoped God would grant her, her wish to die. Those who loved her might think her selfish for taking her own life and would not understand that she did it for her children and Derek. They would mourn her passing, but the mourning period would end. And a simpler and happier life would prevail. Her death would cause her parents great pain, but it wouldn't be long before they would be together. She would never see her children marry. She would never rock her grandchildren to sleep. She would never grow old with Derek. She would never again share fond memories or laughter while enjoying several glasses of wine with her BFFs.

Her choice, her life, and she chose to end it.

"Good night, my sweet princes and princesses." She would watch over them from above. Derek, her beloved, she wished would live a long and happy life.

She could feel herself drifting off. The dream came fast and sweet. She was dressed in a white linen dress. There was a mirror in her hand. She looked at her reflection. Her face was not deformed and scarred. She placed the mirror down and began to dance. She was happy and giddy. The weight of the world has been lifted off her shoulders.

She heard a voice calling her name. From the light, she saw Casey walking toward her. "Hi, beautiful, I've been waiting for you." Kathy ran to embrace her. Casey released Kathy from the embrace and pointed toward the light. The light was bright and warm. Kathy wasn't afraid. She glanced at Casey. Casey smiled and said, "It's time to go."

Together, they walked into the light.

*****

Kathy's only prayer, before taking her life, was that no bells or whistles would go off announcing her demise. She got her wish. Earlier that day, one of the three nurses that were scheduled to work that night came down with the flu. With no time to find a replacement, only two nurses were available when a code blue sounded for room 512. Moments later, Kathy's room alarm sounded. No one answered the call, allowing Kathy to pass from this life to the next.

CHAPTER 37

Elle and Lauren stared at the shadows in the doorway. Peggy, Kathy's oldest daughter, stepped down onto the backyard. Seeing Aunt Elle and Aunt Lauren, she waved.

The women were startled by what they saw. Peggy was the spitting image of Kathy.

Alice took Derek's arm and led him and his other children to where the men were standing. Peggy started to walk toward her aunts.

Eric, Kathy's oldest son, watched his sister but remained close to Derek's side as did Scottie, Mary, and Gabe. Eric was now almost as tall as his father. Derek glanced in the ladies' direction but didn't offer a wave or a smile. He continued his conversation with the men.

When Peggy reached her aunts, she embraced Lauren first, then Elle. "So good to see you, Aunt Lauren, and Aunt Elle, you look great."

Seeing Peggy made Lauren emotional. Elle turned away, so the child didn't see her eyes welling with tears.

"How is the leg, Aunt Lauren?"

"It's good."

"The last time we spoke, Aunt Elle, your doctor wanted you to stop using the cane."

"I was concerned about being on my feet the entire day, so after today, this piece of wood is history."

"I'm so happy for you. Are you still having back issues?"

"No. Actually, the back has been good."

Peggy glanced toward the shore where Liam and Ethan were playing. "Is that Liam and Ethan? I don't remember them being that tall."

Elle smiled. "Growing like weeds." Elle couldn't help but comment, "Peggy, I can't believe—"

"How much I look like my mom?"

Both women nodded in agreement.

"Dad says I'm the spitting image of my mom."

"How is your dad doing?" asked Lauren.

"He's good. He has his moments, like when one of us does something that reminds him of Mom. We can see him tearing up. But we've come to accept that it's a good thing. It keeps Mom close to him. I'm anxious to talk with Kelly. Do you mind if I swing back after speaking with her?"

"Go, she's been waiting to talk with you as well," said Lauren.

Peggy rushed off to talk with Kelly. Lauren and Elle kept a close watch as the girls embraced.

"She is the spitting image of Kathy. I don't think I can—"

"What? You don't think you can stick around for the send-off of Kathy's ashes? This is why I didn't want to come. I told you this was a terrible idea."

"Are you blaming me? If you didn't want to come, you shouldn't have. No one forced you to be here, Lauren."

"Why didn't you support me when I said we should talk Derek out of making this a family gathering? I can't believe he didn't consider how we would feel coming back to the place where we almost lost our lives and ultimately took Kathy's life."

"It was an accident, Lauren. It could have happened anywhere. It was Kathy's request, and I thought it only right to be here to support Derek and the children."

"Did Kathy ever mention to you that she wanted a portion of her ashes to be spread in Cape May? No, of course not."

"Well, she didn't tell you either. She probably didn't want to hear your condescending opinion on why it was a terrible idea. You were always riding her about something when she was alive."

"You're kidding me, right? I loved Kathy like the sister I never had. And if I was such a bitch and you were the perfect friend, then tell me, why didn't she share her final request to have her ashes comingled with Casey's with you?"

"All right, I'm sorry if I hurt your feelings. Let's stop acting like children. I'm here to support the Wilson family. Admit it, Lauren, if you hadn't come, you would have never forgiven yourself. We are here to support our friend. God knows he's been to hell and back. He did everything in his power to help Kathy."

"Did he?"

"What do you mean? Of course, he did."

"You think it was a great idea taking the woman thousands of miles away from the people that could have gotten her through the bad times?"

"I don't know. Maybe it wasn't the best decision, but what use were we to her? You were in Cape Cod mending, and I was of no use to anyone."

"What about the support of her mother and father? The two people responsible for bringing her into the world. I think they would have treasured spending more time with their daughter, before—never mind."

"Stop talking. Derek is heading our way."

"Hi." Derek leaned in and kissed the ladies on both cheeks. "You both look well."

"Hi, Derek. The kids look great. I can't get over how much they've grown."

"Won't be long before they will be leaving the nest for college. Speaking of children, Kelly and Jonathan, do I hear wedding bells? Won't be long, Lauren, before you and Jake are pouncing a few grandkids on your knee. And, Elle, the boys are so tall."

"It's Jacques's cooking and the fact that his mom is five ten and his dad six two."

"Did you hear the news, Derek? Elle and Jacques are moving to Paris."

"Just found out from Jacques. I'm happy for you, Elle. We will miss you, but Paris is only an eight-hour flight."

"That's what I said."

Ethan interrupted their conversation when he fell and started to wail for his mom.

"Duty calls."

Since the memorial service for Kathy, she and Derek had spoken often.

"How's Fanny? Have you spoken to her since she moved to California?"

"Once a month. She's fine."

"Did you hire someone to help with the kids?"

"No. We're doing pretty well on our own."

"Must be hard raising five children, writing during your spare time, and still practicing medicine?"

"I need to stay busy."

Derek's last comment left the two uncomfortable. Lauren couldn't take her eyes off Derek. It seemed the man grew more handsome with age.

"Alice is waving. I think the food is ready."

Together, Derek and Lauren walked toward the others.

*****

After lunch, the time had come to spread Kathy's ashes.

The family and friends headed down toward the shore. Lauren and Elle stood side by side. Derek turned and asked them to stand with his family. They did as he requested.

Scottie read a special poem he wrote for his mom. Peggy told a funny story about Kathy. Eric, Mary, and Gabe remained close to Derek's side. Eric, when asked by his father to say a few words, started by saying his mom was the best, and they missed her terribly. Mary was too emotional to speak. Gabe was young, and Lauren guessed he vaguely remembered his beloved mother, but to keep her close, he held a picture of her in his hands.

The moment had arrived. Derek removed the top from the precious jaded urn that held Kathy's remaining ashes. As he released Kathy's ashes, Lauren remained stoic watching the ashes take flight over the ocean. Sensing that Elle was crying, she handed her a tissue.

*****

Derek leaned on the cement wall that surrounded Alice and Nancy's garden. Jake joined him.

"How you doing, buddy?"

"I have mixed feeling about being here. The place where it all happened. I guess Lauren wasn't too happy with me, but it wasn't my decision. You know, that little part of Kathy has been sitting in my drawer for two years. I guess this puts an end to the mourning period."

"Kathy was a special lady."

"She was and beautiful."

"Have you been getting out?"

"Getting out like dating?"

"Nothing exclusive but sharing a cup of coffee with the opposite sex?"

"I share coffee with female coworkers. I do get hit on often. I'm prime choice for divorced women, widows, and single girls who want to help me move on."

"Every man's dream."

"Not this man. I promised Kathy I'd be there for our children. What woman is going to want to deal with five kids?"

"You'd be surprised."

Derek smiled. "Maybe once the kids are older, but for now, we're good."

Jake knew that it would take a special woman to get Derek to move on. He also knew, this wasn't what Kathy would have wanted for Derek. He was too young to give up on life. But who was Jake to judge. If anything happened to Michelle, and after his divorce from Lauren, he might not want a third run at dating or marriage.

Grace ran into Jake's arms. "Daddy, will you come with me to the ocean. I want to catch a fish!"

Jake smiled at Derek. "Of course, sweetie. Do you have a fishing pole?"

"Aunt Alice wrapped a rope around a stick, and Aunt Nancy tied a curtain hook on the end."

"Then let's go catch ourselves a fish. You have to promise Daddy, you won't be disappointed if the fish aren't biting. They might have gone out to the ocean to sleep."

"It's too early for the fish to go to sleep, Daddy."

Derek remained at the garden wall and glanced at his children enjoying dessert and watermelon. His friends were showering his children with conversation and laughter. They didn't even notice that he was gone.

Once his daughter Mary accepted that Kathy was never coming home, she'd attached herself to Derek. Scottie surprised Derek. The boy who never would leave Kathy's side took a different approach. He was going to be strong for his father. Eric broke Derek's heart by how much Kathy's death had affected the boy. Derek had sought the help of a child phycologist for the children. Eric was still seeing someone to deal with his mom's death. Peggy was as strong as her mom. She didn't have much time to mourn, because her attention was given to her grieving brother, Eric. Gabe was too small to remember, but he kept a picture of Kathy with him wherever he went. There was one in his book bag, one in his sock drawer, one on his nightstand, and a box of pictures in his closet.

Derek duplicated and quad-duplicated pictures of Kathy for their children after her death. Their wedding picture sat beside him on the nightstand, and he spoke with her at bedtime and when he woke.

Thinking of her death, Derek reflected back to that night in Berlin.

He'd arrived at the hotel and immediately went to shower and shave. He set the alarm to go off at five in the morning. He lay in bed for four hours tossing, turning, and praying that Kathy wouldn't change her mind about going into surgery the following morning. When sleep was out of the question, he watched TV. Finally, the alarm went off. He dressed, grabbed his bag, and left the hotel room at five fifteen.

He entered the hospital and realized he hadn't eaten since lunch the day before. His stomach growled. Remembering the hospital cafeteria opened at five, he looked at his watch. It was five twenty. He decided to grab a bagel for later.

He entered the hospital floor at five twenty-seven and walked toward Kathy's room. Opening the door to her room, he found her still asleep. *Strange,* he thought, *shouldn't the nurses be prepping her for surgery?* He went to her. Taking her hand, he screamed. Her hand was as cold as ice. Then he noticed the deep cut on her wrist.

Dropping to his knees, he screamed his wife's name over and over. "Kathy! Kathy! Why? Why, baby?"

Three startled nurses and Dr. Frankel rushed into Kathy's room.

In German, the nurses explained to Dr. Frankel that Derek had slipped past them.

Dr. Frankel knelt beside Derek. "Derek, I'm so sorry."

Derek rose, taking Kathy's lifeless body into his arms; he sobbed. Time passed slowly before Derek laid Kathy back onto the bed.

Dr. Frankel repeated, "I am so sorry, Dr. Wilson."

"Sorry? Is that all you have to say? Someone explain to me how can a woman in her condition manage to cut her own wrist? Which one of you idiots let this happen? Where were you when my sweet Kathy was dying? Which one of you fucked this up? How could you ignore her call for help?"

"Dr. Wilson. We are sorry. A code-blue call left the nurses' station unmanned."

Derek scolded, "You're fucking kidding me. I put my wife's life in your hands because this hospital was the best in the world. And you're telling me my wife died because you weren't fully staffed? You're going to have to come up with a better answer than you were negligent protecting your patient."

"Dr. Wilson, after you've spent some time with your wife, we'll talk."

The staff and Dr. Frankel left the room, giving Derek time to grieve. Two hours passed before Derek emerged from Kathy's room and asked to see Dr. Frankel. He immediately was taken to Dr. Frankel's private office. Derek sat before Dr. Frankel and asked, "Have you prepared the death certificate?"

On his desk was Kathy's file. He retrieved the death certificate and handed it to Derek.

Derek read it. "You will prepare a new death certificate."

"What?"

Derek tore up the death certificate in his hands.

"I want you to prepare me a new death certificate that doesn't say my wife took her own life."

"Dr. Wilson, you know I can't do that."

"Oh, you will do it. If you don't, I'll spend my life suing you and this fucking hospital for neglect."

"Dr. Wilson, you're upset. You know I can't do—"

"Listen to me. I'm well-known. You're well-known in the field of medicine. Do you really want me to ruin you? Because I will. My wife, who is bandaged from head to toe managed to get a knife, not a plastic knife, but a stainless-steel knife, and cut herself. Really? Or did someone at this hospital murder my wife?"

"Dr. Wilson, I swear to you. Your wife took her own life."

"Okay, if you want me to agree that my wife took her own life, change the fucking death certificate. I don't want my children, her parents, or anyone for that matter to know that she killed herself. It's a new death certificate, or I will cry wolf."

Dr. Frankel and Derek agreed that a blood clot to the brain was the cause of death.

*****

Derek thought the worst time of his life was when he got the call that Kathy was in a horrific accident. Second was when the doctors spoke of her facial injuries. The third was when he had to call Kathy's parents to say their daughter was dead. Fourth was telling his children their mother wasn't coming home, and last, telling Lauren, Elle, and Alice their friend was gone.

Screams were their only response. Hearing their sobs, he disconnected each call knowing they blamed him for his wife's passing.

He watched Kathy's coffin being lifted onto the plane from his first-class window seat. A pretty young lady sat beside him. She offered her name and began to make casual conversation. Derek was no stranger to this form of attention. Politely, he explained that he wasn't in the mood for small conversation, flirting, or a quick roll in the hay. Without saying those exact words, the young lady got the hint.

The Palm Reader

The funeral director met him at the airport. He sat beside the young driver in the front seat of the hearse, as together, they drove Kathy's body to the funeral home.

After finalizing the funeral arrangements, Jake arrived to accompany his friend home. They drove in silence.

Entering the house, he was confronted with the grieving parents. He hugged them both. Conversation was minimal. He stared into Fanny's grieving eyes but didn't have the heart to embrace her. His children were off at school and daycare, so he requested some time alone. He asked that his children be sent to his bedroom when they returned home.

Derek entered the bedroom he loved sharing with his wife. He dropped to his knees and muffled the sobs that escaped his body.

When there were no tears left to shed, he lay on the bed and waited for his children.

Slowly, the door to the bedroom opened.

"Daddy?"

Derek glanced at his five children standing in the doorway. Seeing their grieving father, they came to comfort him. They embraced and cried for the senseless loss of their mother's life.

The memorial service was small, just family and close friends.

At the end of the day, after all were gone, except Kathy's parents, Fanny, and the children, Derek dug a hole under Kathy's favorite tree in the backyard, and buried 75 percent of Kathy's ashes in a jaded urn. A plaque was nailed to the tree, which said, "This plaque is dedicated to the beauty that lies within this garden."

Derek would take to his grave the cause of Kathy's demise. With all in agreement that it was a miracle she had survived as long as she did, her family and friends went back to their everyday lives.

Lauren was the only one that asked several times how, insisting that the Philadelphia hospital was aware every time there was a threat of a blood clot. Derek had to explain time and time again, blood clots aren't always detected.

Lauren made it known to him that she didn't agree with his decision to take Kathy to another country for treatment. After speaking her mind several times, she dropped the subject.

Once Kathy's parents had returned home, Derek wanted nothing more than to be left alone to raise his five children. Even Fanny's presence brought him pain. At this time, he needed the woman to help him gain control of being a single parent.

As he and the children returned to their normal lives, he made sure his schedule adhered to the children's schedule. There was aftercare twice a week, which gave him a longer work day. The other three days of the workweek, he was there to greet his children when they returned home from school. Fanny took care of their daily needs, laundry, cleaning, and shopping. Often, Derek would send her packing when he arrived home. Saturdays and Sundays were spent as a family. After a year, Fanny resigned her position and went out West. Derek hired a housekeeper, who took over Fanny's chores. There wasn't a connection with the woman, as with Fanny, so Derek had lost the guilt he felt whenever he looked into Fanny's eyes.

Obviously, Derek was mourning his beloved Kathy. There were times, when he was alone, that he thought of taking his own life. But the children needed him, and he had promised Kathy he would be there for them. He loved his children, and the thought of putting them through the loss of another parent wasn't what he wanted for them.

He sought help for the children, and after a year, it was time he sought the help he needed to go on without Kathy.

Every day, he retrieved the small urn with Kathy's remaining ashes. He remembered the day they had spoken about their final requests. Both wanted to be cremated. Kathy asked that her ashes be placed under the tree in the backyard and a small portion be spread over the ocean comingled with Casey's in Cape May.

"Why?" asked Derek.

She replied, "I don't want her to be alone."

Derek wanted to abide by his wife's wishes a year after her death, but he didn't have the heart to let go of the small part of Kathy that was a short distance from him. He could retrieve the urn and hold it and her in his hands.

He called Dr. Leach and made an appointment. He confessed that he was finding it hard to live without Kathy in his life.

The Palm Reader

After three months of therapy with Dr. Leach, Derek joined a grievance group. He was reluctant at first but was reminded that the family care facility had several grievance groups. He joined the Tuesday morning group.

Every Tuesday, the group went around the room and introduced themselves. They were asked to speak, but Derek never volunteered. He listened to the others tell their sad stories, but nothing hit home. And then one day, Bridgette, who like Derek never spoke, asked to be heard.

"My name is Bridgette Drum. My son, Greg, was diagnosed with blood cancer six years ago. He died two years ago. Today is the anniversary of his death. I joined this group a year ago. Many of you have been here for as long as I have."

One year, thought Derek, *and this is the first time she is speaking.*

"I prayed for the strength to speak about Greg, and thought today was the day. The reason I haven't spoken is because I don't want you to think I'm a terrible person. See, I feel guilty about wanting to save my son's life. He had a rare form of blood cancer. Wanting to save my son's life also cost me losing my husband, a good and decent man." Bridgette reached for a tissue and began to pat at her tears. "Every chemo treatment was a disaster. My boy melted away. His skeleton form should have convinced me there was no hope. But there was another treatment, a more aggressive treatment, and I wanted it for my son, so he could live. My boy begged his father to talk with me. He even told me himself that he didn't want any more treatments. I called my husband a terrible father. I accused him of wanting our son to die, so he could go back to living his normal life. Only a father who didn't love his child would refuse a treatment that could cure his son.

"When my son looked into my begging eyes, he agreed to the treatment. Instead of allowing my son a peaceful death, I allowed him to lay in his own vomit and die in my arms. What mother, you ask, would allow her child to go through horrific pain? That would be me, and my guilt is, I don't regret putting him through the pain. Before you judge me, ask yourself, is there nothing you wouldn't do for the one you love?"

Without a pause, Derek said, "You were right to try to save your child's life. You shouldn't feel guilty."

Bridgette was stunned by Derek's response.

"I too did everything in my power to save my wife. She also didn't want to be saved. She ultimately took her own life, and I've been carrying around the guilt for two years. Two years of telling myself, I was wrong. You ask, which one of us wouldn't do everything in our power to save our loved ones, and I don't believe anyone here can say they would let their loved ones die if there were a remote chance they could live."

When the session ended, Derek felt a weight lift off his shoulders. He asked Bridgette if she had time for coffee. He told her how Kathy had lost her face in a horrific accident. Bridgette held his hand, saying, "I believe my Greg and your Kathy wanted us to speak today. You don't know how your agreeing that I didn't do anything wrong has made me feel so much better."

That was the last time Derek saw Bridgette. He hoped that session gave her the will to move on, as much as it had helped him.

Kathy, in Derek's mind, could never be replaced. He did what he thought was best for her and was sure that no one, not even his children, would fault him for trying.

As he came to the end of his reverie, Lauren stood beside him.

"I owe you an apology, Derek."

"You owe me an apology, why?"

"I've often stated that Kathy wouldn't have died if you hadn't taken her to Germany. I was wrong to even suggest that you caused her death. It was cruel and unjust. I hope you've forgiven me."

"It wasn't so long ago that I had to ask for your forgiveness, Lauren. And you graciously said, I was forgiven. I can't lie. I surmised you blamed me for Kathy's death. But I ask you this question, Lauren. Is there nothing you wouldn't do to save the life of someone you love?"

Lauren smiled. "Did I ever tell you, Dr. Wilson, how special you are? Of course not, because I always thought of you as a cad. But you've proven me wrong. You loved our girl, and even though you had a slight slip, everyone here knows she was everything to you. And those kids adore you, and I see how much you love and adore them. Good job, Daddy."

Derek smiled. Arm in arm, Lauren and Derek joined the others.

CHAPTER 38

Lauren smiled as she listened to her husband, Bruce, whistling show tunes in the kitchen while he prepared their lunch.

At six that morning, Lauren started her latest novel. Before closing her computer for the day, she sat and daydreamed. Four years had passed since Kathy's memorial service in Cape May.

Two years prior, Alice and Nancy purchased a house on Cape Cod. Nancy thought it was time she and Alice moved out of the home Alice had once shared with Casey.

Once Lauren accepted Kathy's death and Derek not being the cause, she had remained close with Kathy's family. It wasn't uncommon for her to travel to Connecticut to check in on her nieces and nephews. She'd often spend a few days with Derek and the children. Derek and the family spent two weeks on the Cape every summer. He often invited Bruce and her to hospital events and, of course, all family functions.

She never questioned Derek about his love life. He had expressed that he was prime meat for divorced and widowed women, but coffee and conversation were all he could muster while the children were living with him. Jake and she were convinced that Derek wasn't interested in replacing his precious Kathy. She hoped in time, he would be ready.

Lauren had three grandchildren that she adored. Josh and Cindy had two lovely girls, and Kelly and Jonathan added a beautiful baby boy, three months earlier.

Lauren had three bestsellers added to her list of accomplishments.

Michelle returned to work full-time, part-time had only lasted a year. Jake retired and enjoyed his new role as Mr. Mom. He now worked part-time to keep his sanity.

Elle and Jacques were happy living in Paris. Elle was back to being her old self. Trudy, Elaine, and Uncle Charlie travel to and from Paris. The Pascal family visited the Cape every other summer. And Lauren had kept her promise. She and Bruce visit Paris each year. Only an eight-hour flight, piece of cake. Elle hinted that she and Jacques were considering purchasing a place on the Cape. She wanted her boys to spend the summers in their place of origin. Lauren was thrilled. She immediately contacted her friend who was a realtor and told her it was a must to find a home close to her cottage.

Elle corresponded with the palm reader twice a year. Bella was in medical school and engaged to the boy the ladies had spied on that day so long ago. The palm reader was baffled by the engagement but was happy for her granddaughter, who had proved her wrong.

Lauren wished life could have been different. She wished her two BFFs hadn't lost their lives so young. She missed them terribly.

She had come up with an idea and ran it by Bruce. He loved the idea. Her latest novel would be of five girls who meet in college and remain BFFs forever. The names were changed, obviously. And the fifth gal was a reflection of how close Alice and she had become.

There would be no death, cheating, or sadness.

While on vacation in Cape May, they would visit a palm reader. The old woman would tell them that very soon they would encounter a visit from a ghost. The women were amused by the old woman. Before leaving for home, a female ghost from the seventeenth century appeared while the ladies were enjoying their dinner and wine. Of course, they were frightened, but the ghost assured them she meant them no harm. She confessed that she had been listening while they reminisce about their lives but didn't confess she was envious. The gals wished the ghost well when they departed, assuming they had left the ghost behind. The ghost, tiring of her surroundings, had another idea. She traveled back with the writer and the housewife. On the trip, she made her presence known. She told them she had the ability to travel through time but neglected to say, she had the power to invade their bodies for a short time whenever the need arises. The ghost began to make periodic visits to the five ladies' primary residence. She came to enjoy the sex, power, fame, and much more. She was complicating the women's lives, which caused them to return to the palm reader and begged for her help, to rid themselves of the ghost.

The book would be filled with antics, surprises, laughter, and an enormous amount of fun.

The title of the book would be *The Palm Reader* by Lauren Hicks Croft.

ABOUT THE AUTHOR

Antoinette Zam was born of Italian descent in Brooklyn, New York, and is proud to call herself a New Yorker. Thirty-eight years ago, she moved to West Windsor, New Jersey. She was once told that if you reside in a state longer than the state you were born in, you are officially from that state. She likes to think of herself as a New York/Jersey gal who enjoys writing.

Thirty-six years ago, she married her beloved husband, Arnold. He supports every crazy thing Antoinette can muster, like her love of writing. They have four children and seven grandchildren, including two nieces, and their families.

As mentioned in her last novel, *Scarred by Death*, it was her mother, before her passing, who inspired her to write. She loved the way her daughter told a story and encouraged her to put her thoughts to paper. At the young age of sixty-three, she began to write.

In the summer, you can find Antoinette lounging on a beach chair, reading, taking long walks along the shore, biking on the boardwalk, and eating breakfast at Rita's deli while watching the boats glide along the bay. The shore is where she creates memories with those most precious to her—her family.

Her love for the Jersey shore and current events brought to fruition *The Palm Reader*.

The question most asked of her is, "When does she find the time to write?" She said that if you're passionate about something, you find the time.

The Palm Reader is her second book, and she hopes you will enjoy it as much as her first novel *Scarred by Death*.

Currently, she is working on a third book titled *A Christmas Awakening*.